WHEN
I Come Home
AGAIN

A Novel
by
Jennifer Rodewald

WORDS THAT EDIFY

Rooted Publishing

But the fruit of the Spirit is love, joy, peace, forbearance, kindness, goodness, faithfulness, gentleness and self-control. Against such things there is no law.

~Galatians 5:22-23~

Jennifer Rodewald

Chapter One

SATURDAYS WERE FOR RELAXING.

This was a fairly new perspective in Brenna Blaum's world. Well, new in the last seven years. Used to be Saturdays were for getting up early, going with Dad so she could watch him come alive during Coach's Coffee Club. He loved talking about football almost as much as he loved coaching it.

Actually, no. That wasn't true exactly. He loved talking about his boys playing football almost as much as he loved coaching them. He loved the game. He loved his boys—his team even more. They were the reason he was so passionate. They were the reason he gave up so many sleep-in-and-relax Saturdays. The reason he rode countless buses until two in the morning. Spent untold hours in front of a screen and a playbook. It wasn't about a pigskin ball, grass turf, ten-yard lines, or uprights. Wasn't even Friday night lights. All of it was for them.

Dad loved his boys. Every one of them. And they loved him.

Time had a habit of wearing things like that away. Those boys—they grew up. Found out life was bigger than a hundred-yard field of turf and lines. Started living it.

And Dad? Dad retired. Early.

Thoughts not super relaxing on a Saturday morning. Brenna banished them, because see above. Saturdays were for relaxing now.

Still wearing her pink-pinstriped jammy pants and old Huskers T-shirt, Brenna stretched near the big window as she looked over Main Street. Her apartment was on the top floor of the old Limestone Hotel—which meant it was three stories up. That was as tall as buildings went in Big Prairie. Her dad had chuckled when Scottie would point to the historic building and call it a skyscraper.

"Wait until we go to the state playoffs, buddy," he'd say. "Then you'll see some really tall buildings."

This conversation would happen a dozen times every year, even though Scottie went to the state playoffs often. Brenna was pretty sure Dad liked the banter as much as Scottie. It never got old for them.

She wondered if Dad still thought about that.

Her phone buzzed from behind her. Usually she had it attached somewhere. Her back pocket. A hoodie pocket. Her palm. But not today. Saturday. Also, she was trying to break the attachment. Grant had said it would be healthy for her and the iPhone to gain a little separation. He was the expert, so she was working on it.

Brenna gathered her bed-head hair and flipped it into a messy bun that was probably not much better as she moved in search of the electronic addiction she apparently had. It buzzed again, drawing her attention from the coffee table in front of her yellow sofa smothered with green pillows. She noted that she had yet to straighten the mess from her late-night date with a Jane Austen story-turned-film. Grant had opted out of that, which was fine. They were not attached at the hip. Which was healthy. They both agreed.

Phone. That was what Brenna was looking for.

Not on the coffee table. Nor the sofa. Did she have it this

morning? *See, Grant. I don't even know where the dumb thing is. I don't have a problem. Unless it's misplacing things. Then yes. I definitely have a problem.*

She'd text him that. He'd smile. Roll his eyes. Text her back something like, *You're cute.* With the correct *You're* and punctuation. Actually, no. He wouldn't use *You're.* He'd type out *You are.* Because Grant was not a lazy texter. He wasn't a lazy anything.

Floor was clear. No iPhones lying about abandoned and lonely.

Hands on her hips, she paused in the big area she called her front room, which was a misnomer, because her whole apartment was three rooms. The kitchen / living room / dining room mash-up that was lovingly called "open concept" these days, the bedroom, and the bathroom. The latter two were actually walled off at the front of the apartment, close to the front door, creating a little hallway/entryway between that and the living space. So. This was not technically the front room at all, but the back.

Grant had pointed this whole misnomer thing out last year when he'd helped Brenna move in. She still called the open-concept living-space mash-up her front room. He lifted his eyebrows a little every time he heard it. Brenna was pretty sure it annoyed him that she was not being technically accurate on purpose. It was mildly amusing.

The phone buzzed again, the vibrating leading her toward the sideboard-table under the wall-mounted TV. Found it. Right where she'd left it all the way back in the past of last night. Right next to the cover for *Persuasion.*

Ha, Grant Hillman. All the way back then. That had been, like, twelve hours ago.

Brenna smirked as she pushed the Home button to find out who was texting on her relaxing Saturday morning. And then laughed, because hello irony.

It was Grant.

Hello, beautiful. I am at Garrett's. Would you like a donut? Or perhaps some coffee?

Did he have to ask? Two years. They'd been dating for two years. In those two years, had she ever turned down either a donut or coffee?

Are you awake? You had better be. I am heading your way bearing treasures.

Brenna's smirk melted into a small smile, and she ran her tongue over her teeth. Yeah, definitely needed some attention. The phone vibrated again as she stepped into the bathroom.

Brenna? Is it really too early? It is after nine.

She leaned against the white quartz of the bathroom counter and texted him back, one hand on the phone, the other operating the toothbrush.

Come on up.
I'm brushing my teeth because I'm thoughtful like that.
Be one minute.

All three texts zipped away. He'd probably shake his head because she'd sent three texts when they were all really part of the same thought.

Yeah. They were different. They worked though. And he made her smile. Especially when he brought her carbs slathered in chocolate frosting.

Come to think of it, that didn't happen all that often.

Still.

His knock echoed through the apartment as she worked up a good foam in her mouth. Still brushing, she wandered the short distance from the bathroom to the front door and let him in. One dark eyebrow lifted as he assessed her from the hallway.

"Do you always make such a mess of your face when you brush your teeth?"

"Huh?" Toothpaste seeped from the corner of her mouth.

"Ew."

"Wha?" Brenna grinned, because his face scrunched into the most adorable *yuck* expression that was too good not to laugh at.

"Go finish in the bathroom before you spit toothpaste all over this overly sweet sugar bomb I brought you."

Brenna shrugged. Smiled. Left the door open so he could come in while she moved toward the bathroom. Grant followed, stopping to lean against the doorframe while she leaned to spit in the sink. Rinse, brush, spit, repeat. Then she wiped the mess off her face with a washrag and turned back to him.

He looked like he'd watched a toddler rub a sucker all over her face and then offered him a lick.

"Seriously, that is how you brush your teeth?"

"What?" She rinsed her fingers and tossed the rag toward the hamper.

"You made a bigger mess than what you started with. Can't you keep the foam inside your mouth like a grown-up?"

Brenna snorted, pushing his shoulder as he rolled off the doorway. "You're kind of boring with all your neat and tidy toothbrushing standards. Did you know that?"

"Yes. Clean is definitely overrated." He nudged her with his shoulder, and a slip of a smile lifted his mouth. "You'll forgive me, though, because I brought you a chocolate sundae donut and a large coffee."

They made it to the tiny island that separated the great mash-up front room into kitchen/dining/living room spaces, and Brenna leaned in to peck the side of his mouth. "Yep. You're forgiven."

He set the bag and the paper hot cup on the counter so he could wipe the spot she'd just kissed. "Sloppy mint. My favorite kind."

She shot him a sassy face and tore into the pastry bag. "Nothing for you?"

"I had oatmeal this morning."

"And you didn't bring me any?"

"How would that go over?"

Sugar melted on her tongue as she sank her teeth into a giant bite of awesomeness. "Not nearly as well as this," she mumbled around the mouthful of donut.

"Brenna. You are a speech therapist. Surely you know not to talk with your mouth full."

She rolled her eyes, licked her lips and then her fingers. Grant handed her a napkin.

"So." She scooped a dollop of cream frosting off the middle of the half-eaten donut and stuck it into her mouth. Grant gave her the *look*. Because he knew she was doing it on purpose. She smiled. "To what do I owe this lovely surprise? Guilty conscience because you skipped out on Captain Wentworth and me?"

He handed her another napkin. "I would not want to come between you and Captain Wentworth."

Carving out another fingerful of frosting, Brenna tipped her head and offered it to him.

He leaned back while simultaneously snagging her wrist. "You really cannot do this if we ever have kids. You know that, right?"

"What?"

"Frosting is not finger food, Brenna."

She slid off the stool and stepped toward him. He sat, knees apart, on the only other stool at the island, and as she leaned into his chest, the slightest pressure of his thighs pressed against her hips. Brenna's grin felt sly and maybe a little sexy as his free hand settled at her waist.

"Kids, huh?" Brenna tipped closer, brushing her nose against his.

"That was not the point I was trying to make."

"Hmm." While he still had one wrist captive, her other hand was available. She happened to know his neck was sensitive. If she trailed her fingertips along the edge of his collared golf shirt, he'd tilt his head to stop the tickle. And that was the perfect moment, when he was distracted.

She smeared the frosting over his top lip.

"Oh! Brenna!" He wrapped her in a bear hug that was meant to contain the mischief. Brenna laughed because he scrunched his face while at the same time tried not to let the frosting inside his mouth.

"Lick it off." She leaned in and nipped a small bit off his lip. "It's yummy."

"That is disgusting."

Grant Hillman was impenetrable when it came to play. Brenna sighed, dropping back to her own stool. "What am I going to do with you?"

"My thoughts exactly." He let her hand go to snatch another napkin, which he used to wipe away the filmy sugar. When the mess was gone to his satisfaction, his arms returned loosely around her. "We're not very much alike."

"Noted." Hooking her arms around his neck, Brenna wondered if he'd ever, just once, let go. Eat some processed sugar. Not straighten every mess he ever encountered. Use a contraction like every other American.

Make out with his girlfriend on a Saturday morning, even if she did taste like donut.

His lips brushed hers, and she thought for a moment that *yes*—today he might cut loose...

Nope. He pulled away, searched her eyes with a seriousness not befitting the whole *Saturday's are for relaxing* vibe, and then settled his hands on her shoulders. Responding to the bit of pressure, Brenna sat back and waited.

His hands covered hers. "Have you seen the school board's recent list of last-minute hires?"

"What?"

"The list the board released this week. It's in the paper. Did you read it?"

"No. Why?"

His thumb traced over her knuckles, and then he moved to cover her knee with his hand. "They have hired a new district music teacher for the elementary and middle school. Recently. Like within the last week."

"Oh." Brenna waved him off. She should have known this was what Grant was stewing over. "Yeah. That."

"So you know?"

"Yes. But I didn't read it in the paper. His mom told me last week."

"His mom?"

"Yeah. She has guardianship of the Fulton boys? You know that—Trent is one of your kids, right?" She didn't wait for him to respond, because technically he couldn't say, and technically she already knew. Grant was big on technicalities, and she didn't want to get into it. "Trent's one of my patients, and I saw him last week. Janet told me then."

"Janet?"

She felt her eyebrows gather. "Yeah."

"Not Ms. Erikson?"

A sigh sagged through her, and suddenly she wished she'd slept in. More. Technicalities were exhausting. "I've known her pretty much forever. We've been close, so..."

"But." Grant shoved a hand through his thick hair. "But things have changed. I mean...you can't still be close. Are you?"

"With Janet? Yes. Janet and I are still close. And you already knew that, Grant."

His jaw worked. Eyes drifted from Brenna's, focusing on whatever was behind her.

"What's going on?" She came off the stool, framed his face with clean fingers, and waited until he looked at her again.

"This is kind of a big deal. I wish you had mentioned to me that you knew *he* was coming back."

"Why?" Things tumbled inside her. Things she'd been

ignoring for the last seven days. Or years—though she wouldn't admit to that. Having Grant react this way wasn't helping.

"I think that we should talk about it," he said. "You should talk about it."

Pulling away, she let her hands slide from his freshly shaven face. "You said you wouldn't do that to me—remember?"

"I'm not speaking as a counselor. I'm talking as your boyfriend—and as the man who cares a lot about you and your heart. Your health."

"That sounds like counselor talk."

"Brenna."

She plopped back onto the stool, reclaimed the half-eaten donut that Grant didn't appreciate in the least, and shoved a mouthful in. "I'm fine."

Grant sighed. Irritated. Because of the mouthful-talking thing. And also.

Nope. He was wrong. She was fine.

"Craig is coming back to stay, Brenna. This is not one of his passing-through gigs. It is full time. You have got to do more than *I'm fine*. Because if that is all you have got, then I—"

"No, Grant. I don't have to do more than that, because that *is* all I've got. That's all there is, all there needs to be. It's been seven years. I'm fine. And this shouldn't change anything for us."

The oversized clock on the brick wall ticked obnoxiously into the silence. Grant rubbed his neck, studying her with an intense look she'd seen him use when he was working on puzzles.

She was *not* a puzzle. Irritation rose up hard and fast. "Grant. Seriously."

"Okay." He leaned in and brushed her temple with his lips. "How about I help you straighten up, and we can go for a Saturday morning walk?"

Straightening up. That was normal Grant. But the twin lines between his eyes gave everything away.

This wasn't fine. Not for him. Because he really didn't think it was for her.

She was though. Fine. Seven years' worth of fine. Craig Erikson's homecoming wasn't going to change all that fine.

Chapter Two

STRANGE HOW A PLACE COULD NEVER CHANGE. AND YET.

Driving into town felt like landing on the moon. Familiar, but so very much not. Like that big white orb up there in the heavens, Craig Erikson, like most, had seen it a million times. Up there, hanging in the sky, reflecting the sun's hidden light. Being normal and awesome all at once. But stepping foot on it? Nope. He hadn't ever done such a thing.

Going back home after a fallout was like walking on the moon. Most never did. Couldn't.

The miles had slipped beneath his tires at sixty-five for near to four hours straight. As he approached the city limits to Big Prairie, his body ached like it'd been a long day.

The unease in his gut said it hadn't been long enough.

The road was the same. Worn double yellow on the faded-black pavement, because the summer sun had its way with the paint once again. Big pothole on the right, just past the *Welcome to Big Prairie, population 6,000* sign. The Department of Roads attempted a yearly conquest to fill that hole. Just as faithfully, the gap returned. Likely as not, the mystery of its stubborn reappearance year after year remained a topic of debate in Mrs. Yuccum's tenth-grade science class.

Craig chuckled. Good times, good memories. One of many, which should have made it easier to drive back into his hometown.

The view hadn't changed. Fields as wide as eternity stretched to his right, like the whole world was one long threshold leading to this quiet little town. Swaying in the gulch to his left, treetops hinting autumn's touch let the population know fall was a turn of the calendar away. Below the canopy, the leaves hid the area's best treasure—the river that was both the stand of tree's lifeblood and the town's.

Somewhere beyond his view, tucked beneath that canopy of trees, the River's Edge Vineyard had been optimistically planted by Lance Carson, a former Big Prairie tight end who had graduated two years before Craig. The field of grapevines had been Lance's FFA project during all four years of his high school career. If the wooden engraved sign Craig drove past and the rumors he'd heard were any indication, Lance's grape project was doing well. And good for him for that.

Up ahead, the three blocks of downtown beckoned, *Come and see my charm.* The well-kept shops and replica yesteryear lampposts supported the *Fighting Broncs* banners. Each displayed a different senior athlete with his or her chosen sports apparel. In a few weeks, they'd be replaced with the burnt oranges and golden yellows of fall displayed on wreaths. After that, evergreen swags would light up the sidewalks with LED white lights.

Craig felt the old draw. The feeling that was warm and familiar—which made it oddly difficult to make this drive. He'd grown up in Big Prairie. Lived every day of his first eighteen years within the boundaries of this little Nebraska town. Tucked into the quaint shops, the tourist-driven outfitter setups, and the guest cabins that lived along the banks of the river, there was a tight-knit community of good people. Friends. In those same folds, his life had been penned. Marked in permanent ink—strokes of glory alongside gashes of shame. Both had been reasons for him to leave and to stay gone, even if in his heart his story was firmly stamped in Big Prairie.

Slowing to twenty-five, Craig passed between those shops. Still charming. Memories swirled through his mind, whether he wanted them to or not. On these three blocks, he and Merrik Petty had trick-or-treated every single year—most of which Craig had worn the red-and-cream uniform of a Husker football player. There were always at least five other guys in the same uniform. Every year. Would bet some cold, hard cash that hadn't changed—and in a few months he'd find out for sure and in person, because this wasn't a visit.

Mr. Applegate was sweeping the dust off the wide sidewalk in front of his Sports Shop. Craig had bought every single pair of cleats he'd owned up until college from him. Mr. Applegate would ask him about the team while he worked on fitting. Were the guys working hard? How was Coach handling this or that situation? How were the new linemen? Blocking for him?

Don't ever forget they make your job possible, son. You'll go nowhere without a good line.

Craig had never forgotten. Never once took for granted the men who protected his job by doing theirs well.

Next to Applegate's, the Garretts were busy inside their family-owned and state-celebrated bakery. Mary Garrett was wiping down the long length of butcher-block counter, visible through the gleaming streak-free window. They were open, but it was slow. Saturday evening. Most people hit The Grill or Hot Stuff Pizza on a Saturday. Henry Garrett was probably back in the kitchen, putting together the specials for the coming week. Best lunch this side of the Missouri. Hands down. Their son, Easton, sat perched on a round barstool at the far end of that counter. Elbows propped up. Playbook open, getting ready for a brand-new year. He'd be a senior by now.

Easton should be playing for Coach Blaum. Craig had heard that he was quite the lineman. Coach was famous for his linemen.

Past Main Street, the high school sat enthroned on a small rise to the right. The center of life in Big Prairie. At least, it had felt that way for Craig and most of the other kids in his class. Once upon a time. He'd lived out some of his best moments there.

And worst. Absolute worst.

The Grill served as a distraction, coming up on his left as the road led him past Main Street. Suddenly, he had a powerful need for some fried to a perfect crunchy-on-the-outside-soft-on-the-inside waffle fries. With a quick turn, he pulled into the parking lot, a smile lifting his cheeks. This, he'd missed, and this, he was ready for.

The smells of fried food and char-grilled meat wafted from the old drive-in restaurant, making his stomach antsy and his steps quicken. How long had it been? He'd come back to visit Mom but hadn't done a whole lot of interacting in town. So it'd been years. Long overdue.

He reached for the long metal handle, eager to remedy that problem.

"Ah. At last, the hometown hero returns."

Craig brushed at the warm blush that crawled over his ears as he turned toward the familiar voice behind him. Hank Johnson had covered every high school game the Broncs had ever played, his animated voice bringing the away games to life for those unlucky few who couldn't make the trip. Turning, he hoped that rush of warmth hadn't painted his cheeks. Likely, it had.

"How are you, Mr. Johnson?" Craig grinned as he clasped hands with the burly, nearly bald man.

"Better now that you're here, Erikson. And you're a grown

man, so it's Hank." He pumped his hand with a firm grip. "You got back not a moment too soon, I'd say. Our boys sure could use some inspiring direction. Things have been looking pretty low over there." He pointed toward the high school perched up on that hill. Or, more specifically, to the stadium.

Craig looked at his shoes, fiddling with the bill of his hat. "Well, sir, not sure you've heard things right. I'm not back in Big Prairie for football. I'm a music teacher, actually. I work with smaller kids."

"Saw that in the paper." Hank dipped a firm nod. "You're a man of many talents, and that's great. But the Broncs have gone under five hundred for three seasons straight. The boys need a coach who can bring back the tradition."

Nope. Not gonna happen. Not here. Not ever.

Instead of speaking his immediate reaction, he held up a hand and shook his head, maintaining that friendly smile he'd been a bit famous for. "They already have a man for that job."

"Hale's not getting it done."

"Some things take time."

Hank grunted. "Some things ain't gonna happen."

True that.

Craig forced a friendly tone when he wanted to snap. After all, the man in front of him had sung his praises for a string of years. And he was offering him a compliment even now, though it came in the form of an insult to a man not present.

"Thanks for thinking so highly of me, Hank. But I'm not here to coach. That's just the way things sit."

With eyebrows pulled inward, a look of curiosity and maybe concern, Hank Johnson let several beats pass before he finally nodded. "Well, Craig, maybe that's so." A smile broke through that concerned look. "All the same, it's good to see you back."

Tension that had arrived somewhere near the beginning of the conversation eased from Craig's shoulders, and he shook Hank's hand again. "Thanks. It's good to be here."

Hank nodded and then passed through the door Craig had

pulled open. The entry closed on his heels, Craig still standing on the outside of it. He turned, his craving for waffle fries now gone. If that first encounter was any indication, he was in for a whole lot of expectations he couldn't meet. Which had been the second biggest reason he'd never come home to stay after college.

The biggest reason...

Well. One hurdle at a time. He climbed back into his Jeep and backed out of the lot. There was a neighborhood tucked into the lip of that small rise beneath the school, and he aimed the nose of his car that way.

The road wound east and then cut south. Five houses down. Yellow siding, six-paned windows, small front porch. It was where he and his mom had battled over homework and chores—in the same little nine-hundred-square-foot bungalow Mom somehow managed to buy when Craig was two. In that same house, he'd realized somewhere around age twelve that single moms had a heavy load and his didn't need him to make life harder. Their relationship changed that winter, and they were still close.

Good thing. Craig needed her. She kept him grounded in places that either had too much air or too much depth. Mom was the solid under his feet. She was the reason Craig was there—coming back to Big Prairie when he really hadn't thought he could return. For her he'd push through it, because right now she needed him too.

That reality had come too soon. The thought tripped through his mind, clattering around with a painful punch, like running into a table while stumbling through the dark. Craig shoved it down as he pulled onto the cracked drive, taking the emotion it provoked in a hard, demanding grip. He couldn't deal with it all at once. Coming back was overwhelming enough for the day.

The air was heavy with warm humidity as he stepped out of

his Jeep Wrangler and stretched. The old house needed a fresh coat of butter-yellow paint. He could tackle that on a weekend. Be good to have something to do. Something to keep him busy and tired.

Craig turned, closing the door to the Jeep as he moved, and watched the life he used to live continue on without him. Ten-year-old boys on bikes, zipping up the lane. One with his father playing catch in their front yard. It provoked memories of Scottie, and the corner of his mouth ticked upward.

Pausing on the sidewalk that led to his front door, Craig turned, took in all that he'd known. All that was familiar and haunting. The life he'd lived, staring at him as if he were a stranger.

Crazy. Big Prairie hadn't changed. And yet it felt completely different. Everything had shifted, and though he'd left at age eighteen as a hometown hero—and would be welcomed back as a twenty-nine-year-old, and, for the most part, that same hero—this home that he'd known and loved for forever was never really going to feel like home again.

It just couldn't. Because he didn't know anyone who had walked on the moon. And he certainly never would.

Chapter Three

"You okay?" Mom delivered a pair of peach iced teas—her specialty—to the table on the back patio. One for Craig. One for her.

The late summer days were still long. Though it was nine thirty, light scattered over the green grass, softer than the intense afternoon heat that had pressed against him when Craig had arrived the day before. Long shadows cast shapes over the yard—the triangle pitch of the roof, round poofs of Mom's rose bushes lining the west fence.

He looked up and smiled as she eased herself onto the cushion of the iron patio chair. As a birthday gift, he'd bought her this set three years ago. She'd gushed about how generous the present had been, how nice the set was, and how he spoiled her. He'd told her she deserved it. Because she did.

"I'm good," Craig said.

Pride made her smiling eyes dance. "It's a big step—coming home. Are you sure?"

He sipped on the drink she'd brought. Oh so good. He missed these little things. With a wandering gaze over the shadows quilting the lawn, he let the moment settle. What an hour before had been a backyard filled with yelling—his and the two Fulton boys who'd lived with Mom for the past three months of the summer—was now peaceful. Trent and Ashton had compliantly showered—necessary after a game of five hundred—while Craig had strummed his guitar, and then they'd been off to bed. School schedule, which was a solemn goodbye to summer.

Big changes for all of them.

"Completely sure, Mom. Did you really think I was going to let you do this alone?"

She chuckled in the easy way that only Mom could pull off in a crisis. "I'm gonna be fine, buddy."

"I know it." He pushed the words around the swelling in his throat. Cancer. Two syllables that wielded the power to make a grown man break. His mom had cancer. "I'm gonna be right here to see that you are," he said, voice tight.

The warmth of her dry, work-worn hand covered his arm. Small. Sinewy. Long fingers. Hands that had held his back when she'd helped him learn how to walk. Fingers that had covered his as they patiently helped him form letters as a little boy. Hands that had selflessly made every meal, cleaned so many messes, washed grass and blood stains from uniforms. Hands that had clapped until they were red at every single game. Hands that, on the day he'd left for college, had cupped his cheeks as she told him to remember who he was—that he had his name and his word, and to never break either. Hands that pressed compassion against his shoulders as he'd wept on the worst day of his life.

He covered that hand. Held it.

She stared at the long fingers smothering hers. Craig wondered if she was scrolling through her own memories.

"You start tomorrow?" she asked.

"Yeah."

"Ready for that?"

"Teaching? Yeah. I love it," he said. "I'm my best me with the kids."

"I believe that. You always were." She slipped her hand away and leaned back. "That's not really what I meant though. This is a big step for you."

Coming back. Staying. That was what she meant.

Craig had missed Big Prairie. In truth, he had never really moved—instead he'd become a tetherless wanderer. Not a vagrant, but homeless nonetheless. For the past several years, he'd traveled from town to town, desperately clinging to the pieces of himself that had survived the last chapters of his Big Prairie story, hoping to find a place that called for him to settle down. To move in and claim as his new home.

Mom, though not wanting him to go far, encouraged this meandering search. "Find a place to transplant, son," she'd say, all her love heavy in her voice. "Set down new roots—and let the things of the past go."

For a few brief days, he'd hoped maybe Rock Creek would be that new hometown for him. Likely, because it was convenient. He had family there—an aunt and some cousins, so that made sense. And there had been a little girl in the kindergarten class he'd taught whose zest for life sparked a little bit of hope into the place that had wilted in his soul. Sydney Brennan. She reminded him of Scottie. Of his energy, his undefeatable attitude, and his smile.

Sydney's mom had been cute too. But that was as far as the attraction went. Kale had fallen in love with someone else—a great guy named Joe, and Craig was perfectly happy for them both.

I tried, Mom. Truly I did. But those things she wanted him to let go? They weren't things at all. They were people.

Brenna and Scottie.

Unforgettable names scrawled across his heart, along with faces and memories impossible to forget. Written in bold strokes, with Sharpie permanence, on nearly every page of his past. Good days—best days.

And worst.

They couldn't be erased. Nor could he let them go. So when Mom's health suddenly took a nosedive and she and the two boys under her care needed help, of course Craig came home. To the place that still burned. To the place that still called. To all those memories that haunted.

Brenna was still here.

Scottie was not.

And his new permanent job would be in the halls that had contained a lifetime of memories of *them.* Which was what Mom was talking about. Was he ready for that?

Yeah, it was a big step. Facing the ghosts. Living in the haunted. Pretending that life had moved forward, gone on, and he was as good as he'd claimed to be with his easy smile and natural kid charm. Could anyone ever be ready for that?

"It'll be fine, Mom. Brenna and me...we've both moved on. Life goes on."

"It does."

Craig wasn't sure if she was agreeing or contradicting something she felt sure was false.

"I really won't even see her much anyway. Probably." He took another drag on the tea. "I'll be hopping from the elementary schools to the junior high and back so much. And how much does she really meet her patients at the schools? Can't be that often. So—"

"She's Trent's speech therapist." Mom tipped her face, concern building in her eyes. "You know that, right?"

"Right. Sure." Craig smiled. He'd had a lot of practice at smiling in awkward situations. Being the single, apparently handsome stranger and kid magnet who happened to have also played a high-profile position at UNL in the not-so-distant past had a way of getting him into awkwardness. "Shouldn't be a problem. Like I said, we've both moved on."

"Hmm." Mom looked over the yard, where the shadows had swallowed the grass and the day was giving into twilight. "You've both been through a lot..."

"*She's* been through a lot, Mom." As he examined the diamond pattern on the table, his voice wilted into quiet because shame still had a way of smothering the perennial optimism of his personality. "She and Coach and Mrs. Blaum. Don't equate their heartache with mine. That isn't right."

"Craig." Her hand covered his arm again.

He shook his head. "I mean it, Mom. Please don't. Don't dishonor them like that."

As night closed in, gentle darkness blanketing the patio, a pull of silence spanned between them. She would forever carry compassion for him about this, and heaven bless her for that. But it made the truth that he carried worse—and she couldn't understand. She didn't know all of it. Didn't know what had happened between Brenna and him and why they would never be able to overcome the tragedy of Scottie.

"She's been dating Grant Hillman for a while now."

"Heard that." Straightening his slouch, he leaned over to hug her. "See there? Moved on." With a tender pat to her shoulder, he let her go and stood.

"Maybe," she said, head tilted to look up.

"It's for the best, Mom. Grant's a good guy, and Brenna deserves to be happy again."

Though so slight it was barely perceptible, her eyebrows lifted.

Wasn't going to play into that silent challenge.

The phone in his palm buzzed with an incoming text. Intending only to see who was messaging him, he glanced at the screen.

Did you make it into town okay? This is a good thing, son. Hard. But good. I'm proud of you. As always.

The knot in his throat tightened. Coach was still talking to him. After Mom called with the news of the C word, Coach had been the first person Craig had called. Maybe that wasn't right. He was certain if Brenna knew, she wouldn't be happy about it. But Craig needed someone...

That night, however, the dips in his life felt like too much. Careful not to sigh against the weight of everything this weekend had been, he stood. With a bend, he kissed Mom's wiry gray hair, which was styled in a trendy pixy because no matter what age she was, she would never be old. "Night."

"Night, son." She patted his elbow and let him go.

When he reached the slider door and tugged it open, her voice caught him one last time. "I'm glad, Craig, that you're back. It's good to have you home again."

Home again...

That remained to be seen. And was very unlikely at best.

***

Two blocks south of her surprisingly small-town-trendy apartment on Main Street, Brenna had landed a private office within her budget. A quick walking distance, plus the benefit of having Garrett's Bakery smack in the middle of her miniature commute, the setup was perfect. When she'd moved into the old Limestone, she had factored that in. Walking to work would be healthy for her. Not physically. Two blocks was nothing. She used to run a 10K pretty much every day. So two blocks? Phsh. But the walk was guaranteed to be littered with people. People who would say good morning as she passed and would expect her to meet their eyes and respond.

Grant had said it was a healthy step. Reentering the land of the truly alive. Participating in the community she had loved.

He was the mental health guy, so Brenna had listened. Well, to that part she listened. Turned out he was right. The simple act of meeting the eyes of her fellow humans, saying good morning, and smiling really did push her in a good direction—away from the emptiness. The depth of loneliness. She should probably tell Grant that he was right on that.

He'd grin a little—not the gloating kind, but the humble acknowledgment kind—nod, and say, "Good. What's your next step?"

Counselor Grant and boyfriend Grant sometimes overlapped, and to be honest, that irritated Brenna. So she likely wouldn't tell him anytime soon. Especially not with Craig back in town working at the schools. Grant's thoughts about next steps would likely involve an honest conversation with Craig, and that wasn't happening. Not the heart-to-heart, let's-dredge-out-everything type of talk that Grant would think was necessary.

Here was the deal: education and personal experience weren't the same thing. While he was a good man and good at his job, the truth was, by no fault of his own, Grant really only had one of those. And for him, Brenna really wouldn't want that to be any different.

But she knew from experience. Some things needed to stay dead in the past. Clearly Craig agreed—evidenced by the fact that he'd left town right after the funeral and had pretty much stayed gone.

Coffee in hand, Brenna pushed through the glass door from Garrett's and stepped into the warm summer air on Main. In her mind, she pushed down the threatening ache of memories triggered by such thoughts. Going back to those dark days wasn't a good idea.

"Morning, Brenna." Sophie Shultz fell into step beside her, meeting her glance with a smile.

Ah, perfect. The girl who wouldn't drag up old hurts because she hadn't been there to witness the damage and therefore had no memories of it. Brenna loved having a fresh face for a friend.

"Morning to you." She grinned, held up her coffee cup as a sort of cheers and question all at once.

Sophie understood the gesture. "Staff breakfast this morning. You know, to celebrate our first day back." Her head tipped backward with an exaggerated "Ugh."

"Whatever, girl. I'm not buying it. You love your job."

Sophie grinned. No. Full-on smiled. "Yeah. But it is hard to go back to a schedule when I've had so much freedom the past few weeks."

That was a bit of an overstatement. Sophie had run band camp two weeks ago. Five days solid with high school kids who really weren't thrilled about giving up a week of their summer break to march on the football field with their instruments. But she'd done well with them. Harnessed the energy. Took their enthusiastic ambition for selfies and great Instagram one-liners and redirected it toward harmonized woodwinds, perfectly pitched brass, and an impressive drum line. Also, she was amazing with them and proved once again that the best teachers did way more than teach.

Something Brenna's dad had shown her and all the kids he'd ever been connected with.

The exhibition marching band performance last Friday had been impressive. Ms. Sophie Shultz would be directing her way back to another State Superior trophy this year. Perhaps even gain another invitation to a bowl parade in January. And her band would love every moment of the journey.

"We have a fresh face in the district music department." Her voice all suggestive, Sophie nudged Brenna's shoulder with a little more excited energy than she'd have expected from her.

What was she hinting at?

"The hometown hero returns." Her wink dropped as if this

news had been a happy conspiracy.

"Yeah." Brenna focused on the hot coffee in her hand, taking a sip even though she knew it'd still be too hot and her taste buds were going to pay for the act for at least a full day.

"Come on." Sophie slipped an arm through Brenna's. "I saw him on camera when they interviewed him his senior year at UNL. You know, with that cute kid who loved him? He was melt-me-into-a-puddle gorgeous back then." Her elbow bonked Brenna's hip. On purpose. "Think he's still that good looking?"

"Probably."

"Did you know him?"

"Yeah. I did." Brenna cut a look at her. "Everyone here knew him. He wasn't exactly shy."

It baffled her a little to see that Sophie hadn't put the story together. Not that anyone ever really talked about it. Not anymore. The accident happened a long time ago, and Sophie had only stepped into their town two years back—about the same time Brenna started dating Grant. But still...

That kid who'd been televised with Craig? He was the high school coach's son. That had been part of the broadcasted story. So full of heart and charm. The reason that kid loved Craig so much? His high school coach had basically taken Craig under his wing as another son—which wasn't so unusual. Coach really loved his boys. Cared more about them off the field than on—which was saying something. And Craig Erikson didn't have a father, so...

Yeah. They were close. Also.

Coach Blaum was Brenna's dad. Sophie probably should have put that together. Brenna Blaum, her best friend for the past two years? Not a common name.

Then again, Dad and Mom had moved away from Big Prairie six years before. Dad retired. Started working at a youth camp in the Black Hills. Hadn't coached since. Sophie hadn't ever met them.

And the town—at least to Brenna's knowledge—didn't talk about any of it. Maybe because she chose to stay in Big Prairie. Or maybe because for everyone, not just the family, the shock and tragedy of it all hurt too much.

So her best friend Sophie Shultz, not native to Big Prairie but now a loved part of the community, didn't know the complications of having Craig Erikson return. And Brenna wasn't going to tell her.

Sophie pulled her to a stop ten steps before they reached her office door. "Think he's seeing anyone?"

"Craig?"

"No. Grant." She rolled her eyes and grinned. "Yes. Craig Erikson, goofball."

"I'm sure you could ask." *Smile. For your friend. Wrangle up a smile.* She hoped she was successful in that.

Sophie snorted a laugh. "Yeah, that's so gonna happen. Because I'm awesome with guys. Who doesn't want to ask out a band nerd girl with frizzy hair?"

"Your hair's not frizzy." Brenna tugged on an ebony ringlet. It bounced right back into springy position as soon as she let it go. "You should ask him. He's nice."

An eyebrow arched. "How well did you know him?"

Unbidden, moments known only to Craig and Brenna flashed through her mind, provoking a heated, visceral response that twisted her stomach and flooded her with both shame and anger. How well? Too well. Something she was pretty sure they both regretted. Once again, she pushed those moments down. Memories that she shouldn't even have, moments that shouldn't have ever been allowed to happen. They needed to stay dead. In the past.

Brenna summoned up that fake smile for her friend, squeezed her arm, and then nodded toward the office. "I gotta go. I'm not even sure who my first client is, so..."

"Right." Sophie's chipper voice didn't change. "I've gotta run too. I'll let you know how it goes." She stepped to her car, which she'd parked in the slanted spot where they'd stopped, and brushed a wave as she clicked the Unlock button on her fob. Another piece of evidence that Sophie hadn't grown up in Big Prairie. No one locked their doors on Main.

Like no one thought Craig Erikson was seeing anyone at the moment. Couldn't imagine it. Or maybe that was just Brenna?

He should move on though.

Her stomach pinged again. *He should*, she insisted into the pain. *After all, I have.*

Chapter Four

"I KNOW IT'S NOT IDEAL, CRAIG. MORE OF A CLOSET THAN ANYTHING. BUT WITH BUDGET CUTS AND THIS BEING THE SMALL TOWN THAT IT IS..."

Craig waved off Jeremiah's concern. "I can play my guitar in a closet. Or the cafeteria. Or gym. Wherever. Music is like that. Mobile. Part of life everywhere."

Jeremiah—actually, he should start getting used to calling him Mr. Colts, as he was the middle school principal—gripped Craig's shoulder. "Haven't changed much, have you? Still the easygoing optimist."

He grunted, a sort of laugh. *Yeah, but if you knew* answer.

"Everyone gets turned around now and then, right?" Jeremiah fist-bumped his shoulder. "Isn't that what Coach would say?" He chuckled. "Remember when I miffed that onside kick? Completely screwed up a kick I'd practiced a million times and had done perfectly most of them? In the middle of a tight game. Man, I should have been benched for the season. You all deserved better than that out of me."

Craig lifted his gaze, which had landed near his shoes moments before. "Nah. You were the guy."

"Not that play. But Coach didn't bench me. Stuck me right back in there the next go-round and had me do the same dang kick, even though everyone in the stands thought he was nuts."

"Yeah, well, you nailed it." Craig shook his head and chuckled. "And didn't miss another kick for the rest of the season."

"Thanks to Coach."

He nodded. Jeremiah smacked his back. "It's good to have you back, buddy."

"Thanks."

"You know, the football team has been struggling. Board keeps talking..."

Both hands up, Craig stepped back. "My days on the field are over."

Jeremiah shook his head. Held eye contact. "That's a shame."

"You're qualified."

He snorted. "Yeah. My wife would pack up and move back to Omaha. I don't see her and the boys enough as it is."

"I'll bet."

"You see Brenna yet?"

Should have expected that turn. "Nope. I'm sure I will soon though. Mom says she works in the schools a couple days a week?"

"Yeah. That gonna be weird?"

"Nah." Craig shrugged, hoping his grin looked confident and relaxed. Not like the churning in his chest—all tight and beyond uncomfortable. Why did everyone keep asking him that? As if Brenna was the reason he'd come back? It was like no one could get over them. Except them. "Mom said Brenna works with Trent twice a week. So I'm sure to see her then. It's all good."

Jeremiah studied him for a beat. Looking for a lie. He nodded. "Good. Like I said, it's good to have you back."

Craig was sure he expected an *it's good to be back* reply. He couldn't muster that response. Not because it wasn't true. But because it wasn't true. Contradiction? Yes. Still trying to figure out how to moonwalk.

Jeremiah turned from the half-sized classroom that would be his music room at the middle school, and Craig followed him out the door. An aroma of fresh bagels and coffee hung in the hallway, drawing them toward the cafeteria where they'd have their first official staff meeting. The hum of voices underscored the smell—energy buzzing with it. First day with the kids was two days away, and they weren't the only ones who stepped back into these halls with nerves.

Jeremiah strode through the double doors into the cafeteria and went left. Craig went right because while J needed to head to the front of the room to run his portion of the meeting, Craig had every intention of standing in the back. He'd blame his size. Tall guy in the front would be rude.

A line of teachers curved around the large room. Some he knew either because they'd taught him in this very building or because he'd attended school with them, again in this very building. A few he didn't, which he took as a good sign. Fresh faces were always welcome in Big Prairie.

Stepping into place in line, he scanned the spread that Garrett's had provided—likely at cost. They were generous like that. Fresh cinnamon bread. Plain and blueberry bagels with cream cheese. A platter of fresh fruit, featuring white table grapes that had likely been grown at River's Edge Vineyard outside of town. Three flavors of coffee, and the plain old kind as well.

A grin played on Craig's lips. This town...

"Hi there." The woman in front of him turned, smiling. Her slender hand extended. "I'm Sophie. Or Ms. Shultz."

Her smile remained friendly and open, her eyes steady on his. Not looking him over. Or licking her lips. Lining up some kind of flirtatious dialogue...

Craig liked her immediately—not unusual. He generally liked people at face value. But this was...comfortable. As far as he could tell, she wasn't making a game plan, which, honestly, was rare.

"Hi. Craig Erikson." He took her offered hand. "I'm the new floating music guy."

"Ah. Yes." Her grip was firm. "I figured. I've heard bits about you. The hometown football hero."

Heat dusted his neck. "Not sure I get to claim that title solo. Took a team..."

Her smile widened. "And now you've come back to teach...music." One dark and defined eyebrow arched.

"Very odd. I know."

"Humble. I like it." She moved with the food line, reaching for a small plate as she went. "I'm the band teacher, so we'll likely be rubbing shoulders a lot. Unless you don't want to. Then I'll mind my business." Her grin flashed up to him with a wink dropping over one chocolate eye, then she focused on the bagel she had grabbed, peeling the halves apart.

"That'd be ridiculous of me," Craig said. "I'd love to rub shoulders. Heard good things are happening with the Big Prairie band."

"You have?"

"Of course. I grew up here, so I keep current on the Big Prairie news."

Cream cheese spread, she moved on to the fruit plate, nodding. "Family still here?"

He followed her down the line, his own plate loaded with cinnamon bread and grapes. "My mom. It was always just the two of us."

"Mmm." She nodded, the coils of her long ebony curls

bouncing with the motion. "I grew up in a single-parent home too. Until I was twelve and my mom remarried. Can make for a tight bond, doesn't it?"

"Yes." He filled a paper cup with ice water. "Well, once I stopped being a punk kid, yeah."

Craig followed her to a table in the back corner and slid onto the bench across from the place she'd claimed. "How'd you land in Big Prairie?"

"Needed a job." She tipped her head and shrugged. "It's surprising how hard it is to find an opening as a band teacher. I hadn't planned on going rural—I grew up south of Omaha—but Big Prairie was one of three openings in the whole state when I graduated a couple years ago. You would not believe how excited I was when I found out that I'd landed the job. Turns out, rural is pretty awesome. I really love it here."

"Aside from the lack of a Starbucks and Target, right?"

She chuckled. "I really thought I'd die without those cultural crutches. But you know? Garrett's is fantastic. And road trips are fun. I found a shopping buddy, and she and I head out about every other month to find a mall."

"That's good. Who'd you snag?"

"Brenna Blaum." She dropped the name so innocuously. Like it was nothing. Like he shouldn't have any kind of breathless, heart-clenching reaction.

Because he shouldn't. Hadn't he been thinking that everyone in this town needed to move past what used to be them?

"She said she knew you." Sophie continued into his mental stall. "Well, of you anyway. Do you remember her?"

The knife was sharp, plunging deep. And unexpected. She knew *of* him? Like he was the boy down the road she'd seen tossing a football every now and then? The kid who everyone talked about because he was fast and had good hands? Like they hadn't spent over four years of their lives thinking about a forever together?

The smolder in his lungs was a bit alarming. It took effort to pull in a breath that would look normal to the woman sitting across from him.

"Yeah, I remember Brenna."

Sophie smiled. So innocent. "She's my bestie here in Big Prairie. Don't know what I'd do without her."

Writhe. Wish that you could figure out how to be normal. Know that, without her, this town couldn't be home. Not ever again.

The potent thoughts blindsided him. Forcing a silence on his inner monologue, he focused on Sophie. The statement—rather, the question of what life was like without Brenna—was meant for her, not him.

He swallowed a gulp of ice water, hoping it would douse the fire in his chest. "Brenna's a great person. I'm glad you found a friend in her."

Sophie continued her easy grin, apparently not suspecting any personal turmoil. "Yep. For sure. Grant Hillman—her boyfriend—he introduced us. You probably know him too, right? He grew up here."

Craig nodded. Grant had been in the class above his, making him three years older than Brenna. Not that it mattered. He'd been quiet. Smart. Proper. About as straitlaced as you could get without being a puppet.

But nice. Grant Hillman, for all his studious seriousness, had been nice.

"Anyway, he's a counselor with the district and is also involved with HR. So when I moved here, he made a point to introduce us, which was so thoughtful."

A screech and an echoey tap cut her off. Jeremiah took the front with a mic in hand. Time to begin. Craig hated that he felt only relief. Sophie was totally likable, and he looked forward to "rubbing shoulders" with her as the two music teachers in Big Prairie.

But Brenna? *Why her? Why is it always her?*

It was like their paths had been irrevocably welded. Several years ago that thought had been the best thing in his life.

Now it only hurt.

***

"How about lunch?"

Brenna leaned back in her office chair, phone held loosely from her face. Grant's invitation hit Brenna as odd. The staff was all back at the schools. As far as she knew, they had lunch catered in the first couple of days. A nice gesture by the district. Then again…considering that from this point forward every employee was bound to sleep, eat, and live Big Prairie public schools for the next nine months, maybe it was due credit. It was a little bit shocking to see how much was expected of a small-town school employee, and Brenna had grown up with a history teacher/football coach for a dad.

"Aren't you eating at one of the schools?"

"Yes. Garrett's is catering. Thought you would like to join us. There's usually plenty."

She sat forward, perching elbows on her desk. "That's not right. I'm not technically a school employee."

"You contract with us."

"Not the same, Grant." This was super weird for him. Grant was big on technicalities.

"Okay, you are right." He sighed. "Would like to see you, is all. I feel like some kind of wedge has been between us all weekend, and I'd rather not have that carry into the week."

Some kind of a wedge? Yeah. It was called he-wouldn't-leave-the-whole-Craig-is-back-in-town thing alone. By Sunday evening he'd brought up the subject three more times, explaining his compulsive and not-normal-for-Grant fixation on Craig's return with yet another round of "You cannot give me 'this is fine.'"

So not her self-possessed, *ask probing questions, but make sure you let them talk in their own time* boyfriend. The more it bothered him, the more the whole thing irritated her.

Which meant that they had ended the weekend divided. Lunch was probably a good call.

"Okay, which building are you in? I'll grab my own lunch and meet you."

"Currently, at the middle school."

Craig's degree was elementary music ed. So he'd likely be at the elementary. Which was not relevant to anything at the moment, so Brenna brushed away the extraneous facts about her very-long-ago ex-boyfriend.

"Okay. I'll be there in twenty minutes. Will that work?"

"Looking forward to it."

Nothing in his voice hinted toward conflict, and the muscles in her shoulders relaxed. He'd let it go, let her be. Thank heaven.

She finished the paperwork she needed to file for her last patient and walked up to Garrett's for a take-out sandwich. Turkey bacon on ciabatta bread with honey mustard and mayo. Favorite. Grant would likely go for the BLT—hold the bacon, add extra lettuce and tomato. Such a weirdo.

The schools were on the other side of town—which was only about a mile and a half away. Perfect distance for a decent walk if she had the time. She didn't.

Her phone vibrated as a text lit the screen right when she parked in front of the middle school.

Last-minute change. I am at the elementary. Meet me at my office?

Perfect. Her stomach clenched, swirling with a churn of nausea.

It's gonna be fine. Just...get it over with.

Right. They were adults. Grown-ups. And over it. Besides, Grant had an actual office at the elementary. Small—perfect for a casual lunch for two, and only two. Craig would probably be out with the group. Laughing. Telling animated stories about something everyone would think was awesome. Because everything Craig said was always awesome—according to everyone in Big Prairie. Or maybe he'd be out on the backfield, tossing a ball around. Organizing an impromptu touch football game.

Yeah. He's not a kid anymore, Brenna. So probably not.

Man, this was so stuck in her head. *Thanks for that, Grant.* If he hadn't insisted they discuss the homecoming of Craig Erikson the Great, she wouldn't be so turned inside out about it.

Right?

She clutched her paper bag and walked across the road to the elementary school. Shoulders back. Head up. Stride confident.

The front doors had been propped open—a sure sign that students were not yet on campus—so she breezed through while pushing her mouth into a small grin. Because...

She didn't know why.

Grant's office was past the front office and to the right. With an even pace, she streamlined toward it, only to have him meet her at the door.

"Hello." He cupped her elbow and leaned in to brush a kiss on her temple.

"Hi." She held up her sack and nodded to the cozy little space behind him where they would be safe. "Shall we?"

His brow wrinkled. "Everyone is eating in the cafeteria. It is kind of a thing, you know?"

"What? But—"

"Besides, I have not grabbed my food." He stepped out, hand still on her elbow, and pulled her along as he walked down the hall toward the murmur of gathered staff. "You don't mind, right?"

Was this a setup? What was he doing?

"Grant, I thought—"

Didn't matter what she thought, because after those last two steps, they entered the cafeteria. A few teachers and support staff turned, smiled, and waved. Mrs. Kline, who taught second grade. Mr. Henricks, PE teacher and baseball coach. Mrs. Liss, the administrative assistant.

Sophie Shultz, whose wave was not simply a hi but a *come over here.*

And that was when the lunch date fell apart.

Brenna's heart morphed to stone. Cold. Hard. The act of breathing became foreign. Because the man Sophie stood beside looked up from the conversation he was having with her and locked his steel-blue gaze on Brenna.

God, help.

Seven years. It'd been seven years. And yet.

There he stood. The storm between them raged. As if not a moment had passed.

Grant had been right. There was nothing about this—about her in the middle of this—that was fine.

Chapter Five

SHE HADN'T FORGIVEN HIM.

The entire reason Craig had stayed gone now stared at him from across the room, and he saw it as plain as an incoming blitz. Seven years hadn't undone anything. Before she blinked, he saw every spark of anger and resentment, still hot. Still fresh.

After she blinked, a desperate attempt at indifference. She shifted the paper lunch sack she'd carried and latched on to Grant Hillman's hand, which had been anchored on her elbow. As their fingers threaded together, she slid her gaze away from Craig's and smiled.

The fake kind. Did she really think he couldn't tell the difference?

They moved together. Grant and Brenna. The chord of their names together hit Craig sharp. Wrong. It had never been Grant and Brenna. Always Craig and Brenna. As their synchronized steps brought them closer, he looked toward the ground, hoping the quick squeeze of his eyes would go both unnoticed and clear the burn of emotion flooding through him.

Grant and Brenna.

That was the reality now. He had known this. He was good with this.

"Brenna!" Sophie's enthusiastic pitch was only what he could assume was her nature. She'd been using it all day, so he had safe reason to assume she was a normally optimistic person. Like himself—normal Craig—in any other moment but this. "I'm so glad Grant talked you into coming. Look who I found." Her hand wrapped around his arm and wiggled, the smile in her voice oh so innocent.

Eyes up, but don't telegraph. Don't let the defense read you.

Was it ridiculous that he still thought in terms of football? No. Certainly it wasn't. Besides, in this moment he was definitely not on offense. Not with the way fire had leapt in her eyes the moment they'd met his. The snap in that glance dredged up a memory. One he couldn't afford to look into at the moment.

"Craig Erikson." Her voice was chill reserve. As if they'd met at some business meeting somewhere in the distant past and she remembered reading his name on a card. The hand she offered—after she untwined her fingers from Grant's—clasped his all casual aloof. Like this reunion meant nothing to her.

Something feral awoke within him. *No*, it barked. *I'm not letting you sideline me. Act as if we were only ever tame friends.* The thoughts, the feeling stirred in equal parts irrational and dangerous. But he moved in, her hand firm in his grip, and wrapped his free arm around her. A move that surely looked friendly, bygones let go, casual friends reunited.

It wasn't. At all. And she knew the truth every bit as much as he.

Her spine rammed stiff. Shoulders pulled back, though she didn't risk causing a scene by stepping away. Breath held. The energy lifting from her stiff frame was as far from *indifferent acquaintance* as Pluto was from the sun. Rather, it was hot warning. Resentment.

Pain.

The wild pitch within settled. Her pain—it still festered. Right where he'd left it. He had no business picking at the wound.

"It's good to see you, Brenna," he said, stepping away. Inside, he folded. Outside, he dropped the hand that had rebelliously drifted down her arm and brushed over her fingers.

She swallowed. Looked toward the floor while her hand sought the safety of Grant's. He stepped closer, secured an arm around her waist. That seemed to bolster her. Steady the reality that Craig had intentionally rocked.

"So..." Sophie stepped in the space he put between them, her chipper tone unsteady.

Craig regrouped. Smiled down at her and then at the couple across from them. "So. Lunch, right? Sophie and I were discussing the genius of turkey, provolone, crisp bacon, and a slice of green apple."

"Brenna's favorite." Grant nodded, his mouth testing a smile that his eyes didn't attempt. Anger didn't linger there. Just...confusion? Concern? Maybe the furrowed brow of study from reading things—people—as he would. Because Grant had a gift as a people barometer. He could gauge the rise and fall of pressure and the oncoming storms that would follow a drastic change.

Craig wondered if Grant had predicted this intense moment of awkward, when the past caught up to Brenna and him and though they'd known a face-to-face meeting was inevitable, neither had prepared for it. Wondered what Grant would do with this silent storm in the private moments only he and Brenna would share.

Block that. Didn't want to think about it.

Craig grinned harder. Because surely that wouldn't look weird to anyone. "Well then, Sophie and I will go grab our sandwiches and join you two."

"Right." Grant nodded, his expression almost neutral. "Except I'll come with you. Brenna grabbed her lunch because she felt wrong about eating off the district's dime even though she works for them."

"No. I don't." Brenna cut a sharp look at him. "I contract with them, and that's not the same. Anyway, I brought my own, so I'll save us a spot."

She didn't wait for his answer, and he didn't seem to mind. Craig pondered what she meant by *us*. The four of them? Her and Grant?

Surely the four of them. Because they were making plans as a group. So that was what she meant. Or not.

Stop.

As they moved toward the tables set up as a buffet, Sophie in front of him, he glanced back at Brenna. If there existed a chance for this homecoming to work, he needed to stop analyzing her. And looking at her.

She'd gone darker with her hair now. Used to be blond. Why had she dyed it? Not that it looked bad. It didn't. The dark auburn absorbed the light, shining back a hint of red, and made her blue eyes appear bigger. A touch of bold highlights weaved around her face. Really, not very Brenna-ish at all. She hadn't been one to do daring hairstyles. Long blond hair kept in a ponytail most of the time. It was easier, she'd said.

Craig had liked her hair down but didn't mind the ponytails. Made for a fun little interlude—sliding that stretchy hair tie from her gathered hair while she twisted and squealed for him to stop. The moment it was set free, her thick tresses would fall over her shoulders, around her face, and his fingers would dance their way through the beautiful mess...

Stop that too.

His heart rate had hiked north a bit. Enough to be

noticeable, which was a bad sign. Those years-ago memories seemed as fresh and vivid as the scrambled eggs and toast he'd had for breakfast that morning. *We've both moved on?*

Clearly not.

"How are the meetings going?" Grant saved him from himself as they stacked sandwiches and grapes on thick paper plates.

"Fine. Just like going back to school."

"I imagine you generally got to skip staff meetings with your old job?"

Craig was fairly certain that was a jab. Maybe not. He was a little wound up. "Yeah, for the most part. Not really necessary when you're a floater."

Grant's chin dipped once—a thoughtful nod. "Perhaps it'll be good to be settled. To be part of the group—the family, as it were?"

"I'm looking forward to that. And to seeing the same kids every day. Building relationships with them."

Grant nodded. With approval? "Yes, I could see how that would be a challenge and maybe something to be missed with your other arrangements."

It was bizarre to be talking to a person you were pretty sure was analyzing you—politely—and likely nailing it, while all you had pounding in your brain was *I was in love with your girlfriend.*

He seemed to not notice Craig's internal turmoil—or more likely, noticed and quietly tucked the information away while he moved on. "Ashton and Trent are good boys, at the heart of it. It was good of you to come back for them."

"And my mom. I need to be here for her."

"Of course. But the boys..." His implied question trailed off.

Craig molded his pressed lips into a smile. "Will stay put. I'm approved by the state, and everyone involved is aware of the situation." He stopped, pinned a direct look on Grant while they waited their turn at the watercooler. "*You're* aware of the situation, right?"

Yeah, that was loaded. Grant was aware of the guardianship Craig would share with his mom over Trent and Ashton. As the district counselor, he'd be in the know.

And the other situation?

His focus drifted from Grant, finding Sophie, who had finished gathering her food and drink ahead of them. He followed her progress across the room until she stopped at a long table near the middle, set her plate and cup down, and slid onto the bench across from Brenna.

"I'm aware of the situation." Grant's voice was low. Controlled. Not threatening, but telling.

Heat churned in Craig's stomach, and a sharp stab flicked near his heart. Yes. Grant had known Brenna and Craig had history. He'd known the agony that had wrecked them both concerning Scottie. He'd known that because everyone in Big Prairie knew. That wasn't why Craig suddenly felt hot and sick and wanting to run all over again.

There were things that the general public didn't know. Things only between Brenna and Craig. The reality was, they'd been wrecked before they'd lost Scottie.

He wondered how much, if anything at all, Grant knew about that.

***

She was gonna kill Grant.

He'd set her up. Knowingly. Willingly. What was his angle on this? Why on earth did he want to throw her into the same room as Craig as soon as possible? It seemed the more logical approach to the fact that her ex-boyfriend—a guy she'd dated for four years and had planned to marry—was back in town would be for Grant (her *current* boyfriend. Ahem.) to keep her away from him as much as possible.

As predictable as her exceedingly neat, healthy, and rigid boyfriend was, she could not understand him. Not with this. And she wasn't about to drop it with him either. Oh no. They'd be having a "conversation" (Counselor Grant-speak) about this in the very near future. And in spite of what he'd request, *that* little chat likely wouldn't be calm.

Side by side, Grant and Craig meandered toward the table Brenna had chosen. One man tall, still built like the star athlete he'd been—though leaner and less muscled, because he no longer played as the starting wide receiver for UNL. The other man of average build and studious looking. Both settled a look on her at different intervals. Grant's unapologetic look searched in a way that made her feel both known and uncomfortable. Craig's...

Hurt. Literally caused pain in her chest. He had no right to look at her like that. All achy and lost and...sorry.

Time was well past for that. Well. Past.

Grant slid onto the seat next to her while Craig stepped to the other side of Sophie, across from Grant. A clear avoidance tactic, as Sophie had left the spot on the end of her bench open for him. Directly across from Brenna.

Guess he read her.

With a clearing of his throat, Grant glanced at her, squeezed her hand, and then looked at the pair across from them. "You guys mind if I pray for our meal—and for the year ahead?"

Craig nodded, one side of his mouth slipping up. "I think that's a great idea."

"Yeah." Sophie beamed at both men. "Wow. This is...I mean I never really thought I'd be surrounded by people who sought God's guidance at work. It's like this little squeeze from God, letting me know that even if I moved away from home all on my own, He's right here with me. Not alone."

With his smile gentle and full, Craig looked down at her,

his eyes all bright with understanding. Brenna's stomach knotted.

"That's good stuff right there." He nudged her shoulder with his own. "Not alone."

Grant approved with a silent dip of his head and then prayed. For God to be with them. To remind them that they weren't ever alone. For them to remain faithful to God's purposes and to reach the kids they worked with to the best of their abilities.

And to learn to forgive whatever lay in the past so that regret wouldn't bind the future.

That knot in her stomach twisted, and Brenna thought she was going to choke.

They were definitely going to have a chat about this. A very long, hold-nothing-back chat. He was tampering with history he knew nothing about.

Chapter Six

TOMORROW THE REAL WORK WOULD BEGIN.

Craig glanced at the setup he'd arranged. In the morning, the semicircle of plastic chairs in his little closet classroom would be filled with squirming kids, all lamenting summer's passing, while at the same time bursting with nervous energy about the upcoming school year.

This was it—the real deal, and Craig felt like a caged beast—trapped in something that felt terrifying and unsafe.

Craig had told a woman—Kale Brennan—back in Rock Creek that the traveling gig he'd somehow landed suited him.

He hadn't told her why.

It wasn't that he didn't like commitment. There had been several things over the years that he'd gone all in for.

Coach Blaum. You couldn't play for Coach Blaum without going all in. Not because he wouldn't allow it by way of punishment but because the man possessed some kind of motivational magic. He was the kind of coach, the kind of man, who drew the best out of his players, both on and off the field. The team had put everything out there because of him. Because how could they not?

His mom. Once Craig understood, at least a little bit, of life from her perspective, there was next to nothing he wouldn't do for her. She amazed him with her stubborn love and giving spirit, and he was resolute to return that kind of commitment.

Scottie. Man, he missed him. Missed his antics. His ever demand that Craig "work until you ain't got no more to give." He missed ice cream Sunday nights, which Scottie had thought was so clever: "Ice cream sundaes on ice cream Sunday!" He'd never missed a chance to say it and to laugh hysterically about how crafty his wordplay was.

And Brenna...

That right there was a simmering storm. Craig shut his eyes. Let the memory of her sink in deep and allowed that long-ago moment that he'd denied at lunch the other day to have its say...

Brenna got in his face. He was playing ball with Scottie and took him down on a tackle—that was to say that Craig hooked Scottie around the waist and then turned, falling onto his back. Scottie landed on top of him—exactly as he'd intended. Scottie belted out a belly laugh, which made Craig laugh, and they were both scrambling up from the ground, when Brenna stormed onto the field.

"What do you think you're doing?" She stepped between them and shoved Craig's chest. "Big man, huh? Picking on an eight-year-old boy with Down's."

"What? No." Horror clawed into his chest. "We were playing."

"I was watching." She inched closer, jabbed a finger into his shoulder.

"Not very closely," he said, leaning over her.

She glared.

Wow. For a girl who seemed only to read and run, she could sure put a guy in his place. Even if it wasn't actually his place. She refused to back down. Her blue eyes snapped and crackled like flaming black powder while she delivered a sound tongue-lashing.

Honestly, Craig hadn't been sure what else she said. Whatever it was, it was fierce and direct—somehow he remembered that. But the actual words?

No clue. He was too mesmerized. How in his multiple years playing for Coach Blaum had he never really noticed his daughter?

Scottie yanked Brenna from her rant, grabbing her by the hand and storming off the field, dragging her along with him. Craig watched them go past the fence and to her car. Watched him slam the passenger-side door shut. She slid into the driver's seat and cranked the engine. Then she paused, shot a glance toward Craig, and drove away.

He'd been a goner.

The brief moments of eye contact the other day at lunch confirmed every fear. Every reason taking a full-time position in Big Prairie, though it had been all that he'd wanted after graduating UNL and after withdrawing from the NFL draft, was a bad idea. So awful, in fact, that coming back had been something he'd only do for his mother.

The twisting of reality and memories sent him off his desk chair. Pacing the closet room became maddening. He needed something to do. Somewhere to go. Back in high school, wind sprints had been his go-to. But the field would be in use right now. The last thing he needed was to show up on that turf when the team was struggling and people thought the Great Craig Erikson should step in and save them.

He had enough trouble brewing for the year.

Cramming his hand through his hair, and with desperation building in his veins, he sought a place to find relief. Garrett's. HotPies. Freshies. No. They were on Main Street, and so was Brenna's office. PerkUp Coffee Stop? Yeah, that made sense, since he wasn't a fan of coffee. The river? Maybe. But a bittersweet tug in his chest turned down that possibility. Too many memories. He was already raw.

The Morris Grill. Ah. Yes. They'd be slow to dead right now, a full hour before the supper rush, and with school not yet in session.

Mind made up, he snatched his phone and ball cap from his desk. This first official day had been a wringer. Perhaps a good visit with Wes Morris would set it straight, and he could go home to his evening, during which he was sure to stumble through as a dad figure without his mind twisted like a pretzel.

***

"I must have spent too much time in front of that fryer. Think my eyesight is gone goofy." Westin Morris grinned, his white teeth splitting a wide contrast to his dark full beard. "I thought for a second I saw the young man I'd hired for a summer in this man standing in front me."

Craig smiled. That had been a hot summer for a seventeen-year-old, and he sometimes had been a wimp about it. "Surely you found another young guy strapped for cash and wanting to impress some girl with a vehicle that has more than two wheels and powered by an engine."

Wes's hearty laugher bellowed, echoing in the kitchen and rolling through the dining area of the Morris Grill. "Jaycee, you'd better come on out of that office and take a look at what the wind blew in."

"I'm working sums, Wes." Jaycee's practical reply sauntered from the office around the corner. "Payroll's due tomorrow, eight a.m. on the nose."

"Ah, come on, Jaycee. You can push those numbers faster than the falls drop water. Get your pretty smile out here. You're not gonna believe it."

"Wes, for heaven's sake." Jaycee rounded the corner, shaking her head, though not once was there a sour note in her tone. When her eyes shifted from Wes to Craig standing on the other side of the service counter, she stopped dead. That curved mouth, seemingly ever bowed by some secret joy, lifted higher, and her gray eyes sparkled.

"Can't be." She edged nearer. "Craig Erickson?"

"That's what I thought too." Wes chuckled. "Then I figured I was seeing history in the heat waves smacking my face from the grill. But since you think it's him..."

"Oh, knock it off." Craig folded his arms but couldn't stop the chuckle. "You had to have heard I was back. It was in the paper."

Jaycee Morris slipped around Wes, giving him a playful smack on his backside as she passed, and nearly skipped to the server's door.

"Coming out!" she called.

Habit. It'd been a hard and fast rule—employees were required to call a warning before busting through that swinging door separating the kitchen and the dining room. Bust through it she did, and after five hurried steps, Jaycee had her arms flung around him.

Craig, a Goliath to Jaycee's David, bent down to catch her hug.

"Good grief, young man." Jaycee squeezed, patted, and then leaned away. "Haven't you stopped growing yet?"

"Yes, ma'am," Craig said. "About the same size I was when I left."

"No." Jaycee swatted the air between them. "Can't be. We sent off a boy to toss around a ball back then. Not a nine-foot man."

Craig shook his head. "Six foot, six inches, Mrs. Morris. Same as before. And I was catching balls, not tossing them."

"Where've you been?" Wes, palms against the counter, leaned into the pass-through window. "One minute you're Big Prairie's biggest news, the next it was like you just vanished. Some of us started to think we made you up."

Craig glanced at the white-and-black checkerboard

flooring, the slip of his smile feeling like dread and regret. "Here and there."

Jaycee stepped back and settled that gaze that could put starch in a T-shirt collar, as only Jaycee Morris could. Probably why the woman couldn't remember Craig's height and build, which, for the record, hadn't changed all that much in seven years.

Even with her diminutive five-foot-two self, Jaycee was a formidable woman. "That is not true. You have *not* been here."

She had him there. Sort of. He had visited Big Prairie to see his mom, but during those brief visits, he'd kept the kind of profile a fugitive from the FBI would keep.

The long pause held in the air like the thickness of a coming thunderstorm. Craig shuffled on his feet, unable to stand still in the putrid stickiness of history that had simmered unattended for too long.

"No one holds you accountable for what happened, son." Wes, still leaning toward the dining room, let his voice drop to something personal and comforting. "You know that, don't you?"

Jaycee's hand, dry and cracked from hours of washing dishes and filling out paperwork, gripped his and squeezed.

Craig dragged in a long breath, drowning the threat of emotions long kept contained in a dark corner he worked hard to ignore. "It was a long time ago."

"They say time heals." Wes lifted his brows, as if they were question marks.

"As if time is some kind of magic." Jaycee shook her head and lifted her brows too, her look direct. "Well, is it?"

He had no idea how to answer that. Some things had healed. Others... Well, there was a reason he'd stayed away. Wasn't what Westin and Jaycee, and probably everyone else in town thought, but yes, there was a reason. And no, that wound hadn't magically healed. Not with time or distance or neglect or any other passive means.

Likely it wouldn't.

Craig cleared his throat. "Seems not much has changed here."

"At the grill?" Wes straightened. "Shoot now. We paint every other year, you know that. Keeps the grease from staining."

Jaycee rolled her eyes. "Every other year the same old eggshell beige. Markus Brant down at the hardware store brings in a stock just for us. We don't even have to tell him when or how much, because you hit that nail square, Craig. Not much changes around here."

"Some people think that's a good thing. Predictability. Makes for fewer ulcers, if you know what I mean." Craig wasn't sure what he'd stepped into there, but it already had the feel of goopy mud. "There is a comfort to the familiar."

Wes gave a firm nod. "Exactly what I'm saying."

Craig slid a glance toward Jaycee. She shook her head. "Oh, he still gets riled—that hasn't changed. A person suggests one little addition to the menu and you'd think someone came in here with a mind to lop off that beard stuck to his face."

Wes eyed his wife. "Now, Jaycee, you know that's not why I got all worked up. You want some kind of weird deal for your breakfast menu, you go right ahead and stick it in there. I won't eat the darn stuff, but that doesn't mean some millennial passing through those doors might not want to give it a go."

"What are we talking about here?" Craig grinned at Jaycee.

"A simple little bit of toast."

"Ha!" West snorted. "That's not the whole deal, and you know it!"

Jaycee seemed to fight for glare, but a laugh trumped her attempt. "Oh, all right. Toast with avocado, and a side of cottage cheese with diced tomatoes, seasoned with a dash of salt and pepper."

"That's the way to come clean." Wes leaned back onto his hands against the counter. "And what do you think of that business, Craig?"

One thing he'd learned as a teenager working at the Morris Grill was not to get between the married pair who owned and managed the place. Palms up, Craig backed two steps and shook his head.

"Come on now, son. Can't believe a big man like you doesn't wanna take a stand."

He kept his attention on Jaycee. "You're still every bit the daunting woman who used to scare the football team into clearing their trays."

"I did *not* scare anyone." Jaycee planted both fists on her hips. "Nor do I scare anyone now. That is a bald-face lie."

"Ha!" Wes barked. "Not a high school kid comes in here but knows they better not trash their booth."

Red seeped into Jaycee's face. "It's just good manners not to live like a slob—especially in someone else's space."

Craig laughed. "That it is."

Jaycee dipped a *so there* nod. "Tell us what you really think."

"About the toast?"

"And the rest of it."

He shrugged. "Sounds trendy. And worth a taste, if you're asking me."

"And there goes the grill." Wes tossed up his hands. "Might as well sell the fryers. No more bacon either. We're gonna go trendy."

"Don't you dare take out those fryers," Craig said. "I came in for some waffle fries and a BLT."

"Now we're talking." Wes smacked his hands together and turned back down the galley kitchen.

"You didn't say what the real bother was." Craig directed his words to Jaycee.

"The real bother? With the toast?"

Craig nodded.

Jaycee sighed. "It's the why behind it. There's talk."

Craig waited. The silence stayed empty, save the sizzle of a fresh batch of fries cooking in the kitchen. "Talk?"

"Yeah. Hear some whispers from the economic development people. Seems one of those chain franchises is looking at setting up in Big Prairie."

"Chain?" Craig tilted his head, trying to wrap his mind around that implication. "Like a...a restaurant kind of chain?"

Oh wow. That was kind of big. Really big. Big Prairie wasn't a chain kind of town. Hadn't ever been, and if it stayed up to the people it'd always been up to, it wouldn't ever be. And that, Craig decided right then and there, wasn't a bad thing.

Hadn't been uncommon to hear a classmate wish for such and such a place around their remote town, especially when they'd come off a recent visit to Lincoln or somewhere else that boasted those kinds of places. Craig might have even voiced such a wish himself from time to time. Back before he better understood small-town economics.

At the end of the day though, Big Prairie had the Morris Grill and Garrett's Bakery and Freshies, not to mention HotPies and the PerkUp Coffee Stop, and he'd heard that Lance's new lodge down at the River's Edge Vineyard was serving more elegant meals a few nights a week.

He'd lived in a city that had offered more. Found out it wasn't necessary.

"Who's bringing a franchise in?"

Jaycee swatted the air. "Don't know. Could be speculation, is all. There are many details yet to be told."

"There is that talk though," Wes called from his post at the fryer.

"So you said," Craig answered.

"Talk that it's Lance."

"Lance Carson?"

"No other Lance in town." Even behind his iconic beard, Wes wore a clear frown. "His vineyard has been doing well. Real well, and he keeps that fancy new lodge busy. Especially during harvest season. People been driving over two or three hours to come and see and taste. Not that that's a bad thing." Wes pointed his spatula at Craig. "And I certainly don't begrudge him his success."

"Well, that is a good thing. Can't be but a bonus for you to have a little more traffic from a tourist increase."

"You're right. Might be, though, that Lance has that traffic thing figured out too. He's no fool when it comes to business."

"Surely he's got his hands full with both the ranch and the vineyard. Didn't his brother take off to be some kind of trail guide in Wyoming or something?"

"Yep. Lane's been away for the past five years."

"So there you go. Lance has plenty on his hands with all that. What makes you think he's the one bringing in a chain?"

"He has the capital to do it." Wes pinned a level, weighted look on Craig. "And the spot said to be the proposed site for the new franchise food joint?"

A hard pause.

"Right on the highway at the turn off for River's Edge Vineyards."

Yikes. Man, that looked bad. What could Lance be thinking?

Chapter Seven

"I DO NOT UNDERSTAND WHY YOU ARE SO UPSET."

Grant leaned against the island in Brenna's front room, hands posted near his hips on the quartz countertop.

Arms crossed, Brenna glared at him from across the room. Her yellow sofa became the force of restraint between them, because at that moment she wanted to grip his starched collared shirt and shake him. "You don't? Truly? Are you new around here or something?"

"No." He sighed, but one eyebrow slid up with a silent *you're being unreasonable* arrogance. "You said you and Craig were fine. I took that as you and Craig were fine. If you were not fine, you should not have said that you were fine."

She felt like he'd done three laps around her with all those sharply emphasized *fines.*

"Yes, Craig and I are fine. That didn't mean I wanted to have lunch with him when I expected to have lunch with my *boyfriend.*"

"We have done lunch with friends lots of times. Be honest here, Brenna, and tell me what you're really upset about."

With a cock of her head to one side, she slid a knee onto the arm of the sofa. "Ah. We've left relationship land and entered the counseling zone. Would this work better if I lie down? Maybe close my eyes, dredge up the past, and let you analyze the bits and pieces I vomit out to you?"

"What is with the snark, Brenna? We have dated for two years, and I have known you since you were twelve. You were not the snarky type. Are not. Except with this. With Craig."

Craig is nowhere in the vicinity, thank you very much. Brenna swallowed back the thought pushing to find voice, the taste salty in her mouth. Snarky? Yes, at the moment. Sometimes she was. When provoked, and the man standing all calm and self-possessed in the middle of her apartment was really, really infuriating her. Had been at it for four days now.

"Okay, you've got me on the snark," she conceded—and wasn't that adultish? "But you've got to admit, you threw me under the bus with the lunch thing yesterday. Didn't it occur to you that seeing Craig for the first time in so long would be a little bit awkward? Didn't you consider that maybe I wouldn't want to do that in the middle of a room full of teachers and staff, over half of whom know some of the Craig-and-Brenna drama and would be watching to see how we reacted? That was mean of you, Grant, and I'm upset right now that you're not willing to admit it."

His shoulders slumped as a long breath passed over his mouth. Looking toward the floor, he rolled his lips together. "Yes, okay. I see your point." His big brown eyes came up, concern and hurt mingling in them. "But when we talked about this, why didn't you say it might be hard—about Craig being back? Why couldn't you admit that to me then?"

She crumpled into the corner of the sofa, pulling a pillow into her chest. "I didn't want to get into it. I didn't want you peeling the layers, reading for things that may or may not be there."

"Why do you assume that's what I'm always doing?"

"Isn't it?" Brenna glanced up and over her shoulder in time to see him jamb a hand through his hair.

He sighed, took the four steps required to bring him to the sofa, and lowered himself onto the place beside her. Elbows perched on his knees, his hands folded, he looked at her sideways, pain and concern in that connection. "That is not what I want for us, Brenna. Don't you know that?"

"What?"

"For you to think that this relationship is me always analyzing, always studying you like you are some kind of puzzle I need to solve, a problem I need to fix. That is not why I'm in this."

Words evaporated as her thoughts whipped and scattered like dandelion seeds on a brisk wind. Truth? She didn't know that. *She* felt like a problem he needed to fix. And, harder truth, she truly believed that somewhere in him, he saw her that way too.

Why else had he set her up yesterday? Especially if he'd known that, really, she wasn't fine. It was like he was testing theories. Trying proofs. Attempting to make her see something that she didn't want to see.

The reality was she didn't want *that*. It wasn't the relationship she wanted either.

This raw moment of honesty. A vulnerability that one really only shared with the people one trusted and loved. It should draw a couple together. Build intimacy and trust. Why was it that sitting there next to Grant, part of their hearts laid bare, Brenna felt an expanse crack between them instead?

***

JOURNAL ENTRY, ELEVEN YEARS EARLIER

Daddy has this number one, you-must-not-ever-break rule with his boys.

Don't ever think about dating his daughter. No flirting. No touching. No even looking at his only daughter. Ever.

Seriously. He has it posted on the door of his office. In bold, all-cap print. Has since I turned fourteen.

Which maybe explains why for the past two years, boys — particularly the football players — treat me like...

Well, like one of them. Except no butt slapping. Because of the no touching — and butt slapping would be a felony-level infraction.

They're polite. They joke with me. Are kind. And that's all.

There's clearly no interest. I'd rather think that's because my dad is their coach — and they know he absolutely means his rules. (There are eight of them, that I know of.) I'd rather think that I'm not of dating interest because Coach will enforce that number one rule with a fierceness none of his boys would like to see. I'd rather not think that it's because I'm mostly a nerd, with the exception of a pair of runner's legs and a set of lungs that allow me to outlast about anyone in Big Prairie.

I'd rather blame Daddy's poster than think that the empty date record in my life might have to do with my fascination with books (which clearly overrides any sense of fashion trends or social popularity).

I'm quiet. Introverted. Academic. A little awkward. And fast on a 5K course. This is me. Think mouse, carrying a book at all times, races being the exception.

But not true when it comes to my brother. When it comes to Scottie, I'm Godzilla. Maybe a little too much.

Daddy says Scottie doesn't need my fierce protection. Scottie has a way of using his innocent charm to make himself loved by all of Dad's boys. Mom calls this charm "the extra chromosome gift." I don't know if that's true. Scottie is the only kid with Down's in Big Prairie, to my knowledge. So I take it on her word.

But the thing is, Daddy and Mom don't understand. Scottie is an eight-year-old boy whose mind will forever be much younger. He is the innocent. The one who cannot defend himself. If Scottie wasn't the coach's son, those boys would probably tease that gift of charm and generous love and ever-

ready humor right out of Scottie's extra twenty-third chromosome. I know. I've seen the cruelty of kids—I live among the natives.

    Daddy says something similar about me and his number one rule when I bring it up. "I know what boys think, Brenna. I have lived among them."

    So. Scottie needs my protection, like apparently I need Daddy's.

    Which means I'll probably be dateless forever.

***

    Brenna didn't know what possessed her to pull down the old journal.

    Toxic thinking, likely.

    There were days back there, captured in ink for all of time to remember, that she didn't want to recall. Days she had sealed from her mind, barred from her heart. Remembering only pierced.

    She missed Scottie though. Especially that night, she missed him like the naked autumn trees missed the green covering of their summer leaves. So much of her had gone dormant—and that fact became a little too stark that night after Grant left.

    He'd let the argument die. Perhaps because neither of them had answers for the other. Or worse, perhaps both had felt the fissure between them break. There were no tears. No apologies. No discussing or pleading. Only shattering silence as he reached for her hand. Brenna had threaded her fingers through his, and they held on as if that connection would halt the gap carving between them.

    Eventually his stomach growled. She suggested ordering pizza, fully expecting him to counter with a healthier option. He kept a stock of frozen protein blends—beans, quinoa, and vegetables—in his freezer. A common go-to in a pinch, and his place wasn't far. The frozen health food wasn't bad, so she rarely argued when it came down to it, though her forever, undying preference would always remain pizza.

Grant shocked her by pulling out his cell and ordering delivery from the local HotPies joint. He even went for her favorite—Italian sausage with mushrooms and black olives. A lump had bulged in her throat while she listened to him place the order. He'd never done that. Not in two years. Which actually worried her more than anything. Because it meant this unraveling in her heart, he felt it too. And it scared him.

***

First day of classes dawned with a red streak on the horizon. Craig wondered if the sailor's adage of red sky at morning carried any validity in the middle of an inland sea of grass. Either way, tension wound in his gut so hard it felt like a full-on blow from a blind-side tackle. Hadn't been that nervous since his first tunnel walk at UNL. By the time he walked into his closet classroom at Big Prairie middle school, his pits felt damp, his hands were shaky, and a demanding voice in the back of his head told him to get in the car, point the nose west, and drive until the fresh dawn had bled into the close of day.

Man, he was a coward.

He rolled his shoulders back as he entered the school and kept them straight while he strode through the halls. "Morning, Mr. Erikson" came from his fellow school staff as he made his way to his music closet.

He answered each greeting. "Morning, Mr. Colts. Mrs. Liss. Mrs. Henry..."

If poise was a lie, he told it well. Bald faced and convincing.

Alone in his tiny classroom, he let the pressure of what lay ahead pull his shoulders down. The morning had already been challenging. Trent was some kind of stubborn, and though Craig was twice his size and usually more patient than most, the ten-year-old boy had exhausted him by the time they'd walked out the front door.

"School be stupit," Trent had proclaimed for at least the twentieth time since his head came off the pillow that morning. "All them people just want to tell me how to live. Why can't they leave me to myself?"

Craig had run out of answers. None of the normal ones that seemed logical sank into the kid. So he'd said there wasn't a choice and to get in the car, and that was the end of it.

Awesome start.

Running a hand over his face, he prayed the pancakes Mom had served that morning would stay put. This whole freak-out nervous thing was odd for him. He didn't react that way usually. It was something Brenna had wrestled with constantly—she had always thought she was going to puke before a race. She'd turn pale and start shaking about ten minutes before the start. Craig's job had been to tell jokes. Or play the guitar he'd slung over his back. Keep her comfortably distracted so she didn't work herself sick or waste all her energy stores on nerves.

Craig didn't think he'd ever properly felt sorry for her. Not until that moment, because he hadn't understood how awful this nervous thing was. Rolling a fist against the threat of shaking hands, he wondered if she still struggled with it. Hoped she didn't. And then hated that he was thinking about her, because he shouldn't. Not simply because he and Brenna were done, but because she and Grant were not.

Desperate for something else to occupy his thoughts, he reached for the guitar, safely stored in its hard case, and picked the strings. When he was about ten, his music teacher suspected that he had a natural musical gift—if not perfect pitch. He'd been in the music classroom at the elementary school, and a couple of the girls in his class were plucking chords on the piano before the teacher came in to begin. The chord wasn't right—though at the time, he didn't even know the name of that particular trio of notes. He just knew it was off—one of the notes was off tune.

When Mrs. Marris came in, he slipped his hand up and said, "I think your piano might need tuned."

She looked at him, head cocked, brow wrinkled. "How's that?"

He pointed to Sharah, one of the girls who had been playing. "Play the second chord."

Sharah shot him a weirdo look. "I don't remember which one I played second."

"Just play those chords again. I'll tell you when to stop."

She looked at Mrs. Marris, who gestured to the piano and then shrugged.

Sharah played. Craig listened. On the third chord, he said, "Stop. Hear that?"

"Huh." Mrs. Marris stepped behind Sharah, placing her hand over the keys she had played. "I'm not sure. Can you pick out what's wrong?"

"Play it again," he said.

She did. He listened hard. When he didn't speak right away, Mrs. Marris played each note individually.

"The second one you played," he said. "It's not right."

"Do you know the name of that note?" she asked.

Craig shook his head. He didn't know.

"Then how do you know it's not right?" Sharah asked, sass in her tone.

"It's just...not."

Mrs. Marris smiled, though her eyes held disbelief. "That note is an A, Craig, and you're right. Right now it sounds closer to a G sharp." She tipped her head to the side again. "You could hear that in the chord?"

"Yes."

"Hmm. That's interesting."

He stared at her, not understanding. But he got it later.

She'd called his mother, and next thing he knew he was spending Monday afternoons in the music room with Mrs. Marris, taking lessons.

At first he hated it. He was a football player. That was his whole goal in life. Sitting at a piano learning what notes were what and how to read sheet music was not a football-player activity. Had no bearing on his life, on his future. But then...well, then he didn't hate it. And by the time Mrs. Marris had slipped a guitar into his hands, he loved music.

Inhaling the smell of school—industrial cleaner, sharpened number-two pencils, and copier ink—Craig made a mental note to thank Mom and to find Mrs. Marris's home and thank her for the music lessons. And also, he allowed a slip of compassion for Trent to edge out the buildup of irritation with the kid. Craig had been a pain-in-the backside ten-year-old too.

As he adjusted the tuning on his guitar, then strummed a few soft chords, the knot of tension in his gut uncoiled.

"Sounds good." Her voice held a smile, and Craig looked to the doorway to find Sophie Shultz grinning as she leaned against the frame.

Craig chuckled, dropped his foot from the chair he'd perched it on, and held the instrument by its neck. "Just tuning, so it can't sound that good."

She folded her arms, a knowing in her bright eyes. "Nervous?"

He gripped his neck. "Nah."

Her eyebrows shot up.

"Okay, yeah. Do I look scared?"

"Your hands were shaking."

"Don't tell."

"Never." She laughed, let her arms fall to her sides as she stepped into the classroom. "Hear this is your first full-time gig, so I thought I'd drop by to wish you luck. And to tell you not to be nervous."

"Were you nervous?" He laid the guitar back in its case. "I mean, your first day?"

She brushed a wayward curl from her cheek. "I threw up."

"No way. Serious?"

"Sadly, yes. Right there in the trash can in my own classroom, so I had to take care of it and pray the room didn't stink like puke when the kids came in. But it was okay. They're just people, you know?"

"Right." This should not rattle him. Wasn't like he'd never taught before. Besides, he was a people person. More, he was a kid magnet. Also, he wasn't a nervous person.

"Here." She reached into the back pocket of her yellow skinny jeans. As she pulled her hand free, her white, flowy tunic top fluttered. The contrast of her cocoa skin and glossy black curls against that snow fabric was a little distracting. Sophie Shultz was a very pretty woman. And her smile loaned him some confidence.

She reached for his hand and slipped a wrapped candy into his palm. "Mint always calms my stomach. Maybe it'll help."

"Thanks."

The pause between them seemed intentional, especially as she studied his face. "You have a story, don't you, Craig Erikson? Not one that is common Big Prairie lore."

"Why would you say that?"

Her vibrant smile lifted again, and she shrugged. "I see something...I don't know. Maybe you'll tell me someday, hmm?" The warmth of her hand filled his, and she squeezed. "Or maybe it's none of my business. Either way, good luck today. You'll do well, I'm sure."

As she turned, that white top drifted around her waist with an easy grace that was calming, and as she seemed to float out of the classroom, Craig wondered what she'd say to coffee sometime—well, tea for him. Maybe even dinner?

He slipped the hard candy mint into his mouth and mulled that over. He liked Sophie Shultz. Especially given the fact that when she was there, he didn't have to think about Brenna.

Chapter Eight

THE THING WAS, CRAIG LIKED KIDS. HE'D ALWAYS BEEN A KID MAGNET, AND TRULY, HE LIKED THEM.

The other thing was, he never actually lived with kids. Not on a twenty-four-hour, full-on-responsibility way. So he'd never before realized how the not-adult variety of humanity really and truly was.

The learning curve, he was quickly discovering, was steep.

Ashton and Trent were like...something. They *did not* stop. Unless they were knocked out in a dead sleep—well earned from all the energy they'd expended by simply living, which entailed constant motion, lots of words, and an enormous amount of arguing. And then after an eight-hour gift of reprieve during which Craig slept, they were up and at it again.

Two-a-days had never been this exhausting. Two-a-days would be a vacation compared to this parenting thing.

And he was only a few days in.

Then there was the full-time teacher gig. The drawback of

being in the classroom full time was that he was in charge. Responsible for everything.

He'd never been accused of being irresponsible and had actually been praised for the opposite. So to discover that this full-responsibility thing was harder than he'd thought—or rather *not* thought—was a bit of a blow to his pride and a whole lot more of a blow to his confidence.

Specifically, he was responsible for not only the plans and progress of his charges, which he liked, but for the discipline as well. This was not his favorite thing. Discipline involved conflict. And facing the reality that he might not be everyone's favorite person at all moments of every day.

Craig did not like this reality.

He really didn't like when the situation was the reality at school *and* at home. Which had been the case with the repetitive predictability of a contemporary worship chorus.

> *You're not my father. No you're not. No you're not. And I won't comply. No I won't. No I won't. Because you're not my father. And I'm not gonna…I'm not gonna…I'm not gonna…*

It was actually alarming that he could hear that in his head, set to music, in Trent's defiant ten-year-old voice.

Becoming a full-time classroom teacher while simultaneously landing the full-time guardianship (read *father-esque*) responsibility for two elementary boys might kill him. If that didn't, Brenna's glacial silent treatment—clearly her attempt at indifference—would finish him off. A fact that was going to get tested after school—4:00 p.m., to be exact.

The perfect storm was set to blow—Trent's behavioral concerns at school (already!), which now rested on Craig's inept guardianship shoulders, would be discussed with the educational intervention team, the members of which included both Grant Hillman and Brenna Blaum.

A sour burn turned near Craig's throat as he put the last recorder into its assigned cubby on the shelf and glanced at the wall clock.

3:45.

He could feel something like a barometric pressure drop. Wondered if Grant felt this tension all the time, the human emotional barometer that he was. Also wondered if he wished, with the same level of desperation that Craig wished with in that moment, that he could sit this one out.

Craig did *not* like conflict. Conflict with Brenna? Worse. So, so much worse.

3:50.

Maybe there wouldn't be conflict. Landing on that distant hope, he turned the possibility over in his mind. With each lap, the probability of non-conflict seemed to increase. Why should there be conflict? They were all on the same team. Pulling for the same thing—Trent's best.

3:55.

He rubbed his hands together, wiping away the dampness, and then rubbed his neck. Time to go. Get this thing done, make a plan with Trent's team. No problem.

He'd convinced himself of that by the time he passed through the conference room door, shoulders square, mouth intentionally relaxed.

Grant stood from the round table and reached a ready hand. "Hello, Craig. Thanks for coming."

"Of course." Craig gripped his handshake, then nodded at Paige, Trent's social worker and a woman he'd met with a few times before. Obviously. And then to Clint, Trent's court-appointed special advocate. "Glad we could all get together."

Paige and Clint both returned a civil look, a small professional smile whisking Paige's mouth. To her left, across the table from Grant, sat Brenna, the silent arctic island, writing something in her notebook. Not looking at Craig at all.

The pressure in the room sank. Storm system moved into play.

He could pretend all he wanted. Brenna wasn't game for pretending. Didn't matter that they were on the same team. There was going to be conflict.

Grant cleared his throat. "Let's get started then." He sat, and though it was a quickly passing glance toward Brenna that Craig wasn't supposed to catch, he saw the reprimand Grant silently shot her way.

Oh man, this was going to be rough.

As he lowered into the plastic chair at the round table, he hoped for the first time since school started that Brenna would stick to the silent-treatment plan she'd latched on to. At least then the conflict would all be subtext and not repeatable.

Not one to waste time, Grant opened the folder he had; cast a professional courtesy glance at Paige, who folded her hands on top of the opened file in front of her and nodded; then dove straight into the situation.

"Trent has loads of potential. I think that's obvious to everyone here. But as has been his pattern, he is only a few days into the school year and already driving his teachers nuts."

Cue the looks at Craig. Because he was responsible for this behavior now.

Craig sat back. "He can definitely wear a person's patience. He's smart enough to know exactly how to do it."

"The question is, why?" Grant lifted an eyebrow.

You're the expert. He kept his tongue pinned in place because he was sure that wasn't going to come off as anything but sarcastic.

"Likely, given the nature of why they were removed from their home," Paige said, "it was and is his attention insurance. The no-fail way he knows to make sure the person responsible for him in any given situation remembers that he's there."

Right. It was more than possible Paige nailed the assessment, since the final straw for Trent's previous home life had been that he'd been left in a locked van all day, windows cracked, with a bag of chips, a cup of mountain dew, and a cracked iPad, while his single mom hung out in the house doing what addicts do.

The reminder of where the boys had come from and what they'd been through pried at the knots of frustration that had coiled a mess in him. Not just with them—Trent primarily—but with several of Craig's other more challenging students. They all had challenges beyond his scope. And while discipline was both necessary and hard, the latter especially true for a guy who liked nothing better than to be seen as everyone's friend, he could still approach it with the mindset that each little soul held inherent dignity.

A few of the tense muscles in his back and neck unfurled. Not all. But some, and that tiny loosening was a relief. The discussion dialed in as Paige and Grant shifted focus, reading the notes that had been shared from Trent's teachers.

Does not engage in appropriate ways. Interrupts both teachers and peers. Does not seem to follow ideas or instructions. Verbally disrespectful. Refuses to do schoolwork.

Grant sighed. "So hopefully now it's clear why I've brought Ms. Blaum in on this team meeting."

Craig swallowed, pushing down the sudden urge to snort. It was laughable that Grant called her *Ms. Blaum.* Not only because—though they were all in their professional capacities—they were all on a first-name basis but because everyone at that table knew Grant was dating *Ms. Blaum.* Craig couldn't imagine Grant and Brenna as a couple when Grant threw down that kind of stiff distance, as if he were a character in one of Brenna's beloved Jane Austen books.

Something deep within lightened. Probably because he didn't want to imagine Grant and Brenna as a couple. He'd forced himself to envision them together on a few occasions—

to the extent that he'd actually pictured her in his arms. Liplocked. Both times had made him angry-nauseous.

Sitting there in that tension-filled room hearing Grant refer to Brenna as Ms. Blaum didn't help convince him that the possibility would transpire. He shouldn't have felt a thrill of victory in that.

"I've been working with Trent on his social language skills," Brenna said, drawing Craig out of his internal—and inappropriate—victory party. She kept her focus planted on Grant.

Still avoiding Craig.

"Yes." Grant nodded at her, his expression as serious and un-loverish as a doctor conversing with a patient. "I think we need to be made aware of what you're doing, and the goals behind the practice, so that we can all be reinforcing them. So that we're on the same team."

Craig held a steady look on Brenna. Silently daring her to look at him. Her attention flicked—involuntarily, he was sure—to him, and he raised an eyebrow.

Same team.

With a stubborn—proud?—lift of her chin, she launched into her therapy plan, which involved storying and language intervention to ease away from what Brenna termed Trent's "street language." Jargon for kids' slang.

Notwithstanding the disrespect Trent was proficient in, Craig liked Trent's slang. It rolled off his tongue with flair, matching his vibrant personality. Mostly, though, in that moment, Brenna had invited a fight with her fiery eyes and cold manner. Unusual for her—she liked conflict about as much as Craig did. But in that moment...

He couldn't resist.

"So when you say 'ease away from his street language,' are you saying the goal is to reprogram his personality?" He knew the answer to that. Wasn't entirely sure why he was baiting her.

Brenna glared. "I'm trying to give him the tools he will need to make him successful in a more structured setting. Such as school. Later, work. Not all of life can be played out in a game. Or on the streets. Getting by on charm alone." Her eyes narrowed.

Three bitter darts. Aimed right at him. Hitting exactly where she'd intended and sinking deeper than any of the other professionals in the room understood.

Her opinion of him still mattered. And her esteem reached the depths of the Mariana Trench. The sting of her jabs provoked an anger that rarely rallied.

"Of course, Ms. Blaum." Craig leaned forward, speaking slow and controlled. "I understand and am on board with that mission. I'm wondering if I'm expected to nix his slang— which is part of that charm you're apparently not impressed with—when we're tossing a football in the backyard?"

"Should have known," she muttered, jaw tight.

"Excuse me?" The space seemed to narrow, and his awareness slipped only to her.

"Should have known that you'd only bring fun Craig to the table."

"What does that mean?"

"It means that you have no foundation to give a grown-up opinion on this. You've been consistent in exactly no one's life. You breeze in like a celebrity, sing a few songs, flash a few charming smiles, look like everyone's best-friend hero, and then take off before any real responsibility sets in. You might think that personality alone gets everyone where you are, but the fact is Trent has zero listening skills. Couple that with his refusal to speak in a way that he knows to be respectful and universally understandable, and we have a problem.

"You want to call it personality? Go ahead. But you're crippling him. Communication is a skill that can open doors—and the lack of good communication will shut them. Trent is smart. He's capable. But he doesn't see the point from his childish view—and you're enabling him." Her face was flushed by the time she finished her rant, and her eyes sparked with more than irritation with the situation.

This meeting had been loaded from the beginning. There was no way either of them could sit there and not bring their baggage to the table.

More than that, though, she was right. About all of it. He'd known the truth before he'd provoked her.

Which left the question swimming in his mind, ready to nag later: Why had he done it?

The reasons had nothing much to do with Trent at all.

***

Grant didn't say much.

Brenna thought plenty on his behalf though. Her mind was filled with his silent reprimands as he walked her up the three flights of steps to her apartment. Once inside, his continued restraint pushed her to the breaking point. She plopped her purse on the island and wiggled her arms from her denim coat sleeves.

"Say it already, Grant," she said.

"What?"

"What you're thinking."

His calm, settled expression barely shifted as one eyebrow danced upward. "Okay, tell me what I am thinking."

Ugh. His self-discipline was infuriating. "Stop that. Just. Stop."

"What now, Brenna?"

"Tell me. Tell me I was out of line back there. That I laid into Craig because I'm mad at him and that it wasn't professional. Tell me I'm supposed to be better than that."

"That is what I am thinking?"

She palmed her forehead, then pushed the hair from her

face. "Grant," she growled.

He lowered onto the stool he'd pulled from beneath the island, never once breaking eye contact. "I thought you made your position clear. I thought you made a valid point." His scowl was the first sign of any real irritation as he shook his head. "I did not think you were out of line. Perhaps more passionate about your position than normal, but not out of line. Craig baited you. You responded. I did not and still do not want to be in the middle of it. The end."

That *was not* really what he thought. Was it? Brenna felt like she didn't truly understand this man she'd been dating for two years. Or perhaps, according to her wound-up mood at that moment, that he'd changed since Craig had walked back into their world. Had shifted to accommodate the fact that he knew she wasn't fine but he didn't want to deal with it.

She wasn't sure how she was supposed to feel about that possibility. Likely, not mad. But she was.

That realization jarred her. Drawing a long breath, she shut her eyes and tried to make her thoughts and emotions align with what they should be. She shouldn't be mad at Grant. Really, she shouldn't even be mad at Craig. Even if he had been provoking her, as Grant claimed, he'd asked a valid question.

Language was as personal as it was universal. How it was used revealed so much about a person, and the uniqueness there should be preserved. Craig was right—Trent often displayed his personality through his use of words. Brenna didn't want to quell that. That wasn't the point of their therapy. The point was to help him be more successful socially. Academically.

The challenge of balance felt overwhelming.

But for all of that, none of it was really why she was mad.

Craig had gotten under her skin. That was the barebones of it, and she'd lashed out in front of a roomful of people who she would rather continue to believe she was fine.

"Brenna." Grant's soft tone beckoned.

When she opened her eyes, she found both of his hands lying open on the island top, stretched toward her. As she fit her palms against his, she forced herself to meet his look. Behind the gentle calmness there, she saw a backdrop of growing concern. Pressing her lips together, she adjusted her gaze to his chest.

"This will not go away, sweetheart." His thumbs moved over her knuckles. "All of this angst, it will not simply disappear because you choose to ignore it."

"I don't understand what you're saying."

"Talk to him. Whatever this silent battle is, the fight is not between you and me."

Talk to Craig? The thought shot panic through her veins, causing her heart to shift into overdrive. She couldn't talk to Craig. Not about the past, about him and her or about him and Scottie. There would be no *talking* about those things.

They were lava. Toxic, scalding lava simmering dangerously below the landscape of the life Brenna had fought to maintain for the past seven years.

Talking to him would open a fault line.

She wouldn't survive the destruction.

Chapter Nine

MONDAY STARTED MUCH AS IT HAD FOR THE PAST FEW WEEKS.

Sophie met him in the little music closet, cup of coffee in hand. She wore bright-orange skinny jeans, a pair of Toms, and a flowery, flowy top thing. And as always, a genuine smile that made her dark eyes glitter.

"Here's to a good week, eh, Mr. Erikson?" she lifted her paper to-go cup from Garrett's.

Craig lifted his Yeti mug to mirror the gesture. "I'll sip to that. Has to be better than how last week ended."

Her full bottom lip poofed out a bit in a sad face. "Oh no. What happened?"

Didn't want to get into it. For all of his memories of a sweet, kind young woman, Craig also knew Brenna had a way of holding on to mad like a prepper would stock canned goods That made him mad—especially since he had yet to squelch the running thoughts and memories he had about her swimming through his mind like they were Michael Phelps in training. Constant. Powerful. Unignorable.

"Let's just say I'm not nailing the parenting thing, and I was called out on it last Friday." Among other things. He had yet to remove the stinging accusation of using the boys for a popularity boost. Brenna's bitter words tripped him up, made him question his heart and motives, and left him feeling upside-down about it all.

"Yikes." She scowled. "Who would do that? I mean, here you are doing a noble thing and—"

"Stop." Craig held up a hand. "Don't do that, okay?"

Her eyes widened, and then after a pause, she nodded. "You got it. But...well, from what I can see, you're doing kind of awesome with a tricky situation. I don't see why anyone has cause to criticize."

If she only knew. Had heard how he'd baited her best friend. Worse, if she'd known the motive behind the barb.

He was sick to death of Brenna giving him the cold shoulder. Of seeing her in the school halls a handful of times and each time having her look the other way. Two weeks of subzero silence had been two weeks too many. Couldn't stand that she was able to walk this town and pretend he wasn't there, that there weren't things between them that were long overdue a good turning over. Brenna's chilled apathy knifed him throughout the weekend as he suspected that her anger didn't have anything whatsoever to do with the two boys under his care.

Man. That so irritated him. Even standing there thinking about it made his pulse slug a little harder.

"Craig, truly." Sophie slid a step nearer and laid her long fingers over his forearm. "You're doing great. I really believe that."

From a distance, this might have looked...contrived. But the thing was, he'd gotten to know Sophie Shultz. She was as guileless as a baby lamb and sweeter than watermelon in July.

And single.

About time Craig moved along. Brenna had.

He smiled down at her, holding that sincere eye contact and waiting for sparks to...well, spark. Though nothing snappy happened, he forged ahead.

"Thanks, Sophie."

Her gentle approval turned shy, though she didn't duck from their connection.

Good.

"Listen, I've been thinking about this morning-meeting thing we've got going here," he said.

Both dark eyebrows arched. "You have?"

"Yep. Thinking maybe we should try it on Saturday. Maybe we could grab something to-go and head to the river?"

"What's at the river?" The light in her expression turned playful.

"Awesome fall colors. And water." He winked.

"Would this river thing be..."

She left the space hang in question, forcing him to define the intent. He shrugged, pushing against the heat crawling up his neck. "Maybe a date-esque kind of thing."

Women had this thing with Craig—they loved to see a big man blush. Apparently this was universal, as sweet, guileless Sophie Shultz stood there, grin steady on him, laughter in her eyes, making him lose the battle against the fire sure to color his face.

"A date?" she said.

"Maybe. If you think that's a good idea."

"Best one I've heard since streaming shows without commercials became a thing."

Craig exhaled. Dramatically, so that maybe this teasing woman might feel a little bit bad for her mischief.

She laughed, fist-bumped his forearm, and winked. "Didn't figure you as the shy kind, Erikson."

"No? Why?"

"Doesn't fit the profile."

"Because I'm tall?"

"Because you're popular. Wasn't more than two people who didn't talk constantly about you coming back to Big Prairie once the word about your return was printed in the paper. It was all *Craig Erikson* this and *Craig Erikson* that for a solid week."

Two people? He knew exactly the pair. But he wasn't thinking about one of them, and it didn't matter with the other. Hanging his thumbs on the edge of his pockets, he shrugged. "I was a football player. Kind of good at it. That's not really being popular. That's just landing myself in the local paper because of a pigskin more often than most."

"Not what I hear. But that's for me to know."

She turned to go, but he stepped to catch up. "That's mean."

Her chuckle felt like a spring rain. Gentle but full of life. "We're out of time, Erikson. Classes start in ten, and I'm not ready for small-town rumors yet."

There was truth in that. Ten-year-olds had a way of jabbering about things that appeared to be one way but maybe weren't exactly that way. Then again, so did every-year-olds.

"Ever wise, Ms. Shultz."

"Perhaps occasionally wise." She stepped past the classroom door, a wave drifting from her hand as she moved.

He stood near the filing cabinet, his attention drifting to the tea in his hand.

It's a date. Though he grinned, that spark he'd been waiting for hadn't lit. Maybe it would. Saturday morning there'd surely be a flicker.

After all, he really did like Sophie Shultz.

***

Grant hadn't been much of an athlete in high school, which was perhaps why Brenna hadn't known him well back then. That, and the fact that he was a senior when she was a freshman. Even still, she'd known and had interacted with guys of all ages back then, but mostly because they were one of her dad's boys. Grant hadn't been that, which seemed perfect now. Brenna had all but abandoned everything football, and she'd ditched running too. Nonathletic Grant was a good thing.

But he loved to float the river in a kayak. He'd won her over to the activity on their first date. It'd been spring back then, the leaves merely bright-green buds on the spindly fingers of branches cradling the river from the baby-blue sky. How could she not fall in love with a leisurely paddle as they'd glided along the river's gentle current?

Telling her she needed a respite from all things town related, Grant had declared they needed a day on the water. Wasn't going to argue that, so after a breakfast of lemon-honey yogurt, dark sweet cherries, and crunchy granola, washed down with a heavily-cream-laced coffee, Brenna loaded her kayak— a gift from her boyfriend—next to Grant's on his roof rack, and they set out for the river.

A chilled northern breeze brought the dawn on that Saturday morning, warning of an early fall and possibly a cold, hard winter ahead. Didn't bother Brenna much as she stowed her life jacket and slipped the kayak onto the silver water below the highway bridge. From there they'd float the day away, covering a leisurely ten miles to a picnic portage where they'd left her car parked the evening before. Inhaling the chilly air, she shut her eyes and savored the sense of floating as Grant's paddles lapped quietly against the water.

"I can see the stress lifting," he said, a smile in his quiet voice.

She smiled. "Can you? I didn't even know I was carrying

visible stress."

"Yes. You have been since school started."

"Hmm." She tipped her head back and exhaled, then sat up and dipped her paddles into the water to pull up beside Grant. "This was a good idea. Thank you."

"I have those sometimes."

"You do," she agreed with a chuckle.

She pushed through the water with five steady beats and then let the morning birds, the rustling breeze, and the rhythmic lap of the water fill the space between them.

"I missed you this week at lunch," Grant said.

A sigh threatened from deep within, and she fought against the rise of frustration. Did he mean to needle at things yet again—things like she was avoiding Craig Erikson—or was this a sincere *I really, truly missed you* kind of thing?

"You could come to my office for lunch sometimes," she suggested, careful to keep sweetness in her tone.

"That is not very feasible. Too many times a last-minute something comes up and I am needed at school."

She knew that. Had had enough lunches alone in his office to bear witness to that fact. Which would make a good counter to this budding disagreement, but the morning felt too fresh for another subtle but tense entanglement. Why were they having so many of those lately anyway?

"Well, this was the perfect solution." The smile she directed toward him felt a little bit like a plea. *Let's not argue again. Please, let this crack between us be. Maybe it will heal.*

He held her gaze, a grin pulling on his mouth, and then reached for her kayak to pull it next to his. When he leaned, she pressed her head nearer, and he held a kiss on her temple. Somehow in that quiet, extended moment, she felt both at peace with what was and trepidation with what was to come.

"I'm glad to be here with you now," he murmured, his forehead now against her hair.

The paradox of emotions stirred anxiety in her gut. She

sighed, leaning into him more. "Me too."

The sun climbed the steep slope of morning, setting out for its daily journey, the rays filtering through the changing canopy above and dancing white off the waters at her fingertips. Warming air calmed the restless breeze, and by late morning, as they drifted into a bend that would open to the swimming hole she'd known well as a child, Brenna was ready to shed her long-sleeve layer. Rounding the corner, she lifted her gaze from stowing the lightweight jacket and found a couple sitting on the shoreline, each with a smile and cup in a hand. Focused on each other.

Her middle twisted painfully, and she swallowed, ducking her gaze as Craig stood.

"Morning!" he called.

Heartburn flared in Brenna's chest.

"Good morning," Grant called, his answer mellower than Craig's, though not less friendly.

A beat settled, the space in which she was supposed to say hello, call out her own good morning or ask how they were. She couldn't manage any of the options.

"How long have you been out?" Sophie asked.

Brenna was being childish. She pushed her attention up, along with the corners of her mouth. "We got on the water a bit before eight, I think." She looked at Grant for confirmation, who nodded, his eyes intent on hers with careful study.

Great. Counselor Grant was bound to make an appearance on the river before the day's end.

"Diehards." Craig chuckled. "Looks like we are the lazy ones, Soph."

Soph? He called her Soph? Like he'd called her Bren. So casual and intimate and... Whoa. She was upset about a nickname? Sheesh. Craig was the nickname king. She really needed to grip some kind of firm sense of reality—and civility—and, sensing Grant's steady watch still buttoned on her, she'd better do it now.

"Saturdays are good for relaxing." Eesh. Since this morning exercise on the river was his idea, Grant could take that as a barb, couldn't he? She tried again, her quick glance not quite meeting Craig's face. "Where are the boys?"

"Mom said she'd take them to Freshies for breakfast and then to the park."

His mom took the boys...so he could go out. On a date? Brenna looked at the pair now standing on the shore. Close. Grinning. She took in her friend's beauty, so unlike herself. Black curly hair glistening in the sunshine. Warm mocha skin, flawless and smooth. Laughing eyes. Ready smile. She was the perfect contrasting compliment to Craig, who was still mostly blond and a bit of a giant. He also had laughing eyes and an easy smile. Once upon a time. Maybe he still did—just not with Brenna.

Not able to take the image of the pair, she looked back down at her hands. Her arms, now bereft of cover, stood out in pale boldness, littered with freckles. In her mind, she pictured the skin of her face, also freckled and smattered with scars left from a difficult battle with acne she hadn't been able to tame until she was almost seventeen and had been put on an antibiotic. Next to Sophie's smooth, rich skin...

Comparison is toxic.

True. Hadn't her days in college proven so? Brenna pushed away the memories, which would trigger guilt. No, they would trigger shame—and that was much worse.

Turning her head, as if taking in the setting around them— the water beneath her, the calm sway of the trees above, the cloudless sky beyond—Brenna pieced together a smile and then looked at Grant. "The Willowgrove Campground is still quite a ways. Should we keep paddling?"

Sympathy lay in his gaze as he nodded. "Onward." He looked back at Craig and Sophie. "Maybe next time we could all float together."

An offer of politeness. And maybe, of real hope. Brenna wasn't sure, and she didn't want to consider it. With a quiet splash, she pushed her vessel with the current, gliding easily away from the swimming hole and the pair now at her back.

If only her life could move forward with so much ease.

***

"The morning is delicious here."

Craig met Sophie's upturned face with a small smile. "There's a little bit of poetry in you, eh?"

"Hmm... Music, mostly, but music is just poetry in notes, right?"

He laughed, shoved his free hand into a pocket, and took in the nature surrounding them. "As are the river and the trees, I suppose. Only not in notes."

"Ah, now we really get into it?"

"Not on a Saturday morning."

Sophie nodded. "And not on a first date-esque sort of thing."

The splash of the paddles dipping and leaving the water faded as Grant and Brenna drifted farther away. Craig waited for relief to settle into the tight spot in his chest. Of all days, of all times, why had that pair passed by this exact place precisely after he and Sophie had arrived? It seemed as if heaven wouldn't let him push forward, move on. Wouldn't let him let go.

"How about something else not typical of a first date-esque conversation?" Sophie's voice had softened as her hand warmed the place near the pulse in his wrist. She tugged with little pressure, and he turned, following her to a twisted ash log angled perfectly on the shore to look upriver.

"That sounds...ominous."

"Hmm." She sipped her latte, released his arm, and settled on the log. "Maybe curious."

He knew what was coming. Pulse slowing to a sharp throb, he swallowed and picked through the facts he'd be willing to share in the promised conversation ahead.

"This tension between you and Brenna..." Sophie studied the shore across the river, her lips pressed loosely together, and sincere curiosity, minus censure, wearing easily on her pretty face.

"You can feel it then?"

"Between her uncharacteristic silence whenever you're near and the way you tense up around her, it's hard to miss, Erikson." She looked up at him.

Nodding, he held those brown eyes for a beat and then bent to nestle his Yeti mug into the silt next to the log. "We dated."

"I figured."

"For nearly five years, in high school and in college."

"That's quite a long time for a dating relationship."

"Yeah."

"What happened?"

A sinking sensation pushed into his chest. There was a simple answer to that—but it wasn't the whole answer. The whole truth was long and complicated, and it might mar the image Sophie had of her best friend. He wasn't willing to do that to Brenna.

Sophie drew in a breath, then nudged him with her shoulder. "Too much for a first date-esque thing?"

"No." He glanced down at her, finding her dark brows lifted. "Well, yeah, maybe."

She nodded. "I'm sorry."

"It's okay. I mean—" What did he mean, exactly? "Maybe it's time I start talking about it. I don't know. No one ever brings it up—except my mom. On occasion."

"Why is that?"

"My mom or everyone else?"

Sophie shrugged. "I don't know. Both?"

"My mom because she worries about me. Everyone else because there's more to the situation than Brenna and me."

"More?"

"Her brother, Scottie. Have you heard of Scottie Blaum?"

He waited only long enough to read puzzlement in her expression.

"Scottie was...something. Special. He had Down's, and everyone in town kind of looked after him. He was a bit of a celebrity around here—initially because he was coach's son and was always on the field beside his dad. But as he grew up, his personality—which was no small thing ever—began to shine. You couldn't help but love Scottie Blaum. He was stubborn and quirky and full of spirit and completely hilarious."

"Wait. Scottie was Brenna's brother?"

Craig nodded.

"The kid on those interviews with you back in college—that was Scottie, wasn't it?"

"Yes." So she did know some of it.

"Brenna has never talked about him. And her dad—he was your football coach?"

He couldn't help but laugh. It was the disbelieving, sad sort of chuckle. "Yes. The most successful coach in Big Prairie history. The one no one will ever live up to. Poor Coach Hale never had a shot."

"Wow." Sophie's expression pinched. "Brenna never said anything. What happened?"

"Scottie was in an accident. He was hanging around the football field on an early January morning. It had snowed all week, and that night another three inches had settled. He was playing on a mound of snow where the plows had been piling it up." The memory of that day crowded in, gripped hard. His voice cracked, and he had to stop. Jaw clenched, he stared over the river, fighting against the chill those memories brought. "Scottie was on the backside of the snow pile, and the plows were working, dumping snow from the streets... The driver never even saw him."

The air felt heavy as a silence gripped what had been soft and beautiful. Sophie's long fingers covered his hand, now rolled into a fist. He waited for the next inevitable question. *Why was Scottie there by himself?*

Because Craig had overslept. Hit snooze when he should have gotten up and gone to the field to run drills, like he had on every other Saturday morning when he'd come home.

"You were close."

He waited for relief that she hadn't asked that loaded question, but instead the need to say it, to own that it was his fault to someone who wouldn't let his popularity haze their perception of the truth, bulged through his mind. "It was my fault," he breathed, the words quivering.

"What?" Her hand folded over his in a warmer grip. "Why?"

"I was supposed to be there. It was our thing—Scottie and me. He loved to *coach* me through drills, and whenever I came home for a weekend, he'd meet me at the field. He was there because he was waiting for me."

"Oh." The warmth of her body seeped into his side as she scooted closer, looping her arm through his. "Craig, it doesn't seem like anyone here believes that it was your fault."

"They don't want to, because I'm Craig Erikson, their hometown football hero."

"No. I know that's untrue." She shifted, her knees poking into his thighs. "I'm new around here and I didn't see this happen, but the things I hear about you..." She gave his arm a gentle shake. "Craig. You're not just a former high school football star. Do you know what people say about you?"

Blinking, he dragged his gaze back to meet hers again.

"They say you are the nicest guy you could ever meet. That you are gifted with kids. And so very generous and kind. That you never let football be bigger than people."

The urge to pull his head down into his arms and sob was nearly overwhelming. Man, if people only knew...

If Sophie only knew. If she understood what had happened between him and Brenna...

"Does Brenna blame you?"

Craig drew in a long breath, willing back the tidal wave of emotion that had swelled, once again hoping it would go away somehow. Magically dissipate by the process of neglect. He shrugged, easing his shoulders back to relieve some tension.

"I can't believe that of her," Sophie said. "She's not the kind of person—"

"Brenna and I had hit some hard places before Scottie's accident," Craig said. "We'd—I'd broken up with her a few months before."

"Oh."

Yeah. Oh. And Sophie didn't even know the worst of it. He wasn't going to tell her either. This had been way too much already.

"Have you two ever talked about it? About Scottie?"

"No."

"And that's why you've been gone?"

Pressing his lips together, Craig let his attention drift across the river and into the trees beyond. Sophie's arm slipped from his, releasing him, and he stood, taking a step toward the river. Man, why couldn't he move on? They were here on a date sort of thing. What was this wall forever in front of him, trapping him in a spot he'd wanted to vacate for years?

A rustling at his back and the sound of leaves beneath her boots preceded the warmth of her hand, once again on his arm. "I'm sorry, Craig. That was so beyond a first-date conversation."

Shaking his head, he managed a half smile and then pulled her into a side hug. "It's okay, Sophie. Well, I hope it's okay."

He studied her, liking the genuine kindness in her eyes. "Is it?"

That full, predictable smile bloomed again. "You think I scare that easily?"

"I don't know."

"I'm a big girl, Craig Erikson. And whether this date kind of thing ever leads to an actual date, I'm your friend. Now I know how to pray for you. And for Brenna. That can only make me a better friend, right?"

He felt as if air had finally broken through, letting him take a clean breath, giving him hope that whatever had kept him hemmed into this hard spot all these years would, in fact, not remain forever. With relief he turned and pulled her into a real hug.

"I'm grateful for that, Sophie Shultz."

Chapter Ten

THE WINDOW RATTLED, CREATING A CONSTANT TAPPING THAT
STARTED IN HER FRONT ROOM AND FOUND ITS WAY TO HER,
SNUGGLED DEEP INTO HER THICK DUVET.

Rain tapped the tin flashing of the roofline above her
bedroom window, creating a symphony in stereo that
accompanied the throb inside her head.

Tylenol hadn't touched the pain.

Seven hours before, she'd declined dinner with Grant. The
headache had grown progressively worse since it'd started
somewhere on the river. She'd blamed it on the shifting
weather. Claimed she could feel the storm coming in. Some
people could, she'd heard, so it made for a good excuse. Never
mind that she'd never before had that particular ability.

After unloading her kayak, seeing her safely into her
apartment, and pressing a warm and lingering kiss on her
forehead, then her lips, Grant had nodded.

"Get some sleep," he'd said. It had been the only advice he'd left her with.

She'd made a cup of soup, downed a couple of mild painkillers, watched two episodes of *Golden Girls*, and crawled under her covers. The rain had started around nine. Now near eleven, it wasn't letting up. And she still wasn't sleeping.

Floating on the river, something had triggered, and that thought—that one lone warning that had pushed through her mind when she'd seen Sophie with Craig—had cracked a vault of sealed memories now waiting for her to examine.

Oh, but she didn't want to pick through them. She'd rather leave them safe and alone in the far reaches of what had been. Seemed the rain, the lack of sleep, and the demand of it in her mind would overrule.

Without her full consent, the scene in her mind shifted from the stormy night to a bright afternoon in November, the heart of football season, now nearly eight years past.

***

The year had been warm, even during the fall, and it seemed that the deep chill of winter would miss them entirely. After the annual Thanksgiving rivalry game, Craig had a couple of days off so that he could come home. A freshman in college, she had come back too, as she often did. If she wasn't in Lincoln visiting him or on the road for a meet, she came home. Her roots were sunk deep in Big Prairie soil, and nowhere else was ever the same.

They didn't know why or who had recorded Craig with Scottie that mild November Saturday morning, but by the end of the weekend, a home taping of the pair doing their habitual workout on the Bronc's homefield had gone viral. Looking for a bright spot in a struggling collegiate team, the local media had taken that video and run with it. By that time, Craig, a junior at UNL, had earned himself the starting wideout position, and he'd pulled in some impressive catches during the early season. Already glimmering on his own, the video of him with Scottie, a preteen kid with Down's syndrome—and massive personality—shoved him into the spotlight. As the season wore on and Craig's team pushed through a hard schedule with inconsistent results, the media continued to focus on this Nebraska-grown wideout receiver and his young friend Scottie.

Craig's hometown-hero status exploded. He became the homegrown Husker everyone loved, and the reporters wanted a feature story.

Craig had been hesitant. Asked her dad and her mom. Talked to her about it too. Scottie, however, had been ecstatic.

How could you not want to be on TV, Craig? You crazy in the brain or something? This is big! This is huge! This better than ice cream Sunday sundaes!

And the decision was made. The interview was sweet. And it went big, making repeat appearances on ESPN. Because who could help but love Scottie? Who could help but love Craig?

Something ugly had grown inside Brenna that winter. Where she should have felt pride in this man doing well on all fronts, she found herself doubting. Finding faults, looking for slips. Every time they walked together on either his campus or hers, she saw the looks of adoration, the flirtatious smirks aimed at the young man holding her hand. And she felt herself becoming less.

He'd become a celebrity in their world. And who was she?

She was *not* the beautiful cheerleaders who stood on the sidelines, slim bodies enviable, bellies bared, makeup perfect. She was not the ostentatious women who boldly approached him, smiles wide, eyes glittering with longing, wanting his autograph. She was not even a girl he saw every day in passing on his way to class, because she'd gone to a different college.

She was still the awkward book nerd from Big Prairie. The girl who, really, all she had going was that she had this quirky ability to run long distances and happened to be a football coach's daughter.

All she'd had with Craig was the history of being his high school sweetheart. Everyone knew that sort of thing didn't survive a college campus. Even if, for three years, it had for them.

***

Comparison is toxic.

If only, back then, she'd understood that. Maybe she wouldn't have been driven to self-doubt that led to her doubting him, which had driven her to desperate logic.

The rain pelted harder against the building, drumming not only the roof but the windows, like Sophie's impressive senior drumline. Against the storm outside, shame leaked through Brenna. Pulling the covers to her ears, she squeezed her eyes shut, hardening herself against the memories and the accusations that whispered into her conscience.

The sun would come up in the morning. The storm would pass. And she'd keep going. After all, that was what runners did.

***

His Bible lay open to the book of James as Craig sat at the table alone. Rare, this moment of peace. He'd read with Trent and Ashton, choosing a Sherlock mystery in a hopeful attempt to find some kind of rhythm in this parenting thing he was stumbling through. Trent had complained even as Ashton had whooped, but a few minutes into *The Hound of the Baskervilles*, and both had been captivated. The transition to bedtime after had gone so much better than previous nights, Craig had decided he'd work to make it a routine.

Just like this. Sitting with the Word of God in front of him, prayerfully seeking wisdom. Something he'd discovered he'd needed desperately his junior and senior years in college. The same sort of desperation he felt for it now.

James 1:27 came into focus again: "Pure and undefiled religion before our God and Father is this: to look after orphans and widows in their distress and to keep oneself unstained by the world."

This shouldn't be a point of wrestling for him. But the phone conversation he'd had with Paige after church had him in knots. Trent and Ashton's mom had walked. Signed her parental rights away. Initially, anger had surged in him. How could a mother forget the babes she'd born? How could a woman turn her back on her children? But then a heavy weight of sorrow—of compassion—had pushed the anger away. How tragic. So deeply tragic. Addiction was simply evil, and it tore him to pieces to think that the hold of it had gripped a woman so tightly that she'd given up. Splintered, his mind had turned to prayer for her and for the sons she'd left, an honest longing for redemption in all their stories.

Then as Paige kept sharing what she could of the woman's situation, an unexpected sense of respect had bloomed. Victoria, the mother, had told Paige her boys were doing so well right then. How could she expect to do better? She wanted them to thrive, and they were. With the Eriksons.

With him.

Before the words were out, he felt the weight of them settle hard.

Trent and Ashton needed a forever home. A father.

This shouldn't be so hard. It shouldn't be.

But he was single. He had no experience as a parent. And he wasn't doing well at it.

But those boys, asleep down the hall...

How could he say no?

Elbows perched on the table, he leaned his head into his palms. *This is overwhelming, God. Not what I saw for my life. How do I do it? I don't even know where to begin...*

As if an immediate answer, the image of Bruce Blaum—standing sideline, almost larger than life, approval etched in his kind eyes—floated behind Craig's closed lids.

I'm always ready to listen, Craig. Always. You're not alone in this world.

Words his coach had spoken to him when he had been sixteen and wrestling with a deep-seated anger against the father he'd never met. A man who had taken advantage of a lonely, confused young woman and left her a single mom to fend for herself—and for her son. Coach had shown Craig a few places in God's Word where God himself had said He would not only comfort the fatherless but would be a father to them. To *him*—to Craig Erikson, a nothing kid in nowhere Nebraska.

His mind had been blown. Heart had ruptured. The God of everything not only knew him but would claim him as a son?

Added to that, Coach had taken on a role he hadn't been obligated to. He'd taken Craig under his wing. Taught him how to be a man of honor, how to study the Bible, how to love all sorts of people. So much more than how to run a play and catch a ball, Coach had given him the learning he'd needed for life, to live well.

And now, there he was...wrestling.

I know it's getting late. Craig typed a text. *But I need some coaching. When you have time.*

There was enough space for him to blow out a breath, rub the moisture from his eyes, and ask heaven once again for the strength and the want-to to do what needed to be done. And the wisdom to do it well.

I always have time for you, son. What's up?

Emotion trembled through him as he read Coach's reply. *The boys' mom has signed away her rights. They are now legal wards of the state...*

Typed out, the statement seemed so simple. The answer plainly obvious. Coach didn't bother to ask the more apparent question, which was rhetorical at best. Instead he went for the heart of Craig's wrestling.

Are you scared?

Terrified.

Why?

I'm already struggling with them, bumbling through this crash course in parenting like a toddler trying to run. What if I screw them up? I didn't have a dad, so...

You have a Father, Craig.

Craig clamped his jaw as the screen on his phone blurred.

You have me too. What can I do?

He wasn't sure where to begin.

You'll need references. Possibly someone willing to testify to a judge about your character and ability to care for and raise both boys.

Leave it to Coach to take the lead. Right. Will you be one?

You didn't even have to ask.

Craig gripped the phone as he pressed his head against the pages of his opened Bible. Relief washed through him as he petitioned once again for strength and wisdom. For the first time in months—since coming back to stay in Big Prairie—Craig felt it.

Real courage rose as the wall he'd sensed before, the one blocking his way forward, loosened.

His plans had been derailed multiple times over in the last several years. But God's plans...there was hope there. And a future after all.

Chapter Eleven

EARLY FRIDAY MORNING IN MID-SEPTEMBER, BRENNA STOOD AT THE WINDOW OVERLOOKING MAIN STREET, ABSENTLY TWIRLING A LOCK OF HAIR AS SHE WATCHED THE ACTIVITY BELOW, THANKFUL THE HEADACHES HAD LESSENED OVER THE PAST WEEK.

Main Street came to life. Not that it was ever dead. For a small town, the heart of Big Prairie stayed lively most of the time. Garrett's kept customers coming and going at a steady stream—Mr. Garrett always inquiring about so-and-so's kid, and *How are they doing in school? Big plans for college? How about after, will they be coming home again? He sure hoped so...* And then there was Jane Tiller's little café, Freshies, which amazingly didn't conflict with either Garrett's up the road and across the street from her adorable little restaurant, or with Morris Grill, located on the other side of town since 1954. In fact, the owners were all good friends, and they found ways to make what seemed like obviously competing businesses complementary instead. Jane sold to the lighter eaters, serving things like fruit and yogurt and vanilla. She also specialized in farm-to-table goods, like in-season fruits and vegetables, fresh-cut and dried herbs, homemade butternut squash soup, and homemade jams, jellies, and sauces.

Garrett's held a firm yet friendly grip on the baking market, which seemed to be fine with Jane and the Morrises. Garrett's specialties were of the sandwich varieties, and it was impressive how many different ways Mr. Garrett could come up with to combine meats, cheeses, and breads.

Then there was the Morris Grill. That was fried-food central and a gem not to be missed for anyone seeking a truly small-town experience. Wes Morris would get ahold of Jane's many home-concocted sauces and would then apply his own genius regarding marinating, sautéing, basting, or slathering when it came to his grilled specialties. The food was art to the taste buds. And the waffle fries. The Morris Grill hands down had the best waffle fries anywhere. Ever. Seasoned with magic and a hint of maple syrup, Brenna, along with all of Big Prairie, population 6,000, could make a meal out of the grill's waffle fries and feel only the tiniest bit of remorse because of the overstuffed sensation they would leave with.

Nope, life in Big Prairie, and specifically on the street below her picture window, was never dead. But that weekend in late September, during Hometown Revival, the pulse of the town elevated.

The sun had dawned in a cloudless sky, spreading a cool, cheery yellow over the limestone buildings. The Main Street shopkeepers peppered the wide sidewalks, selling their wares. A couple of food trucks that were often at the ballparks east of town in the summer, and at the football field in the fall, now parked on the north and south side of the business center, selling funnel cakes and preparing ballpark-style hotdogs and brats, while Garrett's maintained a steady stream of customers seeking freshly baked goods and specialty sandwiches. Freshies also kept a steady beat of foot traffic as the townspeople followed their noses to the handcrafted hot cocoa that could not be matched at any sort of drive-thru cultural icon, and the fall and winter special treat of glazed pecans—something Jane brought in from her family connections in South Carolina and everyone within fifty miles of driving distance was thankful for come fall.

The entire town would have their treads on Main Street sometime during the weekend event. The fair-like atmosphere would be bookended by a street dance Friday night and a hot air balloon celebration on Sunday evening. In between there was the Saturday morning parade, the FFA sponsored ag-challenge series, the Adventure Run sponsored by the high school cross-country team, a cowboy poetry contest in the band shell, and merchants in the park who would sell things like handcrafted jewelry, locally produced wines and cheeses, and meticulously restored furniture. During the day, the local radio station set up live downtown, filling the street with music. At night, the heart of Big Prairie would be lit up with strings of café lights woven from one business to the other over the top of the historic brick drive.

There was nothing like it. At least, that Brenna knew of in her limited experience. She'd only gone away for a few brief years for college. Even then, she'd only missed Hometown Revival once and had sworn she never would again. The charm and feeling of belonging was too good to pass up, and it was one of several reasons she'd decided to stay in Big Prairie even after her parents had left.

There was simply something about it—about Big Prairie—that called to her, telling her to stay.

Brenna loved that she could look down from her third-story window to a view of twinkling white lights, the people of Bronco country smiling and waving, a visual reminder of life after heartbreak.

She needed that yearly reminder.

Coffee mug nearly empty and the remaining contents cold, Brenna pushed off the window frame, struggling against the pull of ache that last thought had tugged. Truth be told, she'd missed that one and only Revival because she'd thought going to it would be too hard. She'd see Scottie's grin, hear his laughter in every stitch of it, because he was all about that little community fair, and she hadn't thought she could survive the emptiness of not having him there. Turned out not being there, not soaking in those sweet memories, had been harder.

For her, Revival also meant remembering. Treasuring. Even in the slowly ebbing ache, there was a gentle joy in taking the time to remember her brother. Unfortunately, that meant often allowing the images of Craig alongside her and Scottie to intrude upon her heart. Oddly, where the memories of Scottie seemed to help heal the hurts of the past, the reminders of Craig only hit her with a hardness she still hadn't managed to name, let alone deal with.

He'd be there this year. In the flesh, not only in her mind. An icy mass pushed in her chest, and she turned away from the scene below, heading to the sink to dump her mug and stow it on the counter.

Didn't mean she'd have to interact with him. Right? He'd be busy with Trent and Ashton—both handfuls enough to keep Craig well occupied. And she'd be with her date. Her boyfriend. Who would, cross her fingers, not push her into another massively awkward encounter—even unintentionally.

There. That was settled. Now, if only her stomach would stop burning.

***

"It's *Revival*."

The word came out as if an explanation was not required. Which it wasn't. He knew.

"I don't want to miss the dance." Mom held his gaze with a stubbornness he knew all too well. Same stubbornness he saw in the mirror on more occasions than he'd like to admit.

"It's chilly, Mom. And the boys—"

"Will love it." She lifted her brows. "I own a sweater or two, and the doctor says that after I start the new treatment in Lincoln, I won't feel like doing much of anything. So I'm taking this chance, Craig. The boys and I are going—with or without you."

Craig folded his arms over his chest, leaning his backside against the counter. The mounds of paperwork he'd been filling out and filing with the DHHS declared that, actually, *he* was the guardian. The parent. "Trent had detention this week."

"Yes. He did." Her forehead wrinkled as one brow pushed toward her hairline. "And he also wrote the apology note you asked him to write and has completed the list of extra chores he was given, not to mention has kept up on his homework. You can't keep disciplining him for the same mistake. It'll backfire on you."

Dread settled into the spot where the fight had been. She was right, as usual. After all, she had raised a boy all on her own—and hadn't done a bad job at that, thank you very much. And though she failed to point it out, he was certain she knew he was digging for every possible excuse not to go. Because he didn't want to.

Brenna loved Revival weekend. Almost more than she loved Christmas. The Adventure Run had been her brainchild, and the street dance had been one of her favorite things. She'd told him once, as they'd held hands under a string of twinkle lights and breathed in the cool September air flavored with barbeque and funnel cakes, hot chocolate, and spiced candied nuts, that it made her feel like she was in a Hallmark movie.

He really hadn't any idea why that was such a good thing, as he'd never made it to the end of one of those cheesy flicks. But that evening almost a decade ago, with her dreamy smile and warm gaze settled firmly on him, the future of them only a joyful haze in her eyes, he'd felt like he'd stumbled into his own happily ever after. Sappy, for sure. But man, it'd felt good.

Reliving that same scene, minus Brenna, minus that happily ever after... He'd rather not. Especially when he was sure she'd be there, her hand in Grant Hillman's, that lovely smile aimed at him. Her Hallmark story playing out without him, while he was struggling even to find footing in a story that hadn't made any sense, let alone was sappy-love-story worthy.

The thought made it hard to breathe.

"Craig." Mom gripped his elbow, her voice, now softer, drawing his attention back down to her. "It's going to get easier."

"What will?" The question leaked out before he could filter it.

"All of this."

Honestly? Probably not.

Mom was going to get worse before—and if—she was going to get better. Her doctor had been clear about that, especially since he'd felt the need to escalate her treatment. Trent and Ashton—well, being a parent wasn't anything like being a kid's hero from a distance. Taking on a dad role had blindsided him. Especially with Trent. Everything from getting dressed in the morning to brushing teeth at night was difficult with Trent, and the kid made things hard on purpose.

His determination to do so seemed to have doubled that Monday past—the very day Craig had started the paperwork to file for adoption. It was as if Trent had known—which he couldn't have because neither Craig nor his mom—nor Paige—had talked to the boys about it, and he was determined to make every stride forward, like walking through wet cement.

Craig couldn't get a grip on why, other than Trent was mad

at the world and determined to punish everyone for it. Ashton was a quiet, more compliant kid, which seemed like good news on the surface, until Craig discovered that compliant could sometimes mean pliable. And Trent knew how to ply. Craig imagined how the fiasco earlier that week had started. Likely went something like...

Guess what would be fun, Ash?

What?

Hide-and-seek with Craig's keys.

Oh! That sounds like a good game. Where should we hide 'em?

The sink.

After frantically looking for ten minutes for his keys, which he always kept on his dresser, Craig had crammed his fingers through his hair, called the boys into his room, and asked if they'd seen them.

We win! Ashton had beamed.

Win?

Yeah! You give up, right?

Sighing, fighting hard to keep the buildup of his temper in check, Craig had squatted in front of both boys. He'd studied them, guessing which had been behind this.

Where are they, Trent?

I dint touch 'em. The heated defiance in his eyes said something else entirely.

I dint! Do I, Ash?

Ashton's grin melted, and his eyes rounded. *You mad, Craig?*

I'm late. We're late. I really need my keys. Where are they?

Tears welled up in his eyes. *Trent say—*

Shut up, Ash. You dit it.

But—

Trent bolted from the room. Next sound Craig had heard was the garbage disposal grinding up his key/fob combo.

He'd used his mom's car the rest of the week while the locksmith ordered and then programed a new key fob that set him back almost two hundred dollars. Made for an awesome week following a decision he was sick-to-his-stomach nervous about.

Though it'd been several days, frustration stirred again. Yes, they'd laid out a discipline plan for Trent, and he had to earn the money to pay for the replacement costs by mowing the lawn and doing some other things Mom had suggested. Yes, Trent had apologized—and it seemed sincere. When Craig had asked him why he'd done it, Trent had shrugged, fighting tears and trembling.

I'm not going to hurt you, Trent.

The boy nodded.

Why did you do that?

Again, a shrug. *Just cuz.*

The storm had settled. But right then, with the pressures of everything being hard and not wanting to go to the street dance to witness Brenna live out happily ever after without him, Craig was sorely tempted to grab back on to that anger, as well as the problem that had happened at school earlier that week, and say they couldn't go. Trent was still in trouble. Craig couldn't trust him to behave.

Excuses, all of it.

"Seeing her will get easier too."

Craig stared at his mom, wishing she couldn't always read him so well. "Don't think so on that one."

"Maybe if you two could find a time to talk..."

"She's not interested in talking." The blade of her angry stare that first week back at the staff lunch still cut deep. The ensuing arctic silence after. At the river, the way she'd cut a hard glance at him and then refused him another look of any kind. Brenna wanted him gone. Made that clear seven years back, and nothing in her position had changed.

Mom rolled her lips together and sighed. "Then...then go for us. For the boys."

"I'm not doing so well there either."

"You're doing fine, Craig. It's just harder than you thought."

"Yeah." He laughed bitterly. "You could say that."

"One foot in front of the other, son. It will get easier. And it's possible that enjoying something fun with them could make a world of difference."

Craig held a long look on her, half hoping she was right but doubting everything. He felt like he was attempting to summit a mountain that he simply wasn't capable of climbing. Feeling exhausted, he nodded, accepting her hug.

For the second time in his life, he'd come up against something that was just too hard. And there was no way to escape it. Running wasn't an option on this one, which didn't matter much anyway. It hadn't worked out for him last time.

***

There was still magic to be had. The white lights dancing in the breeze against a clear, dark sky. Country music drifting along the brick street while couples meandered or danced or talked. The smell of barbeque from the Morris Grill, hot chocolate from Freshies, and funnel cakes...

It was all still there, and Brenna smiled at the things that remained constant.

"My sweet Brenna Blaum," Miss Jane Tiller called from the wide sidewalk in front of her store. The small café tables that lined the area of Freshies' front window all held couples, smiling, some laughing. All with mugs of Mint-Frost hot cocoa—Freshies' special for the evening.

With Grant in step beside her, Brenna switch her path to approach Miss Jane. "How are you?"

"Blessed more'n I deserve to be." This was Miss Jane's standard answer. "I've been thinking about you. And about your mom and dad. How are they?"

Brenna smiled softly. "They're well, thank you. Enjoying life at the camp."

"I so hoped." Miss Jane gripped Brenna's hand and gave it a loving squeeze. "Seeing the boys and girls there—it isn't too hard on your mom, is it?"

Brenna felt the movement of bittersweet ache in her chest. The boys and girls at that camp—they often had Down's. It was a place for kids with special needs to zoom into the independent life they often craved, with the security of a community surrounding them who had experience in helping with that goal. It was also a place that provided parents of special needs kids a short-term respite. Mom and Dad had sent Scottie there a few times—and when he'd gone, they had stayed in a cabin in the Black Hills, breathing in the beauty of the mountains and the deep renewing of a small break. Brenna had gone once and loved the Black Hills, but she'd decided that her parents might deserve a break on their own, and once she was old enough to stay home alone, she did.

She'd never expected Dad and Mom to uproot, so their moving to work as full-time residents of the camp had come as a surprise. And a bit of a dart to her heart. But Mom had needed...something. After Scottie died, something inside Mom had died too. The change, though it had demanded the sacrifice of a lifelong career for her dad, had proven worthy, and Brenna was thankful for that.

"Mom says she sees bits of Scottie scattered around her—all the best parts. His orneriness in a seven-year-old boy here. His stubbornness in a ten-year-old girl there. And his humor, his all-in love for life, it shows up quite a bit."

"So it's been a bit of healing for her?"

"I think so." Brenna sometimes had a hard time wrapping her mind around the contradiction. Mom couldn't handle staying in Big Prairie because she saw Scottie everywhere. But at the camp she saw pieces of Scottie all around her, and it was good. Likely, Brenna would never understand. But she was thankful her mom was resurfacing, that there was more often than not a smile in her voice when they talked these days, and Dad didn't seem so worried about Mom surviving.

"And you, Brenna sweet. Are you doing okay?"

"I am." She put on her best *I'm good, thanks* smile.

"And what about Craig?"

What about him? Brenna bit back the question. In the space where she would have spoken was an uncomfortable lull.

"Is he home for good?" Miss Jane asked.

"That's my understanding."

Miss Jane nodded. "It's not good to run from hard things, you know."

"Yes, ma'am." Brenna wasn't sure if Miss Jane was speaking of her or Craig. Surely Craig, as she had stayed. But then again, Miss Jane had a bit of Yoda in her, even if her grammar was not backward. She spoke in riddles and made statements that seemed simple on the surface but had a way of snagging in your mind like a three-pronged hook.

Miss Jane patted her hand. "You come visit me sometime, sweets. We should chat."

"I'll do that." Brenna muscled her social smile, forcing it to stay in place.

"And you, Grant Hillman." Miss Jane lifted her face to the man beside Brenna. "Aren't you going to buy this lovely girl her favorite?"

"I'd be glad to, if she tells me what it is."

"Hmm." A soft tsk lifted from the woman's lips. "A man should know such things."

Grant cast Brenna a glance that plainly read *help me*.

"Cinnamon pecans with a vanilla latte. Decaf, since it's after dark."

"Same thing every year." Miss Jane nodded at Brenna and then gave Grant a sidelong look. "Hasn't changed since she was sixteen."

Worry snaked through Brenna. Perhaps Miss Jane's seventy-two-year-old mind was slipping and she was confusing Grant with Craig. Seemed inconceivable, as the woman had seemed as likely to live forever as the river was certain to always run east. Or perhaps this was a poignant rebuke mixed in with a comparison between Grant and Craig. Because Craig had never needed to ask Brenna's favorite and hadn't ever bothered to wait for her to make a request of it during Revival. The past couple of years, she'd gone in and made the purchase on her own, meeting Grant up the road, with her indulgence already in hand.

"I'll be back." Grant seemed thankful for the excuse to get away.

Miss Jane watched him as he strode into her café, her expression studious. "He's a nice boy."

"He is a nice man," Brenna responded.

"Always was a nice boy."

Brenna chuckled.

Miss Jane brought her attention back to Brenna. "Hearts are fragile things."

Okay...

"Mending takes time. Be careful not to rush it."

Right.

"Regrets are bondage, Brenna my sweet. If you don't deal with them, well, love, they own you. And the people you care about."

Lips parting, words dried in her mouth as Brenna's mind tripped over Miss Jane's speech. Where was this—

"You come see me. Soon."

"Sure," she mumbled.

Miss Jane lifted her hand, brushing Brenna's jawline with a knobby, work-worn knuckle.

Brenna sifted her thoughts for something to say that wouldn't sound inane or trigger something else from Miss Jane that seemed random and yet dangerously accurate. Revival was one of Brenna's favorite times ever. She didn't want to battle emotions that were becoming harder and harder to ignore this weekend.

Grant returned, a mug and a paper funnel full of pecans in either hand. Handing the mug to Brenna, he summoned a halfhearted smile. "Your favorite. I'll remember from now on."

Dialing up a smile that should have reached midday sun on the radiance scale, Brenna thanked him, said goodbye to Miss Jane, and tipped her head toward the heart of town. "Shall we?"

Grant nodded, and side by side they meandered. Their lack of conversation was made easier to ignore by the soft rumble of people and the music that drifted down to the street from the speakers mounted to a few strategic streetlights. Brenna sipped on her latte as they wove through people, stopping often to say hello to one of Grant's students, one of her clients, or someone they knew from church. Too soon the warm, creamy drink was gone, and she tossed the cup into a waiting trash bin. Energy and smiles met them from every small visit as the music played. In between chats, a slow country love song began. Several couples paired up and swayed.

She slipped her hand into Grant's and tugged against his slow walk. When he looked down at her, she stepped in front of him.

"Dance with me."

"You know I am not much of a dancer."

"It's a slow song. Just move your feet."

He lifted his chin, surveyed the street. "Brenna..."

She sighed, pressing a hand to his chest. He covered it, squeezed, and then pressed a kiss into her forehead. "Let's keep walking."

"Sure."

Her hand in his, she wove their fingers together and

followed him as they moseyed up the street.

There was Shaylee Yost pushing a stroller with an infant seat facing her and her toddler—Alvin?—riding on the little step thing by the handle. Across the way was Jeremiah Colts with his boys, one on his shoulders and one clinging to a leg like a little monkey. His wife, Chelsea, whom Brenna didn't know well, laughed as she held the hands of the boy on her husband's back, dancing.

A group of high schoolers gathered in a loose circle, a few orange-and-blue lettermen jackets in the little huddle, signifying that, yes, those forgotten traditions were making a comeback.

She wondered if Craig still had his, as she'd kept hers.

She spied Wes and Jaycee Morris up by the food truck. The big barrel smoker they'd set up near the bumper wafted a tantalizing aroma of pulled pork, which they served with Miss Jane's fresh peach salsa. Wearing his big leather apron and a giant smile that split his bearded face, Wes answered Jaycee's beckon, easily pushing her into a twostep as she slipped into his arms.

A familiar laugh demanded her attention. How, after all these years, could that deep chuckle still reach inside her and grab hold of something both tender and fierce? There in the middle of the street to her left, with two boys flanking his long legs, Craig held Sophie's hand above her head as she twirled, the graceful move flaring her floral-print skirt. She stopped, Craig released her hand, and she bent to say something to Ashton.

Brenna felt something inside wilt. She also felt Grant's gaze heavy on her. When she looked up at him, pinned smile in place, he turned into her. He began moving his feet as the hand that still held the warm funnel of pecans warmed her back, pulling her close. She tucked against him.

Somewhere there was still magic. The lights, the music, the

everything, they all assured her it was there.

She just didn't feel it that night.

Chapter Twelve

"WE GONNA WIN, RIGHT?" ASHTON BEAMED AS CRAIG KNEELED IN FRONT OF HIM ON THE LIVING ROOM FLOOR.

Craig grinned as he tied a green scarf around his skinny upper arm. "We'll sure try, buddy."

"Trent's fast. Ain'tcha, Trent?"

"Faster'n you." Trent had opted to wear his scarf around his head like a sweatband.

"We're all on the same team, Trent."

He scowled back at Craig. "Don't think that band teacher will be fast."

"Ms. Shultz."

"I like Miz Shultz," Ashton said, impervious to Trent's frown. "You like Miz Shultz, Craig?"

Craig had the distinct impression of an oncoming setup. "Ms. Shultz is a nice lady."

"She pretty."

"She is that."

"She do music, like you."

"Also true."

"Do she like football?" Trent asked, suspicion thick in his voice.

Craig chuckled. "I have no idea."

"If she not fast, and she don't like football, then it don't matter how she look."

This time Craig outright laughed. "Well, I'm sure we'll find out today if she's fast, since she's our team captain." He held his left arm out wide and with his right hand, pushed the last green scarf toward Trent. "How about you tie this on for me?"

An ornery glint danced in Trent's eyes as he took the team identifier. "Tight?"

"Good and tight."

"Watch out." Trent wrapped the fabric around Craig's bicep, and after a pause, he crossed the ends and pulled.

"Oh!" Craig grabbed his shoulder and rocked back like he was in serious pain.

"You hurt 'im, Trent!"

Craig smiled, winking at the younger brother. Ashton laughed, and Trent pulled harder.

"You're killing me!" Flexing, Craig faked a grimace.

"Whoa, mama!" Ashton scrambled onto Craig's bent knee and wrapped both hands around the flexed bicep. "Trent, you see that? Craig, you arm be huge!"

Trent continued to pull the ends tight, growling with the effort. When Craig expected Trent's temper to flare with Ashton—because how dare he be impressed with anyone but Trent?—a sudden grin broke through the boy's concerted effort. Letting the scarf go loose and fall, Trent poked at the muscle.

"That be fake!" He laughed.

"You think?" Craig wrapped his free arm around the brother in his lap and lifted the arm Trent was poking into a new flex pose.

With both hands, Trent gripped the arm. "Where you get this?"

"Out of the closet." Craig winked.

"Come on, man. For real!"

"Lots of years lifting weights."

"You play the guitar." Trent moved from a hand grip to a two-armed hold and then attempted to pull Craig's arm down with his whole body.

Craig leaned away to hold himself upright.

"He play football too!"

"Not anymore." Trent literally hung on his arm now.

"Still could. Right, Craig? You could still play, right?"

"Think my days on the field are over, buddy." Craig tightened his grip on Ashton's waist. "But I can still take on two boys." With a move and a pull, he had Trent wrapped in the arm he'd been using as a jungle gym, and both boys yelped as Craig wrestled them to the ground.

The play ensued for several minutes, both boys laughing. Craig too. When he surrendered, letting them both sit on his chest, it hit him.

For that moment, the hard had eased. And Trent's smile...

Worth every ounce of the struggle.

***

She'd had no reasonable or dignified way to decline. Standing at the tree line, a few feet away from the start and finish line, Brenna felt like a cornered bird. After all, the Adventure Run had been her baby. The now-ten-year-old tradition for Saturday morning's activities during Revival weekend had been her bright idea when she'd been sixteen. No, she hadn't run it all those years—or even most of those years—because she'd hung up her running shoes a while back.

But when Sophie had to bow out of her Green-Means-Go Team with a cold and had asked her to step in, Brenna lost the battle to stay out of it.

"Come on, Brenna," Sophie said, a small garble in her voice from the headful she'd woken up with. "I saw your picture in the trophy case at the high school. State cross-country qualifier four years in a row and two-time champion? This should be your jam, girl!"

"Should be," Grant agreed. "Especially since it had been her idea in high school. This whole gig happens because she made it happen back then."

"What?" Sophie crossed her arms, a smirk poking the corners of her mouth north. "No is definitely not an option."

"I'm really not in any kind of shape for a race," Brenna said.

"Your leg is only a half mile."

Brenna looked down at her feet. Tennis shoes. She'd worn runners, so that excuse was out. Still looking at her feet, she let a faint memory of the course pass through her mind. The shorter leg—that half mile—went through a pasture, crossed a creek, and wound through a stand of trees. It was a fun part of the run. Actually, she'd thought once upon a time that all of it had been fun. Had been so by design.

"All right. But don't let your team have high expectations or anything. Like I said, I'm not really in shape for this."

"Of course. Craig and the boys will be glad they're still in."

A sick feeling pushed over her. Should have known. How had she not figured that when Sophie had said she and another teacher had made a team that she'd meant Craig? Face hot, Brenna refused to look at either Sophie or Grant, both flanking her sides.

"Thank you so much, Brenna!" Sophie pressed the green scarf in her hand and then swung both arms around her. "I can't wait to see what you've got. I mean, seriously? You won state twice?"

"Yeah." She pushed the word out around the bulge in her throat and forced a glance at Sophie.

"The things you learn..." Sophie shook her head in a mock rebuke, then smiled. "I'll go tell the boys."

Great. Brenna stared at the green material in her hand until Grant removed it from her fingers. He wrapped it around her arm, above the elbow, and secured it with a knot.

"You okay?" he asked.

"Of course." Cue the sweetest grin possible. "You'll cheer me on, right?"

"Always." His study seemed too intense for a good-luck-go-get-'em pep talk.

She ignored the dread and anxiety. "It's only a half mile. So shouldn't be a problem."

He nodded but apparently missed her hint to quit looking at her with such deep concern. "Not for a cross-country star like you."

"That's the past, Grant. Some things are in the past and that's all." She wondered if he was listening to her. Didn't seem like he really heard, the way he watched her, face shadowed with something that seemed troubling.

Either way she was determined not to jump into the deep. She had enough to deal with being on Craig's team, and wasn't that going to be awesome? Grant could work through whatever he was thinking on his own. With a quick kiss on his clean-shaven cheek, she held on to the grin that was making her face hurt.

"Meet you at the finish."

***

If Sophie hadn't been so sweetly innocent, he would have sworn she'd done this on purpose. After all, he'd told her that he and Brenna had dated. She'd witnessed their awkward interaction at the river not long before. But sly or manipulative simply wasn't her style. She'd come down with a cold and found a sub. Obviously she'd chosen Brenna because they were good friends. Not because she'd decided to see what would happen when she shoved two jagged edges together and gave them a good rub.

Craig doused the budding irritation in his gut. "I'm sorry you're not feeling well," he said, rather than the *Of all the people in this town you could ask to take your place, why did you ask her?* he'd been tempted to say.

"Just a cold, but the state marching contest is coming up. I really can't let down my kids, you know?"

"Of course not. You're doing the right thing."

"Brenna's a good runner, right?"

One of the best out there. Should have made the trials, if not all the way to the Olympics. Guilt sank where irritation had carved a trench through him. "Yes, she was quite good."

"So you should be golden." Sophie smiled.

Craig nodded as the woman of discussion strode toward them, a green bandanna tied on her left arm and Grant near her side.

"Ah, here's the team that's going to win." Sophie stepped back, allowing Brenna a clear line to join Craig.

Brenna stopped beside her, giving him only the smallest of glances. "Now, Sophie, I told you, I haven't run in years, so..."

She hadn't? Brenna had been one of those truly, strangely gifted people who actually loved running.

"I have the longer leg, Bren," he said, forcing her to look at him. "But you can take it if you want. You'd be better at it."

"Like I said, I haven't run in a long time." This time, she held her gaze on him—cool, challenging, and hard.

"Okay. It's up to you."

"I'm good."

"Good."

"Unless you're not good with this?"

What was *this* exactly? With this situation? No. No, he was not good with this situation. But he hadn't been good with any of his *situations* in a couple of months, so that hardly mattered. With running the longer leg? He'd be fine. Wouldn't put up the kind of time he knew Brenna was capable of, even if she hadn't been running. But he'd finish, and he wouldn't be knocking on death's door by the end of it.

"I'm good." He muscled a smile into place and whistled for the boys. As the pair joined them, the bullhorn blared, signaling the start time.

Good. Sooner, the better.

Trenton and Ashton would run the first two legs, which could be ran as one leg or broken into two, depending on the team's preferences, and were more obstacle courses than running courses. Brenna had designed it that way on purpose, all those years ago. That way Scottie could participate in something he thought was fun. It worked well for other teams too, because it allowed them to get their little kids involved, making it a family event. After the boys finished their part, Craig would run the longer leg—a full 5K. Brenna's specialty— though he knew she could go so much farther and usually did when she competed at the college level. Last, he'd hand the baton off to her, and she'd run the leg she'd originally designed for him—a half mile of sloshing through the creek, dodging yucca in the pasture, and weaving through trees near the finish.

Why did she insist on doing that part? She hated wet feet and had never been a good sprinter. Probably to stick it to him because he'd offered a switch. Just to be difficult.

The thought poured sadness through him—an odd reaction when he'd been frustrated only a moment before. Brenna hadn't always been difficult. In fact, that had been rare for her. Stubborn? Yes. Feisty? You bet—especially when it had come to protecting Scottie. But straight-up difficult? Not usually, and from what he'd seen and heard around town, she still wasn't normally. Only with him.

And she had her reasons.

The start horn blared, and the kids starting the race tore off, Ashton and Trent scrambling, jumping, climbing, and running, perfect little-boy grins plastering their faces, providing Craig with a much-needed distraction from introspection and the past that seemed to float to the surface whenever he allowed his thoughts to linger on Brenna Blaum.

They were in third when Trent slapped the baton into Craig's palm with a "Go fast, man! We can win!"

Chuckling, Craig took off after the two in front of him—Jeremiah Colts, who by nature had more distance in him than Craig did, and Candace Sherman, a woman who, when they'd been in school together, could outswim anyone. Winning looked a little more optimistic than realistic, but he settled into a faster-than-normal stride and hoped the other two weren't quite the athletes they'd been back then.

The thing about running was that the body could settle into a rhythm, allowing the brain to do its own thing. Like think. Craig would have preferred not to, but it happened all the same. And his thoughts turned back to Brenna. Back to the past. And back to the things he wished he could take back.

"I need a break." He couldn't look at her, sitting over there on the other side of the bench. Instead, he clenched his fists and watched while his knuckles turned white.

"A...a break?" Her whisper trembled. "Like, you're breaking up with me?"

For a full five seconds, he couldn't speak. His throat was too swollen, the panic in his chest a seismic rumble.

But the past year—especially the past few months... Man, they'd become something he couldn't recognize. Full of passion and fury. Making choices, doing things that two years ago he'd swore would not be them. But every time he'd tried to right the ship, a fight had broken loose. If anything, the roller coaster had been a warning. Added to the talk he'd had last week with his coach, things had clicked. They needed this. He needed this.

"Look, right now, Brenna, things are just...too complicated. I've got this opportunity in front of me, and I can't afford to blow it. I need to focus, to cut out distractions."

"Distractions? I'm a distraction now?"

Nausea rolled through him, and he pressed his head against his fisted hands. "Brenna, I don't mean it like that. But—" He inhaled, steadied his breathing, lined up the words he hoped would make her understand. "Look, I think we could agree that lately we haven't been good for each other."

That blow hit her hard, but instead of crumbling into tears, her expression hardened. "I see."

"No, I don't think you do—"

Reading that angry expression, he was certain she didn't. Weeks before, they'd thought there was a baby, and he was wholeheartedly ready to marry her. When it turned out there was no baby, she'd been completely relieved, and he thought they'd find their way back to the way they'd been before. Didn't happen.

"I get it, Craig. Suddenly the NFL is interested, and you've got bigger fish on the line."

"That's not what's happening."

"You have to focus, right? Me too. I've got dreams of my own, you know. They're not all centered on the Great Craig Erikson. So maybe you're right."

He looked at her, heart shattering over the mask of indifference she wore. "Brenna, I don't mean that we—"

Jolting to her feet, she twisted the ring she'd worn on her right hand since her eighteenth birthday. When it came free, she pressed it into his palm. "Now you can focus on anything you want, Craig. We're done."

Back then, he'd felt trapped. Didn't know what to do. The first time they'd slept together, guilt had nearly seared a hole through his soul. He'd promised her. Promised her dad. Promised himself. He'd never wanted to be like his own DNA donor—a man whom he'd never met, who'd used his mom and left her to raise a kid on her own.

Turned out, making promises and keeping promises were about as much the same as wet was from dry. So even when he'd sworn to himself it wouldn't happen again, it happened again.

Repeatedly.

Instead of facing it, addressing the things he'd suspected were going on with her and the things that were driving them apart, he'd run, breaking more promises.

Not to mention her heart.

***

Brenna took the baton from Craig, not looking at anything but that large hand that had once held hers. Which didn't cross her mind. Much.

Turning, she took off after the young man in front of her. He was at least five years younger and had been a runner in high school. But that didn't mean she couldn't catch him. After all, she usually beat the boys, back in the day.

"Go, Bren! You've got this!"

Suddenly time shifted, and she was in perfect racing condition. And that voice cheering her on?

His. Sent from heaven above to be all the encouragement she needed.

As her body moved faster, legs striking the ground at a pace that brought her closer to that boy out in front, she smiled. Couldn't help it. Remembering the joy of running and the mysterious lightness she'd known when Craig had been the voice of encouragement propelling her forward...

It was like all the good that had been in her life before returned, and she felt the swirl of God's pleasure in her, in this gift of running that he'd blessed her with, and in the love...

No. She'd focus on the sensation of God smiling on her as she ran. Wow, she hadn't realized how much she missed that—the feeling that she was using what He'd given her, and it made

Him happy.

Craig had felt that way once too—they used to talk about it. About how amazing it was to think, to feel, to *know* the joy of their Creator as they exercised the gifts He'd built into them. For Craig, he knew that pleasure with music and when he worked with kids, more than when he played football, which had made his switch of ambitions toward the NFL odd back when everything fell apart. Still, she would have supported him. Would have remained his biggest fan. How could he have not known that?

"You're amazing, Bren! Keep going!"

This time Craig's encouragement pulled sadness from a place beneath the anger she'd felt toward him. At the same time, her heart awakened. Leapt, where before it had seemed flat and dead. Irreparably unresponsive.

That could be dangerous.

It could be glorious.

Avoiding the conflict in her mind, Brenna switched her distance stride into a faster turnover as she closed the space between her and the leader. Five yards. Then three. Two. The finish was just ahead, and years of competition kicked in. Pulling beside the younger man, she focused every muscle on forward momentum, pushed that turnover into a full sprint, and...

Adrenaline surged through her veins as she slowed to a jog, then a walk, and then turned to shake hands with the other competitors.

She'd won! Goodness, she'd forgotten how much she loved to race. This feeling...it was excitement, a thrill that wasn't just victory but true—maybe holy—delight. How could she have forgotten this joy?

Her smile stretched, and she laughed.

"Nice race," she repeated as she smacked hands with those crossing the line. Her breathing and heart rate were fast, and she was certainly not in top condition, but that was still *fun*.

A cattleman's whistle sailed on the air, also something firmly pressed into days-gone-by memories. Unable *not* to look, she lifted her gaze to the spot she was certain he'd be standing. Left of the finish line, wide grin aimed on her, warming her in a way that running never could, his blue eyes took her captive. She found herself caught in a moment that should have been lost in the past.

When he jogged toward her, both palms up, she was nineteen and enthralled with Craig Erikson all over again. Thrilled with the run, with the boy who—beyond reason— liked her, and with life. With both hands, she high-fived him, and then those strong arms surrounded her, and she was tucked close, right next the steady beat of his heart.

"Nice running, Blaum," he said near her ear, same as he'd always done. "You killed it out there."

No. This wasn't the same as always. She wasn't nineteen, and they weren't in love. Seven years' worth of resentment rushed forward. Inhaling, his familiar scent made her dizzy. She froze against the nostalgia that had tricked her mind. Blinded her heart. Instead, she switched her thoughts toward Grant. Steady, reliable Grant—who surely was around there somewhere. *He* was the boyfriend of the present, who was about as likely to let her down as the sun was to refuse to set that evening.

The illusion of a long-since dead moment shattered, and she pushed out of Craig's embrace. Stepping back, she focused the gaze she seemed incapable of stealing away from him into a glare. His smile faded; the joy in his eyes collapsed.

After licking his lips, he nodded, as if their silent exchange had been audible, and then looked toward the ground. "Nice run, Brenna. The boys are excited about a win."

She couldn't respond.

He peeked at her with half a sad smile. "Thanks for being a good sport. You didn't have to."

"For the boys," she croaked.

"I know." Eyes hidden under the bill of his hat, he turned and walked away.

She didn't want to admit how much she wished things were different.

Chapter Thirteen

"Sit, Brenna my sweet. Now is our chance to have that chat."

Miss Jane winked over her cup of hot chai tea and motioned to the cranberry white chocolate cookies she had mounded on a plate placed in the center of the table.

Brenna wrapped her hands around her own mug—a large floral something containing rich white chocolate mocha—on the house because Freshies' owner sometimes did such generous acts. While gratitude for the drink made her smile, a sense of foreboding also stirred within Brenna's mind. This little Monday chat, while random—Brenna had stopped in for an afternoon snack when her two o'clock canceled with a cold— had the makings of something loaded. Just the word *chat* carried a weight that came with a warning label.

Thunder rumbled through the darkly overcast skies hanging ominously above Main Street just outside the big picture window—one of the reasons Freshies was currently vacant, save

Brenna and Miss Jane. The downpour of the morning had subsided, but if the color and consistency of the clouds were telling truths, they were about to get dumped on again.

"It was so lovely to see you running again on Saturday. Do you know, I've missed watching you race? Pure joy. That's what it is on your beautiful face when you run. Just pure joy."

Oh. That's what this is about? Well, goodbye trepidation, hello friendly chatter. Brenna breathed a small giggle while at the same time hushing the memory of Craig's encouragement and the effect it had had on her. Her mental efforts proved lackluster as a thrill at that particular recent memory shot like a bottle rocket through her system.

"It did feel good, actually," she said, proclaiming to herself that it had been the run that surged a mild high through her body that day. Which, to be fair, it had. Just maybe not all...but she wasn't admitting that. "Though *lovely* must certainly be an overstatement. I'm completely out of shape and was covered with mud. By the time I crossed the finish line, I was a royal mess."

"You were beaming, my love. Simply radiant. Oh, my heart wanted to burst with praise to see you smile like that again."

She had smiled, but surely it wasn't radiant. That was a word used almost exclusively for a woman walking an aisle in a white dress, and they were definitely not discussing any such matter as that. Miss Jane had a thing for embellishments. Always leaning toward good and beauty, but embellishment nonetheless.

"Do you know"—Miss Jane's wrinkled but firm hand grasped hers—"I went straight home and called your mother. She delighted to hear it, that her girl was running again. And smiling. Oh, Brenna! How we have been praying for you to find that smile again!"

What? "I didn't realize you kept in touch with my parents."

"Of course I keep in touch! Goodness, girl. What kind of

friend do you think I am?" Miss Jane squeezed her hand again and then swatted the air, as if to brush away such an insulting comment. "Your mother and I have been prayer sisters since the day you were born, little miss. I'll have you know a few hundred miles are certainly not going to end such a beautiful relationship." She huffed.

Feeling heat feather her cheeks, Brenna laughed. "I'm sorry, Miss Jane. I didn't know, is all."

"Well, now you do. And you may as well know also that I pray for you. Daily. And have taken your mother's request to look out for you seriously."

"That would explain the occasional soups and salads you deliver to my house, wouldn't it?"

Miss Jane tipped her chin up.

Brenna cocked a sassy smirk. "And the mild rebuke you issued my boyfriend on Friday night."

The pair of sliver eyebrows went up next. "A man should know those kinds of things."

"Grant's not one hundred percent in favor of my little indulgences." Brenna sipped her mocha, as if in subtle defiance.

"Grant Hillman would eat cardboard every day if he thought it would deliver enough nutrients for him to survive. The man must have had his taste buds removed sometime in his childhood."

Brenna laughed. "Possibly. But in his defense, he is healthy."

Miss Jane's dark eyes lit as she leveled a look on Brenna.

Oh no. Here it comes... Yes, this was a *chat* thing, not just *chatter*.

"And you, Brenna my sweet?"

"Me?"

"Are you healthy?"

She cleared her throat. "I might like this a little more than is good for me"—she held up her mug—"and I have a deep affection for pizza. And donuts. But I do eat salad fairly often, and fresh peaches when they're in season is a personal favorite, so that's something, right?"

Leaning forward, Miss Jane settled a look that seemed to peer into Brenna's heart. "I am not talking about your eating habits, young lady. Nor do I mean your exercise habits, although as I said, it was lovely to see you running again. But, also as I said, that had more to do with the joy in your smile than your heart rate and endurance."

Another drumroll from the sky preceded a bursting of the clouds. Rain smattered the window beside them, playing a tapping tune that sounded cleansing and mournful all at once.

"I'm doing okay, Miss Jane."

With a pleasant set of her mouth—though not a smile—the elderly woman leaned back in her chair in a way that did not disrupt her perfect posture. Her gaze drifted from Brenna and became distant as she watched the washing of the streets outside.

"I wanted to tell you a story," she said.

"Is it a true one?"

"All of it. It is something from my younger years."

"Does it involve a man?" Brenna had always wondered about Miss Jane's younger years. If there had been romance in her life, and if so, why the quirky, funny, outspoken, beautiful woman had never married.

"No, this one does not involve a man. Not entirely, at least. Perhaps someday I'll tell you that story. When you're older."

Brenna swallowed a laugh. How much older did she need to be?

"This is a sad story." Her focus came back to Brenna, sharp and clear.

Her heart squeezed. "Do I already know it?" *Please, let's not talk about Scottie.*

"You do not. Not many left around here do, because I'm not proud of it."

Yikes. The makings of a confession. Why to her?

"Back in my schooling days, I had a friend. She and I were close—closer than sisters, we used to say. As we grew up, we were inseparable. *Jane and Evelyn*, they would say, *if you're looking for one, might as well look for both.* We shared secrets and dreams and lunches and walks. Used to promise that when we married, we would marry brothers so then we would truly be related. We also said we'd never let anything come between us. Not boys or parents or achievements, nothing."

The friendships of young girls...

"But something happened when we were seventeen. Evelyn knew I liked a boy. But she also knew that the boy I liked did not love Jesus and had a reputation."

"Like, a bad reputation with the girls?"

"Yes. And also a tendency toward violence."

"Oh."

"But I liked him. He was older, and handsome, and strong, and for some reason, he noticed me. Evelyn told me I should be careful."

Her study wandered again, back out to the street, though Brenna thought perhaps Miss Jane saw history replaying in that windowpane and not the rain pouring onto Big Prairie.

"Then she came to me one day, after I'd been spending time with this boy for a few weeks, and said she felt like we needed to talk. I didn't want to, because I knew what she was going to say, but I followed her to the river, to our special spot by a clump of ash trees. It was hard for her—I could tell. She could barely look at me, and she pulled in many deep breaths and fiddled with her fingers. Finally, she just said, 'Jane, I'm scared for you. Alton is saying things that I know aren't true. I really don't think he's good for you.'"

"You know, Brenna, I felt sick at first, thinking Alton might be spreading rumors. But then. Well, then I got mad—and not at him. I stepped right into my best friend's face and shouted at her. That she was jealous. That she had no business telling me what was right and wrong. And that I didn't want to speak to her again."

A tremble moved Miss Jane's mouth, emotion misting her eyes. The depth of impact caught Brenna off guard. This story was likely over forty years old, and still it provoked such a potent response in Miss Jane.

"What happened?" Brenna whispered.

"Evelynn honored my wish. I gave her the coldest silent treatment ever known anywhere south of the North Pole, and she let me be. And I stayed mad. Even after I found out that what she'd said about Alton was true and I stopped spending time with him. I held on to my anger with her, told myself it was justified and that if she wanted to be friends again, she should make amends. After all, she didn't even try to smooth things over when she knew I was so angry, nor after I cut things off with Alton. A year later, Evelyn met the man she would marry, and they moved away."

"Did you ever make up?"

"No." Fully present again, Miss Jane met Brenna's eyes. "No, we did not. Because I didn't try. I let anger ruin a relationship that had been beautiful, one that had meant more than I can tell you. Once I realized how ugly I'd been, I was too embarrassed to reach out to her. And here's the reason I'm telling you this shameful part of my life: It could have been different. There is every possibility in the world that Evelyn would have forgiven me and we could have found new footing in our friendship. But I let regret dictate my actions."

"But if you regretted it, then why—"

"Because often regret isn't the same as repentance, Brenna. Regret is a hateful captor—it's bondage. It allows shame to dictate what you do and what you don't do. But repentance? Repentance is hard because it requires true humility. But it is also freedom." She leaned in again, emphasizing the word *freedom*. "Repentance is telling the truth about what has been.

It is taking charge of regret, not allowing shame and anger to be regret's chains, and owning up to what you did wrong. It is admitting to not doing things right and asking for forgiveness. Repentance is the chance at fresh footing and a clean slate."

Eyes watery, Brenna blinked, not sure whether the emotions Miss Jane's story stirred were entirely about Miss Jane's story alone.

"What if I had told Evelyn that I was sorry?" Miss Jane asked. "What if I had the courage and the humility to tell her that I had been wrong?" Her voice broke, and she let the space between them go empty for several long moments.

"Why are you telling me this?" Brenna whispered.

"Because for a long time your smile has lacked joy. And because I've seen you around lately—since a certain young man has reentered our small town. I recognize the frozen look I've seen on your face."

That nausea returned, roiling in her gut. Pricking emotions stung. Fear. Shame. Anger. Who was Miss Jane to bring this up? She didn't know all of Brenna's past. Didn't know what really happened between her and Craig. What place did this woman have to...

Miss Jane's time-worn hand smothered Brenna's, and then when Brenna looked into her eyes, her fingers moved to cup her jaw. "Brenna my sweet, hear an old woman's tale. Do with it what you think best. And know that I love you, just as I have your mother. With all my heart."

The buildup of anger evaporated. In its place, tears. As one dripped onto her cheek, she nodded.

Because Miss Jane was right. Regrets bound her heart. Had for a long time. Maybe it was time to look into them with some courageous honesty. And to tell herself the truth about the things she hadn't wanted to admit before.

Chapter Fourteen

THE RHYTHM OF THE SCRAPER LULLED HIS MIND, ALLOWING HIS THOUGHTS TO WANDER WHILE HE PEELED THE OLD PAINT AWAY FROM THE WOOD SIDING OF THE HOUSE.

Around the corner, Trent and Ashton painted, their voices drifting to him as they discussed and then laughed. He'd likely need to go over some spots—do some touch up and some thinning. But as he listened, he felt his heart settle.

Things were okay. Had been okay for a whole week. No trouble at school. Nothing more major than a sour attitude here and there at home. It was as though the Adventure Run last week had stitched them together as a team.

Ah. The race. They'd won, but that had hardly mattered. And, scratch that anyway. He'd only narrowed the gap between himself and the two in front of him by the time he'd finished his leg. Brenna had won. Man, though, that woman could run. For all her claims about being out of shape and over that particular activity, she ran like there were wings on her feet and a fire in her heart, fascinating him with that strange way she smiled though a race.

Just remembering the joy on her face sent gooseflesh over his arms. Because in that brief few minutes, he saw her again. Brenna Blaum, the girl who had always mesmerized him in a way that he'd found delightfully addicting.

Still addicted, apparently.

Especially when he thought about those brief moments at the finish line, when he rushed her as she'd stood there catching her breath and congratulating the other runners. A high five would have been appropriate. They were teammates, after all, but after he smacked her lifted palms, he wrapped both arms around her and hauled her in close, just like he had after every race he'd ever watched her run. And she...

Man. With an arrow of panic, he tried to cut off that part of the memory. The part where her arms gripped his shoulders as she pressed into him. The part where the pound of her heart throbbed against his chest and the warmth of her still-labored breath tingled against his neck.

He stepped back from the house, let his arm fall to his side as he fought against the way his own pulse responded to a moment he shouldn't have been dwelling on—one that shouldn't have happened in the first place. That was all it had been anyway. A moment. As soon as she realized who had scooped her up, she'd stiffened. Pushed against his shoulders, and he'd lowered her back to the ground. And they were back to awkward, chilled silence.

What had he been thinking? Pressing a palm to his head, he pocketed the scraper with his other hand and leaned against the house. Yellow paint flecks dusted his arms and peppered his jeans. Slick sweat covered his body. This work was supposed to keep him from thinking.

A whistle sounded from the windowsill ten feet from where he was currently *not* working. His phone—hadn't realized he'd left it there. Growling at his lack of mental self-discipline, he walked over to retrieve it.

Good grief. He'd missed four calls. How was that even possible? The phone was set to *whistle*, for crying out loud. How did a guy get that lost inside his head? Worse, all four calls had been from Sophie.

Feeling about as awesome as roadkill, he hit the Call Back button. She answered on the second ring, her smile, as always, evident in her voice.

"Hey, I'm sorry to be such a pain."

"You're never a pain. What's up?"

"Oh, didn't you get my messages?"

"No, just saw I missed some calls."

"Well, no worries then. Crisis averted."

"There was a crisis?" Flattened roadkill. With his tongue hanging out and vultures picking at his carcass. "I'm sorry. What happened?"

"Nothing to worry about. I just went for a drive, and I found myself on a muddy road. Didn't realize how much it had rained, you know? Anyway, I'm stuck—"

"Tell me where you are, and I'll be there soon." Man, he was such a jerk. Lost in his head about a woman who despised him while the woman he was sort of dating had been trying to call for help. He deserved to be roadkill.

"No, that's what I was saying just now. Crisis averted. There's a guy here, and he's in his four-wheel-drive pickup. My car is gonna have to stay put for the day because I really dug myself in trying to get out, but Lance says he'll get me back to town. So no worries."

"Lance Carson?"

"I think so?"

"Are you out toward the vineyard?"

"Yes. How'd you know?"

"Lance owns the vineyard. You're in good hands—he's a nice guy."

"Thought so. Seemed like a good guy."

"I'm really sorry, Sophie."

"Why? You didn't get me stuck."

"You tried to call me for help, and I—" *Was too busy thinking about Brenna to hear my phone.*

"It's not a thing. Seriously, Craig. I'll catch up with you at church on Sunday, okay?"

He blew out a sigh. *Such a jerk.* "Yeah. Maybe we can do lunch after?"

"Maybe." There was hesitation in her response, even with the smile he could still clearly hear.

"I owe you."

"No, you don't, Craig. You don't owe me anything, so don't worry about it. Okay?"

Don't worry about it? Yeah, right. "Okay."

And that was that.

After ending the call, he pressed the back of his phone against his forehead and slouched against the house, an ooze of defeat draining through him. Man, he was not doing any of life well these days. School, Brenna, Sophie, the boys...

Uh-oh.

Craig stepped away from the house. Work. He was supposed to be painting the house, and he had two boys to oversee. Last he knew, his mom had gone in for a nap. They'd gotten awful quiet out back. How long had it been since he'd heard a shout? An argument?

Not good.

With an uneasy sense that his mental checkout was about to cost him something on the peaceful front recently established, Craig strode through the back gate and into the yard. Snickering—the quiet kind that was sure to indicate trouble— put that sense of concern into full-on alarm. What now?

Oh.

Oh man.

Craig stopped several feet from the back patio, wide eyes

glued to the two boys—now splotched heavily with yellow paint. Brushes abandoned, they had resorted to the bare-handed smearing method. Finger-painting the house, leaving yellow paint as a splotchy, chaotic trail all around them. On the grass. The patio. And since finger-painting the house wasn't fun enough, both boys, with maniacal grins stretched wider than ever and feverish delight lighting their every move, had taken to pressing their yellow painted hands against the glass patio door.

Good grief, were they crazy?

"Trent!" he barked.

Both boys froze. All delight and laughter snapped into wide-eyed fear. Ashton lowered his paint-smeared hands. His little frame shaking, he slipped behind Trent.

Defiance hardened every muscle in Trent's body as he straightened, rolled his fingers into fists, and glared back at Craig. His stance, and the challenge in that stare, all but dared Craig to come after him. *Go ahead*, the snapping silence of his position screamed, *go ahead and just try to break me.*

How did a kid all of ten years old get here?

Craig inhaled. Exhaled. Allowed the pain of the reality in Trent's body language to sweep away the surge of anger. Fisting and then unfisting his hands, the tension diffused from his shoulders, and after a silent stare-down that lasted too long, Craig removed his ball cap and lowered into a squat, bringing Trent's defiant glare to his eye level.

"Trent." Craig disciplined his voice into a low, steady calmness.

Trent stomped his foot. "It not just me!"

"I see that." Craig shifted his look to the boy trembling behind his brother. "Ashton?"

"No!" Trent moved to shield his little brother. "It were me! I do it. Ashton just spill some, and I say we clean it up, and then..."

Ah, this kid. A rush of compassion had Craig blinking. Poor heart, trying so hard, not sure how to make his life work, but determined that Ashton wouldn't take the smackdowns that had clearly littered his own path.

"You spilled?" Craig asked gently.

Trent's lips trembled, but he pressed them firmly and refused to respond. Allowing the beats of silence to pass, Craig watched both boys.

Timid as a scared puppy, Ashton peeked around Trent's shoulders. "I kicked the paint bucket," he whispered.

"It were a accident!" Trent's defense was passionate and loud, and again he stepped to shield Ashton.

Craig nodded. With a long breath, he looked around the patio. Such a mess. Paint streaks, handprints...

He owned a hose. Had some soap. And, actually, maybe a few handprints might not be so bad. Might be...well, a memory. His attention fell back on the two young men, both obviously certain that wrath was about to fall on them with painful ferocity.

"It was an accident," Craig repeated. "That happens. How about next time, just tell me?"

The tension in Trent's mouth eased, but he watched Craig with an untrusting stare, one hand tucked behind him, holding his little brother in place.

"You can tell me when you make mistakes, boys. We all do, and I'll work really hard not to be unfair about it."

Ashton leaned around Trent's shoulder, eyes glazed. "You not gonna..."

The end was left hanging wide open for Craig's imagination. He didn't want to envision what they thought he'd do—what they'd experienced before. He reached to touch Ashton's arm, but Trent shifted, blocking the move.

Craig's vision blurred as his hand fell back to his knee. *God, please heal this.* After lowering his gaze, breathing out in silent prayer, he slowly pushed up to a stand and replaced his hat. "How about we clean this up?"

Two pairs of rounded eyes stared up at him.

"You..." Ashton inched around his protector again. "You help us?"

"You bet, buddy."

"You not..."

"No." Craig reached again, this time for Trent. The shoulder his hand covered was tight and trembling, but he didn't jerk away. "We'll just clean it up, is all. And then we'll finish the back part of the house together. Okay?"

He held Trent's look, longing for the boy to soften. While he didn't, and that felt like a loss, he also didn't smack Craig's hand away either. A win. Craig brushed his thumb over the bundled-up shoulder and then moved toward the spigot in Mom's flowerbed. "We'll spray it down, get the big push broom, and clean up what we can. What we can't...well, it'll be okay." He paused after he had the hose attached and checked the boys over his shoulder. Still standing there, statues of anxiety, watching him. He smiled against the ache pressing through him. "And now that I'm looking at it from here, let's not wash the door, okay? We'll keep those handprints right where they are."

"We will?" Ashton's voice was almost all happy shock and nearly no fear. A good transition.

"Yeah. We will."

Maybe next year, they'd add another set to see how much they'd grown. And the year after, another...

Maybe.

***

With the paint fiasco cleaned up and behind them, the boys scrubbed, read to, and now tucked into bed, Craig sat back against the swing he'd hung on the pergola covering the patio. Mom had sat outside with him for a time, grinning at the handprints on the door.

"I'm glad you didn't wash them," she'd said. "Wish that I had a set of yours from when you were little right there alongside them."

He'd chuckled quietly. She'd risen, her movements a little slow, walked over to him, and warmed his cheek with her work-worn hand and held a silent gaze before she'd told him good night.

Now he was alone, with room and quiet to think, and his mind reviewed the day. Though it had ended well, it had been a bit of a disaster. His fault. Because he'd checked out. Let himself obsess about a woman who didn't want him in her life. With that thought, a sour burn stirred in his gut. He hadn't even thought to check on Sophie, to make sure that Lance got her out of the mud and home okay—once again proving that he was stuck in a place that wouldn't do her any good. What was wrong with him?

Sophie was beautiful and fun, and he shouldn't have one bit of trouble keeping his mind on her. Same story that had repeated itself many times over the past seven years. He'd met some great women. Kind, selfless, fun, loved Jesus...

Not one of them had wiped away the memories of Brenna. Or the longing. That didn't seem fair. He'd been a lot of stupid stuff in his life, but after knowing his mom's backstory, he'd determined he would not be *that* man. Never a player. Never careless with a woman's heart. He didn't want to answer for that sort of unkindness.

As a breeze blew cool against his neck, his mind drifted over the coffees and the two meals he and Sophie had shared since the river-coffee-date-esque thing. He had to own the truth. She was great company. A great girl. But the relationship wasn't going anywhere past the friend zone.

Maybe he was being too...hasty? Measuring this against how he'd felt with Brenna, expecting the same kind of magic. The same kind of spark that lit his veins. The kind of sweet burn he hadn't felt since.

Perhaps he'd been holding on to a fairy tale that hadn't lasted and he needed to let it go. Besides, he had the boys to think about now...

A completely selfish thought.

A different memory sparked, an afternoon when he was seventeen. Though time and tragedy lay long and hard between now and that first time Brenna had laid into him, he remembered clearly the electricity zapping through his veins while he'd watched her stomp away beside her indignant little brother after she'd caught Craig wrestling with Scottie on the field and had immediately pinned Craig as a jerk.

He hadn't been a jerk. And for the record, Scottie had started the playful tangle and had laughed his way through the whole deal. Brenna had missed that piece somehow, as she had told Craig off and stormed toward her car with Scottie in tow.

Man, she'd been something. He smiled as against sound judgment, he indulged the replay of that day long past.

"I saw that."

Craig sucked in a breath and probably jumped a little before he turned to the opposite sideline. Coach Blaum, arms crossed, strode forward. Shaking his head, Craig swam against the hypnotic fog that had swallowed him and stuffed away the wish that Brenna was still standing there—even if it was to give him a butt chewing—because he could stare into those bright-blue eyes forever.

Seriously. He could.

"You have trouble written across your face, Erikson. Don't think I don't know."

The tips of his ears burned. "I swear, Coach, I was being careful. I'd never let Scottie get hurt." It was the God-honest truth. Scottie had latched on to Craig his freshman season, and in season and off, he'd become one of Craig's best friends. Truly.

Kind of a weird pairing maybe, but it was a fact nonetheless. Scottie had a way about him. A special gifting. Observant and blunt, he could tell you off with the fury of an angry bull, but also oh so funny. And loyal. Man, you'd never seen that kind of loyalty. If only all men had been blessed with his oak-like resolve when it came to the people he loved.

If ever Craig could learn anything from little Scottie, he wanted that to be it.

"I know that, Craig," Coach said, his stance relaxing. "And Scottie thinks you're the best thing since ice cream—and we both know how big that is." He cocked his head, and Craig was pretty sure there was a touch of amusement in the crinkled corners of the older man's eyes. Maybe about Scottie and ice cream?

In the next moment, the look Coach pinned on him shifted to the one he wore when Craig had misunderstood a play call and had gone right when he should have cut left. Serious and none to impressed. "That's not what I'm talking about."

"What?"

"I'm not talking about you and Scottie."

Without thinking, he glanced back to the road Brenna had disappeared down.

"Rule number one," Coach said.

"Huh?" Craig turned back to him.

"First rule."

Craig studied him. He had blue eyes, shaded by a Big Prairie Broncos ball cap, and Craig knew exactly where his daughter's eye color had come from, though Coach's weren't nearly as intriguing as Brenna's.

Not nearly as snappy as hers had been either. Rule number one...

Oh. That rule.

"Don't think about dating your daughter?"

"That's the one." His mouth twitched. Not in an angry way. "Can't make exceptions, Craig."

An inexplicable pain sank through him, like his greatest wish had just been revealed. Staked into the landscape of his heart and driven in with a solid whack. Interestingly, that wish had very little to do with football. Had everything to do with Brenna Blaum.

His life focused. The future of everything had just been flung wide open, and Craig knew exactly what he wanted.

"Sir—"

Coach held his hand up. "Not while you're still playing for me. It would undercut everything else."

Was that a loophole? "Season's over in two months," Craig said, a little bit shocked at his boldness.

With a serious stare, Coach nodded.

Craig raised an eyebrow. "And I'm a senior."

"That's true."

"So?"

That twitch moved the corner of his mouth again. Craig waited in the torturous gap of silence, suspecting the older man was rather enjoying this awkward moment.

He clapped Craig's shoulder and then turned toward the sideline.

Agony. "Wait. Coach?"

He kept walking. Craig jogged to catch up. When they passed the thick white band marking the out of bounds, Coach glanced at him, and an actual grin lit his face. "We'll see."

Snapping blue eyes filled Craig's mind as hope swam in his chest. "Sir, what about homecoming?"

"Homecoming? What about it?"

"It's coming up. Before the season ends."

"So?"

Craig dared to snag his elbow as they came to a stop. Coach also paused, turned to face him.

"I swear, Coach, I'd be a gentleman. You can ask anyone. I'm—"

Coach laughed. "I know, Erikson."

"So..." Craig shifted, the nerve that had driven him up to that point suddenly a splat near his shoes. "Would it be okay...I mean...if I asked her—would you be okay with that?"

"You want to ask Brenna to homecoming?"

Craig forced himself to peek at him. *Make eye contact like a man.* Nodded.

"Seeing as you're one of my favorite young men, I could bend that much. But the thing is, you'll have to dig yourself out of the mudhole you just landed yourself in with her. See, Brenna's got a rule number one too. It's don't mess with her brother."

The interesting mix of approval and challenge in his voice resurrected the boldness in Craig.

"And if I manage to get myself out of trouble with her?"

Coach's expression went back to stern, though it looked like it took some effort. "Then yes to homecoming." He chuckled. "You'll have earned it."

Craig smiled and had to restrain himself from fist pumping the air.

Coach pinned him with severity again. "Just homecoming, Erikson."

"Right." Craig tamed his grin

Coach smirked, a warning in the lift of his brow. "Don't blow it, son."

Shutting his eyes as the swing rocked its gentle sway, Craig could still feel it. The magic. The way his body tingled with the kind of thrill he couldn't forget. Coach had given his permission. Well, for homecoming, anyway—but had hinted that after the football season, Craig could come back to him, ask to date his daughter. That was special—everyone knew it. While Coach loved his boys well, every last one of them knew he adored his daughter.

Craig had played his guts out that season, determined to not only impress Coach Blaum but Brenna as well—who had only agreed to go to homecoming with him because Craig had been persistent, and Scottie hadn't let up either.

Had he ever been so thankful that kid was his fan? For so many reasons, Scottie had had Craig's heart, and he hadn't ever been one bit ashamed of that fact.

Scottie's sister...

Coach had been right. Craig had dug himself into a hole, and Brenna had a hard time letting it go.

But he hadn't ever been a quitter. He'd started to watch her races. Traveled as much as he could so he could cheer her on as she won most of her meets, and he'd found it beautifully bizarre that she looked delighted as she worked through a 5K.

The first little smirk he'd gained from her was a win. When he managed to wrangle a full-blown smile—the kind that made those blue eyes seem like a warm June afternoon all clear and beautiful and perfect—he'd known he had been right that afternoon on the field after she'd stormed away.

He was a goner.

As the memories settled into the tender spot where he'd kept them safe, all second-guesses vanished. Just like with the other women he'd tried to date—he and Sophie weren't gonna happen.

Even if Brenna never smiled at him again, he was still a goner.

Chapter Fifteen

THE DREAM LINGERED STUBBORNLY, STILL AS VIVID AS IF SHE WAS
RELIVING THOSE MOMENTS. AND AS PERSISTENT AS THE REPETITIVE
WARNING ORIGINATING FROM MISS JANE'S STORY.

Regrets are bondage.

Maybe. Probably. And honestly, she'd like to be free of hers.
Sooner rather than later, thank you very much. But...

Well. Miss Jane wasn't always right, was she?
Repentance...that was hard. Way harder than simply stewing in
regret. Wasn't it?

Maybe not. Couldn't she just maybe sort of repent. To God,
silently just between the two of them. And maybe not in detail,
because He already knew anyway, right? He didn't need the full
spectrum of it, did He? Anyway, she could just take that
honesty to Him, because after all, sin was first and foremost
against God, right? So. Including others in said repentance was
not necessary.

That same logic had been pounding through her mind for
five days now. And for five days she'd laid the things that she

was ashamed of out in the open—to God. Most of them. Things like...she'd idolized Craig. Looked up to him and admired him too much in a way that crossed the boundary between what belonged to man and what belonged to God. And then she'd become obsessive and jealous, always believing every young woman who ever laid eyes on her boyfriend was devising a plan to seduce him. Which was followed fairly quickly with, he was seducible.

She'd stopped trusting him—something they'd argued about. He was offended—but he didn't understand. Didn't know how it felt to be with someone who was well above your level. Worse, not just being with that someone, but barely hanging on to him while loving him fiercely.

Those things, she had bravely put out there. To God.

So where was the freedom?

Why did she keep having these dreams that put her back in the past, in places that had become bittersweet and left her feeling even more captive to something slimy and cold than before she'd shut her eyes?

Why?

Answers lay on the fringed edges of her mind, but a hazy fear kept her from searching them out. Instead she let the images that had played while she slept, provoking an ache that was both longing and regret, replay yet again.

He was nice. There, she admitted it. Following Craig Erikson to an empty spot on the gym floor, under laser lights and with a country love song sounding from the speakers turned up way too much, she studied the hand that held hers. It was large, strong. The hands of a receiver—able to bring in a football, even on a wonky pass, and hold it firm even when the defense tried to punch it free. Honestly, that big hand swallowing hers was kind of sweaty. Because he was nervous—had been from the moment he'd picked her up at her house, his smile a little twitchy and his voice cracking a time or two. Especially when Daddy had pinned a look dead on his face and said, "I like you, Craig.

Don't do anything to make me not like you."

Pretty sure she'd heard him gulp before he eeked out a "Yes, sir." And he'd blushed.

It was a little bit adorable. This big six-foot-six football star all edgy because of her. And come to think of it, a lot a bit crazy. Why would he be so nervous about her? She was just...the book nerd who could run a long way. And the coach's only daughter.

"You'll see, Brenna. And then you gonna feel silly." Scottie had put a sassy set of hands on his square waist and waggled his head as if he were telling her off good. "Craig is the best man in this town. 'Cept Dad—but it's close. You gonna see and wish you didn't act like a monster at him."

She was beginning to see. Craig had been the perfect gentleman all evening. Opening her doors, holding her elbow as she hopped over a puddle, telling her she was pretty, and he was sure glad she was willing to give him this chance.

Then again, it was homecoming. Boys were always a little bit sappy at homecoming. Usually had an agenda behind all that nice.

So. She'd best keep that in mind. That little reminder played through her thoughts as Craig turned, pulled her into a respectable hold, and moved them into a twostep—which truth be told, she was nervous to death about because she'd only had one crash course with her mother on how the thing was done.

Hadn't planned on dancing. Or on liking her daddy's star wideout—not to mention Scottie's live-and-in-the-flesh superhero—quite so much.

She slid her left foot back when it should have been her right, and Craig collided with her, causing her to stumble. His light hold slid around her back, and he steadied her against his chest. Face brushing his crisp white shirt, she inhaled.

Wow. He smelled good. And...oh goodness. She did like how this felt, held against him. Tipping her forehead, she pressed farther into that place where she felt his heartbeat kick. It kicked a little harder, and she felt his sharp inhale the same moment the hand that held hers gripped harder. His body curled around hers in a way that was deliciously protective, and she slid her arm to hook him closer.

Forget running or calculus. Who cared about college or a job someday? Barely moving to the music, she figured she could just stay curled into him forever, because it was lovely.

"Brenna." He spoke from just above her ear, the sensation of his breath against her skin sending a shiver down her neck.

"Yeah."

"I like you."

She didn't fight the small grin. He couldn't see it anyway. "Why?"

He chuckled, provoking another delightful shiver. "There's something about you..."

She tipped her head up to meet his gaze. "Sounds like a line. Use it much?"

"Not once. Until now."

"Hmm." He was adorable, all serious faced. Probably acting, but cute. Too cute. She should probably cut this gig down. Tilting her head, she pursed her lips. "How many girls have you kissed?"

"None."

"Liar."

"No. I'm not lying. Have you heard of me having a girlfriend?"

"Well..." No. Actually, strangely enough, she'd never heard about him dating anyone. Which was bizarre.

"I've only been to homecoming one other time—my freshman year."

"Who did you go with?"

"A few other guys—we just went to see what all the hype was. None of us had dates, so we left. Went over to Morris's for ice cream, then down to the river to toss rocks. Was home by eleven."

"Doesn't sound like a football star's life to me."

"Huh."

"Doesn't prove you've never kissed a girl either."

"Okay. You've got me." Though the lighting was dim and the lasers messed with the coloring of everything, she could see a blush shading his cheeks. "I've kissed one. Once."

She slid her eyebrows toward her hairline while she fought away a sudden and stupid surge of jealousy. "I see..."

"Allie Sharps. Second grade. At the church playground, by the monkey bars. We were waiting for our moms to finish Bible *study, and she dared me to kiss her."*

Brenna couldn't help but laugh. *"That's it? That's all you're going to confess?"*

"It's all I've got. I swear, on your dad's approval of me, that's it."

"Not sure if I can believe you."

"What if I beg?" He finally smiled again, letting the solemnness of his expression slip.

"Why would you do that?"

And just as fast as it'd come, the teasing grin on his way-too-good-looking face faded as he held her gaze with an earnest intensity. *"I told you why. I like you."*

This bantering was a little bit addictive. Who knew Brenna Blaum had it in her? Not Brenna, that was for sure. But there they were. *"Hmm...what if I dared you?"*

"Dared me..."

"To kiss me." Her face felt like fire. That was probably a bit far.

When she thought he'd smile the way he did when ran in a touchdown or made an amazing catch downfield, he only stared at her with the kind of serious look that made everything in the room fade away. Slowly, he leaned, the muscles in his arms tensing, and her lips tingled, anticipating his.

"Don't tease me, Bren." His words were a feathered breath over the bridge of her nose.

She tilted her face.

He froze, leaving the most agonizingly small space between their mouths. *"Your dad trusts me."*

"Okay."

"And I really, really like you."

"You said."

He lifted his head, taking with him the promise of his kiss and leaving her with gaping desire. Stepping back, prying the space that had vanished between them back into place, she looked at the floor and then shot a glare up to him.

"That was mean, Craig Erikson."

"What?"

"You set me up." She glanced around. *"Are your friends out there watching? Laughing at the way you can play a nerd as well as you run the field?"*

"Brenna, no! Why would you think that?"

Why would she? Because...there in his arms, she'd been mesmerized. Vulnerable. And he'd...what?

She felt stupid, that was what. He'd made her want his kiss, and then...just...nothing. Like it was a game.

"Why did you do that?"

"You're mad I didn't kiss you?"

She glared at him, working hard to keep only anger on her face and none of the hurt.

Though the music kept going, Craig stopped dancing and studied her as if she were a complicated problem in advanced chemistry. Slowly he stepped away but wrapped one large, sweaty hand around hers.

Not wanting to cause a scene, though she suspected she'd already had several eyes staring at her, Brenna followed as he led her toward a sideline that was sparsely populated. When he turned to look at her again, his hand kept hers in a gentle but firm grip.

"I can't screw this up, Brenna." He didn't hesitate, and his voice, though low to keep the words between them, was confident. "That's what that was. Don't think for a minute that I don't want to kiss you, because if the total fit going on in my chest didn't tip you off, I really wanted to. But I don't want to mess this up. If I screw this up, your dad will never give me another chance. I like you too much to risk that."

He didn't waver as she looked at him, searching for his angle. If he was playing her, he should be in theater, because he was a better actor than he was a football player—and he was a really, really good football player.

The hand that hung at his side came up, and then the back of his fingers drifted down her cheek. "Don't stay mad at me. Please?"

It was that part of the memory, of the dream, that lingered most. The scene that replayed more than the rest. Seventeen-year-old Craig would often morph into twenty-nine-year-old Craig, standing there with his heart his eyes, hurt on his expression, and tenderness in his touch.

Pleading with her to not stay mad at him.

***

"How's Craig doing?"

Still upset about the dreams that would not go away, Brenna swallowed against a growl. Of the few things she wished her dad knew not to ask, that question was near the top. Hanging out up there with *Why are you still stubbornly hanging on to Big Prairie when I know you're not happy?* And *Do you ever think about running again?*

She drew a calming breath, careful to make sure her voice would sound neutral when she used it to answer that loaded and unwelcome inquiry. Couldn't he ask about Grant? Shouldn't it be a standard question to ask about your daughter's actual boyfriend and not her ex?

Goodness, she was in a mood.

"I'm not sure, Dad." She kept sugar in her voice where she was likely to put salt. Those pesky dreams were one thing, but this? Ugh. "I don't see him much."

"Big Prairie's a small town, punks. And you're Trent's speech therapist, aren't you?"

"How do you know—" Brenna cut off the ill-thought question.

Too late.

"He told me."

"You...he..." She gripped the phone as her jaw grew rigid. "You talk to Craig?"

"About once a month. Sometimes more."

"What?"

"That a problem, punks?"

Salt overtook the sweet she was terrible at faking. "Since when?"

His long sigh whispered through the speaker, making her irritation spike. She was tired, confused, and now...now betrayed. "Dad?"

"For a while, Brenna. I don't know how long. Just...for a while."

"Why?"

"He called me four, five years back? I don't know. But he wanted to make sure I was okay. Wanted to have some things cleared up between us."

"What things?"

"About Scottie."

"Scottie?"

"It wasn't his fault, Brenna. That day—Craig just overslept. Hit the snooze button, and that's why he wasn't at the field. He didn't know Scottie would be there."

"Scottie was always there when Craig was home. Craig knew that." As bitterness coated her tongue, she wondered why she was arguing this. She knew that day had been a tragic accident. Hadn't been Craig's fault, or the snowplow driver's fault, or Scottie's fault. There was no fault. Only devastation.

But dang it, she was still mad at Craig. Felt like a treachery that Dad wasn't.

The drift of silence extended on the other end of the call. It felt like distance and disapproval. Hurt and defeat. Dad had suffered enough over this, and she was clearly not helping. Though it made her wonder why Dad would feel it necessary to defend Craig, she wasn't willing to clang swords with him about it.

"I know, Daddy," she said softly. "I know it wasn't anyone's fault. But I still don't understand why you're asking about Craig."

"He's in Big Prairie—which you should know is not an easy place for him to go back to. This is his first full-time, all-in-one-place job. His mom is sick. And he's got two boys he's hoping to adopt. I assumed you'd care a little."

The barb bit. Everything Dad said were all things Brenna knew. Whoa. Except— "Adopt? No, Dad. He's their foster-care provider. Actually, that's not entirely true. Janet is—"

"He's working on adoption." Dad's voice held that don't argue with things you know nothing about tone.

As he let that sink in, the silence began to ring. Craig? Adopt the Fulton boys?

Made little sense. Why would a single twenty-nine-year-old man adopt two rough-around-the-edges boys? Why would he even consider it when his mom was so sick? Why did Craig Erikson continually feel the need to look like the superhero in every story he entered?

Didn't he understand that long-term things required long-term commitment? He couldn't just bail when a shiny new opportunity danced across his path?

"Brenna, I don't understand what happened between you two exactly, but this ugly image you've attached to a man that, at one point, you thought you were going to marry just isn't the truth. Seems to me that you're looking at him through a lens of bitterness and regret."

And that was too much. "Don't go there, Dad. You don't know."

"You're right. I don't. I know Craig is human and he's messed up some things, but still a good man. And I know he's serious about those boys."

"I don't even know how you know about those boys."

"I told you, he told me. Asked me if I'd be a reference for him."

Unbelievable. Brenna stared out the window overlooking Main, thoughts boiling about a man she couldn't shake. One who invaded her dreams, robbed her of the peace she'd fought hard to grab hold of, and now apparently had her dad taking his side.

"Brenna. Punks. I'm your father, and I adore you. And I think you need to hear this: some people live with regret their whole lives, never realizing that they don't have to."

She couldn't find an answer that wouldn't bite at her dad.

***

"You have some kind of nerve."

Craig froze at the doorway of her office after sending Trent on ahead to the car parked out front. It took two full beats before he turned to face Brenna, his expression all balled up in contrived confusion.

"I do?"

Brenna crossed her arms. "My dad, Craig? Are you serious?"

His hand braced on the doorframe while he shook his head.

"You asked my dad to be a reference for you?"

"He was my coach," he said slowly, almost sounding unsure. "And the only father figure I've had in my life."

"He's my dad! Don't you think he's been through enough after Scottie? Couldn't you just leave my parents alone?"

As Craig blinked, pain passed over his face as clearly as if she'd just slashed a razor over his skin. While that should have made her feel bad, Brenna gave way to the rising anger that possessed her when it came to this man.

"And adoption, Craig? What do you know about raising kids?" Something in the back of her head told her to stop, but she couldn't. The full vent of fury had opened, and she was a Vesuvius of unreasonable rage, Craig the Pompei of her scalding words. "This isn't something you can just walk away from. Do you realize that? You can't just use those boys as a popularity stunt and then drop them when it's no longer convenient."

His lips parted, shock morphing into offense. "Is that what you think?" As he stepped toward her, his hand fell away from the doorway and livid confusion lit his blue eyes. "Brenna, that was never—"

She held up a hand, dropped her focus to the floor. "Just

leave, Craig."

"Are you kidding? You can explode on me like that, and then demand that I leave? I don't get to say anything?"

Pressing her lips together, Brenna shook her head.

His stare felt like sharp jabs, but as he stood there, nailing her, he said nothing.

"You should go," she whispered.

He remained like stone. When she looked up, meeting his unwavering gaze, her stomach quivered at the storm of emotion. For several hard-to-catch breaths, she was lost there with him, frightened in the chaos of waves and thunder, sinking into the deep darkness of things that seemed to never surrender their fight.

Once more, he blinked, and the tempest in his eyes eased. The anger drained, though the ache remained, and in the place of the first came something so much worse.

Pity.

How could he look at her like that—like he knew this storm she battled daily? The heartache of lost dreams, of lonely grief and love buried?

He'd left. Hadn't gone through it.

He couldn't know, and Brenna hated that he pretended he did.

***

Deciding which was worse—Brenna's stony silence or her harsh accusations—took full occupation of his mind as Craig drove Trent home. The events of seven years past dragged him backward, into a dark spot of confusion and frustration, and later, massive heartache, and he was defenseless against the pull.

Would it always be like this with her?

"You cuttin me' out?"

"What?" Craig glanced at the boy buckled in the seat beside him.

"Not even listenin'. Just like everyone."

"I'm sorry, buddy. I was lost in my head. Say it again, will you?"

"Forget it."

"No, really, I'm listening now." And relieved for it. Brenna was tying him into knots, and he hadn't been ironed out to begin with.

With another glance toward Trent while they drove the last few blocks home, Craig caught the rare openness of vulnerability in his look.

"I say, what gonna happen to us?"

With that, he had Craig's undivided attention. "To you and Ashton?"

"Yeah." His tone cut hard, losing that uncertain openness. "I'm good. I handle things. But Ashton...he can't."

Man, this kid was *ten*. Ten years old, and claiming he was fine with his life of never really knowing where he'd land after the next seismic rumble of his world. Still a kid, yet trying with all his scarred little heart to protect his brother from the fallout.

"Do you know what Ms. Blaum and I were talking about just now?" He really hoped Trent hadn't hung around the front of the office instead of going to the car like he'd asked him to. But there was a distinct possibility he'd done exactly that, and overhearing even part of the not-so-calm conversation could easily be why Trent was thinking about his future.

The boy shrugged, then leaned against the door.

Craig waited until they'd turned into the driveway, parked, and shut off the engine before he twisted in the seat to look at Trent. "I've started the paperwork for adoption, Trent."

He winced.

"That's not okay with you?" Craig worked to keep surprise

and hurt from his tone.

Trent shrugged. "It's fine."

"I'm not sure fine is good enough for this, buddy. Talk to me."

A long silence settled over them as he studied the house beyond his window. The buttery paint had dried nicely, their handprints a daily reminder that chaos didn't have to end ugly, and the memory of working on it with the boys pricked an ache in Craig's chest. He wanted this with them—an answer to prayer—but knowing what was best for everyone hadn't ever been Craig's strong suit. The woman who'd just unloaded on him was exhibit A, and she clearly didn't think Craig's pursuit of adoption was anywhere in the ballpark of a good idea.

But what would happen to the boys if he didn't? He couldn't handle the strong possibility of them bouncing around the foster system until they aged out. Older kids were hard to place and even harder to find a forever family for. Besides, there was this tenderness growing inside his chest. Daily.

He couldn't imagine letting them go.

Trent remained uncharacteristically silent. Man, Craig wasn't good at hard things like this—which meant maybe Brenna had a point.

"Is there somewhere else you'd rather be?"

When Trent finally turned his face back to Craig, all he could read was division in dark eyes that had a much more worn look to them than any ten-year-old kid ought to have. "Why you do that, Craig? Why you wanna be stuck with two bits of trouble like us?"

"I've never thought of you and your brother as two bits of trouble." Well, actually, he had. Trent, especially, had a specific talent for finding trouble. But not the way he was implying—that Craig didn't want to be a part of their lives.

"Ms. Blaum think it a bad plan."

"No." Craig sighed, fighting back the irritation with

Brenna that simmered in the back of his mind. She always did have a temper, especially when she'd been stewing over something for a time. And like as not, that Adventure Run, and their hug that followed, had her stewing. "Whatever you overheard today, Trent, you need to know that Ms. Blaum is upset with me. Not you or Ashton. She's mad at me. Because of some stuff in the past that happened between her and me."

The skin around Trent's eyes pinched, and his mouth seamed tight.

"I promise you, buddy." Craig leaned toward him, palming his shoulder. "Ms. Blaum likes you quite a lot. And more importantly, I swear I'm petitioning to adopt you and Ashton because I want to. I want you both."

Trent's eyebrows folded in, and he blinked several times.

"We're a team, Trent. You and Ashton and me. We're a family now, and even though there are times that are hard, I want that to be the way it always is."

Craig waited, afraid Trent was going to shove his hand away. Fly out of the car and into the house, slamming the door in his face. Wouldn't be the first time he'd come unglued when Craig had tried to reach his heart. Paige said it was the trauma reaction in him—the need to preserve his heart because he was certain it would get ripped up again. Craig didn't know but that she was right, but that sad fact didn't help him know what to do.

He was so out of his depth when it came to the hard things.

So there he sat, afraid that Trent was about two seconds from a blowout. Which left Craig shocked speechless when a single tear flicked onto the side of his nose, and he connected with Craig's gaze.

"Think they let us?" he whispered.

"Be a family?" Craig had to muscle the words past the vise in his throat.

Trent swallowed.

"I sure hope so, Trent. I'm trying everything I can to make that happen. Would that be okay with you?"

Those glazed eyes held steady, and in the next moment, he was huddled up against Craig's chest.

God help me, he thought. There were so many ways all of this could go south. He needed it not to. Trent and Ashton needed it not to.

Even in that moment, with this awesome, broken, frustrating, incredible kid tucked up in his arms, Craig couldn't stop thinking about Brenna, about the anger she'd clung to when it came to him. And about whether or not she was right.

After all, he'd failed her. Massively. And there was no going back on that.

These boys couldn't afford that kind of disaster.

Chapter Sixteen

GRANT WAS ORDERING PIZZA. AGAIN.

A girl should be excited when her guy called and invited her over for her favorite non-healthy dinner.

Brenna's stomach churned, and thoughts whirled through her mind. Not the *isn't my boyfriend the best—willing to sacrifice his rigid meal expectations for me* kind. More like the *this isn't like Grant, and the last time he did this it was because something happened between us that neither of us could understand or fix* way of thinking.

So naturally Brenna summoned her most enthusiastic "Wow, Grant, that sounds so good. Thanks. I'll be there in twenty" when he asked, and was working on the most believable, innocent girl-in-love smile as she trudged up his walkway.

He must have had the same game plan, because he met her at the door, his look intense as he leaned against the frame, hands stuffed in his pockets—all enchanted boyish and sexy. Brenna stepped into the house and laid a palm against his chest. He leaned when she leaned, and his mouth lingered over hers.

The kiss felt...forced. Pretend. She gripped the material of his button-down, fighting against the feeling of estrangement.

His hand rested on the curve of her waist as he pulled away from her mouth. The sigh that passed over his lips and forced his eyes shut didn't seem like contentment. Everything about that moment felt like goodbye.

Brenna preferred the pretense.

"So." She stepped into the house and smiled. "Pizza, huh? It's like you know me or something."

One corner of his mouth twitched upward. "Yeah. I think I do." His study held so many contradicting things. *I know things that maybe you don't realize, and I wish I didn't. This is actually the last thing I want...*

The pain in her stomach surged. Pizza didn't sound so good.

The door clicked shut, and then Grant's hand was at her back. He leaned to kiss her head as they moved together into his small house. Brenna knew the layout of the older cracker-box setup. The crisp gray walls of his living room, which remained clutter-free with only a wall clock and four framed prints of landmark architecture—two on each side of the clock, maintaining perfect symmetry.

The same gray paint continued throughout because if Grant Hillman was anything, he was consistent. In the dining room, on the old architect's desk he'd converted to his table, the box of HotPies waited, seeping its baked bread and saucy deliciousness through the small room. She wanted so much to appreciate this moment—that he'd done it for her at a sacrifice to himself. But all she could think was *why?*

Hand still on her back, he guided her to one of the four metal stools flanking the table, and after she slid onto it, he took the one next to her. Without a word, he opened the box and served them both a slice. Without a word, he poured her a coke and him a water. Without a word, he shut his eyes, rubbing his hands down his jeans, and pulled in a long breath.

She couldn't. Not anymore.

"Grant, what's going on?"

He looked at her. Reached over the table and brushed her knuckles. "Let's pray and eat, and then we can talk."

She didn't answer, but he bowed and prayed anyway. Asked to bless the food that she knew good and well he didn't think they should be consuming because it wasn't good for them. Asked to bless their night together.

Asked for wisdom. For them both.

He looked up and so did Brenna. Sipped his water while she fingered the rim of her plate. There was no way she could eat now. Not with the fire in her gut and the spinning in her mind.

"Grant..."

He sighed again. Was that the third time in less than ten minutes?

"I know. We should just get into it, because dinner is not working." His eyes connected with hers. Held. "*We* are not working, Brenna."

She blinked. Pulled back. "What?"

His hand forked through his hair and then gripped his neck. "I did not want to admit it. I have been wrestling with it for weeks. Trust me when I say that this is the last conversation I really want to have with you."

"Then why are we having it?"

Lips pressed, one corner of his mouth lifted. It was the saddest half smile she'd ever seen. "Because I care about you too much to not have it."

Brenna stared at him, trying to figure this enigma of a man she'd been dating. He smacked his thighs, pushed himself to standing, and tugged her up. "I cannot do this across a table from you."

When she stood, he studied her face in that way that made her sick with fear.

"Can we sit in the living room?"

"Okay..."

Her hand tucked in his, he moved, and she followed. They landed side by side on the same couch they'd snuggled up together on to watch *Gifted Hands* and *The Pursuit of Happiness* and all of *John Adams* on Netflix. His house, his choice. That was how they did things. When they were at her house, they watched her picks. *Pride and Prejudice*, *Father of the Bride*, and reruns of *Dr. Quinn*.

He sat straight, and there was a three-inch gap between their bodies.

"Grant, what are you doing?"

"Facing reality." He turned to look at her.

"Which reality is that?"

"You and me."

"You and me..."

"Are not going anywhere."

"What? Why would you say that?" Flustered, and with all the messy, mixed-up emotions that had been building in her since the school year started, she angled to him. Without any filter, she let her words gush. "You're the one who's held back. Every time. When we kiss, you're the first one to pull away. When—if—we ever make out, I'm the one who initiates it. And two years, Grant! Two years!" She held up her empty left hand, letting the naked ring finger finish the statement.

With a gentleness that was infuriating, he wrapped her wrist suspended between them and slowly lowered it to her lap.

"I have said *I love you*." His low statement was calm, measured.

The most devastating retort she'd ever heard. What did that mean?

His touch abandoned her skin, and he pressed his palms together between his knees. "Do you realize you have never said it back?"

A beat that was like silent thunder crashed between them.

He peeked at her.

She had. She'd said *I love you*. Hadn't she?

Hadn't she?

She did love him. Didn't she?

Her heart ached as she looked at him, lips parted. Ready to argue, but without any words that she could say for certain were true.

He shook his head, as if he'd read her screaming thoughts. "No, Brenna. You never have. You say *me too* or you kiss me. But the words? Not once. Do you remember the first time I said them to you?"

She swallowed.

"I asked you if you wanted me to go with you to visit Scottie's grave on the anniversary last winter. You said that was sweet but you would rather go alone. I nodded, and then we just stood there in your apartment in awkward silence. It felt like there was this part of your life you did not want me touching. So I said it. I told you I loved you, because I thought if you knew how I felt, you would feel safe to let me in there."

She remembered. Looking away, she struggled under the misery, pulse throbbing as the memory ran its course. He didn't finish it for her, because he didn't have to. She remembered it all clearly. How she'd given him a closed-mouth smile—tight and pretty much false—and then leaned to kiss his cheek.

And that had been it.

Ten months had passed, and still, that was it.

Her insides crumbled, and she felt like she was flailing around, trying to find something to grip while her world caved in all over again.

Grant's palm warmed hers. The hold she'd searched for an irony of razor edges.

"Brenna..." A pause. An ache. A breath for courage and truth. "I have wondered for many months why I cannot reach that place. Why you cannot say those words. And I think now I see why, and it is not going to change while we stubbornly pretend it is not there."

"What do you see?"

"Craig."

"What?" She sniffed, jerking her hand from his, and stood. "I told you—"

"You told me you were fine, but you are not. Clearly, you are not."

"Craig and I are done. We've been done for a long time. Why can't everyone just get over it? Why can't *you* get over it?"

"It is not mine to get over."

"What does that even mean?"

He stood and took the steps required to be in front of her. "It means that *you* are not over it." Both hands wove through his hair, and he gripped his head, as if trying to hold himself together. Forcing himself to do what he'd determined was right. "Why can't you stand to be in the same room with him? You cannot even look at him, Brenna. That is not you. It is definitely not you being *fine*."

Brenna's jaw clamped so hard and stiff that sharp pain shot through her skull. Thursday's team meeting flashed through her mind. Brenna had actually prayed for a headache so she could legitimately opt out.

She couldn't face Craig again. Not only because she was still mad that he'd gone behind her back, talking to her dad for *years*, but because now he had leverage on her. She'd been out of line last week, and the ugly words she'd spewed at him in her office needled her conscience.

Of all the times to come down with the flu, that afternoon would have been perfect. Unfortunately, heaven did not agree.

Brenna had taken her place at the round table moments before Craig strode in. The glance he'd landed on her was stormy, and she'd hardened against the guilt that poked her heart. He needed to think through this thing. That was a fact.

You hang on your mad like it your best friend, Bren. Craig a good man.

She had wanted to cover her ears, as if that could shut out the faded memory of Scottie's rebuke from so many years past. She and her brother would argue occasionally, but the only time their mild disagreements ever got to her had been when it'd been about Craig that fall before homecoming. Scottie would not let it go—wouldn't leave her alone about it. It was like in his head, he'd seen the future and it was Craig and Brenna forever and ever, amen.

Her head spinning with memories and anger, she'd glared at Craig for half a heartbeat and then refused to look at him—or speak to him—for the duration of the meeting. Apparently that had not gone unnoticed by Grant.

Sitting on his sofa, turned to face her, Grant's eyes lit with an angry passion rare for his consistent nature. "If you had treated him with any sort of casual friendship, that would be something else entirely. But you cannot even talk about him, let alone to him. You say you are done? I say you are refusing to deal with the truth. I think you have never been done. Now the past is here, staring you in the face, and you just want to shut your eyes and deny anything ever happened."

"You don't know what you're talking about!" she seethed, tears cresting her eyelids and running over her cheeks. "You don't know anything about it."

In a breath, he returned to calm Grant. Steady, even Grant. Grant who could read between the lines, even when no one else could. His palm cradled her cheek, thumb traced over the wet path of tears. "You are right. Because you will not talk about it. For weeks I have waited. I have tried to give you both the space and the security to know that I am listening. I am here. But I think I am not the guy you need to work through this with. And I know I do not want to be the guy who was too selfish to let you work through it with the one you should."

"With Craig?"

He nodded.

"Grant, I've told you—"

He shook his head. "You are not being honest with either of us—mostly with yourself. You are not fine, Brenna. You are not anywhere near fine."

***

His declaration reverberated in her mind, but the voice within her thoughts lost Grant's gentle rumble, and the words simply became monotone brandings stamping through her ears.

You are not anywhere near fine.

As she lay in bed that night, alone in the dark with the words haunting the silence of her room, she felt the slip of stability she'd managed to grasp after Scottie's accident slide through her fingers.

No, she hadn't been fine. Not in a really, really long time. She'd learned to fake fine. Mastered pushing through daily living with an act that looked very much like fine. After all, she'd had to. Mom and Dad, they weren't okay. How were they going to deal with their agonizing grief and her slide into deep...whatever the darkness was called? They couldn't, and she didn't ask them to. She just put her head down and pushed through.

But now, with that thread of stability of *fine* loose and beyond her grip, she felt a sense of falling.

Her heart was ash. The ache felt hot and familiar. A smolder she'd known intimately and had run from with everything she had. And she was good at running.

The thing about running was that no matter how much distance you had in your legs and lungs—and Brenna had a lot—eventually you got tired. Everyone got tired.

No one can run forever.

The notion of it—of her running from the things that had seared so painfully in the past—seemed a bit absurd on the surface. Here she was in Big Prairie. When her parents said they couldn't stay anymore—that every corner of this itty-bitty town held Scottie in it in some way or another and they just couldn't do it—Brenna had stayed. Stubbornly. Against all logic and even some advice. She had remained in the town where her heart had been shattered for the second time in less than six months.

She had stayed. Claiming that she wasn't going to run.

That had been a loaded proclamation—rich with double meaning. She'd quit on her dreams to reach the Olympic trials. Quit the university team. Finished her classes online, then dove into her practicums. All so that she could stay in Big Prairie. Because she wasn't running.

And yet there she was, achingly exhausted.

***

"The thing is, Craig..."

Wow. He knew that intro. Had used it a few times himself—and had actually been composing something similar in his own mind to open a conversation with Sophie.

It'd been over a week since he'd come to fully and completely realize that no, he wasn't over Brenna—and likely at this point, would never get there—which meant that this casual dating thing he had going on with the lovely and kind Sophia Shultz should go back to a friendship-only thing if he was any kind of gentleman at all. Which he hoped with all his heart to be. More than seven days passed with that firm knowledge, and he'd done and said all of nothing about it to her.

Nice.

Heat blazed up his neck, sure to splash his face with color

within the next two breaths. With a palm, he covered his neck, and wished to high heaven looking at his shoes would hide his face. At the towering height of six six to Sophie's five three, there would be no such luck.

"Oh dear," Sophie breathed, a catch in her words. "I really, really don't want to say this..."

Put on some man clothes and save the lady.

Sometimes he could be such a coward. Not this time. With a determined focus, he lifted his gaze to meet hers. "It's okay, Sophie. Actually, if you're going to say this isn't working, then you should find some comfort in knowing that it's mutual."

Her eyes widened. "What?"

Great. It wasn't mutual. What an idiot...

That smile widened on her face. The one that could warm a frosty room and ease a guy standing on needles, and then she laughed. "Oh my goodness, are you serious, Craig? I've been agonizing over this!"

"I'm sorry for that."

"Yeah, me too!"

"I should have said something sooner. I just...really do like you, but—"

With a warm hand, she gripped his elbow and then leaned her forehead onto his shoulder. "But we're not going to make it past friends."

"Right." He exhaled the word, feeling relief and appreciation for the lovely, vibrant, fun woman at his side.

Sophie smiled up at him and then made a mocking motion of wiping her brow. "Whew. Glad to have that established."

"Me too."

She leaned away, patting his arm. "But we're still good for morning coffee sometimes, right?"

"I'm actually not a coffee drinker, Sophie. But I'd be disappointed if I didn't see you with your mug at seven forty-five at least two or three times a week."

For a moment, she looked stunned at his coffee deficiency—

which he'd discovered was a typical reaction from a coffee addict—and then she grinned. "Right. And I'll still get a dance or two out of you at homecoming, right?"

His heart stalled, and a hint of nausea bulged in his gut. Homecoming. He had to fight off the urge to shut his eyes and sigh. He definitely did not want to attend homecoming. Even if he had been assigned as a faculty sponsor.

Rumor had it, Grant had been too, and he'd asked Brenna to go—also as an official supervisor.

Should be awesome. Because seeing her at the river with Grant, and then hugging her after the Adventure Run—minus Grant—hadn't made things even more awkward at all.

"Craig?"

"Yeah." He spat the word out, trying to cover up his slip into...whatever it was. "Yeah, we'll definitely have to work the floor."

The furrowed brow Sophie studied him with threatened more questions. But then she smoothed on a grin that whispered sympathy—which didn't make him feel any better—and nodded.

"Good. I'm glad we're friends, Craig Erikson."

"I am too, Sophie Shultz."

She waved as she moved through the door. "See you at the dance."

Chapter Seventeen

MISERY MUST INDEED LOVE COMPANY, BECAUSE THERE HE WAS.

All handsome and dangerous, just as he'd been nine years before, when he'd taken Brenna to her sophomore homecoming dance. She couldn't believe he'd asked back then—and couldn't believe Daddy had agreed to it. Broke that number one rule. Not just cracked it. Splintered it to pieces.

Craig's special. That was all Daddy had said.

Couple years later, at her senior prom, when she'd brought up that first homecoming date, Craig had turned a warm tomato red, laughed a little, and then looked into her eyes with that deep *I love you* stare.

"He said he'd remove any part of my body that infringed upon propriety with a dull, rusty knife."

"And you still asked?" she'd wondered.

He'd leaned down, those muscled shoulders curling over her just like they had that first dance two years before, making her feel like she was all he wanted in the world, and his nose brushed hers. "I had to. Something in me needed to know you."

Ah. The romance of an eighteen-year-old. So innocent and lovely. Breathtaking and falsely secure. Never once had Brenna doubted that she and Craig would last. They'd been Big Prairie's William and Kate. At that point, they still had never really fought. Imagine that? Two years of dating and the hottest argument they'd ever had was about whether Brenna would miss a cross-country meet to go see Craig's homecoming game at UNL.

Such bliss.

Eighteen months later, everything had changed. Everything. All the fears that had quietly rooted in her mind somewhere around Craig's junior year in college—Brenna's freshman year at a different school and the year Craig's football success gained massive momentum—became a strangling vine, smothering her trust, suffocating them. The love she had been sure would be steady and everlasting splintered. That no-fight record morphed into constant struggle interrupted by brief periods of peace. Daily insecurity plagued her mind.

She'd felt him pulling away, distracted by the demands of more pressure than either of them had ever expected him to shoulder. After the video of Craig and Scottie had gone viral, all that unforeseen pressure reached a boiling point. She'd been certain his distraction had led to a wandering heart. Jealousy hadn't even been the right word for it. She'd become saturated with suspicious envy. As time slipped on, everything she had done as an attempt to avoid the fruition of those worst-case scenarios that poisoned her heart had blown up in her face.

She'd lost him. Worse, long before she'd lost him, she'd lost herself.

Now, there they were. Right back where they'd begun. This

time, miserable.

Brenna glanced toward the far wall where she'd glimpsed Grant's profile. He was handsome. A bookish, gentle kind of handsome that seemed steady and safe. A twinge scratched at her heart. She was supposed to be here with him. Chaperoning this event at his side. He was supposed to be her forward motion. Proof in the flesh that she'd moved on and would not, for a single moment, step a toe into the past. Not with Craig.

An upbeat Taylor Swift song blared from the DJ's set up—certainly a song that should have been put to rest by now. Who understood the trends? High school kids bopped and moved, not a care in the world. Oh, for such a moment. Brenna meandered the sidelines, focusing her attention on the girls and their pretty dresses, fancy updos.

Lord, make them wiser than I was. Let them embrace the fun of this season and leave the hard stuff for later. Let them make better choices, hear good counsel.

She blinked, her heart stuck in grieving. For the innocent girl that she'd been. And for the innocent young man Craig had been. For the things that they'd chosen. The way that they'd broken. The dream between them that had died.

"I haven't seen you out on that floor once." Sophie sidled up next to Brenna with a hip check. "And that boyfriend of yours has been on the opposite side of the room all night."

Drawing a breath, Brenna trained her attention back to Grant. "There's a reason for that," she said as quietly as the loud music would allow.

Sophie's hand wound around Brenna's elbow, and she tugged. "I was afraid of that."

Brenna's bottom lip trembled, and she looked at her peep-toe shoes. Nodded.

"Why?"

"It's complicated."

"Isn't it always?"

A hard, sad chuckle shook her chest.

"Are you okay?"

Another long, deep breath filled her lungs, and she looked back at her friend. "Not today. But I will be." Forcing a smile, she straightened her shoulders. "Did you come with Craig?"

A studious look passed over Sophie's expression. "No. That wasn't going anywhere, and we've agreed that a professional buddy friendship would be of more benefit to us both right now. So he's here and I'm here, but we're not here together."

"I'm sorry," Brenna said.

"Don't be. I'm not." Her beautiful smile stretched full. "I've gained another good friend out of the deal, and that's no small thing."

Brenna leaned into Sophie's shoulder and wrapped an arm around her back. "You are something pretty special."

"Thanks."

Taylor Swift got done shaking things off, and the DJ switched gears. As Chris Young started in on "Think of You," Brenna crumbled inside.

Please no.

Grant looked up and across the room. Of all times during the evening, when he'd avoided eye contact with her the entire night, he'd set his attention on her for that song. Brenna sighed and turned away.

"You okay?" Sophie's hand fell from her shoulder as Brenna moved.

"Yep." *Not at all.* Her heart throbbed with pain. The air in the room seemed heavy and hot and suddenly hard to breathe. In her narrowed view, she found the doors at the far end of the gym, one of them propped open. "I think I'll go grab a few gulps of clean air. These boys really doused on the cologne, you know?"

Sophie laughed. "Every. Single. Day." She squeezed my hand. "Want company?"

"No." She pinned up a grin. "I'll be back in a minute, and we can pick out our favorite dresses of the year."

Brenna moved, and with a wink, Sophie let her hand fall away. It was cheesy and ridiculous, this physical reaction she was having to a sappy pop song. All the same, she straight-lined for the open door and kept going until the darkness of the cool night engulfed her in its embrace.

***

"A homecoming game loss." Jeremiah shook his head. "Poor Hale. Can you imagine living in this town with a losing record like that?"

Craig shrugged. It was getting harder and harder to avoid the football coach issue—and it hadn't been easy to begin with. "He's finding his stride. Don't think Coach Blaum had a winning record for, like, five years."

"Yeah, but he didn't move into a town that launched the likes of Craig Erikson."

Craig gripped the back of his neck. "Let's not be ridiculous with that. I had a good team. Both in high school and in college. No man can do great things alone—isn't that what Coach always told us?"

J nodded, his gaze serious. "See. This is what everyone sees in you, Craig. You know the game—but you know so much more. You know kids and life and—"

Craig held up his hand. "Hale is the coach. Respectfully, this conversation needs to end there." Setting his glass of water on the table, he pivoted, looking over the pulsating clump of teenagers in the middle of the floor for someone who wouldn't try to pin him into something seriously uncomfortable. Like a conversation involving him, football, and coaching.

The T-Swift song switched to something slower. Sadder. A story way too familiar.

What happened to the old country sets? Something to twostep to. Something meaningless and dumb and without any emotional threats waiting within the lyrics? This was a high school dance, after all.

Actually, Craig didn't mind the pop. Listened to a mix of genres on a regular basis. There were only a handful of songs he really couldn't stand in any of them. This one was one of them. Especially when he could feel the eyes of every adult in the room—at least those who knew his history—slide over him. As if they were waiting, breath held, to see what the lyrics would do to him.

Knifelike twisting in his chest, that was what it did. He slipped out of the room, through the front doors of the gym, down the hall, and out of the band room exit. The whisper of a gentle breeze swept away the toxic lyrics as it cooled the heat on his face.

It's just a song. He drew a deep breath. Let it go, long and slow. The pinch in his lungs eased.

Brenna had been there tonight. He'd seen her slip in somewhere around ten, a little black V-neck dress accentuating the beauty that had beckoned to him since he was a teen. Man, she was unforgettable.

The only way out of those thoughts, and that physical reaction, was to summon the memories that blotched regret in his heart, which would remind him why he could never have her again.

The way he'd let things go too far, becoming much too much like the man who had fathered him and less and less like the man he'd wanted so much to please—more, to become like. Coach had been everything good and honorable. And not only had Craig not grown into that same man, but he'd let him down. Abused his trust. Broken his daughter's heart.

That was cold water right there. A glacial waterfall.

A mild gust from the north blew against his face, combing an added chill through his hair and pulling his attention toward the direction of its birth. Down the straight line of bricks that was the west wall of the school, leaning against the rough end at the corner, a lone figure gazed out into the dark eastern horizon. By the light of the fluorescent bulb beyond her, he could make out the black of her dress, the shape of her athletic frame, the twist of her fancied-up hair, and the profile of a face forever embedded in his mind.

As if sensing his gaze, she turned. Didn't look away.

In that moment, she became gravity to his wandering heart. He could no more look away than he could stop his footfalls from closing the yards between them. She watched as he closed the space of night, their connection unsevered every step. Old fires blazed as her soft skin, blue eyes, became more visible as the distance of separation vanished.

"You okay?" Craig whispered past a growing lump in his throat.

"Fine." Her voice cracked, betraying the truth.

One more step and he was in front of her. With a lift of his hand, he could trace the silky curve of her jaw. With a half step forward, the evening chill between them would disappear. His whole body remembered the feel of her, and with the memory came a craving. A demand. He rolled both hands into fists, desperately fighting to retrain his thoughts, his desires.

"Mom said something about you and Grant—"

"There's no more me and Grant."

The rush of her words seemed a mystery. He thought she'd hide the truth. Thought she wouldn't want him to know because Grant was her chosen shield against his unwelcome reentry into her world.

She blinked several times, folded her arms against the breezy night, and curled against the brick wall.

"I'm sorry." His fists balled tighter while the magnetism between them grew. "About you and Grant."

"You are?"

What was he supposed to do with that? "I'm sorry you're

hurting."

"That's a first." Her face lifted, hard stare found his eyes again.

The wall of self-preserving control within him shivered. "You know that's not true."

A tear seeped from the corner of her eye. "How would I know that?"

He should walk. Back away and leave. The tension between them billowed, and he knew the ache of yearning for her way too well. The moment he slid a foot backward was the very one she brought herself straight.

"Prove that you're sorry, Craig Erikson." Anger and tears salted her voice.

Fire flashed through his core. This woman had been the world to him. When he had thought about his life beyond the field, she was it. Everything. He inhaled, hoping for a cleansing breath of chilled autumn air. What he got was a full, heady dose of her.

All the memories blazed to the surface. All the defenses crashed. Before he could think through the disaster that might follow, his fists unrolled, he slid his fingers over the curves of her face, and he gave in to the powerful longing that seven years had failed to crush. Lifting her face, he dipped to find her mouth with his own.

Seven years of missing her flowed into that kiss. Seven years of regret. Of wishing he hadn't done what he'd done. Of wishing that they weren't excluded from the second-chance types who could find their way back home again.

She kissed him back. Ache and passion and confusion. They all wove between them. She trembled as she pressed against him, and he held her tight as instinct overtook all thought.

And then she pulled away. His mouth tingled, heart throbbed. Their ragged breaths rattled the small space separating her mouth from his. Not satisfied, he shifted to find her lips again. She pressed her palms against his shoulders.

Reality snapped. The daze he'd slipped into evaporated, and as he studied her, she became rigid. She stepped back, colliding with the bricks again, and he let his hands fall away.

"Brenna—"

"Don't." Her voice cut. Iron set her jaw. She glared while her breath settled.

Craig shifted, widening the space between them, and then lifted his fingers, searching out the softness of her cheek once again.

She grabbed his hand before he touched her and shoved it to his side, and before he could react, her free palm smacked his face.

The click of her heels against the pavement joined with the throb in his ears as he stood stunned, watching her march away.

Chapter Eighteen

HER MIND SCREAMED TO FORGET. NOT TO RELIVE THAT KISS YET
ONE MORE TIME. DWELLING THERE WAS TOXIC.

Why'd he have to go and kiss her? Why had he even been out
there in the first place?

Why had she been there?

She should have been with Grant. Grant was supposed to be
her safety net. Her out. Her reason not to remember.

She didn't want to remember. Seemed she didn't have a
choice.

The insanity of this circular thinking pressed on her. By the
time Craig showed up with Trent for their scheduled visit,
Brenna's head had ached for a day and a half, her muscles felt
about as tight as the day after a ten-mile untrained run, and
she knew she'd likely snap.

She couldn't snap. She was a professional. Snapping was not
in her job description.

"Brenna, your four o'clock is here," Angel called from her

front desk—which was the barrier Brenna fully intended to maintain between her and Craig.

You're a professional.

Straightening her posture, she pulled in a long breath. Face the man. *Yes. Go out there and get it over with.* Then maybe they could both move the heck forward with their lives without the past clinging like static to their backs.

With measured steps, she left the office, dialed up a welcome-to-my-professional-space smile (for Trent), and took herself to the front. "Okay." She spoke without really seeing. "Trent, shall we get—"

She looked up. Sophie met her plastic grin with raised eyebrows.

"Sophie..."

"Craig was working on tuning the guitars for me. We start our strings unit next week, and I found out he has perfect pitch."

"Oh." No. She was so not disappointed. Surprised. Not disappointed. "That's great."

"Did you know he had perfect pitch?"

There was so much about Craig that Brenna knew that she wasn't going to own to. "How handy for you, right?"

"You okay, Bren? Haven't seen you since Saturday night, and—"

"I'm quite well." Cue the plastic smile again. "Trent. Shall we get started?"

"Sure, Dawg."

"Trenton, I'm not a dog, and we're not going to start this way."

The slouching ten-year-old shrugged like he wasn't listening and didn't care.

Sophie sighed. "It's been a day. Craig will deal with it when he picks him up."

"He'll be done in an hour?"

"Hopefully. Either way, he said he'd come get Trent." She rested a hand on his shoulder. "Try not to drive Ms. Blaum crazy."

"It what I best at," Trent said.

"Some days I think that's true." Sophie tipped an eyebrow and gave him an eye-to-eye look. "But Craig says you have about a million other amazing talents. You've used up your allotment of crazy-driving for the day." She smiled at him— that grin that could pull a kitty-cat purr out of a hungry lioness.

Bolstered by Sophie's charm-the-kid magic—a trait she shared with Craig—Brenna walked with Trent back to her office. Their project that day: storytelling. The goal: learning how to listen, to take turns, and to stay on topic.

This was life to her—a therapy angle she'd grown up with and had engaged in pretty much daily with Scottie. It was their game, their language. In many ways, their bond. Because even though she'd understood at a young age that Scottie needed help with the social communication skills, she'd also understood what he did for her.

He told the best stories. Scottie could tease a belly laugh out of her more than anyone else, and he did it with the kind of smile that turned a glacier into a pool of hot springs.

Trent could be that way too. She'd seen his lighter side, folded within the depths of his hard, stubborn shell. Likely, Craig had seen it too—because he had the same kid-charming DNA Sophie possessed. Which would have been a convenient match between those two...

A double edge of jealousy and relief cut through her thoughts. Sophie had said she and Craig were keeping things in the friend zone. A fact Brenna had no business feeling relieved over, any more than she should feel jealous over the things that Sophie and Craig had in common.

Sheesh, that kiss really had messed her up. Meeting Trent's

scowl, she shook off her mental meanderings.

She was supposed to be working.

"Well, buddy, I guess it's story time for you and me. Let's get to it, shall we?"

"What kind of stories?"

"I was thinking dragons. What do you say?"

"Don't get why we tell stories for this junk." Trent waved his hand at her and then over her office. "I don't even get why I have to do this dumb ther-py. I know how to talk."

"Social interaction, buddy. We learn to listen, to wait our turn to speak, and to stay on topic."

"Sound dumb."

She smirked, resting a hand on his bony shoulder. "Of course it does. But someday you'll thank me." With a nudge she moved them toward her office while looking back at Sophie.

"Best of luck," Sophie said with an *I'm sorry—it's been a day* look.

So it'd been a day for all of them. Ugh.

Brenna settled cross-legged on the red carpet across from Trent, and the storytelling began. For the first five minutes, Trent sighed, rolled his eyes, stretched backward on the floor, but after ten minutes and a hard story twist she'd planned beforehand, he sat straight, fully engaged.

They exchanged the plot. Listened carefully so they could repeat the previous action back and then added to the unfolding adventure. By the time the hour was up, Trent was capturing the dragons of fear and rejection in his mind while becoming the warrior for the good dragon of hope. He hadn't noticed that he'd dropped his street English. Didn't notice that he'd lost his *I ain't listening to you* attitude. Had no way of knowing that his dark eyes glittered with adventure and engagement as he held Brenna's gaze.

Trenton Fulton transformed into the ten-year-old boy that

he was.

Brenna breathed in as the weight of the day—of the days since homecoming—sagged from her being. She smiled, eyes still locked with Trent's.

"That was quite a tale, buddy."

"We should write it down."

"I think that's a splendid idea, and you should do it."

His eyebrows pulled together, mouth pursed. Suspicion reentered his expression. "Why we do this, Miss Blaum? Why you care how I talk?"

"There is power in language, Trent."

"But you understand me fine."

"Yes, I do. And, honestly, so does everyone else right now. But the thing is, someday the way you speak will allow people to make assumptions about you. What you say and how you say it can open and close doors for you."

"That ain't fair."

"Perhaps not. But it is what is true, whether it's fair or not. Like I said, there is power in language. And just like you were being the warrior protecting our dragon of hope, Craig and Janet and me and so many others are fighting to protect you. And to make sure you have the opportunities in your future that can help you succeed."

Trent crossed his arms. "Maybe I don't want your succeeding ways."

How quickly the defiance returned. Brenna fought against the argument trap Trent was so good at putting down. With a bright expression, she shrugged. "Up to you. Ultimately, no matter where we come from in life, we will start being responsible for our choices. At some point we don't get to blame others for the paths we walk. At some point, no matter where we've come from, we'll have to choose for ourselves where we will go." Her words warmed the room as she heard them. As though it was not she who spoke, but another, and it wasn't Trent who needed to listen, but her.

"Ten years old. Miss Blaum, I be ten. And a foster kid. You know how many choices I got?"

Brenna swallowed the hard lump of conviction she didn't want to deal with and embraced the compassion flowing from her heart instead. "Right now, not many, buddy. I get it, and your life hasn't been all roses. But guess what?"

"Shoot." His hard look said he wasn't listening.

Brenna finished anyway. "You get to choose how you speak. How you use language."

"Man." Trent's arms dropped to his side like lead weights. "Shoulda knowd you circle back on me."

A small chuckle left her mouth and then died as the chime rang outside her office. The signal that someone had come through the front door. Trent was her last client of the day. Craig had come.

A pulse of panic zipped through her. "All right, Trent. We're done for the day, and it sounds like Craig's here, so—"

The tap at the door cut her off only a moment before the passage swung open. And there he was. Stormy blue eyes grazed Trent, sending the boy a tight smile, and then landed on her. Held. Her chest knotted, making it difficult to draw a breath. Thoughts scrambled as anger and longing collided, making an incomprehensible mess in her mind.

"Hey. How'd it go?"

Go? What go? Where?

"Brenna?" He stepped into the room, reached for Trent's shoulder, and stopped at his side, making the ten-year-old seem much younger with the scale of difference between Craig's athletic bulk and Trent's little-boy body.

"Good," she spat out, willing her brain to pick up and move.

"Good?" Craig shifted his study to Trent. "That so, T-man?"

"I done good." Trent nodded. "Like Miss Shultz tell me. No crazy-driving."

Nearly fully recovered from the mental wall she'd labeled *Craig's in the same space and I can't deal with that*, Brenna cleared her throat. "How about trying that again, only not in your street English."

Trent's shoulders slumped, and he flailed his hands to his sides. "Dang. Give a man a break."

"Man?" Craig chuckled. "Men don't toss themselves around like a limp rag like that, buddy."

Trent looked up, all fire and fury, the tip of his head required to meet Craig's challenge almost amusing. At the cock of one eyebrow on Craig's face, Trent chilled. One side of his mouth scrunched, and he held Craig's look. A slick grin moved Trent's mouth, and an ornery glint sparked his expression. He cleared his throat, rolled his shoulders into an exaggerated posture, and blinked.

"I was an excellent student, good sir," he said with a hilariously inflated attempt at an English accent. "My behavior was exactly as the beautiful band lady say. Perfection was my name."

Brenna blew out a laugh, and Craig snorted.

"That is excellent news, my good fellow." Craig tilted a small bow and covered Trent's head with his hand. Returning to his native midwestern non-accent, he finished, "Now, head on out to the car. I need to speak with Miss Blaum for a minute."

Suspicion returned to Trent's eyes. "Am I in trouble?"

"Nope. Not one bit. Just give me a minute, okay?" Craig rolled a loose fist and held it between them.

"Yaman." Trent bumped his knuckles as he moved toward the door. "Laters, Miss B."

"I'll be seeing you, Trent." Brenna kept her attention on Trent even after he passed the doorframe, pulling the door shut behind him.

All laughter evaporated, leaving only the tension between

her and Craig.

"Brenna."

"Yep?" She summoned that professional smile she thought she'd mastered, and grazed Craig's eyes, as if that would suffice as actual eye contact. "He really did do fine today. We did storytelling, and after a few minutes he fell right into it. Truly, he does know more than he lets on. Also, where on earth did he get that accent?"

"We've been listening to *Sherlock Holmes*. He and Ashton are both into it."

"Oh. That's a good idea. Do they follow it? I mean, the English is quite a bit different and—"

"Brenna."

She stopped short, realizing that she had launched into a full-on babble fest while simultaneously backing herself up against her desk.

Craig stepped toward her.

This office was too small. Too hot. Too...

"We need to talk." Craig slid another half step closer, his voice low.

Curling her fingers around the lip of her desk, Brenna swallowed. She took the five heartbeats of silence to order her thoughts and reerect the walls she'd had firmly in place last week. With a lift of her chin, she met his steady gaze. "Unless it's about the boys, then I disagree. We have nothing to talk about."

"I kissed you."

Her heart punched hard against her ribs. Craig hadn't always been this...direct. He wasn't the confrontational type. He preferred smooth waters and easy laughs and for everyone in the room to feel comfortable.

This was anything but comfortable.

Brenna pressed her lips together, and though she knew she should, she couldn't hold her look on him anymore. She shook her head. "Forget it—"

"You kissed me back."

Suddenly his fingers—strong and yet gentle—were under her chin. Lifting her face. A tremble shuddered over her. When she leaned back away from the touch that both burned and soothed, he dropped his hand. She reached into the stores of anger she'd kept for emergencies such as this and crossed her arms.

"I also slapped you," she said.

He rubbed his jaw on the side that she'd struck. "Yes, you did that too."

"So..."

The strain between them was a fury of ache and a swirl of anger. It was memories they didn't want to pick up again and feelings that neither had been able to bury. Grant had been right—she couldn't move on because she hadn't let go.

"I can't forget." His whisper teased the frayed places in her heart.

She shut her eyes. "Why?"

"I don't know. Do you?"

She refused to cry. Lifted her face again but could only make herself look at his chest. His question implied that she couldn't forget either. An assumption on his part. A denial on hers.

Her fingernails bit into her palms as she squeezed her hands tight. The clock on the wall ticked absurdly loud into the death-grip silence.

"Trent's waiting," she finally said, hating the slip in her voice.

Craig nodded, the feel of his unwavering gaze heavy upon her as he backed away. "I'd leave again, Brenna, if I could. So that this wouldn't be so hard for you. So that you could live again. But right now, I can't. You know I can't."

Her head snapped up, anger firing through her veins. "I'm sure that would be easier for you."

The sadness weighing his expression, dulling the blue of his eyes, smothered the heat within her. He shook his head, held the connection between them for another breath, and then turned for the door.

As she watched him walk from her office, she remembered the defeated posture he carried. Not because it was normal for him. But because it wasn't.

She'd only seen him defeated twice before. Both times he'd been walking away.

Chapter Nineteen

HE DIDN'T USE IT AS AN EXCUSE.

He promised himself, that was not why he called Brenna instead of Sophie. Besides, Sophie had been occupied with something recently. He wasn't sure what, but last weekend she'd gone on another solo adventure into the country. Since then...

Well, since then she'd smiled. More than usual—which had already been a lot. And she'd also been busy.

Who was he to interrupt that? Especially when Brenna had a connection with Trent and Ashton anyway. He wouldn't be there anyway. So. Choosing to call her wasn't him setting out an excuse. It was a true ask for help. Nothing more.

That whole stream of logic ran through his mind while he listened to the phone ring, waiting for Brenna to pick up. Expecting that she'd let it go to message, considering their last conversation.

"Hello."

Huh. How about that? She answered. Delayed, and she

sounded entirely suspicious, but an answer nonetheless.

"Hey, Brenna, it's Craig."

"I know. Caller ID."

"Right."

She waited, the line between them still. "Well?"

"Yeah. Uh, I kind of need a favor."

"What's that?" More suspicion.

He should have called Sophie—was Sophie even an approved care provider though? Or even Grant—he would be approved. Either one would have made more sense. Less mess.

"Mom needs to go to Lincoln on Friday for some treatments, and I need to go with her."

"Oh." Her tight voice unwound. "You need someone to stay with the boys?"

"Exactly. I mean, I can call Paige, and I'm sure she'd find a respite provider, but the last time I did that, they had to go to a house in a town over an hour away. You're listed as an approved caretaker, right?"

"Yeah, I'm on their team list."

"I thought that's what Mom had said. Anyway, I'd rather they not have to go so far away and to another stranger's house, if I can avoid it. So...so I thought I'd ask you."

She inhaled—he could hear the long draw of air.

"Listen, I didn't mean to make assumptions. It's okay for you to say no."

Her pause felt like the stretch of time between the singing of the national anthem and the first snap of the game. An eternity of tension-swathed silence that made him antsy.

"What time do you need to leave?" she said.

What? Blinking, he repeated her question in his mind to make sure he'd heard correctly. "Early." Surprise pitched up his voice. He cleared his throat. "By seven at the latest."

"And you'll be gone all day?"

"Most likely."

"Okay."

He dropped onto the kitchen chair, relief washing through him. Pulling the phone from his ear, he looked at it to be sure he'd called the right person. Yep. Brenna Blaum. Only Brenna he knew. He slipped the screen back against his whiskered face. "Okay?"

"Yeah. I'll be there at a quarter to seven. Will that give you enough time?"

"Should be perfect." He leaned forward, resting his head between his thumb and fingers, trying to douse the little flame of hope that flickered where it should not. "Brenna, I really appreciate—"

"I'll do it for the boys." Her tone turned stone. "And for Janet."

Not for you. Water to that small spark. She couldn't be much clearer.

"Okay?" And that sharp jab sank her point in deeper.

"Yeah. Okay." So did he still say thanks? See you Friday morning? How did he end this awful...whatever it was?

"I'll be there," she said.

"Good. Uh, thanks."

He felt about two feet tall.

***

Brenna stalled at the front door in the gray predawn morning. She'd been in this house a million times. Knew the shadows and textures and creaks nearly as well as she'd known her own home. But it had been years since she'd stepped over the threshold. Years since she'd ever wanted to.

Beyond that door was a million memories. And as many dreams that she had fingered like soft feathers, all with gentle promise and hope. All of them with him.

The recent memory of his lips on hers smashed through her

mind, making her heart jump and her mixed-up emotions tangle. Mostly mad surfaced though. Mad that she'd let that happen, mad that she defaulted into play mode, where that memory should have been deleted. He'd had no right to kiss her. He'd resigned that privilege long before, of his choosing, not hers.

The doorknob before her rattled, and before she'd banished all thoughts of disturbing, lingering passion between her and Craig, the barrier between them swished open.

"Hi." Craig leaned against the door for a moment, his gaze serious and intense before he seemed to shake off whatever passed through his mind and then smiled. Straightening, he pulled the entry open. "Thought I'd heard your car out front. Come on in."

She did, nerves firing like an electrical pulse. Following him into the kitchen, she inhaled in through the nose, out through the mouth, as if struggling to settle into the second mile of a long run, fighting off the urge to quit before she really got started.

Craig stopped beside the fridge. "The boys are making their beds. They're dressed and ready for school but haven't eaten yet. Mom put a batch of pancakes in the freezer, and I set the butter and syrup on the counter." His tone carried only the level of interest one would have when talking to a babysitter.

That struck her as irritating. But she couldn't say why and fought to cover it with a smile and a nod. "Easy enough."

"Hope so."

"Do they have anything after school today?"

"Nope." Craig lifted half a grin. "I cleared their appointments and let Trent's football coach know he'll miss practice today."

"Why? I could have gotten them there."

His shoulders rose and fell with a long breath. "Ashton sees Grant on Friday afternoons, and Trent got into a fight with a teammate during Tuesday's practice. Wasn't sure you were up for either of those scenarios, and I didn't want to abuse your help."

Oh.

"How did you know about Grant and me?"

His eyebrows tucked together. "You told me."

Right. At homecoming. Had he known before that night? Before he'd come over to her in all her misery and all his...magnetism? She felt her jaw tighten.

Craig stepped closer, then his hand warmed her elbow. "You okay?"

She snapped her head up. "Of course. I'm sure the day will go fine."

"No, I mean—"

"Ah, Brenna love." Janet's soft, soothing voice cut him off. Thank God. "Good morning, hon."

"Morning, Janet." Brenna turned to her with a smile that faded when she saw the woman she'd known well for half her life. Where there had been a woman full of energy and spunk and life, there now was exhaustion. Thin, sagging pale skin bore testimony to her battle, and the scarf wrapping her head told the story of why, in case Brenna had somehow managed to forget.

Craig's mom had cancer.

A sharp pain cut through her chest, making her eyes sting.

This was why Brenna was here. For Janet. And for the boys. So that Craig could take care of his mom, because despite all that was broken and ugly between him and her, she adored his mother. Still.

Pulled in by an unbroken friendship, Brenna stepped nearer and wrapped Janet in both arms. "How are you?"

"I am..." The breath through Janet shuddered. "I am fighting."

"You are. And we're glad."

She chuckled. "I am happy to see you standing here in my home, sweet girl. It's been much too long."

It had been quite some time. But standing there felt...dangerous.

"And I am thankful," Janet continued, "to you for taking on the boys today. It means so much to Craig and me to know that people who know them, who get their story and love them in the middle of it, are willing to help us like this."

"You know I would do anything to help," Brenna said.

Janet cupped her face and smiled. Beauty and light danced in her gaze as she held Brenna in it, giving her a glimpse of the woman Brenna had known. "Such a good girl."

Those soft words pelted her. She fought off the assault with a fake smile and a determined refusal to look at Craig. Craig, the one who might refute that claim. Craig, the man who knew more of her than anyone else and therefore possessed the ammunition to tear down that illusion of goodness.

No. Craig, the man who had shattered her world and then left her to sift through the ashes alone. That was the issue. The reason to stay mad. Only when that reminder locked firmly in place did she look at him. And scowled.

So that he would remember it too.

***

She wondered if it would have been more or less work to take on football practice that evening. Maybe more running around. More hurry up and wait. But then again, that would have been ninety minutes of Trent being occupied, which would have meant ninety minutes less of him antagonizing his brother.

Heaven help the boy moms.

Or maybe all the moms. She had no real experience to differentiate. But goodness, their bickering could drive a woman mad.

"Trent, have you started writing down our story yet?"

Yes, she was desperate. What ten-year-old boy honestly wanted to spend his Friday night punching a story into a computer? But the rain was picking up outside, and the escalation of traded insults between brothers warranted some kind of diversion.

"What story?" Ashton asked.

"None your beeswax," Trent said.

Ashton crossed his arms. "That ain't fair. I like stories."

"Isn't fair, Ashton," Brenna said.

The younger Fulton boy turned up a puzzled look. "You gonna work on my talk next, Miss Blaum?"

She laughed. "Every chance I get. Tell you what. Let's make up a new story. All three of us together."

"That be dumb for sure. Ashton only like baby stories, like *Paddington* and that dumb pig named Mercy something."

"*Mercy Watson?*" Brenna clapped. "Oh! I love that little pig!"

Trent rolled his eyes. Ashton's frown flipped into a smile. Well, she had one boy, so that was like batting .500, right?

"What else, Ashton?"

"Stories?"

"Yeah, what other stories do you like?"

"Craig reads a *Frog and Toad* book to me."

An image of Craig stretched out on the couch, Ashton tucked up next to his chest, his darker hair a beautiful contrast to Craig's, and *Frog and Toad Are Friends* held up between them nearly made her sigh. Easy to picture. She'd seen him read to Scottie often enough. Could still hear the low, soothing cadence of his story voice. Could still see the delight on Scottie's face.

"Miss Brenna?" Ashton's hand on hers startled her.

"Yes?"

"I axed if you like dat story?"

"I do. That book is a favorite."

"Then we can read dat?"

She glanced at Trent. He rolled his eyes again, but the tension in his shoulders loosened, and he plopped onto the couch.

Hmm. *Someone likes stories, just like his little brother.*

"Would you rather read a book than make up our own story?"

"Yes." Ashton grinned, punching the air, then running down the hall. "You do the voices too, 'kay? Like Craig."

"Uh..." She glanced at Trent. "I'll try. No promises though."

As Brenna lowered onto the couch beside him, Trent's eyebrows shot up in a challenge. "Know how to do the voices?" he asked.

Maybe. She sort of remembered them. "Like I said, I'll try. Want to help me?"

He snorted, turned his gaze away. Hard little bugger.

Ashton raced back from his room, three books bundled at all sorts of angles in his skinny little arms.

"Whoa, that's three stories, buddy."

"Yeah!" He flew to the couch and jumped. The cushion bounced with his impact, and his laugh made her chuckle.

"Ugh." Trent snatched the books from his brother. "See? What I say? All baby books."

"Well, let's read a *Frog and Toad* book, and then we'll talk."

"'Course we will. That's what you do."

Brenna smirked down at Trent. For all his protests, there he sat, waiting for the story. By page five, she remembered Craig's Frog and Toad voices perfectly, and her mimic of them was pretty close, if she did say so herself. The boys leaned onto her arms as she read. Both of them. When she read *the end*, they both dropped back into the cushions.

Trent crossed his arms.

Ashton jumped up. "Now *Paddington!*"

Brenna grinned, brushing his cheek with her fingertips. "How about Trent picks the next one?"

"I don't like books."

The last several minutes begged to differ.

"What kinds of books don't you like?"

"The kind with words."

"The kind with words you're not sure about?"

"No. The kind with words I don't care nuttin' 'bout."

"Huh." She held his gaze, keeping a mild challenge there, but a smile as well. "Name a book you don't like."

"*Paddington.*"

"Right. I got that loud and clear. *Paddington* is out. Sorry, Ashton."

"And that dumb Mercy pig one."

"All right, no *Mercy Watson.*"

Trent's lips pressed closed.

"What else?" Brenna pressed.

His arms tightened around his chest.

"I see," she said. "Well, I remember Craig reading often. Even in high school."

"Craig played football." Trent said. "He didn't read dumb stories."

"No, not dumb ones. But he did read. Quite a lot."

"You messin'. Not even being true."

"How about if I find one of his old favorites? We'll try one of those."

Trent squinted hard at her. "How would you know what be his favorite?"

Something hard clamped inside her. Should have seen that coming. Why was she doing this anyway? She could flip on a movie and call it good. Surely Craig and Janet would be home within an hour anyway. What did it matter?

Ashton bounced on the couch. "I know his favorite!"

Trent let his body drop back into the couch with yet another solid eye roll and a loud "Ugh."

Brenna ignored it and looked at Ashton.

"*Narnia*! Craig likes Aslan!"

Her smile was both relieved and genuine. "Yes. Craig likes *Narnia*. He also likes *Harry Potter*. So, Trent"—she looked back at the slumped-over boy—"you pick."

"I don't like either."

"Have you read either?"

He looked away. Right. "Okay, last chance for you to pick, and then I will."

Trent pushed himself up, looking at her like she was asking him to do a silly dance in front of his football team. "Which one be cooler?"

"They're both awesome. Magic, a faraway land, an epic battle. You can't go wrong."

Trent looked to Ashton. "Do you know which one is better?"

"The lion! Pick the lion!"

Brenna laughed. Trent shrugged. "Don't matter none. I probably fall asleep."

Wouldn't be a bad outcome.

Finding the book tucked into the shelf lined with children's literature made her heart do strange, twingy things. Scottie had loved to come to the Erikson home. He was the one who picked the stories. And Craig had never once denied him. Never once complained.

How could Craig so easily forget? He'd walked away, didn't look back. Moved on with life as if the devastation hadn't touched him.

Of course he had. After all, Scottie was her brother, not Craig's. And Craig had proven his motives with his friendship to Scottie to be less than honest.

He'd used her special needs brother.

Her hand shook as she gripped the spine containing C. S.

Lewis's classic novel. The sting in her nose made her eyes itch. *That's not true.*

She tried to ignore that deep-seated whisper. It was true. Near the end, Craig had used Scottie. And everything had changed. Craig's disappearance after the accident only proved his guilt. The fact that he stopped pursuing a professional football career also indicated his shame.

Tears pushed against her lids, and her stomach hurt.

"Miss Brenna?" Ashton called from the couch.

Glancing back at them, she found Ashton in a headstand, his legs draped over the seat of the couch, and Trent with his arms shielding his chest like armor, his eyes squeezed shut while he pretended to be asleep.

"Right." She blinked. "I've got it, buddy." Lowering in between them, she swallowed, hoping the turning in her stomach would ease. "So are we ready?"

Ashton scrambled upright and back into his seat. Trent held like stone.

"Go!" Ashton commanded.

They began. By the time Edmund had betrayed his siblings to the White Witch, both Trent and Ashton were truly asleep. Brenna tucked a three-by-five note card she'd found in the back of the volume at chapter 10, then closed the cover and sagged back.

Oh, Edmund. Why?

The thought no sooner settled than one answered back. *Oh, daughter of Eve. You know why. Will you continue to nourish this anger too?*

Squeezing her eyes shut, she felt the warm liquid rim near her lashes. *But, God, do you know what he did? How it hurt?*

It was a silly thing to say to the Sovereign of heaven. Brenna's theology contained a certainty that the God and King of all things did in fact know all things too. But there was this pain. This anger. This brokenness. And she couldn't reconcile it.

To whom else could she say what she truly felt?

There she'd laid her heart bare—at the throne of both holiness and love. There she'd found a kind shelter. A gentle touch.

But that night? The response was not as soft. Not as indulgent. Not as easy.

Do you know Craig's pain?

She snorted softly. "No," she whispered into the stillness. "How could I? He left. Walked away and didn't look back."

Ashton inhaled and then breathed a long sigh. Brenna turned her focus to his sleeping face. Peaceful and content, without any sign of the messy life he'd already survived. Oh, that he would never lose his zeal. That the world would never erase his smile. Take away his joy.

Seemed like a long shot, given his messed-up little world. Brenna knew, all too well, what pain and disillusion could do to even the stoutest of hearts.

Chapter Twenty

THE FRONT DOORKNOB RATTLED SOFTLY, AND THEN GENTLE FOOTSTEPS SOUNDED AGAINST THE WOOD-FLOOR ENTRY. BRENNA BLINKED SEVERAL TIMES, BANISHING ALL EVIDENCE OF HER INTERNAL BATTLES.

"Hey there," Craig whispered from the other side of the room. He nodded at the two charges snoring softly beside her on the couch, his mouth curving into a small, tired grin. "Looks like you did well."

She summoned a tight smile. "We survived."

He chuckled. "That's a win. I'll get them to their beds. Do you mind helping Mom? She's pretty exhausted."

"Sure." Brenna stepped across the cozy living room and curved an arm around Janet, who leaned against Craig. His hand brushed hers as they shifted his mom between them.

"I'm so sorry, hon," Janet mumbled. "You'd think I could get myself to my own bed."

"No need to be sorry, Janet. I told you I want to help. I'd be honored if you'd let me."

They shuffled slowly toward her room while Craig saw to the boys. Feeling the slightness of Janet's body against her own broke something painful in Brenna as she guided the woman to the bed.

"Do you need to stop at the bathroom first?" Brenna asked.

Janet sighed. "I'd better."

"What do you need me to do?"

Eyes full of humiliation and exhaustion looked up to her. "Just get me there, I think. I'll manage."

"I can help," Brenna said, careful to keep the wobble out of her voice.

"I feel so off kilter. So tired. And a little dizzy."

"It's okay, Janet. I'm here, okay? And this is only us girls."

She nodded. It was awkward. Hard. And yet somehow sacred. Together they managed, and Brenna got Janet decent and settled in her bed by the time Craig passed into his mom's room.

He squatted near Janet's head, placed his large palm over her head. "You okay, Mom?"

A faint smile covered her mouth, and she raised her hand to press against his chest. "I am good, son. Just need sleep."

"You sure?"

"Go away now. Let me rest."

He leaned forward and pressed a light kiss to her balding head. "I'll check on you later."

From her spot at the doorway, Brenna shuddered. This Craig she remembered. Gentle. Humble. Kind. This was the man she had loved.

With quiet steps, he left the room, and Brenna followed. Silence dwelt between them as he moved toward the back of the house and out to the patio. The October evening brushed against her skin with the breath of fall. The sweet smell of harvest drifted as a subtle undertone on a breeze floating off the river and from the vineyard beyond town. It was an evening that, in years past, would have hummed with romance.

Brenna wasn't sure Craig was aware that she'd followed him, especially when he leaned against the siding of the house near the glass patio doors—one of which now had an array of yellow, little-boy-sized handprints. There was a story to that...

She thought to ask about it as Craig raised his hands to cover his face. Her heart shivered, breath caught.

He was breaking.

She'd seen it once before. And the contrast of this beautiful evening to Craig's unraveling crashed through the stone-cold indifference she'd tried to maintain concerning him. A tear trickled near her nose as she watched this big man—still built like the solid wide receiver that he'd been all those years back—tremble with a powerful swell of emotion.

"My mom is dying, Brenna." His voice came tight, the words strained.

She had no words. Nothing. When his hands fell away and his tear-glazed eyes met hers, she felt frozen in a glacier of moments from the past that both of them would have rather not known. Their intertwined lives had been frayed at the ends with pain. With nothing to say and only hurt making her heart ache, she stepped into him. His arms tightened around her.

"She's a fighter, Craig," she whispered.

A draw of air rattled his solid chest as he clung to her, his muscled hold trembling. While the crickets chirped from beyond the light spilling from the house, their song a constant reminder that life exists in the darkness, she held him, felt his pain deeply.

Slowly his grip loosened, and she realized how tight his embrace had been. Like a man clinging to a raft in the middle of a raging sea. Desperate and lonely.

High emotions. Oh, they'd so been there before.

When his fingers wove through her hair, the tips pressing into her scalp, warning flared through her mind. Moving her arms—arms that she had wrapped around him before he'd clung to her—she settled her palms against his chest and pushed away.

"Craig." She breathed out his name like a sigh, edged with a winter frost. "Look, this…"

He dislodged his fingers, leaving the places where his hands had been cool and tingly, and more than a little bit of her wished back his touch. His study of her face was serious and intense, his lips pressed flat.

She swallowed, took another step back. "I'm not sure what you're thinking."

"I told you what I was thinking."

Scraping her bottom lip with her teeth, she fought away the warning to leave her thoughts unsaid. They needed said. She couldn't go backward with him, and he needed to get that.

"About us. You and me."

The corners of his eyes pinched.

Lifting her chin, she plunged ahead. "I can't go back to where we ended. Not after everything else."

"I don't want to go back to where we ended, Brenna. I don't want that for you or for me. Not ever."

The spear of his words pierced clean through. "Good," she spat, anger filling the painful hole he'd cut. "I needed to make that clear. Especially after you kissed me the other night."

"I was not the only one involved in that kiss."

"I was emotional. You took advantage."

"Is that what you think? Is that what you think about everything that happened that last year? It was all me, taking advantage?"

"That is exactly what happened, Craig. And you know it. Why else would you have left and never looked back? Just own the guilt."

"What?" He stepped closer. "What exactly are you charging me with here?"

The past reared up, the massive wave of all of it terrifying and infuriating all at once. "You used us! You used Scottie. And then when he died, you..."

His lips parted, eyes widened. "How dare you." Though not much more than a whisper, his words seared. "How dare you say that, Brenna. I *loved him*! You know I loved him. Every plan you and I ever made for the future included Scottie. Every single one of them. Because I loved him too."

"Then how could you have—"

"No." The anger on his face darkened as he shook his head. Anger like she'd never seen on him before. So strong it rippled through his muscles, blazed from his eyes. "If you think there hasn't been a day in my life over the past seven years that I haven't wished with the kind of desperation a man would rather never feel that I could go back to that day and *not* hit snooze, than you're completely delusional."

She pressed her lips closed because they trembled too much. That hadn't been what she'd meant. Scottie's death had been an accident. A tragic, horrible accident that was no one's fault.

Did Craig get that?

"I know that day was an accident," she whispered.

"One you hold me responsible for."

"No." She blinked, and the tears flowed.

"Don't lie." His voice rose as he plowed a hand through his thick hair. "I know what you think. What you thought. You couldn't even look at me, and when you finally did, the accusation was clear. You wanted me to leave. Never wanted to see me again, because you thought I was responsible. *That* was why I left. *For* you."

The unbidden and unwanted memory of Scottie's funeral played through her mind. He was right. She hadn't looked at him. Not until the graveside service. And when she did, she'd found him off by himself, near a tree, shoulders half turned, as if he were already gone.

Leaving her alone. Again. This time to deal with something that pressed thick and dark against her already broken heart. An abyss she had no idea how to navigate.

She had glared at him then. As if it had been his fault, because yes, for a time, maybe...

"I was hurting, Craig. We'd just buried my brother, and I could barely breathe, let alone think straight."

He took two steps back, and the rippling tension in his shoulders eased. Eyes locked somewhere on the floor, he shoved his hands into his pockets as his breathing slowly leveled into something more normal.

"That kiss the other night was...was unfinished business," he said.

"What does that mean?"

"You and me..." He peeked at her. "I never intended our breakup to be permanent. For me, it was never really over."

She scoffed. "What did you think a breakup was?"

He raised his chin. "It was me trying to figure out how to get things back to where they should have been."

"No. That's a lie, Craig. It was you deciding that I was a distraction. You finding out that you had a shot at the draft—thanks to all the attention you'd gained because of Scottie—and then removing anything and anyone who might have gotten in the way. Me, in particular."

The muscle in his jaw clenched, and a moment of fire passed through his eyes before he looked away and nodded.

His silent agreement hit her like a black-powder confession, exploding the old anger all over again. "I was your biggest fan—next to Scottie. I loved watching you play. Loved seeing you continue to get better and better. If the NFL was what you wanted, you should have told me. I would have done everything to back you. Instead, you decided I was a distraction. Something you needed to set aside until you got what you really wanted. And I was supposed to embrace that?"

One hand covered his forehead, and his fingers rubbed at his temples. "I lost myself back then, Brenna." He turned to meet her gaze again, sorrow and regret, and some kind of gentle rebuke, stirring in his eyes. "You're right. I messed up. But if we are being honest about it all, I think you'd agree that we were both off the rails and had been for months. I didn't know how to make it right."

Crossing her arms, she felt her face go to stone. "You broke my heart, Craig Erikson. I gave you everything. All of me. And you...you walked away. That's all I know. You broke me, and I still don't know what to do with that. Which means we cannot pick up and start a relationship all over again. There is no *unfinished business* between us."

His grunt sounded like defeat. Surrender. "A relationship, Brenna? No. No we most definitely can't do that." With a cool gaze that spoke of frustration as much as it did of regret, he shook his head. "How could we? We're not honest. There's no trust. You and I, we aren't even friends."

***

Night had long-since taken over, and Craig lay in his room, darkness a flimsy shield against the day passed.

Man. It'd been brutal. Watching Mom's body respond so violently to the treatment. Seeing her, feeling her slowly drain from the woman he'd always known to a struggling shell. Didn't matter how much the doctors had tried to prepare him. He'd not been prepared, and the very recent memory of it made him feel like a rickety old shed getting battered in a spring storm.

And then Brenna.

Why had he asked her to help with the boys?

He knew why. He knew all the reasons. Some more selfish than others.

She was awesome with special needs kids. She got them, saw their stories, felt their struggles. Not that Sophie couldn't, but he had a history with Brenna that guaranteed that she did. And he'd been convinced that Trent and Ashton needed not only Brenna's heart but her unique experience she'd gained from being Scottie's sister.

But there was the other reason. The *unfinished business* reason. Didn't matter that she'd been vehement when she'd declared that they had no unfinished business. Didn't matter that he was completely sincere when he'd said that they weren't even friends.

Things between them were not finished. Though he didn't know exactly what that meant, he was certain of its truth.

He groaned as he rubbed the throbbing spots right above his eyebrows. The muscles in his neck refused to unlock as he lay flat against his bed and willed both the tension in his body and the headache away.

Fight as he might, he couldn't block away the memories, and as he shut his eyes, they crowded his mind, demanding another review.

"You wanted to see me?"

Coach Yancy, whose main purpose on the team was to hone the passing game, waved him into his office and motioned to the chair across from his desk. "Have a seat, Craig."

He'd been there several other times, especially after he'd been named one of the team captains the year before. But as Yancy lifted his look, gripping the armrests of his office chair, a sense of unease filled Craig.

"What's up, Coach?" He aimed for an easy tone. Because the brewing sense of conflict seeping into the office made him edgy.

"I'm gonna get right to it, Erikson."

"What's that, sir?"

"Are you serious about this NFL bid?"

Craig sat back, the tightness in his shoulders easing. He'd been worried Coach was going to lay into him about the yards he hadn't been putting up in the first couple of games. Craig was the first to admit, his rhythm was off. Couple of dropped catches. Misreads. Hadn't been a stellar start to the season. But that happened. Coach Blaum always made a point to remind his team that they were men. Men didn't do perfect, but they could get back up and keep taking aim for better.

"Yeah," Craig said.

"Then what's this rumor I'm hearing?"

He felt his eyebrows fold in. "What rumor is that, sir?"

"You're thinking about getting married?"

Then he wanted to laugh. That what this was about? Not his game? Not how he looked at practice? he sat back. "Not sure where you heard about that, but yeah. Brenna and I have been together for—"

"Now's a really bad time for distractions, Craig."

"What?"

"Look, I know young men will be young men, but the deal is, over the last several months—since the spring game, and into this new season—you've been, well, distracted."

His shoulders coiled. There had been some things that had him...concerned over the past several months. And yeah, all of them had to do with his relationship with Brenna. And yeah, they were big reasons he'd been looking at engagement rings. But he really didn't think those things had anything to do with his game.

The chair beneath him squeaked as Coach sat forward, leaning his elbows against his desk. "The thing is, Craig, there are some opportunities that are once in a lifetime. Things that if you miss that chance, you'll never get it back. Other things? They can wait. There'll be time later."

His stomach hurt, and his chest pinched. He couldn't hold Yancy's long look anymore. Looking at his hands locked together in a tight grip, he let the silence in the office extend. A month ago he would have said it didn't matter. Nothing would have changed his mind. Because a month ago they thought there would be a baby.

Now...

There wasn't a baby. And things between him and Brenna

were still not right. Hadn't been right—not since the spring game last April. Not since they'd started sleeping together. He still loved her. More than anything, he loved Brenna and wanted a life with her. But he also wanted them to be right—he wanted to quit being weak about something he knew wasn't okay for them.

And.

Well, and though he'd never actually thought the NFL was a real possibility, now it was. After last season and after a lot of national attention he'd gained thanks to Scottie, there was a lot of legitimate talk of getting selected in the spring draft— especially with the projected thirty spots opening up for his position that year.

"Look." Coach sighed, finally breaking the leaded silence. "I'm all for marriage, Erikson. Been married before myself. Twice, actually. But this thing with the draft—you've got a real shot, kid. Do you know how many guys would die to have this chance you've got in front of you? Do you get what they'd trade to be in your place right now? I'm just saying, don't let something that can wait distract you from this. This can't wait. This won't happen again."

His stomach twisted embers, Craig still couldn't look at the man. But he nodded. Stood up and took two steps for the door.

"Erikson."

He stopped. Forced himself to look at Coach. "Sir?"

Yancy studied him as if Craig were a defense he wasn't expecting. Finally, he picked up his pen and started working on whatever he'd been doing before Craig came in. "See you at practice."

He did. Craig worked his butt off, like he did every day. Spent the whole week in undivided focus. Football became his complete obsession. Missed Wednesday night Bible study, which was a bit of a relief, since he'd felt guilty every time he'd gone for the past six months. Missed Sunday morning service.

And didn't talk to Brenna. Not until they had the talk. The one where he'd broken her heart.

After, Craig looked for the relief he thought he should feel. Not only could he focus, but he could stop feeling guilty over the fact that he couldn't stop sleeping with her, and he couldn't bring himself to talk about what had gone sideways between

Jennifer Rodewald

them.

Reasons to feel relieved.

But he didn't. He loved her. Had for years, was pretty sure he always would. Missed her from the moment she'd walked away that night.

Maybe, after next April, after I have the future secured, she'll understand... *It took some work to convince himself, so he kept saying it over and over in his head.*

At the end of it all, though, he only felt miserable.

That old hollow ache settled on him as the night deepened, the feeling familiar and heavy. Shutting his eyes against it only made the memories come through more clearly, so he stared at the shadows above his bed.

Regret was a weighty thing that apparently refused to fade.

Chapter Twenty-One

WE AREN'T EVEN FRIENDS.

The words slashed at her mind, cutting her peace and keeping her awake as she lay in the lonely darkness. They were blades of truth and conviction joining with the blunt force of Grant's confrontation about her behavior toward Craig. She could barely look at him without scowling. Couldn't have a conversation with him without an edge of anger in her voice. Could hardly stand to be in the same room with him.

Unless, of course, she was kissing him.

Suddenly Grant's perspective focused in with sharp clarity. Brenna made a point to be friendly with about everyone. Mom had taught her that kindness always counts, and people more often than not needed a smile and a word of encouragement.

But with Craig...

The day of the Adventure Run came to mind. When she realized he was hugging her, that it had been his encouragement that had made her smile, she'd shoved away from him as if he were the enemy. The hated.

Did she hate him?

Regrets are bondage, Brenna my sweet. If you don't deal with them, well, love, they own you.

Regrets were one thing. Hate? Hate was a strong, foul thing. A parasite that slowly killed. It seeped in, permeated the dark corners of a person's being, and settled in with deep, sharp-pronged hooks. And it brought its slow, withering death without bothering to warn its host.

Did she hate Craig?

She was angry. Still so, so angry with him.

Did that amount to hate?

Hate fed on the former affections—the things that also took captive hearts and minds. It took that deep attachment and ripped it inside out. Twisted what had once been beautifully mesmerizing and made it hideous. And still, somehow in its dark ugliness, remained mesmerizing. Hate was an angry fixation. An obsession that reviled its object of passion.

Did she hate Craig?

She did not want to hate him. Didn't want to hate anyone. Lying there in the tumultuous silence, only able to be starkly honest in the plain nakedness of midnight, she had to own that her anger had grown deep hooks. Sharp holds that felt dangerously like a parasite seeking to destroy.

A tear bulged from the corner of her eye and rolled down the side of her face. As the moisture seeped into the folds of her hair, she allowed the crevasses of her heart to be probed with a painful, honest light.

She refused the instinct to shrivel away from it, to continue to hide.

I don't want to hate. God, I don't want this anger anymore.

How did one remove such a stubborn leech? Perhaps this was why Craig came back—to force the reckoning. To make her see what seemed dormant and harmless but had slowly been rotting within. Grant had been right, which was not unusual. There were things she needed to deal with. But maybe he'd been wrong—maybe she did need to process through some of it with him. Who better to talk to than a trained and experienced counselor?

Was that fair to a man who'd said he loved her?

Likely not.

So who? Not Sophie. That'd be so awkward.

What do I do? The thought turned to a prayer. A plea pushed up with both hands. Painful and yet somehow like the first opening of a flower—the moment when the first petal fights itself free to yield to the sun.

The first break away from the darkness.

Show me what to do.

***

The river slipped by as if almost indifferent.

Same as it had always been. Unchanged from the days of his youth, when he and his posse of fellow ten-year-olds had crashed through the brush to toss rocks or fishing lines beneath the surface of the glass-smooth water. The same as those cherished afternoons with Brenna and Scottie under this same canopy of birch and ash, her hand in his while they watched Scottie launch from the rope swing into the swimming hole below, ever laughing at his brilliant way with facial expressions and self-commentaries.

These waters had witnessed some of the highlights of his life. Which oddly moved a current of pain in his chest as he watched Trent and Ashton skip rocks across the same flawless surface he'd disturbed as a boy. How could life change so much and yet not at all?

The conversation he'd had with Brenna on his patio the week before replayed, and he didn't even try to banish it from his thoughts. Instead he lowered himself to the crumbled shale shore, kept a watchful eye on both boys, lifted a prayer for his mother's rest and recovery as she remained back at the house, and allowed the exchange between Brenna and him to roll unhindered through his mind.

He didn't want to go back to the way they'd ended. He'd meant that with all his heart. They'd been damaged long before he'd broken up with her, and though he knew some of the reasons, he still couldn't understand completely why. Why had she pushed for physical intimacy when they'd promised that they'd wait? Why had she turned from a confident girl, content to hold his hand, to an almost desperate young woman to whom he'd never seemed able to pay enough attention?

What had happened that final spring that had forced a change between them that he'd had no idea what to do with?

It'd been like this river—the same on the surface. But the depths beneath? Those waters had turned. Gone cold and riotous, and he still didn't know why.

That's not all true. The thought turned his gut sour. An accusation he couldn't defend himself against, because he knew, at least in part, why she'd been the way she'd been. And he'd... just gone with it. Let it happen. Had been too spineless to dare to open a conversation with her about it.

Now... now there they were, caught in an awkward place again, and he wasn't sure what to do.

All he knew was what he'd said the other night was heartbreakingly true. He and Brenna weren't even friends.

She'd been his best friend. For the years that they'd dated, she'd been his confidant, the dreamer at his side sharing the same hopes for the future. The one he'd delighted to laugh with. The single person he couldn't wait to talk to every day. His *very best* friend in the world.

The world had become so lonely without her, and it was her friendship he'd missed the most. Admitting, out loud, to both himself and her that they were no longer friends was like finally lowering the coffin of *them* into the concrete vault. Time of death long past. Autopsy inconclusive. Result undeniable.

Dead.

Craig folded his hands, balling them into a single fisted bundle, and pressed his forehead into them as he leaned against his knees. Surrendering to the truth had been something he'd not been brave enough to do. He'd consoled his trembling heart seven years ago with the promise that they'd stay friends. No, more than that—a selfish promise that the break was not the end of them. It was only a break. Not only would they stay friends but the plans they'd planned, the future they'd seen together, would still happen. Just, after. It had been his way of dealing with what he didn't want to deal with. Avoidance.

It'd taken seven years away from home to finally admit what had been true the moment he'd broken her heart.

He'd broken all of it.

Inhaling the muddied, stale hints of leaf decay and autumn musk, he shut his eyes as moisture rimmed his lids.

He'd committed the final act that had wrecked them. It hadn't been the tragic accident that had taken Scottie—that had ensured that he'd have something to hide behind and a reason to stay away. But really, it'd been himself. Only himself.

The sound of water crashing ripped him from that introspective moment, sparking alarm that blazed through his veins. The boys had promised to stay onshore. His gaze ripped from the silt beach to the muddied bank, finding Ashton and Trent yelling and jumping but safe on the shore. The splashing continued about four feet into the current of the river, the culprit small and brown and adding a yelp here and there to the thrashing of his four legs in the water.

A dog. An ugly one at that.

"Craig!"

He suddenly became aware that both boys had been calling for him.

"Craig! He gonna drown! Get 'im! Get 'im!" Ashton ran toward Craig, panic in his dark eyes.

"Yeah, come on." Trent edged toward the lip of the water.

That set Craig in motion. "Stay put, buddy. Don't go in the water."

Frustration boiled in Trent's expression. "But you doin' nothin'. He gonna die."

"I got it." Craig gripped Trent's shoulder, patted Ashton's head. "I'll get him, but you have to promise that you'll stay out of the river. Got it?"

"We already promised." Ashton said, his voice a wire of nerves and maybe a little hurt.

"Yeah." Trent folded his arms, as if daring Craig to call him out on a lie he hadn't told.

Craig nodded, kicked his old tennis shoes off at the shoreline, and moved into the water. The lazy current swirled around his calves with a chill that made him shiver. The dog must be pretty young to be unable to get himself to shore. Or hurt. Maybe both. Either way, Craig had promised the boys he'd make sure he was safe.

Beyond that...

Man. He couldn't do much more. A dog? Probably more accurately, a puppy? Between his mom, the boys, the new job...

This is too much, God. What are You thinking?

Chapter Twenty-Two

"WE GOT A PUPPY!"

Trent's eyes lit like the night sky on the Fourth of July as he bounced on the rug in the middle of Brenna's office.

She sat back, eyebrows lifting. "A puppy?"

"Yeah! Craig saved it. It be floppin' around that river like it gonna slide down under an' die."

"Really?" A real smile smoothed her face. "Could you tell me again, please?"

Trent only half scowled at her mild reminder to speak correctly, his sky-high joy unhampered. He cleared his throat. "Craig rescued a puppy," he began, using the voice she now knew he'd taken from listening to *Sherlock Holmes* with Craig. Amusing all on its own. "He ran into the waters of the river and saved the little rascal from being dunked to death."

Brenna laughed. It moved a lightness in her heart that she hadn't felt in quite a while.

Seeing Trent grinning like the ten-year-old boy he was and not scowling like a sulking seventeen-year-old made her feel a little freer. A taste of joy she used to ingest daily and hadn't realized until that exact moment how much she'd missed.

With a little startle, she realized there was more to that joy than Trent's smile. Something deeper whispered into her soul. There was a glimpse of redemption sitting right there on her office floor. Her thoughts turned...

It was crazy how much having Trent in her office made Brenna think about Craig.

Never used to.

Then again it was also crazy to realize that she and Trent were making some real progress since the Friday she'd stayed with the boys. Take this moment—Trent didn't argue with her, rebel against her, throw a fit. Nothing of what would have happened months before. He'd given her a mild scowl and then complied. With humor. More, Trent, all on his own, was making some positive strides in his life. Their last team meeting, which she'd declined to go to but had asked Grant to forward her notes from, noted that Trent's teachers had seen a better attitude from him. There was even a comment in there, ironic as it might be, that Trent was beginning to show a real aptitude for writing—for stories.

How about that?

She'd like to take a little smug credit for that. Maybe would too, but she knew full well that a large portion of the nod should go to Craig. He was good for Trent—for both the Fulton boys. Just as he'd been good for Scottie.

She shouldn't be surprised. Craig had always had some magic about him when it came to elementary-aged kids. Always.

"Miss Brenna?"

"What?" Her gaze snapped back to Trent, only now realizing that she'd not only drifted away mentally but had been staring at the door of her office, as if waiting for someone to appear.

"I axed if I did it all right?"

"You *asked* if you did what all right?"

"Tell you 'bout that puppy."

"Oh." she chuckled. "Yes. You did splendidly."

"That's a funny word."

"Splendidly?"

"Yeah. Real peeps don't talk dat way."

"Well, I just did. Am I real?"

He reached across the rug, gripped her arm, and gave it a jiggle. "Yep. Solid as stone, Miss Brenna."

"I'm relieved."

"Know what I be thinkin'?"

She couldn't guess. But it was a delight to engage in a conversation with this kid that was not initiated—or more accurately, forced—by herself. "I'd love to know what you've been thinking."

"I be thinking that Craig like you."

She sat up straight, the ease of this exchange suddenly gone, like the last beautiful red leaf on the bushes in front of Freshies after a hard freeze. "You think—"

Trent smirked, mischief ablaze in his eyes. "Gotcha, Miss B."

"What?" Her breath felt hard and short.

He rocked back, slapped his leg, and laughed. Brenna searched for reason, and finding none in his sudden proclamation, looked for a solid grip on something else instead.

"Have you decided to try on Cupid's wings?" She attempted a tease. It felt false, but maybe it came off as true.

"I don't know no Cupid, lady." He smiled, as if the contrary was obviously true.

"Oh?"

"Just wanted to see how you be if I say dat." He laughed again.

"Is that so?" She leaned in, forcing herself to play in his mischief even if it was a little painful to do so. Not Trent's fault—he didn't know anything of the past. "And how I be?"

This time he drew up. "Miss B! You used my street talk!"

She raised her eyebrows.

He crossed his arms. "Ask me again, and I might say."

Ha. How about that proper sentence? "Okay." She mocked his sassy scowl. "And how was I?"

"Shocked." He tipped a little closer, drew his tone into a whisper. "And your cheeks turned red as a watermelon, Miss B."

"Did not." Her protest slipped out too fast.

Trent rocked backward again, laughing. A tap at the door came as a rescue. Brenna chuckled along with Trent, determined not to show the wound he'd accidentally uncovered, as she answered.

And there was the man. His blue eyes took them both in, and though the etches on his face penned to her a tired tale only the two of them really knew, his smile spread warm and genuine.

"Both smiling," Craig said, stepping into her office. "That's a good sign."

Trent popped off the floor. "I made Miss Brenna speak correctly," he announced smugly. "And also turn watermelon red."

Craig's grin faded to half. "Not sure that sounds good."

Brenna held her breath, silently begging Craig not to ask and Trent not to tell.

"I told her about Rascal."

He did? Rascal was... She searched for someone named Rascal in their session. *The puppy.* They must have named him Rascal.

Craig laid a hand to Trent's back, and the boy leaned into the man's space a tiny bit. As if it was his safe zone. The place he wanted to belong, even if he wasn't sure how to do it. Though subtle, the move spread a sweet ache across Brenna's heart.

Yes, Trent was making progress. And yes, Craig was good for him. So very good.

Do I hate this man? No. She couldn't possibly hate this man. That left her with anger. An anger she was beginning to desperately wish she could smother until it died forever and ever, amen.

The raw truth of it hit her hard. Once upon a time, not really that long ago, she and Craig had been good together.

And she missed him. Missed them.

Which left her in a gaping space of uncertainty between the reality of her still very active anger and the fresh realization of the truth Grant had obviously discerned in her daftness—she missed Craig.

His gaze felt warm on her as she stumbled through the silent process of emotions. But though she feared he was reading her, evaluating her as Grant so often seemed to do, when she looked at him again, she found only an honest, yet reserved, waiting in his eyes. As if that was a crack in the wall between them, a shaft of light flickering there, she mentally moved toward it. Took a risk she didn't know she was brave enough to take.

"I wanted to talk to you," she said, certain her face glowed red.

A slight upward move of his brows preceded a nod. "Trent, buddy, you want to head out to the car for me? I'll be a minute."

Trent's grin faded into a suspicious stare pinned on her. "I ain't in trouble?"

"Not at all." Brenna held a smile and hoped that the thread of connection she and Trent were pulling on would grow stronger. "You did very well, Trent."

The boy nodded, looked up at Craig, who offered a fist bump that Trent responded to, and then he sauntered from her office.

And the door clicked.

The feeling was different this time. Her cold, determined

hostility had thawed again, awakening her to exactly how harsh she'd been to this man. It was time to chip away at that crack in the wall.

Craig shoved his hands into his pockets, holding his silence and that reserved gaze.

Be brave.

"I hear you've adopted a puppy."

Not so brave.

Craig's mouth dipped. "Yeah, well, not really adopted." A hand lifted, pushed through his hair as he sighed. "Poor Trent. I explained to both boys that we couldn't keep him. Honest I did. And I wish we could, but I can't do a puppy right now, and I really can't put that on my mom, so..."

"Oh." Concern and compassion wove through her. Craig was right—anyone could see that. A puppy in his world right now would be way too much. But Trent. But Ashton. Those boys could really use a break too.

The smack of Craig's hand against his thigh cracked the silence between them. "Brenna, I promise. I told them we couldn't keep him—"

"Craig." She stepped forward, laid a hand on his arm, the move an instinct. "I wasn't criticizing you."

He winced, the look both painful and maybe a little needy, and he searched her as if looking for something to hang on to.

"I believe you," she said. "And I agree with you."

"You do?"

"Yes." She slipped her hand away.

His attention drifted to her fingers as they fell to her side, and his brow furrowed. "Trent's convinced the owner won't claim the dog." In his pause, Craig pressed his lips closed and looked across the room. "What will I do then?"

"I can take him." The words were out before she'd really considered it. But actually, maybe having a puppy would be okay. Maybe it would be more than okay—maybe helping Craig this way was exactly what needed to happen.

"You could?" Doubt edged Craig's response. "Don't you live in an apartment?"

"A loft above the Limestone Hotel." Her small grin made her feel lighter. "But they allow pets."

"He's a puppy, Brenna."

"So I've heard."

"Do you know the kind of messes puppies make? The energy they have? The work they take?"

"Did you know how much of all of that two little boys would demand from you?"

The wall between them split a little more, and the reserve in his expression lowered. Behind it she saw what she should have known was there all along. Craig was struggling. Maybe sinking was more accurate. As he blinked, his shoulders rolled inward, and he gripped the back of his neck.

She reached for the arm that was still at his side. "Let me help you."

His study was shock and yearning and confusion and hope. Several breaths passed between them before he squared to her, forcing her hand to fall away as he moved.

"Why?"

The edge in his voice threatened to beckon the anger she'd maintained where he was concerned. It took intentional control to not allow frustration to oblige. "Because you need help."

"No, why do *you* want to help me?" The rawness of his low words was wrapped with vulnerability.

Be brave. She didn't feel brave. Honesty took courage—and this particular kind of honesty had been something she hadn't even been brave enough to employ when they'd been together as so much more than friends.

"Brenna?"

Her tummy pulled tight as she sucked in a breath. "Because of what you said the other night."

"What I said?"

"That we aren't even friends." Warm moisture pushed against her lids, and she desperately wanted to turn away. Give him her back and let him figure out what to do with the things still broken between them, if he cared to mess with them at all.

But that was what she'd done before. Seven years later it was becoming plainly obvious that tactic hadn't done either of them any good.

He stared at her, lips parted.

"You're right," she whispered. "We're not friends, and that's not all your fault. Maybe it's not your fault at all—I don't know. But I don't want us to stay that way."

His brows pulled in as his weighted look kept her pinned to the spot. Barely able to breathe. Suddenly she remembered her rejection of him after Scottie's death. The way she'd glared and then turned away from the grief and pleading she'd recognized in his posture, his pain-filled eyes. He'd silently been vulnerable to her, and she'd soundly rejected him.

Now there she was, the moment familiar but reversed. He could take this risk she'd stepped into and give her his back. Turn the rejection on her with a silent but firm *No, we cannot be friends. Not ever again.*

Why hadn't it been clear to her all these years? This great emptiness and loss—it hadn't all been put upon her. So much of it she'd taken in all on her own.

At some point she'd need to own that. Right now might be a good time to start.

Her father's words whispered into the thread of silence between her and Craig. *Some people live with regret their whole lives, never realizing that they don't have to.*

Craig cleared his throat, shaking the stillness in the room. "Are...are you serious, Brenna?"

"About the dog?"

"No. I mean, yes, that would be really helpful, if you mean

it." He edged closer, his watchful look a little less guarded. "But I meant..."

She crept nearer too, halving the distance between them. "I don't want the end we've had to be permanent. Not anymore. This regret...it's been too heavy for too long. I don't want to live with it anymore."

"Me either," he whispered.

His hand wrapped hers, and a fresh softness moved between them before he let himself out of the office.

***

Would it work for me to come over tonight to pick up Rascal?

Craig blinked, reread the text. Shock number one: Brenna had texted him. No, that wasn't the first shock. He was still grasping at their exchange yesterday afternoon. Trying to convince himself that it had been real.

Could they be friends? After everything that had existed and then blown up between them, was friendship even a remote possibility?

Jesus had said all things were possible with God—even the theoretical problem of a camel going through the eye of a needle. Or a rich man being saved. What was truly impossible with man was possible with God.

Even still, this new ground beneath him felt risky at best.

It'd be easier to shut the door. Text her back that he'd changed his mind. *Don't worry about the dog*—he'd take it to the humane society, deal with the tears and disappointment and probable angry explosion from the boys. Tragic as it might be, that would, in fact, be easier than risking a hope for any kind of relationship with Brenna again only to have that hope cut down.

But she'd stepped out into the neutral zone yesterday. He could see in her eyes how scary her move into the difficulty between them had been, hear it in the waver of her voice. That kind of courage deserved to be honored.

Sure. Tonight would be fine. Six?

He sent the message before he could talk himself out of it, and he put his phone into his desk drawer. Still had half a day left to teach. Didn't need to focus on a distraction.

Ironically, the hours that seeped by felt way too long. What he'd thought he should be dreading took entirely too much time to happen. Even when the school day ended, he found himself wishing away the two hours before she'd arrive, and filling the gap with the boys' schedule hardly served as an adequate distraction.

That couldn't bode well, could it?

He was way too mixed up with Brenna Blaum. How was he supposed to find friendship with a woman who tied him into knots with a simple offer of *I'd like to help you out?* Made him feel awkward and inside out and fourteen years old all over again?

He didn't want to go back to where they'd ended, but he couldn't seem to get out of the past. Made any kind of future of anything with her feel impossible, which made him feel defeated.

And there he was, in the middle of his childhood house, antsy for the girl accidently pummeling him to walk though his front door.

All because of an ugly puppy.

Whatcha gonna do about that?

A sense of mischief filled him—but not his own. Nope, definitely not of him. Rather, it was almost as if the One on the throne had cocked an eyebrow while His mouth quirked into a smirk. And His answer settled silent and clear.

What am I going to do? Watch Me.

As a small chuckle touched Craig's mind, a knock sounded on the door, sending that ugly puppy they'd named Rascal into a frenzy of yelps and jumps. After asking the boys to grab the dog and take him out back, he moved toward the front door.

You ready then? Craig thought toward that throne.

The smile pressed into his heart felt as certain as the ground beneath his shoes.

So then. It would begin.

Chapter Twenty-Three

LAUGHTER DANCED IN HIS EYES WHEN CRAIG OPENED THE DOOR FOR HER.

Not what she'd expected. But, oh, such a relief. And also, wow—she'd forgotten how amusement made those blue eyes shine. How she could lose that kind of crystal recollection, she couldn't say, because seeing him smiling at her right then provoked a flood of memories. More than ample evidence that Craig had laughed often. As he should. Suited him so much better than the careful, guarded looks she'd seen from him since his return.

"Six o'clock exactly." He stepped back so that she could enter. "Is this a new thing with you?"

"What's that?"

"Being on time."

She rolled her eyes even as a smile poked up one side of her mouth. "I adult quite well, thank you very much."

"Nice."

"I was always responsible." She met his mischievous raised brows, crossing her arms.

"That is true. You were quite responsible. Just usually five minutes late for all of your responsibilities."

Brenna couldn't help a laugh. "Well, if you must know, I still am often late. But I do try harder. Though for the record, I wasn't late on purpose all those years."

"I know."

Craig moved beside her, nudged her shoulder so that she turned toward the living room, then walked toward the backside of the house. Brenna trekked beside him.

"Mom is feeling better. She's sitting on the patio—was hoping you'd stay and visit with her awhile."

"I'm so glad." Relief washed through her knowing Janet was able to sit up for a while. That was a good sign. Brenna paused before Craig opened the back door. "I didn't ask the other day about how she was doing. I'm sorry."

"She's recovering from that last round of treatment finally." He glanced out the window, the corners of his eyes tight. "Thank God. It was pretty rough. Scared me pretty good."

Brenna nodded. She remembered how the anxiety had pressed him. How the strain of his life had rippled through his arms and chest when he'd held on to her that night.

"I'm sorry," she said. "I should have been more helpful."

"You helped." His gaze settled on her again. "You helped more than you know. I'm grateful, and Mom is too. Now, especially with the dog."

Words fell away as a silence drifted between them. Not exactly comfortable, but not hard either. A resetting. A figuring out of something that was and then wasn't, and where to begin something entirely different.

"You're sure though?" he asked, breaking that awkward drift.

"Sure?"

"About the dog. Now that you've had some time to think about it, it's okay if you've changed your mind. It's a big ask— and actually, I didn't ask, so—" The laughter faded from his eyes, and his mouth sagged.

"I haven't changed my mind. About any of it."

At her words, the unease smoothed from his face. "I'm glad."

"I did think about some things last night though." She swallowed, looked toward the floor. "I feel like we need to talk. I mean, I feel like we need to keep talking." Heavens, she was messing this up. And being a coward again. Lifting her face, she forced herself to meet his look again. "I have some things I need to say to you. That's what I'm trying to say. Not tonight—I'm not ready yet. But—" Wow. For a speech therapist, she was really bad with words.

Though caution had carved his expression, pressing a set of lines between his brows, Craig nodded. "Whenever you feel ready, I'll listen." His hand moved to the handle for the sliding glass door.

"Craig."

He paused, looked back at her.

"It's not—I'm not going to lay into you. That's not what I mean."

He studied her, brow crumpled with thought lines. "Okay. But you can. If you want to."

"I don't want to."

Though confusion settled on him, he nodded, and after another breath, he opened the back door.

The boys were posted on either side of the yard, a football sailing between them. On the grass spreading from boy to boy, a brown shaggy mutt ran and yelped, chasing the shadow of the ball as it sailed over the yard. Between them was the kind of noise that felt like comfortable chaos. Like home.

Janet sat near her metal weave table, her reclining chair freshly cushioned and angled to prop up her feet. She leaned heavily against the backrest—a position that seemed odd for a woman who had sat straight and prim through every quarter of every football game Craig had ever played.

"Hey, Mom." Craig moved across the concrete beneath the vine-covered pergola, and Brenna followed him toward the table. "Look who came to visit."

"Brenna." Janet smiled, her look sincerely happy, though tired. She patted Craig's shaved jaw as he leaned down to peck the place where her kerchief met her smooth forehead. She then found Brenna again. "Come sit with me, my girl."

Something warm and soft slipped into her chest as Brenna lowered into a place across from Janet. Belonging. That was what that sense was. She'd hardly realized that it'd been missing, but feeling it now was like encountering a long-lost friend.

"How are you feeling?" Brenna asked.

"Alive again, so that is good." Her smile lifted, making the laugh lines at the corners of her eyes crinkle beautifully. "And delighted to see you at my table after such a long time away."

Yes. A very long time.

"Craig!" Ashton shouted, though he ran the short distance from the yard to the back patio. "Now? You can play now, right?"

His low chuckle brushed the space like music. "Yes. I can play now. What do you want to do?"

"Monkey in the middle. You're the monkey. But Trent and me get to run around. 'Kay?"

"Right." Craig winked at the boy tugging on his hand, glanced back at his mom and Brenna, and then stepped into the fading Saturday evening sunshine.

"Listen to that." Janet chuckled. "Nearly flawless. Your work with Trent is rubbing off on Ashton."

"Glad we're getting somewhere with someone."

"Oh, I think you're making quite an impact."

"I think Craig and his love for books is doing more good than anything."

Pride and contentment shone on Janet's face when Brenna glanced at her. Even with her skin pale and her body frail and thin, it was good to see the light of joy replacing the undercurrent of concern that had been a part of Janet's countenance for the past several years.

"It's good to have him back, isn't it?" Brenna asked, her tone low.

The smile faded as Janet slowly shifted her attention back to Brenna. "I think so, of course." Her hand slid across the empty space between them, and she brushed Brenna's arm with her fingertips. "More than that, it's good to see him return—at least a little bit—to the young man I once knew. That *we* once knew."

Brenna swallowed as she shifted to watch the activity in the yard. "Had he changed much?"

The sigh left Janet with a reserve that spoke of hesitancy. A concern for breaking a trust. A worry for adding another burden.

"He...drifted. Not changed like he was rebellious. But changed, as in he was lost. He couldn't find a place to settle and to begin again. Now..."

"Now?"

The lack of her answer settled like an implication. The boys ran circles around the man as he shuffled in the grass. He laughed and played as if he'd always been this. Been the Craig she'd known. It was hard to imagine him any other way, and hearing his mom's sadness at the memory of something less provoked a fresh wave of guilt.

"I'm grateful he came back—heaven knows he wasn't sure he could," Janet said. "But we needed him. I didn't want to admit it and felt bad when he told me he'd applied for and accepted a job with our schools." An honest weight entered her story. "I'd hoped he'd find a place to settle down. Somewhere to put down some new roots and start over. So he could move forward."

That stung, though spoken with a soft kindness intended to take the poison out. Brenna inhaled, tried not to wince.

"Brenna, sweetie, I wanted you both to find peace again. To be happy and to move past the hard places you'd been."

Brenna nodded. "Now here he is." The words felt tight and hard against her throat. "In a hard place all over again." Though she'd dropped eye contact, unable to meet Janet's gentle look or to watch Craig be the boy she'd once loved right there before her aching heart, she pushed forward. "He's scared for you."

"Hmm." The sound was an acknowledgment when words could not suffice.

A wind drifted up from the far-off river, the smell full of crisp yellow leaves. It danced with Brenna's hair, tossing strands across her face, and she lifted her chin to catch the updraft of life and play that it brought. She shut her eyes, let the current fill her with something fresh and pull away that something old and dull.

"Hard places and soft places. Life is full of them both." Janet's soft voice harmonized with the sound of leaves and grass dancing in the breeze. "Heaven knows you already know that."

"What do we do with the hard places?" It was an honest question—one seven years in the making, fermented by time and still unanswered. Slowly Brenna opened her eyes.

"I don't know that there's one right answer to that," Janet said.

"What about now? This cancer, in the midst of you trying to raise these boys? Hardly seems fair or right. What do you do with that?"

The floral pattern of Janet's kerchief moved as if it had become a live garden, while the breeze flicked at the ties at her neck. *What would that feel like on a nearly bare scalp, the coolness of autumn fingering skin that for her whole life had been covered?*

"Here I am," Janet said, her expression drifting into wistfulness. "Watching my son be what these boys of my heart need in this moment..." Her pause was more than a breath. It was as if the life they were sharing in that moment stood still. As if truth flickered as darkness peeled back. "I hate this cancer. Hate the pain that keeps me from doing the things that I've loved. Hate the thought that I might not see next summer with these young men I adore. But this—" She gestured to the game on the grass. "This moment is beauty and hope. Healing, even if it's painful. Is it hard? Yes. But the God I love can bring beauty into hard places, and I trust Him to do it."

Brenna rolled her bottom lip under her teeth and resisted the instinct to shield herself from Janet's words. To say to herself, *She doesn't really understand the pain I've known.* To justify her resentment.

A hand, thin and weak from an illness that was never merciful, covered Brenna's. She turned her palm to take a gentle grip as she borrowed Janet's faith, pressing it up against the long-standing doubt.

"How do you do that?" Brenna whispered.

"What's that, love?"

"Trust God for beauty when all you see is darkness."

"Hmm..." That hum again. The hand in Brenna's squeezed. "I think it's knowing God that lets us trust when life is hard. Allows us to see past the darkness."

"Knowing...what?"

"Him. Who He is."

"Like, that Jesus is my Savior, knowing?"

"That's a good start. But no. That's not really knowing Him. That's a little like me saying Craig is my son and expecting there to be a given that I really know him—which I do—but not just because he's my son. He could be my son and a virtual stranger to me at the same time, if I didn't take the time and make the effort to really know who he is. To know that he loves my peach tea but has never liked coffee. To know that as much as he loved football, he's loved music too. To know that his love for me is usually expressed physically—that he's a hugger. But he's not really much of a gift giver. To know that as much as Craig is a people person, he doesn't always understand the complexities of others. He's straightforward and open, and he doesn't always understand when others aren't. He's generally an extrovert, and sometimes he misunderstands the introverted. A hundred other things that make Craig who he is...I know them because I've come to know him as a man and not only as my son."

This made sense. How many times had she been frustrated with people because they assumed they knew her because they knew of her—Brenna Blaum, Coach Blaum's daughter. Brenna Blaum, the runner. Brenna Blaum, Scottie's protective older sister.

"Okay, so what do you know about God beyond Jesus died for our sins?"

Janet chuckled softly. "My sweet girl, this knowing takes a lifetime. I could tell you things, but they would likely be little more than me giving you a list. Probably of things that you've already heard. Things like He is good. And kind. And loving. And just. And merciful. And gracious."

Brenna pressed her lips together.

"Me knowing Him is an entirely separate thing from you knowing Him. I can't hand you a list and accomplish the knowing in a single conversation."

Disappointment weighed against her heart. "But how?"

"Do you remember what you thought of Craig when you were fifteen?"

A soft laugh jolted through her chest. "That he was a stuck-up bully. An arrogant high school A-lister who thought he could do whatever he wanted."

Janet chuckled. "Since you dated him for five years after

that, I assume you didn't always have that opinion."

"No." She leaned forward, attention set on Craig again. "No, I was wrong. He was kind. He never worked for his popularity, and honestly it rarely affected him. He liked people, and people responded to his vibrant personality. You're right about football and music. For the most part, football was a game to him. He loved playing it, but it rarely possessed him. Music, though—he could lose himself in music. And he loved my brother." A ragged edge caught on that last statement.

"Ninety-five percent of the people in this town don't know half of those things about Craig. Not really—not by experience. So why do you know them?"

"I spent time with him."

"Right."

"How do you spend time with the God of the universe? It seems like He's too busy and I'm too small."

A yelp from the yard snapped the flow of their conversation, and within three heartbeats, Craig and the boys were moving toward them from the yard. The puppy—Rascal—wriggled in Craig's arms, whining and panting in intervals.

"What happened?" Janet reached for Trent, her slim hand curving over the boy's shoulders.

Though clearly worried about the dog, Trent's posture took on a defensive edge. "Rascal got under my feet. I didn't mean to hurt 'im."

"Of course you didn't," Janet soothed.

Craig squatted between his mom and Brenna, the dog sprawled over his forearm. "He's all right, big guy. I think he's mostly just thirsty. You boys managed to wear him out, and congratulations on that." With his free hand, he held out a fist bump offer to Trent. "Not a job easily done."

A ghost of a grin pried at Trent's mouth. "Well then, that proves it. We can handle 'im here, right?"

Craig looked up at his mom and then dashed a *help me out*

glance toward Brenna. "Trent, we've talked about this. You and me, buddy, we're gone a big part of the day, and that leaves Rascal to Mom. We can't do that to her right now, you know?"

Trent cast his eyes toward the table.

"I'm going to take him, Trent," Brenna said, an ache for the boy's hurt needling her middle. "He'll stay with me, but I'm going to need help. He'll need someone with more energy than I have to play with him. Preferably a couple of boys. Know of anyone?"

"Us!" Ashton bounced on his feet, hand shooting up in the air. "That's us, Ms. B!"

"I hoped so." She laughed.

"Doesn't seem like it be any better for Rascal to stay with you." A scowl wrinkled Trent's face. "You have a job too."

"That's true." Brenna leaned forward. "But my office is right down the street from my apartment, and I can go check on him a couple times during the day."

"He'll get bored. Chew up your favorite shoes and maybe even your couch." Trent tipped his head. "You got a couch, right?"

"I do. But I've got a kennel for him."

His eyes bugged out with accusation. "You gonna keep him on lockdown like a bad guy all day long?"

"No. Like I said, I'll go check on him. Take him out to the park to play on my break."

Trent crossed his arms and huffed. Ashton, his mini-me, mirrored his disapproval. "Not gonna be enough."

"How about this? I'll get up every morning, nice and early, and I'll take Rascal on a good long run."

"How long?"

"A couple of miles at least."

"Yeah right." Full doubt coated Trent's response, punctuated with an eye roll. "You ain't gonna run no miles, lady."

"Yeah." Ashton again mimicked his brother. "How you

gonna run miles?"

Craig's laugh filled the space with a mixture of challenge and pride—the sound of it having an effect that, though distant in memory, was thrillingly familiar in Brenna's belly.

"Oh boys. You have no idea." He sat back on the concrete, laying the puppy at his feet, and sent the brothers a set of raised brows before he turned to Brenna and winked.

She tried to deny that the sensation zipping through her was pleasure. For about three seconds, she tried.

"You think she can run miles?" Ashton peeked up at Brenna, his little expression loaded with doubt, and then studied Craig, as if this might be a test.

"Ash, I know she can." Craig's hand covered her shoe. "This woman can outrun about anyone you know—including Trent. And likely Rascal too."

"No way," Trent said.

What was Craig setting up here? Didn't much matter, as judging by the smile she felt lifting her face, she was rather delighted with it.

"Way," Craig said. "Didn't you see her go at the Adventure Run? Didn't she win that race?"

"Yeah, but you do the long part," Trent argued. "That ain't no miles."

"Ha!" Craig laughed. "She could have kept going for hours."

"She could beat Trent? Let me see!" Ashton said.

Trent scowled down at him, shaking his head. "I ain't racing no girl."

"Chicken."

Brenna wasn't sure how grown-up it was for Craig to bait Trent. Then again, there were times boys needed to learn they weren't nearly as invincible as they liked to believe.

"I ain't chicken."

"A race!" Ashton whooped. "We have a race! Where will you race?"

"What do you think, Bren? You want to go the distance or start with something smaller first?"

Brenna smirked, trying to hide a conspirator's laugh. "I don't remember agreeing to this."

"I didn't hear you protesting."

"You chicken, Ms. B?" Trent latched on to the possibility with the enthusiasm of a sportscaster calling a Hail Mary in the Big Ten playoffs.

"Might be," she owned with a full smile. "It's been a long time since I've really run much more than a block."

"Ah, come on." Craig shuffled to his feet. "Class C state champion two years in a row. Ran in college—trained for the Olympic trials. You still have it in you."

He'd listed her résumé with pride, which somehow felt like a mixed bag. He'd always been proud of her. Even in the races where she'd locked up and hadn't run well. He'd said she worked harder than most of the guys on his team. Said she deserved so much more applause than he did and wished people understood what it took to run the distance.

At the end of the day, what other people thought hadn't mattered. She didn't like being the focus of attention anyway, and she didn't think she could handle it the way Craig had. Running was something that was in her—she had done it because she'd loved it, because she felt the warm smile of God in her heart when she ran. But Craig's pride in her? That had mattered. For a time, it'd been maybe too important. An addiction she didn't like to own to. An idol she would rather deny.

His approval had meant too much. His attention had become...

There was probably a name for it. Grant would know. He'd pin it on her, see how it fit. And then with that gentle way of his that she'd sometimes found infuriating, Grant would have nudged her to look at it herself.

Maybe that wasn't true. Grant had said she'd assumed things of him that weren't true. That she thought he was always analyzing when really, he just liked being with her. Assumptions had set her on a downward path before. Maybe she'd better stick with what was clearly true.

In that moment, it was clearly true that Craig was still proud of her. It was also clearly true that Trent was itching to prove that the woman with whom he met two days a week to "fix his street talk" could not, in any realm of possibility, beat him in a foot race.

It was on.

"All right, Trent. We could run."

"Yesss!" Ashton threw a fist into the air, celebrating like they were about to see a big game.

"You on, lady." Trent wobbled his head to the beat of his smug words. "To the fence and back. Ashton says go."

"Not so fast, buddy." Craig laid a hand on Trent's shoulders. "We were talking about miles, remember? You didn't think Ms. Brenna could go miles with Rascal."

"I ain't runnin' no miles." He leaned back, eyes wide again. "You crazy you think I gonna run miles. I ride me miles in the car. I ain't no fool, runnin' miles."

"So we're not running?" Brenna molded a frown that was actually sincere. In the space of two minutes, she'd been given a reason to run again and had it jerked away, which was surprisingly disappointing.

Eyebrows puckered, mouth pursed, Trent studied her. "How far?"

"Around the block?"

His expression smoothed, grin resurfaced. "Around the block? Easy." The wave of his hand was the exclamation point.

"Great. Around the block it is."

"I say go!"

Craig laughed. "Right, Ash. You say go. Mom? Do you want

to watch?"

"You know I do." Janet held a hand toward Craig, who met her grip and then with the tenderest of care pulled her forward until he could slip an arm around her slight frame.

The picture they made shot an ache through Brenna. This man—he was good. Not flawless, but good. And his mother? A gem. A woman who had been both a friend and a mentor to Brenna through the years that she'd dated Craig.

That sense of having lost something beautiful burgeoned as she looked upon the pair. If she were to be brave and honest, she'd have to own the truth: She'd put herself on the outside. The wall between her and Craig had been her creation.

His mom safely anchored at his side, Craig looked at Brenna, the initial tip of his mouth a silent *ready, then?* But as he caught her settled gaze, the silent exchange became much more personal, and the crinkled laugh lines near his eyes smoothed.

They would talk. Later. And Brenna would remember to be brave.

***

"Go!"

With an enthusiastic command, Ashton sent them off. Trent shot forward like a dart from a nerf gun—his instant speed reminding her very much of a younger Craig and provoking memories of early mornings when they'd met at the football field, Scottie along to "coach" them both.

Scottie loved early morning workouts. It was why he'd shown up at the field, even in the middle of a snowstorm, that early January morning. There was not much he loved more than to coach his favorite football player through speed and agility drills. Well, there was ice cream. That, Scottie definitely loved more. And Craig himself. Then Mom and Dad, and maybe Brenna. But she might have fallen below the early morning practice passion. It had been hard to tell.

A chuckle—a concoction of love and sadness—passed her lips as she held a steady pace. Trent's burst of speed trickled as they neared the first corner, and Brenna easily met his side as they made the turn. So familiar. This was her and Scottie, racing while Craig high-kneed his way through those dumb old tires. The warm-up Scottie had insisted for them both.

You're letting me get too much in front, Bren. Faster starts. That's what.

Every. Single. Day. And her response every time? *Right, Coach. I'll get there.*

There's ice cream in my head, Bren. That's why I start so fast. Put some ice cream in there, 'kay?

Forget speeches, heroic stories of perseverance, and goals that could drive. Ice cream was the supreme motivator. It was a wonder other coaches hadn't caught on.

Trent's breath came in loud huffs, and his feet scuffed where a minute ago they'd been a confident pounding.

Brenna slowed her pace, put a hand to his shoulder. "Come on, buddy. Halfway there."

With a glance that was torture and a smidge of humiliation, Trent shook his head. "Can't."

"Not true." Brenna locked her arm with his and kept him on his feet and moving.

"I gonna die."

"Nope. You're still talking, so you're okay."

"When I fall down dead, you gonna know different."

Brenna laughed. "When you finish with me, you're going to know different."

He threw his head back and sagged on her arm like a limp sack of flour.

"My brother used to talk me out of quitting," Brenna said.

"You got a brother?"

"I did." She swallowed, ignoring the fact that this was the

first time in seven years she'd really allowed the memory of her brother to spring up voluntarily. "He was kind of awesome. And sort of my honorary coach when I was running. Want to know what he told me when I wasn't working hard enough or when I wanted to quit?"

"What?"

"No ice cream for you."

There was a pause. Trent glanced at her, a silent *are you serious?* And then...

He laughed. Tossed his head back and let a shout of amusement fill the block, provoking a belly laugh of her own as they turned the final corner and strode the last twenty yards.

"I get ice cream if I win?" Trent asked between heaving breaths and grinning lips.

"Think we both get ice cream either way." She released his arm and turned to jog backward. "But I'm not going to just let you win." Waiting until he looked straight at her, she dropped a wink, spun back around, and pushed her stride into a sprint.

"No way, lady!" Trent's pounding feet picked up in a staccato rhythm.

They pounded it out to the end, where Ashton cheered loyally for his brother, Craig yelled for them both, and Janet wore a smile of days gone by.

Brenna won, but only by a few strides. "Ice cream it is." She turned, hoping that Trent wouldn't fall into a sulk.

Sucking air, the boy flopped onto the grass at Craig's feet and smiled. "Ice cream." His small fist lifted, a weak but determined celebration.

Heart pounding more than it should for a run around the block, Brenna hadn't felt quite this alive in far too long—the end of the Adventure Run being a recent exception. There was Craig's deep laugh. Ashton's whoop of joy. Janet's sweet smile.

And there was Scottie in her head. Grinning. Saying that she'd done good. And to hurry up, because ice cream should not be delayed.

***

Wes grinned from his place at the grill while Jaycee took their order. Craig nodded with a smile of his own.

"That's a full order, young man." Jaycee peeked around the window toward the booth the rest of Craig's party had taken. A smile slid onto her mouth, and she looked back up at him with loving approval.

"Four small chocolate swirls and a frozen lemonade," she said. "You got it."

"Thanks." He slid the payment across the counter, accepted the change, and walked back toward the booth.

"Coming out!" Wes pushed through the kitchen door before he made it halfway. "No waffle fries, Craig? What's the matter—you 'fraid you'll lose that girlish figure?"

Chuckling, Craig patted his abs—which, by the way, were still firm, thank you very much. "Nope. I filled up on my beef stroganoff about an hour ago, which wasn't half bad, if I do say so myself."

Wes put a hand to his chest. "A man who can cook is a man after my own heart. I'll try not to be insulted about the fries."

"You know I'll be back for some before long."

Still grinning, Wes turned his attention toward the booth. "Ah..." The sound was low and of approval. "There's a sight."

Yes. Indeed there was a sight. Brenna sat next to Mom, talking easily while the boys sat across from them playing with the wooden pegboard game that waited at every table. A small pain pinched his chest as he let that image imprint in his mind. Because it was perfect.

Wes leaned in and, dropping his voice low, said, "For there is nothing lost, that may be found, if sought."

Craig turned a sharp gaze back to Wes, as surprised by the

fact that this burly man whom he'd known all his life had quoted Spenser's epic poetry as he was by Wes's bold implication.

"You are not the only multilayered man in this small town, Craig Erikson." Wes smirked, then winked and patted him on the shoulder. "I'll bring that order straight out."

"Thanks." The word dropped lamely from Craig's mouth, still caught in shock as he was.

Mom's glance at him and the quirk of her eyebrows snapped him out of it. The week had been strange all around. But not in a bad way. Might as well embrace all the gloriously weird moments. And linger over the quote Wes had whispered. The things thought to be worn away and lost...were perhaps not. Maybe they were just different.

The thoughts turned slowly as he lowered next to the boys.

"I think it helps to really read the Bible rather than simply depending on a daily verse, Brenna." Mom continued her conversation, her attention focused on Brenna. "Don't get me wrong—a daily verse reading is a good start, but there is so much missed if that's all you do."

"Then what? I wouldn't know where to begin."

"Read the stories. Take them as a whole. And come to them with a different focus."

"What kind of focus?"

"Most of us approach God's Word rather selfishly. We come to it asking, *What will You do for me today? Lift me. Inspire me. Feed me.* Which isn't wholly bad. But what if we began with *What will You reveal about Yourself?* What if we came to God asking Him to let us know Him?"

Caught by their conversation, Craig flicked his gaze to Brenna, warily watching her reaction.

She wore a thoughtful look, easing the tension he felt about walking into such a deep conversation. Then she nodded.

"That's why you know Him so well, isn't it? Why you can

trust Him? Because you've studied to know who He is."

Mom's small smile spread warmly, and Craig latched on to a deeper knowledge about her. This woman who raised him—her strength, her character—she gleaned them from a deep knowledge of God, which gave her a profound love. Longing stirred within to follow in her legacy.

"Scripture has been given for our learning," Mom said. "Sometimes we need to take a fresh approach. God already knows us. The real mystery to me is that though He knows all my failures and all my weaknesses, He continues to invite me to know Him. That's what a relationship is, isn't it? Not only Him knowing me and me asking Him to tell me nice things about myself so I feel good. But Him doing those things because He loves me—and *also* allowing me to know Him. Though I will never understand all that He is, the fact that He opens up to me what I can grasp—there is deep wonder in that."

Profound things for him to think on. And he had no doubt, given the studious look on Brenna's face, that she would be ruminating on the words as well.

"Here we are." Jaycee slipped through the grip of the conversation as she delivered a tray of goodies. Six cups, rather than five, slid onto the table.

"I think Wes forgot how to count," Craig teased.

"No." Jaycee held a solemn look on him and then turned it toward Brenna. "No, he didn't, but he did say I was probably overstepping. But I can't...well, the thing is, I know..." A tentative look bounced from Brenna's face to Craig's. "Scottie's birthday is this month. It's been too long without a celebration of him, and since you're both here, I thought perhaps you would take this time to remember the joy he brought into all of our lives."

The air grew still. Craig's throat swelled, and when he dared a glance at Brenna's face, he found her eyes sheened.

Brenna blinked, and then with a wobbly smile, she nodded. "You're right. It's been too long, and this is the perfect way to remember him. Over ice cream."

Jaycee laughed. "I love remembering the way he'd order his favorite. *Choc-it, choc-it, choc-it, Ms. Jaycee, and don't forget the cherry on top!* Every. Time. That's what he'd say, with the best smile you ever saw in all of Big Prairie."

Janet chuckled first, quickly joined by both Craig and Brenna. The boys looked up from their game, but something innate held them still as they listened.

"Oh, but he loved his ice cream!" Brenna laughed. "And football. Couldn't even sit during a game, because he had so much energy about it."

"He loved his dad—that's why he loved the game," Craig said. "Coach was Scottie's hero—just as he was for the rest of us boys, and Scottie inspired us as much."

Brenna nodded.

"But he wasn't only about football and ice cream." Mom's smile settled on Craig. "Remember how he loved to hear you read to him? And how he begged you to show him how to play your guitar? I would dare to guess that he was the reason you chose to go into education."

Craig looked down at the table, blinking against the warmth. "Yes, he was."

"Frog and Toad," Brenna said. "He loved Frog and Toad. Said it was like you and him, Craig. You were Frog because you were so tall, and he was Toad, and you were best friends. He also told me I was not allowed to read it to him, because I never got the voices right, no matter how hard I tried."

They all chuckled. The teary sort that hurt and healed at once.

Jaycee lifted the extra cup, filled with a triple chocolate swirl. When Craig looked up, he saw tears leaking beneath her eyelids.

"I don't think we should pretend to forget such an amazing boy," she said. "He was a gift to all of us, and I think he'd be pretty disappointed if he got to looking down from heaven and saw all of us pretending that life moved on, all of us on our own. Think he'd like better to see us enjoying these ice creams, laughing, living, and remembering. Even if it makes us cry a little bit."

Sniffing, Craig moved his gaze to the young woman across from him. Hers was already soft and on him. Risking exposure and rejection, he moved his hand across the space beneath the table. When he found her fingers spread over the jeans covering her knees, he brushed them gently. Her hand moved to grip his and held.

"I think you're right," Brenna whispered. She blinked, a tear dropping from her lash, and then looked up to Jaycee. "It's been long overdue, but you're right. Thank you for honoring my brother."

Chapter Twenty-Four

SUMMER DECIDED NOT TO LET GO QUITE YET.

While the hues that edged the river sang of autumn, reminding one of pumpkins and apple cider and corn mazes soon to come, the temperature left the impression of late July. This happened in October, as she never knew which season she liked best and often chose both.

When it came to Friday night games, October's inkling about weather mattered little. The games were on either way. Well, it mattered, as those suited-up young men were going to end the night red faced and drenched in sweat whether they spent most of the four quarters on the field or holding down the sidelines. But the outcome would be the same: they would play. There would be a winner and a loser and a new tally on the records. And almost everyone in Big Prairie would be there to bear witness. Including Craig Erikson and, interestingly on that particular Friday night, Brenna Blaum.

Craig had heard that Brenna didn't go to the games. Grant often did—he was on staff with the district, so there were expectations there. A fact evidenced by Grant's presence at the bottom of the stands where he was posted for crowd-control duty—a job Craig would take on the following week, as it would be his turn. But according to chatter, even when they'd been dating, Brenna didn't fill the seat at Grant's side. Little insights into the goings-on of Big Prairie while he'd been away that Craig didn't necessarily seek out or actually need to know. But they'd found him nonetheless, and the knowledge hooked into his curiosity as he watched her step down the stairway to his right, attractive in her dark skinny jeans rolled at the ankles, white Cons, and an orange Broncs T-shirt, looking for a place to sit.

He hadn't spoken much to her since their ice cream treat at the grill the week before, and given that the evening had ended on the deeply emotional side and then there had been a long, hollow silence between them, he wasn't sure what to think. Sure, they'd interacted. For therapy appointments and when she'd invited the boys to the park to play with Rascal on a handful of evenings. But that didn't involve much talking between the two of them, leaving him with a sense of lostness that made him frustrated all over again.

Face shaded by a ball cap, with her ponytail pulled through the back, Craig caught her profile and sucked in a breath. Speechless. In that moment he was eighteen and lovesick, watching the girl who owned every inch of his heart come down the steps to wish him good luck in his last home game.

Man, he'd loved her. Although at that time they weren't officially dating—because of that rule number one on Coach's office door—Craig had been sure of it. He loved her. Hadn't been able to imagine life without her.

That truth was like a blow to his gut, an explosion in his head. They'd been young, and after they'd started dating on the record, there had been many adults who had told them they were too young to know love, too young to make that kind of massive commitment. They'd been well meaning, and possibly, to a degree, right. But sitting there in the middle of a crowd watching the girl he'd let go singed the still-raw places of his heart that had belonged to her.

He *had* loved her. He should have never considered the idea that she should or could come after football. Never should have thought that setting her aside could be justified.

She turned and searched the crowd until she came to him. Uncertainty played in her expression as she bit the corner of her lip, but then a small grin eased the hesitancy away and she lifted a hand to wave.

"Ms. Brenna comin'." Trent pointed. Amazing how in a few weeks' time Trent had gone from resenting his speech therapist to apparently thinking Brenna was on par with Superman. At least. The afternoons playing with Rascal helped. The fact that though she hadn't let him win, she'd refused to let him quit in their little race also did something. Likely, though, it was the ice cream that sealed the deal.

Scottie's legacy lived on. Heaven bless him for that.

"She gonna sit with us, Craig?" Ashton wanted to know.

"Don't know, buddy." He tracked her progress the rest of the way down the stadium steps and across the base of the bleachers, heading toward Grant.

Drawing in the next breath pinched.

Grant smiled, his greeting both surprised and genuinely glad to see her. Brenna looked to the ground, nodded at whatever Grant had said, and then tipped her chin up to meet the other man's eyes. His hand cupped her elbow. She smiled. He did too.

Craig looked away. It wasn't his business. He'd let her go a long time ago, and how selfish could a man be to wish that she'd not gotten over him the way he'd never gotten over her?

"She comin'!" Ashton grabbed Craig's hand and wiggled it. "I knowd she would!"

The boy was up on the bleacher below them, stretching tall and waving like he was flagging down a ride. Craig looked to where he'd last seen her with Grant, but found her instead halfway up the steps that would lead her to them, her expression light and with a wave for the little boy bouncing in front of him.

"Ms. Brenna!"

"Hi, Ashton. How are you?"

"You sit with us, right?"

"Absolutely." Her attention shifted to Craig. "If there's room?"

"Of course." Had his voice cracked? Awesome. Worse than still being eighteen. He cleared his throat, reached for the manliness that must be in him somewhere, and diverted his attention to Trent. "We've got room for Ms. Brenna, right, buddy?"

"You know it." Trent slid a step away, opening a space between himself and Craig.

Not what he'd meant. Craig swallowed, lifting his ball cap and readjusting it on his head before he dared peek at Brenna.

Her face was tucked under the bill of her hat as she slipped in front of Ashton and Craig to reach the seat next to Trent. And Craig.

"Thanks, Trent." She kept her eyes focused on the boy. Away from Craig. "How was school today?"

"Nailed it."

"Yeah? Ms. Everson told me you were working on a story."

"Aw, man. She didn't." He swatted at the air between them, but the smile in his voice betrayed him. "Ain't right she rats me out like that."

"No one was ratting." Brenna laughed. "She said it's good. I was hoping you'd bring it sometime. I'd love to hear it."

Trent couldn't keep his grin from leaking onto his face. Then suddenly she was looking up at Craig.

The splay of faded freckles across her nose and cheeks begged his study, calling up old habits. He'd loved tracing the path of constellations with the pads of his thumbs, and he stepped into the memory of the first time he'd done so.

She'd brushed at her face after a race, clearing the sweat that had gathered near her nose, and made a comment about wishing the moisture would wipe away the freckles that made her look smudged all the time. He'd taken her hands from her face, shaking his head, then traced the path across her cheeks with his thumbs.

"Stop wishing that," he'd said. "I would miss them too much."

He had missed them. So much. As well as her determination. And smile. And the way she could look at him and he'd feel like everything that mattered in the world was right there in front of him.

"Craig?"

He blinked. "What?"

Twin lines carved between her brows as she held him with curiosity. "I asked if you've heard Trent's story."

"Oh." He battled the heat spilling from his ears onto his face. "No. Hadn't heard anything about it until tonight." Tilting to look around her at Trent, he was thankful for somewhere to refocus. "You're going tell me about it, right?"

Trent shrugged, but his expression betrayed his pleasure. Craig held out a fist, and Trent smashed it with their signature pound.

"I want in on this." Brenna held her fist out too.

Trent turned up a sly grin. "Only if I get to play with Rascal."

"That's not even a question. You know you can anytime."

"Tonight?"

Brenna sent a questioning glance toward Craig. He nodded, though internally he began bundling up unreasonable hopes and packing away memories that would be sure to push him off balance again.

"Sure." Her attention fell back on Trent as the announcer welcomed everyone to the game.

The motion of the night took on a familiar path—the national anthem, the starting lineup, the coin toss, and the opening kick-off.

Friday night in Big Prairie. Same as it had always been, but Craig hadn't experienced it like this during high school. In the stands, not on the field. Next to Brenna Blaum, with the longing to take her hand going painfully unanswered. With two boys on either side of them, cheering on the Broncs, though the scoreboard made it known to all that the season, which had started poorly, wasn't getting better anytime soon.

It was surreal, and Craig couldn't help but swim in the sense of things that should have been and weren't.

This was what he'd wanted. Even back then as that eighteen-year-old football player who had already had several serious visits with scouts from UNL, he'd seen the long game, and this was the end he'd wanted. Brenna at his side. Big Prairie their forever hometown. And a pair of kids with them—their uncle Scottie keeping them continually entertained, not to mention the promise of ice cream always in sight.

His utopia.

A bittersweet ache moved in his chest, and Craig couldn't resist a glance to his right. Hers, timed by coincidence—or not—collided with his, and the movement of time became fixed. In that breath, *then* was no longer the past. *Then* was now, and the hope for that dream burst through soil that had been crusted with frost for way too long.

And then she looked away. Watched the game, though the set of her jaw, the edge of her profile told him her mind was not on the field. She could recognize play calls and defensive formations better than most of the sofa coaches in America and probably as well as any safety on the field, but she wasn't fixed on any of those details.

"I don't usually come to these." Her stare remained static on the game.

Craig searched her profile. "I've heard that."

The smile she'd worn to the game melted.

"Here you are though," Craig said, keeping their conversation quiet compared to the roar that made up small-town football.

Nodding, she scanned the scene as if it was new or she was searching for something long lost.

"I started running consistently again. After that night with Trent. With Rascal."

Craig rolled one hand into the other, tucked the loose fists under his chin. There was a releasing in her. A softening. Had been for some weeks now, and he'd prayed it would continue as much as he'd prayed he'd have wisdom in how to handle that cracking if it were to happen.

Here she was, slowly cracking. And he, still vulnerable. He wondered if she was intentional about tearing down the walls or if it simply was breaking inside her and she couldn't keep the pieces in place anymore.

"Had heard you'd quit." Rolling his lips together, he kept his focus on her, begging her attention to come back to him.

When it did, there was a squall in her gaze, though her features didn't harden the way they had when she was truly good and angry.

"Why?" He pressed, tempting the storm he knew was brewing.

She studied him and then scanned the crowd again. When he followed the direction of her focus, it landed on Grant. His lungs seemed to collapse.

"He seemed glad to see you tonight." Shoulders tense, Craig sat up, fighting to keep a casual air in his voice.

"He was surprised."

"He smiled. Looked relieved...and happy."

"You were watching?"

How could she not know that it would have been impossible for him not to watch?

"How will he feel about you sitting up here with us?" If the roles were switched, Craig knew without a wisp of doubt he'd be crazy-jealous—and that probably wasn't a good thing. Knowing that, he didn't want to be the point of friction between Brenna and Grant if they really weren't done.

She pinned him with a look that hid none of the irritation his meddling had provoked. "Since he broke up with me, I'm not sure that it matters. Anyway, he's a grown man, and a good one. I'm sure he'll deal with it in a grown-up sort of way."

Was that a jab?

Yeah. A jab for sure. He hadn't asked her to come. Didn't beg her to sit with them. They hadn't even spoken in a week— not really. This friendship thing she said she wanted—was she kidding with that? Why was it that even when he felt a thawing between them, he managed to irritate her without the slightest intent?

This emotional volleying was tiresome.

"Why'd you come here, Brenna?"

"I didn't want to spend another Friday night at home alone."

"Sophie is over with the band." He pointed across the field, where the band sat in their marching uniforms. "Why didn't you sit with her?"

Her lips pressed, chilled gaze locked on something—or nothing—somewhere across the field. This was familiar too. Their last year together had been littered with this kind of simmering-under-the-surface conflict. Seemed back then he couldn't do anything right. Hadn't called often enough. Didn't notice when she'd gotten a new pair of jeans. Had let his attention drift somewhere...

Back then he'd let her fume. Had backed off, said nothing,

waited for whatever was needling her to let up so they could move on. Maybe that'd been passive aggressive. Or maybe it was being nonconfrontational. He didn't know—was certain Grant could give it some kind of label.

He was sick of the thought of Grant making him tense. The man didn't deserve it—had nothing to do with this ongoing Brenna-and-Craig fiasco. Also, there was a strong possibility that turning his frustration toward Grant was him deflecting.

Had been pretty good at that seven years ago too.

"Brenna." Angling his shoulders toward her, he kept her name low and quiet.

She continued to stare forward.

"Brenna, let's not do this."

Her chin moved, jaw tightened. Man, he was good at making her mad. Whether he meant to or not.

You meant to.

Sighing, he shut his eyes, rubbed the bridge of his nose. Yeah. He'd poked at her because he'd thought she was jabbing at him. Maybe she was. And round and round they'd go. Forever.

Or.

"Brenna, I'm sorry."

The granite of her expression softened a bit.

"I'm glad you sat with us." He leaned closer to ensure she heard him. "I always want you to sit with me."

Whoa. Words were falling off his tongue without his consent. She turned to him, a question in her eyes. Pain touching her expression.

The crowd around them erupted as the Broncs ran for a touchdown. Across the field, the band launched into the school fight song, and every person wearing orange and blue stood, clapping to the beat. Except Brenna and Craig.

Her study was a silent plea. A white flag and a begging for truce. "I don't want this anymore," she said, her voice tight.

"What?"

"This bickering."

Had her voice faltered?

He leaned closer still. "I don't either."

The song wound down, and the people around them began to sit as the kick-off team set up in formation.

Brenna shifted, stretching a hand toward his. Her fingers, warm and soft, brushed over his thumb, his knuckles. "Is it possible to find our way back to friends?"

Ah...the conversation that they'd left hanging, unfinished, and brewing in the background of their tentative truce. Tension in his shoulders eased, making him suddenly aware of how rigid he'd been. "I hope so, Brenna." He moved his thumb across the fold of her palm.

The tipping of her mouth was slight, but it was there. A phantom smile, not full of hope, but enough to fuel his.

"Maybe this is how," he said. "Maybe we need to stop thinking that relationships have to be easy in order to be valid."

Another burst of cheers and clapping filled the stadium, finally drawing Craig's attention from Brenna. The kicker had sent the ball deep but not through the endzone, and the ball had been downed at the seven-yard line.

A near-perfect kickoff. Perhaps the tide was turning for the Big Prairie fighting Broncs.

"Maybe." Brenna's whisper floated through the applause and cheers, settling a new calm deep in his chest.

He was all for turning the tide.

Chapter Twenty-Five

THE MORNING AIR WAS CRISP TO HER LUNGS, SEASONED WITH THE SPICE OF FALL AND STIRRED BY THE BREEZE.

Brenna pushed her stride as the dirt road wound around a bend that paralleled the meandering path of the river to her left. Ten days now. This made the tenth day she'd stretched her legs into a run, pushed her heart rate and breathing past a brisk walk down some street in town.

The road was quiet, allowing for the gentle symphony of swishing leaves, still clinging in their fall adornment to the arched branches above; the call of a meadowlark, soon to be missing as he migrated for the fall; and the gurgling of the river. She and Rascal were the only ones to disturb nature's exclusive little show with the rhythmic pounding of her new running shoes and the controlled staccato of her breathing countering the puppy's.

Another five days and hopefully she'd find the stride that felt more like flying than like jabbing the ground.

Rascal kept up with her and seemed happy to be out. Their first time at this together had been a fairly ridiculous scene that made her glad she'd decided to take up distance running again out of town's sight. The mutt had yelped and jumped, tried to nip her heels, and nearly toppled her with a quick dart in front of her path. The only reason she hadn't landed in the dirt was because she'd spun out of the leash's wrapping, essentially following the dog in a circle.

It'd been tempting to quit right then.

But she'd pushed through, and by the beginning of that second of three miles, Rascal figured out what they were doing and became a good dirt-road companion.

She glanced at him galloping to her right on a loose leash, his flapping tongue and doggy smile making her grin. If only she'd had a running partner like him before. Maybe she wouldn't have quit.

Maybe.

Likely not so. She'd quit because her world had crashed. Piece by piece, it'd crumbled, and some of that had been by her own hands.

As that thought pinched another pang of regret in her chest, she tilted her chin upward. The yellow-and-orange canopy overhead allowed for only splotchy glimpses of the clear blue sky.

It was the perfect fall morning, and yet she wanted to cry.

Might have to do with the argument she'd managed to find with Craig last night at the game. Even though it had resolved, even though he had apologized. The fact that they'd fallen right back into the petty bickering that had marked the last eight months of their relationship before he'd ended it had made her heart sick and frustrated.

Then again, this ache…might have more to do with the constant grip of regret.

How did one get out of that?

Her pace slowed as her focus shifted. Absently, she checked her GPS watch, hit End Workout, and noted without a whole lot of interest that she'd only gone a mile and a half. This run was more for thinking and for praying than for training. She needed to sort through things that had been cluttering her up for way too long.

Grant had asked why she was so mad. He'd meant, why was she so mad at Craig? Why did she become a cold stone wall whenever Craig was in her presence? Reaching for the superficial answer had been both instinct and habit. Craig broke up with her. Chose football over them and broke her heart. Broke his promises. Broke their dreams. Should be reason enough for her to stay mad at him forever, shouldn't it?

It's been seven years, Brenna. You still can barely stand to be in the same room with him. Seems like maybe there's more.

She'd wanted to shove Grant for saying such a stupid thing.

Turned out, however, that when she gathered enough courage to honestly examine the root of her anger, he was right. There was more—and it hadn't all been Craig's fault.

Regret is a bondage that holds many captives. Sometimes for life. But there is freedom in repentance.

A tug at her right hand drew her attention down as Rascal yelped, his energy pointed at something through the trees.

"What is it, boy? Smell a coon? Maybe a deer by the river?"

Rascal jumped, his motion turning her off the road and to a foot trail. With a quick glance around, she realized the spot was familiar; the trail led to a swimming hole often used by the youth of Big Prairie. A place she'd rarely visited in the last seven years.

As her feet left the gravel and pressed into the black earth, sand, and shale unique to the river's extended banks, she passed through the border of forest. The trail pulled them gently through the stands of birch and ash, the sound of the gently moving waters now only an undertone to a mix of laughter and the distinct *skip, skip, skip, plunk* of stones skimming the water's surface before sinking.

The laughter was of three, and she knew the owners even before the final bend of path dumped her and Rascal from tree stand to open bank.

Rascal yipped, and two boys whipped around, grins ready.

"Rascal!" Ashton dropped his stones and ran toward them.

Trent turned to skip his final stone and then followed his little brother. "You runnin', Ms. Brenna?"

"We are." She stopped when Ashton and Rascal collided, now ten feet from the water's edge, and handed the leash to Trent. "Well, we were. Rascal told me someone was at the old swimming hole, so we came to investigate."

"Swimming hole?" Trent had bent to love on the exuberant dog but stood to tip up a questioning look.

"Yes, swimming hole." Brenna shifted her attention from the boys and dog to the man who'd remained beside the river. "You mean you haven't taken them swimming?"

Shaded by a red ball cap, Craig's expression, which had been watchful, eased into a grin, and he stepped toward them. With a shrug, he shook his head. "Haven't braved that activity yet."

"We ain't swimmers," Ashton said, barely glancing from Rascal.

"What do you mean, you aren't swimmers?" Brenna asked.

Trent stood full, his look serious. "He means we can't swim. Don't know how."

Brenna pushed out her bottom lip and glanced back at Craig. His hand cupped his neck, and she wondered if he was expecting a scowl from her. That regret she'd been wrestling with tightened in her chest. She'd really left him with a sour version of herself. The worst possible version.

That ended. Here. Now. This constant animosity she'd stirred between them was going to die. Starting right there on the riverbank on that perfect fall morning.

After a quick check to ensure that Trent did in fact have a good hold on Rascal, who was dancing between the boys, tongue busy licking one and then the other as fast as he could move, Brenna moved to meet Craig where he'd stopped five feet away. When she smiled, relief washed through those stormy blue eyes.

"Did you know"—she turned back to the boys—"you are living with one of the best swimmers in River Bend county?"

"No way." Trent raised a suspicious eyebrow directed at Craig. "You played football."

"I did," Craig said. "And Ms. Brenna is exaggerating."

"Not at all. Craig did swim team in the winter. Many of the football players did. My dad thought it was good training for his boys and encouraged them to do it."

"Your dad?" Ashton asked, surprising Brenna because she really hadn't thought he was listening. Too busy wiggling around with the puppy who mirrored his energy.

"Yeah. My dad was Craig's football coach."

"What!" Trent dropped the leash and marched toward them. "Why didn't we know that?"

She felt Craig tense beside her. Certainly waiting for her to stone up. Grip the mad she'd kept at the ready for any occasion involving Craig and anything football-past and hurl it at him.

"It was a long time ago," Craig said.

Brenna turned her face back to him, kept her look gentle. "It was."

Right there in the crisp breeze scented by the gently moving river, something happened. The beats of silence that passed were like a bridge, and Brenna stepped onto the crossing, hoping for a better beyond. She felt the muscles in her face relax, the corners of her mouth shift upward, and a piece of herself she'd thought had died rise up and breathe.

It felt like joy.

Craig watched her, the hint of caution between them evaporating at her grin.

"It was a long time ago," she repeated. "But there were good times that shouldn't be forgotten." Coming back to the present, Brenna looked back at the boys, who now watched them with interest, the dog panting but settled between them. A touch of heat crept onto her cheeks. "Craig actually taught my brother how to swim, and Scottie struggled with learning some things—swimming being one of them—but eventually he came to love it. I have no doubt Craig could teach you."

Craig chuckled, his hand gesturing toward the bend of the river that had been their swimming hole. "Maybe not here in the middle of October though."

"Afraid of a little chilly water?" She eyed him with sass.

"Yes, actually." He winked. "I'm not eighteen anymore. Unless, of course, you'd like to test the water out for me. Then I'd definitely reconsider…"

Eyebrows up in a challenge, he moved as if to scoop her up.

"Not on your life!" Brenna launched the opposite direction, her able legs taking her around to the other side of the boys. Craig stood his ground, amusement lifting his lips.

"The rec center has a pool!" Trent jumped from his knees to his feet, lit with excitement.

"It does!" She pointed at Craig, a silent warning.

He held up his hands in truce and then shook his head. "Puppies and pools and stories and running…anything else you think the boys and I need?"

Me.

The thought blindsided her. Jolted the reality she'd started to enjoy and left her speechless.

***

She'd been there, standing by that river, laughter in her gaze and the old smile on her lips toying with dormant things in his heart. Craig couldn't get those rare moments out of his head.

Brenna. The old Brenna. Smiling at him. Teasing him. Laughing with him.

"Hey, music man." Jeremiah tapped a cursory knock on the door as he passed into Craig's classroom. "How's the weekend?"

Craig lowered the guitar he'd been absently strumming

while his mind had lingered over that woman, wishing he'd snagged her in that teasing moment. Just to feel her in his arms again. With a force of discipline, he shifted his thoughts to the present and wondered if he shouldn't be a little more thankful that Jeremiah had intruded on the memory of Brenna's laugh and the rise of longing she stirred.

"Good." Craig cleared his throat. "Boys and I had a good weekend, and Mom seems to be on an upward trend, so it was good."

Jeremiah nodded. "Saw you at the game Friday night."

With Brenna. He nodded while he held his breath, bracing for the questions.

"What'd you think?"

She and I still have some things to sort out. Starting with why this shift all the sudden? Was J really meddling with this? Craig shrugged, turning toward the chairs to rearrange an arrangement that had been perfectly fine.

"Coach Hale keeps trying to force a passing game," J said.

Oh. Of course, J was talking about the game, not... Man, his head was not right.

"Boys will get it."

"Not likely," J said. "Haven't for four years. Always been better on the ground—and the running game is what got you in as a Husker."

Smothering a sigh, because the subject of the good old glory days was not his favorite, Craig set a chair down nearly in the same spot it'd been and squared back to J. "What are you hinting at?"

"I told you at the beginning of the year—board's not happy."

"I'm not getting in the middle of it. Think I told you that when you first brought it up."

"Hale's resigning."

Crossing his arms, Craig felt a scowl creasing his bow. "Voluntarily?"

Silence.

"Leave me out of this, J. Hale is a good guy, and I came back here to teach music. To take care of my mom, and so those boys would have someone. My deck is full, and football is in the past for me."

"Doesn't have to be."

"Yeah, actually, it does."

"Keep up with Coach much?"

Craig's gaze remained steady—probably had heated into a glare at J's switch in topics. "Yeah. I talk to him about once a week."

"Well, I talked to him too. On Sunday, after Buck called me to say the board had received an email from Hale. He was informing them that this was his last year in Big Prairie. I called Blaum to see if he'd consider coming back."

"Hardly considerate of you. Don't you think they've been through about enough?"

"He didn't seem to mind." J stepped closer, hands anchored on his hips. "Honestly, Craig, I think he's dealt with everything a whole lot better than you have. And Scottie was his son. At least Coach is still living. Still the man he was back then, even with the scars. You're walking around like a shell. Engaging with the kids, but that's about it. Everything else is surface for you, like you're drifting on the river of life waiting until the ride's over."

Craig pressed his lips together. J had no idea how hard it had been to come back, for reasons J, nor anyone else in Big Prairie save one, would understand. Not to mention figuring out how to be a single dad to two half-grown boys who had some pretty big trauma issues, while watching his mom deteriorate at the cruel hand of cancer. Anger coursed through him during the beats that hummed between them.

"That's not what I wanted to say to you though." J's hands fell to his side, and the hardness in his expression softened.

"Blaum said no—not because he can't come back but because he said the man we need is already here."

"So go talk to Hale."

"He meant you."

"No he didn't."

"Last I knew, you were Erickson."

Another handful of tense moments passed. Craig unfolded his arms, drew in a breath. "Look, J, I know you mean well, but this needs to stop. I have a class to teach, and this conversation is done. Please don't bring it up again."

A frown tugged on a corner of J's mouth as he held Craig in a long look. Shaking his head, he shoved his hands into his pockets and turned. At the door, he paused. "Scottie loved life, buddy. He wouldn't miss a moment of it."

Back turned to J, Craig tipped his head back and shut his eyes. There was Scottie, big ol' smile, mischief on his face, energy flooding his eyes.

"Doubt he'd want you to miss it either. Especially on his account."

Knife placed. Turned. But yet again another misunderstanding. Craig hadn't run because of Scottie.

And Brenna had recently started to smile at him again.

Chapter Twenty-Six

"ARE YOU GOING TO THE GAME TOMORROW?"

She'd barely seen Craig, and only slightly more of the boys during the week. The old insecurities flared as he stood in her office—*he's got someone else*—which logically was ridiculous because she and Craig had no understanding between them. She had no business being...jealous?

Yeah, that was what that had been, back then. And then...manipulative.

Being that person again...not a good option.

Oh, but she'd missed him. For four days she'd been chasing thoughts and memories involving Craig Erikson. All of the what-could-have-beens. The regrets. They'd clamped down on her in a way that had felt nearly paralyzing as she'd remembered the way she'd been suspicious of him, the way she'd manipulated and clung and ultimately had destroyed.

For several nights she'd allowed herself to really look at what had happened and to be humbly honest about what she'd done.

Back then she'd known the vulnerable places in Craig's heart. He'd shared them with her with open trust. Resenting the father he'd never known, the last thing Craig had ever wanted to be was a man like that. A man who would sleep with a woman, taking something Craig believed to be sacred, and then leave her broken and alone. Craig had been determined to be like *her* father instead—the coach he'd nearly idolized. Dependable, kind, and above all, a man of honor.

She'd become so wrapped up in her own fears and too self-focused to understand what she was really doing. She'd taken that trust and twisted it.

Last night, tears had seeped from the corner of her eye as she remembered. Confessed. All of it she'd blamed on him. She had refused to own her faults back then and for the years up until now.

That thought about him missing her in his life had spun her in an entirely new direction. No, that wasn't right. It had reset her in an old direction. One that had their paths aligned. But there were things that needed said. Owned. Repented of.

Unfortunately, their paths hardly crossed during the week. *Because he doesn't want to see you.*

More stomach fire.

Make me wiser. Better.

Her prayers lifted silently as she glanced toward the window on her right, desperate for an anchor within so that she would not be tossed back into that chaos again, dragging Craig along with her as he stood across from her.

Craig rolled his shoulders back as if to ease tension. The brief glance he met her with seemed... distant. "No, I wasn't planning on making the drive. Three hours one way seems like a lot with the boys."

He silently put distance into the space that had only begun to close between them. What had she done? Said? Had she already given him signs of the clinging girl she'd become with him before?

Maybe he didn't want reconciliation. Maybe she'd been too ugly. Too hard. Maybe it was too late. Seven years was a long time.

The press of panic and despair those possibilities triggered was a bit of a shock. For seven years she'd clung to an anger that hadn't been reasonable for the sole purpose of keeping him away. Now? Now, when she'd decided to pry her fingers loose of resentment...

This life. Misery sagged through her. She was really good at making life harder than it likely needed to be.

"I'm sorry." Craig cleared his throat, shifted his feet like he was still uncomfortable. "That must sound lame to a woman who grew up going to every single game, no matter the distance."

She lifted her eyes to search his face. Yes, he looked uncomfortable. And also...lost?

"That's not what I was thinking," she said.

"No?"

"No. And I liked going to my dad's games, for the record. And to yours."

He nodded. The pause lengthened.

"I was going to see if I could ride with you and the boys if you were going," she said, drowning in the strangeness of this undefined place whose currents were strong and frightening.

"Oh." His expression slid from uncomfortable to a little confused, but the study of his gaze deepened. "We could make that work." A pause. Another roll of his shoulders. "If you wanted to."

"No, I only wanted to go if you were planning on going."

His lips pressed, attention drifted from her face to something behind her.

"Craig, are you upset with me?" Such a loaded question. Yes. He should be upset with her. There was a stack of calendars, each page filled with reasons he could be upset with her. Not to mention the past three months during which she was an all-out frosty to him.

"No." He formed a plastic smile.

"You're not?"

"No." The fake attempt of a grin faded, but his attention latched back on to her, and he nudged away a bit of the space between them. A beat wove with hesitation, then he shoved his hands into his jeans pockets. "Trent did okay today?"

"Yes. Like I said when he was still here, he's doing awesome."

Craig nodded, eased backward again.

He did this. Folded in on himself when something was bothering him but he didn't want to deal with it. Didn't want to fight.

"Craig..."

"You could come over and listen to the game with us." His offer came out in a rush. "If you wanted."

She bit her bottom lip, trying to read between the awkward spaces of silence that throbbed between them.

"The boys would like that," he said. "And Rascal—they haven't seen him since Saturday."

"Right." Wrapping her arms around her middle, Brenna considered declining. This was exhausting. This struggling.

"So." He swallowed. "Five thirty?"

"Okay." No, probably not okay. Why was she pushing something he clearly didn't want?

His mouth curved again. This time less plastic, and it somehow managed to cool the flame in her belly and warm something deep in her heart.

"Okay," he said. "You still eat pizza, right?"

Ah. Solid ground. Well, muddy. A little squishy. But ground nonetheless. She chuckled. "Of course. But I'll get it—my treat."

"No—"

She held a hand up. "My treat. Because I invited myself."

That hard-won grin on his face faded, and he stood there

silent yet again, before he turned. With a "See you then," he left her alone in her office. Not saying things.

Because he didn't want conflict.

And she'd insisted she'd bring the pizza, so now she had to go.

***

"Two hundred." Craig rocked the football back and let it fly high. Trent and Ashton ran with every bit of speed they could muscle out of their little legs, determined to catch it.

This was round three of the game he'd promised them after dinner. By the time they finished playing 500, the sun would be tucked safely behind the western horizon, the boys would have run off all of that energy that had them bickering in the car on the way home from Trent's appointment, and he should have dusted the week's frustrations from his mind.

Two out of three, likely. Because the drain of being tired and locked in a situation he hadn't signed up for had stuck him hard and fast into a bad mood. Had nothing to do with the boys though, so he worked to keep it light. Upbeat.

Trent lined up for the catch but bobbled the ball on impact, resulting in a fumble. Ashton dove on it and tucked it in tight for the recovery. In this version, with two little boys, that counted.

"Two hundred to Ashton," Craig called.

Both boys, sprawled out on the grass in a sort of scrum on the ground, wrestled for possession. At Craig's call, Trent scrambled to his feet and held out a hand to his younger brother to help him off the ground. A marked difference from the boy Craig had first encountered a few months back.

"I like that, Trent." He touched the older boy's sweaty head after the pair came running back to him. "Good job."

"Did you like my dive?" Ashton asked, tugging on Craig's

hand.

"I did. You were right in there, buddy. Good hustle."

"I got two hundred!"

A big deal for the smaller brother.

"Sure do."

Ashton jumped. "Do two hundred again. It's lucky for me."

Trent bent around Craig's body to talk to Ashton. "If he do two hundred and I get it, the game's over, Ash."

"That's true." Craig waited to see how the boys would call this one.

Ashton scrunched up his face, working the math in his head. Craig wondered how those numbers were lining up in that young mind, wishing he could hear the math out loud, the way Scottie would have done.

"Don't do two hundred," Ashton decided. "Only do one."

"One?"

"Yes."

Craig chuckled. "Just one point?"

"No!" Ashton jumped again, this time wrapping his arms around Craig's waist and clinging to him like a monkey. "One hundred, silly. Do one *hundred*."

"Oh." Craig continued to laugh. "I see."

"Ashton, you a goofball." Trent launched into Craig and Ashton like a linebacker with a good angle.

The impact barely touched Craig's balance, but he rocked back with a dramatic "whoa!" and the next thing he knew, they were in a full wrestling match on the grass. Two against one, laughter warming the cool evening, game of 500 forgotten.

After several minutes and a few accidental scratches stinging his arms and back, Craig lay on his back in surrender. Evening faded, and the porchlight flickered on. Mom had probably stood at the glass patio door, watching. Likely wishing she had the strength and energy to come out and play too.

But she was getting better. Stronger. Had even made supper that evening. Things to be thankful for.

"Craig?"

He turned his chin to look at Trent, breathless and lying on his back to Craig's right. "Yeah, buddy?"

"We gonna stay here with you?"

Suddenly he couldn't breathe. He'd told few people about his petition to adopt. Though he and Trent had talked about it once before, there were too many uncertainties to broadcast it, so he hadn't brought it up again, and neither had Trent.

Recovered, Trent sat up, turned on his backside, and looked down at Craig. With the hand that had been resting over his head, Craig reached, brushed the back of his fingers down that stubborn jawline.

When tears sheened Trent's brown eyes, Craig about came undone. He'd move heaven and earth if he could. Would fight with everything he had for this kid who, in spite of their struggles, had rooted strong and fast in his heart, alongside his brother. For him and Ashton both.

"We ain't." Trent's whisper cracked. "When people don't answer, it's bad news."

"I'm working on it, Trent." Craig sat up and tugged on Trent's arm. That body that had been so hard, so distant, so difficult, tucked up against his side, burying against him. Not to be left out, Ashton crawled onto Craig's lap, wrapped his monkey arms around his neck, and laid his cheek on Craig's shoulder.

"I want you both." A raw ache ballooned in Craig's voice as he folded them in his arms. "You got to believe me, I want you both, and I'm working on it."

***

The chain of the porch swing creaked while Brenna toed the

cement beneath her Converse, keeping the tiny sway in motion. Big Prairie would be in mild mourning over the weekend, as another loss put the fighting Broncs below .500 for the fourth year in a row. Small Nebraska towns didn't accept that kind of record with a whole lot of grace. Especially when that town had gone to the state championship game seven years in a row, winning three of those trips, in the previous decade.

Which was why rumors were circulating. Coach Hale was getting the boot. Or quitting under threat of getting the boot. Coach Blaum was coming back. Or more likely, the returned hometown hero would take up the old legacy. Mr. Erikson would wear the title of coach and bring back the tradition he'd played under.

Yep. Lots of rumors. Brenna had tried to shut her ears to them. Especially since she knew at least one of them was absolutely untrue. Her dad wasn't coming back to Big Prairie. He and Mom had settled in their little cabin in the Black Hills, and working at the youth camp had become his new passion. Something healing for both him and Mom that felt like honoring Scottie's memory.

Visiting them was bittersweet, but she'd gone a few times. They were okay—her parents. It'd taken some time, and there was something different in their smiles. A sadness. A longing. And yet a firm hope. Scottie loved Jesus with his whole heart— and wow, that boy could love. They'd see him again on heaven's side.

Mom once said that while she knew Jesus healed every disease, took away every hardship, but she couldn't help but hope that didn't mean He'd take away Scottie's extra chromosome.

There are things that you can learn only when life requires you to take a different view. Scottie has so much to teach us, and we are all better for it.

Brenna had been fifteen when Mom told her that. A

response to a timid question about if Mom regretted having a Down's baby. Brenna never forgot it.

Mom didn't want Scottie to change. Brenna quietly held the same hope, because Mom was right. Life looked different because of Scottie. The work she did now, the way she saw each kid in their glorious uniqueness, and the man Craig had grown into—so much of it was because of Scottie.

Exactly the way he was, he'd been a gift from heaven, and they were all better for it. Even after his death, his life continued to be a gift. Scottie left a mark of love and delight and enthusiasm on the lives he touched, and he made them see the good things in the world where it seemed only the hard could exist.

A teary chuckle left her chest as she searched for the Big Dipper up there in the night sky. The swish of the patio sliding door redirected her view to find Craig stepping through.

"Boys all tucked in?"

"Good and tight." He gripped the tall glass of tea he'd tucked into the crook of his elbow to shut the door and held it out to her.

"Thanks." She slid over, making room for him on the swing.

He lowered slowly, and she noted he'd kept a sure distance between their places. Though he'd been more himself that night—and she didn't regret coming as she'd worried she might—he was also careful around her.

Figuring out this friends business. That was what they were doing. And not doing it very well. But then again, sometimes there was beauty in hard things. Brenna pulled her posture straight, drew a breath, then looked at the man on her left.

"Craig?"

"Yeah?" It was a couple of heartbeats before he lowered his gaze from the heavens to her.

"Something was wrong yesterday."

"It was?" He waited for her to answer. When she didn't, "What?"

"I don't know. You were upset though."

"Oh." His attention drifted away, settling on the fence line across the backyard. "Not at you though. I told you that."

"I know. But, well, maybe you need someone to talk about it with? You're carrying a lot all on your own."

"Not doing great at it, am I?"

"I didn't say that."

An eyebrow hitched as he glanced at her.

"Okay, I did. That one time. But—" But at that point, she had been finding things to be mad about. She swallowed, the words pasty against the back of her throat and refusing to come out.

He breathed a chuckle that likely was supposed to relieve her of a response. "Coach Hale is leaving Big Prairie." He sighed, and his weight shifted against the backrest of the swing. "Some people want me to step in. Actually, a lot of people."

"Oh." A weight floated off her chest. He really hadn't been upset at her. "I heard something like that."

"Yeah."

"And you're upset?"

"I am. My football days are behind me."

There was that weight again. Heavier. Responsibility and regret. Shackles she hadn't been able to pray herself out of. Apparently he wore them too. Her jaw felt stiff as she forced out words that clawed her throat. "Those days don't have to be over."

The gentle sway of the swing halted as the muscles in his arms tensed, his grip on his tea glass white knuckled. With a look that felt like lead against her heart, he held her for a long, silent moment.

"Yes they do." His words felt as heavy as that stare. "And you know why."

Tension bound the air, cementing the moment into the ever-growing realm of hard places between them. Brows drawn together, he searched her, not hiding the storm of emotions that clouded those blue eyes. Though tempted, Brenna refused to hide away, and somehow the stone between them cracked in the silence.

His expression eased, and the swing began its sleepy rock-a-bye yet again.

Brenna tried to muffle the long draw of air as her heart stuttered against her ribs. "Craig?"

"Yeah, Brenna." His whisper was strained.

"Think this is going to get easier?"

Twin lines creased between his brows, and he turned back to her.

With two fingers, she gestured between them.

He blinked. "Is it too hard?"

"Feels like drowning, to be honest." She searched his face, reading concern and confusion there. "You don't feel it?"

"I feel..." He gripped his tea glass with both hands, leaning to anchor his elbows to his knees. "I don't know, Brenna. I feel overwhelmed with everything." Slowly, he turned his chin back to her. "But not necessarily because of you. I'm sorry I had to come home though. I mean—no that's not quite what I mean." That weighty stare locked on her again. "I mean, I'm sorry my coming home makes things hard for you."

A small tremble shook inside her chest. "You don't need to be sorry about coming home. Not for me."

"Grant broke up with you."

She pressed her lips together and stared at her shoes.

"Because I came home," he pressed. "Right?"

Her eyes slid shut as she inhaled. "No."

"He wouldn't have if I'd never come back."

"Also not true."

"No?"

"I didn't love him." She sat back, leaned against the chain of the swing. "I played at it. But...well, I never could say the words. Then when you came back and I couldn't hardly look at you without exploding, Grant kind of cornered me about some things."

"Things..."

She swallowed.

"About us? About...college?"

"No. I never told him those kinds of things." She met his eyes for a moment, the seal of their secrets both a bond and a wound between them. "No one knows, Craig."

The pound of her heart hurt, and she wasn't sure he couldn't hear it sitting there at her side. But he remained quiet and rigid, the distance between them jagged.

"I'm sorry you had to come back," Brenna whispered. "Not because I don't want you here though."

As she glanced again at his profile, seeing his jaw work, she wondered if this riptide of hurt and resentment would forever drag them through this sea of bitterness. But then he nodded, the muscles that had drawn his deep frown easing.

"I'm glad you're here." He gripped the chain on his side of the swing. "I'm glad we're trying to figure this out."

"There's a *but* in that, I think."

A long sigh emptied from his lungs. "I wonder if you'll ever forgive me."

The muscles in her back and legs tensed. A pair of crickets began a duet somewhere near the house, and the porch light flicked off—the sensor must have decided all were safely inside.

Nothing to see here. Just two splintered hearts searching for a cure for the past.

"You can't, can you?" His low whisper was broken.

"It's...it's more complicated than that."

"Because of Scottie?"

"No. But...maybe. I don't know."

"I loved him, Brenna. I still love him. Every memory of wrestling in the grass, of morning workouts, ice cream sundaes, reading his favorite stories, playing How Great Is Our God, and feeling his pudgy fingers on the strings beneath mine, they all hurt and make me smile and miss him all at once. There was no way I'd have let those interviews happen if he didn't want to do them. I never meant to use him—never imagined that scouts would come looking because of those videos."

With her free hand, she rolled a fist. "I know that, Craig. I know all of that, and I never should have said what I said."

The feel of his stare fastening on her was intense. Deep and frightening. Salted with anger but flavored more of need.

"But you said it. You thought it."

She nodded. Rolled her lips together and summoned the bravery to be honest.

"I was mad at you. I've been mad at you for so long, it feels like that's all I know how to be."

Leaning, he set his tea on the patio near his feet, the glass clunking softly against the cement. Though he sat up, his posture remained curled as he pressed his arms against his knees. "I know that, Brenna. I don't know what I can do about all of it now. I told you there's not a day goes by that I don't wish that I hadn't hit snooze that day. Or ask God why Scottie had to be playing on that pile of snow, or even at the field at all." Both hands raked through his hair, and then he held the back of his head. "I have no idea how to tell you I'm sorry so you know that I mean it. So that you can forgive me and maybe then I can look at you and have it not hurt to breathe."

It all rushed back, dumping grief into her heart, chaos in her mind. That day had been awful, first not being able to find Scottie, and then the call. She still saw the way her dad's face had gone sheet white as he listened. He'd said nothing. Lowered the phone and then turned away. Slowly the man

whose broad shoulders had carried Scottie after football wins;
who had handled both the pride and the sometimes over-
enthusiasm of a football-crazy small town as he led their high
school to one state playoff after another; this man who had
been, in her mind, invincible, caved. Those strong shoulders
rolled in as he folded, doubled over, then fell to his knees, sobs
quaking the solid man she called Dad.

Mom had crumpled by his side, asking what happened.

They'd found Scottie. A strap of his backpack had been seen
peeking out of a pile of recently plowed snow at the practice
field. First responders scrambled, dug as fast as they could, but
Scottie had been missing for hours. By the time they pulled
him out, it was too late.

Brenna stood behind her parents on that snowy day in
January, watching as their world turned to ash. Feeling the
flames scald her as well. And bearing it alone.

"I needed you." Her voice was a wisp and a cry, and then she
crumpled, just like her dad had that day. A little broken mess,
unable to pretend wholeness anymore. "When Scottie died,
everything fell apart. I lost my brother, and for a long time my
parents, and it was like no one seemed to notice me. And
you..."

"Brenna." He shifted, turning toward her, and his hand
curved over her head, the touch soft and the answer to the
longing she'd had since that awful day. Breaking her more.
Clearing away the jagged pieces.

"You never came back." It was as much a revelation to her as
to him. She'd been too mad to really understand why. Too hurt
and too alone to process how much she'd ached that he'd left
her, as, it seemed, had everyone else.

Every pushed-away shard of grief resurfaced, bringing with
it gut-deep cries until those sharp pieces wore into blunt
remains, and the sobbing eased. As the billow of things
unhealed eased into a gentle rain, she realized her fists gripped

fabric. The sleeves of Craig's shirt.

And the man she'd both loved and resented so deeply held her securely in his arms.

Chapter Twenty-Seven

"You go, son."

Mom's hand covered his on the breakfast table, her tired smile as warm as her touch.

"Mom, I hadn't planned on it, and you still look—"

"Sick?"

He exhaled. "Tired, Mom. You still look tired."

"I am still alive, Craig. The boys will help me."

Craig arched an eyebrow.

"They will." Her lips drew into a line—the kind that he'd known many times as a kid. The kind that said *do not argue with your mother.* "I'll have you know, my overbearing son, that those boys and I got along fine before the C word became a household curse. I'll also have you know that I've raised a rambunctious, ornery boy once before, and he grew into quite a fine young man."

"That's debatable."

"Not in Big Prairie."

"Depends on who you talk to."

"Okay, we'll start with Brenna Blaum."

Ice slid through his chest. The way she'd broken the weekend before haunted him. Holding her while she fell apart had been long overdue. If he'd known back then... Too much there to think about now while he was debating his Saturday night plans with his strong-willed mother.

"Yes." He turned away, pretending to retrieve something from the floor near his feet, hoping the tightness in his throat didn't affect his voice. "Start there and see."

"Oh, I see things, young man." Mom's hand cupped his arm, drawing his attention to her. Looking up at him, her eyes lit. "I absolutely see things."

Heat crawled over his neck. "Sometimes, my intrusive mother, you see what you want."

"Hmm."

"And sometimes, my hopeful mother, you want what you can't have."

A grin slipped up one corner of her mouth. "Sometimes, my stubborn son, you have to simply mind your mother."

"That so?"

"Indeed it is. And this is one of those times. I want you to go to the pickers' picnic. Without the boys. I want you to run into that girl you used to blush about. I want you to unearth that charming boy you were with her and make her smile. And then if you've done all of the above satisfactorily, you may come home, and I may allow you to think that you are in charge around here once again."

He tried—truly and honestly—to give her a deadpan glare. But a laugh bubbled up instead, coming out as a sort of snort-chuckle that made her laugh as well. "Well, that is about the sum of it, isn't it?"

With a sassy wink, she nodded. "For today." Mom pushed both palms against the tabletop and then leveraged herself to stand—a sign of her depleted strength that made Craig's heart lower.

"Mom..."

"It's one night. You'll be fifteen minutes away. And it's good for the boys to take up some responsibility. Encourages that tender seed of manhood you've been sowing in them to sprout."

Craig watched while she straightened her back, walked to the sink, and began rinsing her dishes. Man, it hurt to see her in that scarf, her body thin, her gait slow. But also, man, he loved his mother. She was one strong, determined, love-hard woman, and those boys would be all the better for her pouring into their lives.

He certainly was.

"There's a Proverb about you, you know?" he said, following her to the sink with his own plate of cleaned-up eggs. "Her children will rise up and call her blessed."

Her small chuckle couldn't hide the fact that she blinked. Craig wrapped his arms around her bony shoulders and pulled her in as tight as he dared.

These women in his life. Tough and fragile. Hard to understand. Impossible to let go.

He spent the day reorganizing the garage, Trent and Ashton popping in to help for twenty minutes here and twenty minutes there. Their week had been full of testing, and they'd been faithful about chores and reading and bedtime through it. There were days—like that Saturday—when boys needed the freedom to be boys. To toss a ball in the backyard, and dig up earthworms, and climb the trees. So when they volunteered their services in bits and pieces on a day he'd given them that freedom, Craig's heart moved with pride. And love.

Which stirred anxiety.

He needed to check on the adoption process. Man, it took forever, and the silence in between was maddening.

As the warmth of the day melted, the sweat cooling against

his spine, the faint pull of a headache settled near the base of his skull. Tension had strained his jawline and shoulders, most of which had nothing to do with the work he'd been doing.

This stress. It wore on him, and he couldn't escape. Seemed every corner of his life had blurred into uncertainty, and nothing was left to his control. Tired from so much more than physical labor, Craig eased onto the step between the garage and the house.

He'd been reading through the Old Testament, and interestingly, his attention had snagged on Hannah in 1 Samuel. A woman who had known her God well enough to lift up her pain *and* her most treasured possession, trusting Him with both. A woman very much like his mother.

He had some pain and some treasures, and he wasn't able to lift up either. Not completely.

God, I'm not there yet. Please help me with this weak faith.

He wouldn't go to the vineyard. He'd tell Mom he had a headache, and hopefully she'd let it be. No one really expected him there anyway. Gripping the spot on his neck that tugged pain from his brain, he leaned against the door at his back and shut his eyes.

Brenna.

What was there between them? Things had shifted again, no longer walls of bitterness. Now, it seemed, there was rubble. There was her and him and broken pieces of them scattered in the space between, almost as impossible to wade through as seeing past that wall had been.

He guessed she felt the same, because he'd barely spoken to her that week. With the exception of Trent's two appointments, he'd have not spoken to her at all. How did that happen? How did you hold a woman while she shattered one night and not speak to her for the next six days? Answers didn't filter with any kind of clarity, but he'd guessed it had something to do with him being a coward. Again. Still too afraid of more conflict to deal with the conflict that had been.

Shouldn't seem like a conflict, should it? He'd let her down. Multiple times over. Own it, apologize, and hope for forgiveness. That was the formula, right?

Except, if he'd known back then what she'd told him last week, he wouldn't have left. He'd packed up and wandered like a homeless man for seven years because he had been certain she didn't want him in Big Prairie. Didn't want him anywhere near her and the heart he'd had a heavy hand in breaking. Everything from her cold silent treatment before Scottie's accident, when he'd come back home to try to mend things between them, to the furious stare she'd leveled on him after the graveside service, told him she wanted him gone. For good.

So he'd left.

Now, knowing she had wanted him—needed him—back then? Man, he was confused. Frustrated. One more misjudgment. One more bad decision that had taken him farther away from home and driven deeper hurt into the people he'd loved.

"Why?" He ground out the word into the emptiness, knowing answers were likely not going to fall from the sky.

Still. Why did everything have to fall apart the way it had? Why had he and Brenna gone from the couple everyone adored to the pair who could barely look at one another? Why had he chosen football—something he'd never envisioned as career until that awful year—over the girl he'd loved?

Why did God take Scottie in the middle of it all?

And why, seven years later, was all of it still so hard?

The phone in his back pocket buzzed. Craig sat forward to retrieve it, half hoping it was something that would give him a distraction. Score updates for the Big Ten. A weather notification. News from Rock Creek—maybe Joe White passing along another Sydney story that would definitely make him laugh, or Craig's cousin Paul sending him a picture of his growing son. Any of the above would have been perfect.

But it was a text from Brenna.

Are you going to the pickers' picnic tonight?

What on earth? She'd been silent all week. Well, he assumed she had been. He hadn't texted or called either, so...

Not sure.

The boys might like it.

That was a little nuts. It was an adult thing with the late-evening start and wine tasting and all.

Don't think they'll go.

Oh yeah. Of course. Sorry. Your mom mentioned that you were thinking about going. I assumed...

Fisting the phone, he pressed it against his forehead. Of course his mom had talked to Brenna. They'd have a chat about this. About the fact that he was nearly thirty and didn't need his mother arranging things for him. Yeah, that would happen, since he was so good at conflict.

A buzz vibrated near his hairline.

I was going to tell you that I'll be there, if you needed a hand with the boys.

They'd already established that the boys weren't going. Hadn't they?

Thanks anyway.

The little scroll dots rolled at the bottom. He waited. They kept scrolling. He braced himself for whatever was taking her so long to say. Finally, the phone vibrated again.

Craig?

That was it?

I'm still here.

I'm glad.

She was glad...glad for what? Brenna had been right—trying to wade through this friendship thing felt like drowning.

That you're here.

He stared at that final text, and the scroll dots beneath it disappeared. Conversation over. And he still felt lost at sea.

***

Brenna set the phone on the blue comforter on her bed, her mind whirling and heart dropping. Every day since last Friday, she'd hoped Craig would call. They needed to talk, didn't they? How could he not call her after she'd broken to pieces in his arms?

The text sound tweeted from her phone, and relief zipped through her. Finally, he was saying something.

Or not. Sophie. Not Craig.

Want to ride out with me?

Though frustrated and hurt, a smile pushed on her lips. Sophie was a keeper. Though Brenna had been distracted lately and probably seemed distant, Sophie kept it light. Kept her smiling. And this offer was sweet, because Brenna was pretty sure Sophie had a whole other reason for wanting to go to the picnic tonight than anyone else in town. That reason spent his days wearing a cowboy hat and tending grapes. And lately he'd been spotted hanging out around the high school marching band during football games.

No thanks. You might want to stay later than me.

What?

Brenna snorted. *Don't play innocent. I know you've been doing some solo dirt-road driving lately. Gotta be a reason that a city girl such as yourself has taken a liking to country roads. One road in particular.*

Huh.

Is that a denial kind of huh—which I won't believe—or is it a my-friend-is-insightful kind of huh?

Just huh.

Brenna shook her head. *Huh.*

You're coming though, right?

Planned on it. Had hoped that Craig would want to go too. Maybe even ride with her. Maybe they could actually talk like grown-up people without one of them having some kind of emotional outburst from which they either ended up hoppin' mad, liplocked, or sobbing.

Maybe that was just her.

The phone chirped again. *Good. We should catch up. Been a while.*

Brenna blinked against the sudden stab into her consciousness. When she got sucked into an emotional hole, she really got sucked in. *I agree. Miss my friend.*

Miss you too. Come find me, okay?

Gonna be with Lance?

Lance who?

Brenna rolled her eyes. *LOL. Not buying that, Sophie.*

So I'll look for the owner. Shouldn't be hard. He wears that cowboy hat and stands about a head taller than everyone.

Except Craig.

Ah. So you do know Lance Carson.

Dang. You're sneaky.

Small town.

Yeah. Speaking of which...

Oh no. That sounds foreboding.

Coming out with Craig?

The lightness that had eased the chaos in Brenna's mind evaporated. *No.*

Huh.

Please don't go there.

You never told me about the two of you. I wish I'd known.

I didn't think it mattered.

I wouldn't have gone out with him the few times I did if I'd known. Now I feel kind of dumb.

That's ridiculous. No reason to feel dumb. I was dating Grant. Craig and I broke up a long time ago.

You're not dating Grant now.

A sigh rolled over Brenna, sagging her posture.

Another text from Sophie chirped. *Sorry. I'll mind my own business.*

Don't say that. Brenna paused, staring across the room. Goodness, she was really bad at relationships in general. How come no one told her so before?

You there? she typed.

Yes.

I'm sorry I didn't tell you. It's kind of messy, and I tried to forget most of it.

I'm guessing that didn't work.

No.

Maybe that's a good thing?

I don't know. It's still pretty complicated.

I'm sorry.

Thanks. Can I ask you something?

Sure.

Brenna flopped backward on the bed. *Do you think we're stuck living with our regrets forever?*

Like you regret breaking up with Craig?

I didn't break up with him.

Oh.

Nothing else surfaced on Brenna's screen for several long moments, giving Brenna time to soak in that question. The conversations with Miss Jane and then with her dad from so many weeks ago kept resurfacing in her mind.

She thought she'd been repentant. Had asked God to forgive her for the things that made shame run hot through her veins. Where was the freedom?

Craig looks at you like he has regrets.

Brenna read the text, and it only bundled up more anxiety. Thing was, she wasn't talking about Craig's regrets. She really couldn't do anything about them on his behalf.

Except forgive him for breaking her heart. Like he'd asked her to.

Didn't know you could see that in him, Brenna typed.

Only in select moments. Like at the game a couple of weeks ago, when you were talking with Grant.

He'd gotten frustrated with her pretty easily that night. Had he been wading through regrets?

Can I tell you something, Brenna? As your friend?

Always.

You never looked at Grant the way you do at Craig when you think no one sees.

Great. She gripped her phone and squeezed her eyes shut. That was sure to keep her up with more guilt.

The text chirped again. *Maybe the only way to deal with the regret is to talk to him about it.*

Sounded like something Grant would say. And she should probably listen. Grant cared about her and was an expert. Sophie was her best friend. Not to mention, Dad had told her something similar. Good reasons to pay attention.

Thing was, she'd been trying. It was hard though. There were layers there—a lot of them—and getting through each one was like holding her head underwater. It'd been a week since the last time she'd gone under.

That was a long time to hold her breath.

The phone in her fist chirped one last time. This time, though, it was Craig.

If you're going still, can I catch a ride?

Air. Brenna dragged in a long, deep breath of air. Who knew when she'd get to take in another.

Chapter Twenty-Eight

HOW COULD A SIMPLE COUNTRY DRIVE TWIST HIS NERVES—NOT
TO MENTION HIS GUT—INTO A TANGLE OF KNOTS?

Not like he'd never been alone in a car with Brenna Blaum.

From the moment he'd sent that *I'll ride out with you* text,
the churning in his gut made him doubt his ability to make
good choices. The silence smothering the inside of the car only
made the heartburn worse.

They'd started out with the normal social niceties.

Hey.

Hi. Thanks for the ride.

Sure, no problem. Glad you're going.

Yeah. He wasn't glad. Hated this kind of awkward and
would have preferred peeling gum off the football bleachers
than being stuck with the feeling of being an idiot.

So...have a good week?

Survived. Boys did well this week, so that's good. You?

Uh, sure.

And that was where the conversation hit a brick wall. If her
pressed lips and her grip on the steering wheel were an
indication, Brenna was wrestling with her own anxiety about

this little excursion together too. They were both apparently addicted to emotional punishment, because here they were again.

Maybe it was time to step up. Be the first one to start wading through the slime that oozed between them. Trying to ignore it wasn't getting either of them anywhere.

"So listen." His voice cracked like he was sixteen. Awesome. He cleared his throat before he tried again. "This week was...uh...well, I...I should have called you."

Her mouth twisted to the side, a look that said she wasn't sure what to say but was irritated at him. "Yeah. I guess maybe Friday night was too much. I should apologize."

"No." Actually, yes, Friday night had been heavy and more than he thought he could handle, but that wasn't her fault. Processing everything—their past, the grief that had welled up like a tidal wave, realizing he'd failed her more than he'd thought, which had already been quite a lot—and still trying to figure out this new life teaching full-time, taking care of his mom and the boys, and wading through a child welfare system that seemed more complex than sending a man into space... Not to mention the building pressure from the rumor about him and the football team that had spread through town like the flu.

Should he tell her all of that?

"Brenna, the thing is, I'm really bad at this."

"At talking?"

"Uh, maybe. Yeah. I just...I don't know what to say or do when things get hard. It's not that I don't want to say something. It's that I don't know what or how. But I should have called you."

"Yes. You should have." A bite snipped her words. "I thought..." She sighed as she turned off the highway and onto the dirt road to the vineyard.

Something twisted near his heart, and he reached across the

space to brush the length of her arm. When she glanced at him, he saw vulnerability and pain. His doing, again.

"Can you pull over?" he said.

After a breath, she nodded and guided her little Versa toward the ditch.

They were on the path to a fairly large gathering. The pickers' picnic—a slight misnomer because it didn't actually involve any picking—had grown to be an anticipated and well-attended event in Big Prairie. Big enough that even he knew about it after a seven-year absence. Likely, someone would be by within minutes. Given the nature of their community, they'd stop to make sure the car on the side of the road and the people within were okay. They weren't, actually— but not because of a vehicle problem.

Man, he had such bad timing.

He turned, burrowing his shoulder into the seatback and reached to trace her arm again. "I'm sorry, Brenna. For so many things, I'm sorry."

"Why didn't you call me this week? Gosh, Craig, I spent every day growing more miserable than the last, thinking you were appalled at me or something."

Nodding, he looked at the gearshift while waves of guilt rolled hard and fast over him. "I'm sorry. I didn't know what to do. Everything feels overwhelming—and not only the stuff between you and me. My mom. The boys. This...football situation I didn't ask for but can't seem to shake free. All of it."

"I get that. But just talk to me." She twisted in the seat to face him. "Why is that so hard? We dated for five years. You should be able to do that, don't you think?"

Staring at his knees, he nodded. He raised his face to meet her eyes. "Here's the thing—I've spent the past seven years believing that you hated me. Seriously thinking that I was dead to you. Do you know how that feels, Brenna? To think that someone you cared deeply about has decided that to them you may as well be dead?"

"Dead to me? Why? What does that even mean?"

"Seven years ago I came home that January to see if we could mend things. To apologize. I walked away from that sports agent, ignored the advice of my coaches, and came home so I could see you. Do you remember what you did?"

She sagged against the seat, looked toward her hands twisting in her lap. And said nothing.

"This. This is what you did. You shut me out. Completely ignored me. Every time I approached you, you gave me your back. Every text I sent, message I left, you returned with icy silence."

"So this week was payback?"

"No." Craig raked a hand through his hair and blew out a frustrated breath. "This week was me being stupid. Again. And overwhelmed. Me not knowing what to do or say or being too...scared of what might happen if I said the wrong thing. So I did nothing." He rolled a fist, focusing the tension building in his shoulders into that clench, and then splayed his fingers over his jeans. "I did nothing, and I'm sorry."

The road rumbled behind them, and a white pickup trailed by a dusty cloud eased around Brenna's car. As predicted, the taillights lit, and the driver came to a stop twenty feet ahead.

Brenna flashed a look of panic at him, and he covered her shoulder with his palm. When the man walked through the billow of white dust, the pinch in Craig's gut squeezed tighter.

Grant Hillman stopped at her window and bent while Brenna lowered the glass.

"I thought this was your car." Grant glanced at Craig and then refocused on Brenna. "Everything okay?"

"Yes, thanks. Needed to take a phone call, is all." Red crawled up the side of her neck as she lied to her ex-boyfriend.

"I see." Grant held a measured look on her, and then his attention slid back to Craig. "So you are good?"

So many ways to take that comment. For almost all of them, the honest answer would be *no*. They weren't good. But there was nothing wrong with their vehicle.

"Yes, everything's fine." Brenna worked up a grin. "We'll follow right behind you."

Grant was slow in straightening, and Craig wondered if he could tell Brenna's faking-fine smile from her real one. As the man strode back to his pickup, Craig sagged into his seat.

"Sorry for that, too," he muttered.

Brenna cleared her throat and shifted into Drive. "I'll live."

"I'd rather you be happy."

The car eased back onto the road as they followed Grant.

"Right now I'd be happy to breathe."

Craig squeezed his eyes shut, feeling an acute stab at the base of his head. *The tension headache strikes again.* "Maybe I shouldn't have come."

"Maybe we should try being honest."

He rolled his head and looked at her profile. "I thought that's what we were doing. Feels like it's making things worse."

The gravel popped and crunched under the tires as the final mile rolled beneath them. Once again Craig shot up a series of *whys*. Why did God force him back to Big Prairie? Why couldn't he and Brenna figure out how to communicate without frustrating each other? Why didn't Brenna marry Grant so they could both move on?

Why did that thought make him want to puke?

One of those questions had a clear answer. The same answer to the question of why he hadn't had a serious relationship with another woman in the seven years since they'd broken up. Wasn't ready to really examine that yet though.

Brenna guided her car to the spot next to where Grant had parked. The evening was sure to get more uncomfortable, as Grant had come alone and more than likely would wait for Brenna and Craig before he walked toward the Overlook

Lodge. She shifted into Park and cut the engine, then rested both hands on top of her steering wheel.

"Some things have to get worse before they get better," she said, her focus on the windshield.

"What's that?"

"My dad used to say that. Sometimes things don't get better until you deal with the ugly parts. Clean up the mess."

"Oh." Craig leaned forward, glancing toward Brenna, then catching a glimpse of Grant looking toward their car, running a hand over his head and then turning away.

Poor man. Craig couldn't help but feel bad. This time last year, Craig would have bet Grant saw his life looking a whole lot different than it did right now.

"I'm giving you permission to be honest with me, Craig."

He found Brenna watching him, wondered if she knew what he'd been looking at and thinking.

"I want you to keep being honest," she said. "Even if it makes things worse for the moment. It's got to get better, right?"

"This friendship thing is not getting easier."

"No. Not yet. But maybe it will."

On an impulse he probably should have disciplined, he reached across the space until the pad of his fingers skimmed the line of her jaw. Unexpectedly, her eyes drifted closed, and her mouth eased into a soft curve.

Those lips... He'd known them well long ago. Had never tired of their softness or the way he felt both alive and completely captive to her when those lips moved against his.

Friends. We were working on a friendship.

Why couldn't he keep himself in check? Remembering the impulsive and passionate kiss they'd shared not much more than a month before at the homecoming dance sent a flash of heat down his spine.

When it came to Brenna, keeping himself in check had been an area of devastating failure. Something that, even with the long space of time between them, was clearly still a weakness.

He sat back, lowering his hand, breaking contact. Her eyes fluttered open, meeting his gaze and holding. And then her hand closed over his.

How honest, exactly, did she want him to be?

Chapter Twenty-Nine

BRENNA SAW HER FRIEND FROM HER PERCH ON THE OVERLOOK LODGE'S DECK.

Well, to be more exact, she spotted Lance Carson standing in one of the rows of vines, his white cane cowboy hat poking up above the crowd. It'd taken only a slide of Brenna's view to Lance's left to spot Sophie, her ringlet hair glossy and beautiful, cascading over her shoulders in a stunning contrast to her white tunic.

Didn't that pair look happy? And maybe a little bit perfect together, as Sophie grinned up at him, and as Brenna caught the advantage of his profile, Lance looked down at Sophie like she was the best thing ever to wander through his increasingly popular vineyard. If Brenna was any judge of men at all, that good-looking cowboy-turned-vineyard-owner was falling in love with her best friend.

How had that happened, and Brenna was just now seeing it?

She hadn't meant to neglect Sophie. Hadn't meant to be so taken by the undertow of Craig's return to Big Prairie. In fact, her plan had been to avoid him at all costs.

Making him feel, once again, that he was dead to her.

How awful. Never, not once, had she thought about it that way. That treating someone who had once been such a massive part of her everyday life as if they didn't exist anymore would be like telling them *You're dead to me.*

That was wrong. So wrong. Almost like...murder. Was that what Jesus had meant when he'd equated hate to murder?

Add it to the list of wrongs she'd done him. She was tired of living with it all.

God, I really need this emptied from my cup.

She and Craig should have stayed in the car. Turned around and headed toward their spot on the river—to the swimming hole—where no one would interrupt. No, not there. Not where she'd watched him teach Scottie to swim and had experienced for the first time the dizzying power of Craig's mouth against hers.

But the football field... Where it all began. And where it had ended. They could have gone, sat in those bleachers, and ripped off the soured bandage of time and regret. She could have poured out her remorse, and maybe he would too.

Didn't happen that way though. Jeremiah Colts and his wife had parked beside them, the pop of their car doors slamming, drawing Craig's attention. As he'd freed his hand from her grip, Craig flashed her a look that she wasn't sure she knew how to read and then exited the vehicle. Stat.

Maybe for the best. Truth be told, when he'd brushed her face, all tenderness in his touch, he'd relit some longings. When it came to her and Craig, if she was honest, talking wasn't the only thing that had entered her mind.

That might be too honest. And definitely wouldn't be helpful, not when they were still figuring out the landmines they'd scattered in the past, trying a go at being friends.

So there they were, at River's Edge Vineyard. As friends.

Actually, Craig had sort of disappeared on her. Probably to breathe. Heaven knew she needed some air too. Hopefully, it would help her think straight when she drove him home later that night.

"Brenna my sweet." Miss Jane's fingers, slim, wrinkled, yet strong, slipped into Brenna's hand. "How is my lovely girl?"

Warmth enveloped her heart as she turned a smile down to Miss Jane. "I am better now that you're here with me."

"Things are always easier to face with someone else. Two are better than one, yes?"

"I think that's how it goes." This woman. Yoda in a lovely old-lady's body. Her long gray-white hair was swept back into a girlish French braid—as it often was—and her eyes danced with a sort of secret joy that somehow always made Brenna think of Jesus.

"Do you know, I was thinking the other day that you and I need to redefine our relationship."

Brenna laughed. "That sounds serious."

"It is. And here are my terms. I think you need family in this town. And since I am an independent woman and always have been, I believe I need you."

"Me?"

"Yes, you. I am officially asking you to be my granddaughter. Of the heart, of course."

Heat rimmed her eyelids, and Brenna gathered Miss Jane in a hug. "You want me?"

"Well, isn't that what I said?"

"I would love that, Miss Jane."

"Then it's settled."

"Can I still call you Miss Jane?"

"Of course. And you must visit me. At least once a week. And you must tell me what I can pray over you about. And if there are any needs—money, or counsel, or anything—I will be utterly offended if you choose not to tell me."

Hands now clasped with Miss Jane's, Brenna nodded. "Understood."

"Good. There are some perks."

"I thought those were the perks."

Miss Jane swatted the air between them. "No, child. Real perks. Like I will show you how to make my sunset jam. The recipe is a family secret."

"How thrilling. When do we start?"

"As soon as you join me in my kitchen. Next week?"

"Let's do it."

"And now..."

Uh-oh. Brenna's end of the deal.

"And now you'll want to know about Craig?"

"Why would you say that?"

"Because he came with me, and now I'm standing here alone?"

"Well, that is news to me, Brenna my sweet. Interesting, but not what I was going to say."

"Oh." Warmth dusted her face.

Miss Jane led them down the walking path toward an empty round table where they could sit overlooking a view of both the river and the vineyard. "I was going to say, 'And now for the grapes,' but I like your idea better. Do tell."

Brenna slipped onto the bench nearest Miss Jane, her hands sliding over the smooth wood of beetle kill pine that had been varnished to a gleam. "Do you remember the story you told me a few weeks back? And what you said about regret?"

"I do." Miss Jane kept a steady, gentle look on her.

"I keep thinking on that. And, well, the thing is, I've been trying. With Craig, I've been trying to free up those regrets so that maybe both of us can move forward in freedom."

"How is that going?"

"Hard. Badly. I don't know exactly why."

"Hmm." Miss Jane's eyes lifted, scanning the view behind Brenna. Certainly it was a lovely view, with Lance's rows of neatly maintained vines, the stand of trees at the opposite end of his field, and the colorful display of the lowering sun as a backdrop. "This place, it's so wonderful, isn't it?" A soft smile set off the best of Miss Jane's well-earned wrinkles. "But I remember young Lance doing the work. Years of preparation even before he sank the first roots into the ground. And then after several more years of tending, pruning, hoping, praying. All of them fruitless at the time. We outsiders think this vineyard is six or seven years old. Truth is, Lance has over a dozen years put into those fields, and he is only recently benefiting from the harvest."

Brenna listened, following the story, searching for the threads of wisdom that were woven into Miss Jane's tale.

"Brenna, there is beauty in the hard places. Don't miss the breathtaking wonder because you are too afraid to go through the painful work of getting there."

Biting her lip, Brenna blinked. "I *am* afraid, but also, I don't know how to do it. How do I break free of something that seems complicated and unclear?"

"Is it that complicated?"

Yes, Brenna wanted to say. Yes, the things that broke her and Craig were many and complicated.

"Sometimes," Miss Jane said, "it's easier to pin the blame on something that won't argue with you than to be honest about your own failures. Sometimes we want to call something complicated when actually the truth is, that complicated something is simply ourselves."

Oh. The words stung as they hit the sore part of truth. Looking to the gleaming tabletop, Brenna winced.

Ever the gentle woman, even when being bluntly honest, Miss Jane's warm hand soothed as she covered Brenna's. "Do the hard things, Brenna my sweet. Be honest and forgive."

After a long draw of fresh evening air, several blinks, and a squeeze of the aged hand that held hers, Brenna looked up and nodded. "You'll pray for me?"

"Always."

"Then I think I should call you Grandma Jane."

"That would be my favorite thing ever."

***

"Well, there he is after all." Wes clapped a massive hand around Craig's and pumped his arm while slapping the opposite shoulder. "Glad to see you changed your mind."

Craig returned the handshake. "I'm a little surprised to see you here. Thought you were mad at Lance."

"Not about to miss this town gathering, no mind the matter of things. And besides, I can keep an eye out on the doings and an ear to the developments."

"Ah." With a lift of his brow, Craig studied his old boss. "What if it's all just a rumor? What if you're all stirred up about nothing?"

"Doubt it."

"Huh."

"Speaking of rumors..."

Craig crossed his arms and sighed. "Think we've had this talk before."

"I think you need to think about it. Brent Blaum would be mighty proud to have one of his own boys carrying on his legacy. And you, you're like a son to him."

Knife in chest.

"My hands are pretty full these days, Wes." Craig tried—maybe not successfully—to keep the bite out of his voice. "And I don't even have a coaching endorsement."

"Don't need one. Not in this state."

Man, they'd been over this before. Why couldn't they all let this go? Like a dog on a bone, gnawing away at something already dead. Craig closed his mouth, his lips sealing tight.

Wes held up his hands, took a step back. "Okay, son. Okay.

I'm sorry. It's your decision."

Well, thanks for that. Craig drew in a slow breath.

"Look, don't hold it against me, okay?"

Despite the irritation, Craig felt a smile tickle his lips. Couldn't stay mad at Wes. "Deal."

"Good. And you'll bring those boys in for ice cream soon?"

"You know it."

"And you'll let me know if you hear anything about that franchise?"

"Not making that promise." Craig scanned the milling crowd of almost all the adult population of Big Prairie, seeking a white cane cowboy hat on a man who equaled his own height. Finding it, he also spotted Sophie, and he smiled in earnest. He looked back at Wes. "Lance is right over there, buddy." With a quick gesture, he pointed toward the vineyard. "Maybe a conversation would clear this whole thing up right now."

"Huh." Wes grunted. "Look at that. My lovely wife is over there, and I think she's looking for me."

Craig followed the extended path Wes had already begun to scurry down, finding that, yes, Jaycee was standing there. Not looking for Wes at all while she chatted among three other women. He couldn't help a quiet chuckle.

Seemed every man had a bit of a chicken hiding within.

Under the shade of his hat bill, he scanned the activity moving through River's Edge Vineyard. Lance had made quite a deal out there in a field that had once been used for corn and soybeans. Straight, beautifully kept rows of vines waved softly in the evening breeze. Every other row had tall posts, which he'd heard were actually for fans or something that would help with late frosts or early frosts or something that had to do with frost. Craig wasn't sure. But at the moment, those tall posts supported café lights, strung with precision over the vineyard in graceful inverted arcs that danced above the green vines and milling people.

The lodge, newly built within the past three years, was a massive cabin-style building, windows covering more surface than the logs, and the oversized French double doors currently blocked open for people to easily move between indoors and out. Round tables, handcrafted from beetle kill pine and varnished to a shine, scattered on the expansive deck that stretched toward the vineyard and the river beyond it. More tables salted the borders of the walking path that wound from the lodge, to the vines, around the field, through the trees, and to the bank of the river.

The transformation from a common field to this tourist hot spot was impressive. Craig made a mental note to tell Lance. But for the moment, that path through the trees beckoned, and given that he'd already had two other brief conversations about coaching football besides the one he'd had with Wes, he was up for a few moments on his own.

Since the vineyard—the grapes and the food—were the main attraction, once he wandered several yards away from them, the friendly chatter became lost in the breeze, and the smell of cool water cleared his head. He followed the meandering trail until it dumped into a beach. Probably the Carsons' old swimming hole. He could picture Lance and his brother, Lane—a year younger than Craig—spending hot July afternoons in that very spot. Stopping near the waterline, Craig rocked back on his heels as he closed his eyes.

You still have me, right? he prayed.

The playful toying of a breeze through what remained of leaves in the canopy above him was the only response. That was okay. This moment of peace was something. More than what he'd had all week, and he was grateful.

"It has been an interesting homecoming for you, hasn't it?"

The voice behind Craig was low, kind, and forced his spine straight. As much as Grant Hillman was nice, he was also direct. That last part being exactly Craig's opposite, and maybe if Craig had some of Grant's ability to deal with uncomfortable situations in a non-passive yet non-conflict-bearing way, maybe his life would have been smoother.

All of that, while something to consider later, hadn't any bearing on the moment. And in any case, Craig's gut twisted as he glanced to his left. Grant stepped beside him on the shoreline, the field of grapes at their back and the lowering sun beyond the tree line.

"I imagine nothing about coming back was easy for you," Grant said, his face pointed toward the trees and the sky beyond.

"No," Craig said. "No, nothing about coming back has been easy. Honestly, Grant, I didn't plan on any of this." He didn't doubt that Grant understood the double meaning.

Grant shoved his hands into his pockets and nodded. "I know that, Craig. And like I said, I know that it could not have been easy for you. I do wonder, though, if it is getting better?"

Craig studied his profile for a moment. Decided that the direct route might be the best. "Well, that depends on how you define better. Brenna isn't giving me the silent treatment anymore. So that's better. But she and I still have some hard conversations ahead of us."

"I'm glad she decided to have those conversations with you," Grant said. "She has been needing to work through some things for quite a while."

"I kind of thought she would have worked through some of them with you."

Grant chuckled—the sad sort of *I'm sorry and I wish* chuckle. "Brenna assumed that I was always trying to figure her out. That I was always trying to be her counselor, trying to analyze what she was thinking, what she had been through, or why she is who she is." He sighed. "She needed to work out whatever she was battling with the people she was battling with. That was not me." He turned a lifted brow toward Craig.

"Me?"

"Apparently. Since she could hardly look at you without seething." Again, Grant passed a glance at him. "That seems to have changed."

Craig shrugged, battling the discomfort that begged him to pivot and walk away. "Like I said, we're working through some things. It's hard. We weren't very good at working out differences even before everything went south. In the years that we dated, in the beginning we really didn't have any differences, and in the end, we were too scared to deal with them."

"I think that happens a lot. People would rather think that their problems will disappear if they do not mess with them than to go do the hard work."

"I guess you could say that I am the passive type. I didn't really understand that until now. And it's kind of cowardly of me. I'm not proud of it."

"Maybe we have to know ourselves before we can let somebody else truly know us." He paused, kicked a stone that had been lodged into the silt mud until it came free, and then stooped to pick it up. "But then again I do not know." The stone sailed low over the water, touching it, jumping, touching it again, skipping, and then sinking beneath the surface. "I am just a single guy out here avoiding the crowd. Just like you."

Grant turned a wry grin at him, and Craig chuckled. Suddenly the unease morphed into something more comfortable. A couple of guys out skipping stones.

"I guess that makes us an interesting pair, doesn't it?" Craig loosened a stone of his own and sent it over the river with a side-arm fling.

"I hope that means that despite what happened between you and Brenna, and me and Brenna, and now you and Brenna again, that we can live in this small town and not be enemies."

Craig dusted the damp earth of his fingers. "Since I'm the one who came back and ruined your life, I'd say that's big of you."

"I do not know that I would say you ruined it. Maybe you made me see what I did not want to see. Maybe that is for the best."

"Are you always this optimistic?"

Grant chuckled again. "One of my more irritating qualities, I guess."

"So since we're standing here in all this awkwardness, can I ask you something else?"

Grant shrugged, his gaze once again drifting back to the treetops. "I cannot promise that I will answer, but you can ask."

"How long after Scottie's accident was it before you came home?"

"I was finishing school and then some practicums. About three years maybe."

"I see."

"Not the question I was expecting."

"Yeah, I know." Craig lifted his hat, let the breeze dance through his hair for a moment, and resettled it on his head. "Brenna said one of the reasons she was mad at me was that I had left her alone to deal with the grief." He inhaled, dug up some courage to keep talking. "I thought she didn't want me here. For a while I thought she blamed me. And then, well then I thought she hated me. But she said that she'd felt completely alone. I guess that surprised me, given who her father is, what he was to this town. Given how much everyone around here loved Scottie and the rest of the family."

Grant waited, ever the listener. When Craig didn't continue—because he didn't really know how to ask what he was asking, Grant nodded.

"I was not here to see it, so I cannot say. But it is not

uncommon for a person to experience a deep loneliness after a sibling's death. It is rather a unique kind of grief. Not only did that person lose someone they loved, but very often they lose their parents for a time too. We worry about the grieving parents, and sometimes the surviving children get lost."

Craig crossed his arms, an instinct to protect his heart as he let this information sink in. He should have known...

"Craig," Grant turned, faced him for the first time in the conversation. "You and Brenna... Maybe you both think that you should be able to move on in life. From this grief—this ache that is both about Scottie and about the two of you. But that is a misconception. You move forward, but you do not move on. You do not get over it. You do not just forget the people you have loved because things have changed."

Moving forward. That was what he'd wanted. Wished for when he'd been a traveling music teacher looking for another place to begin again. That had been his attempt at moving forward, hadn't it?

Always, in every place, it was like a wall stood in front of him, blocking his way out.

The scuffle of dirt and rocks snagged his attention, and he realized he'd been hiding under the bill of his hat, staring at his feet. Grant stepped forward as Craig brought his eyes up, and with an outstretched hand, offered yet again a friendship Craig was certain was difficult for Grant and undeserved by himself. Gratitude moved in his heart as he accepted the handshake.

"And on other topics, for the record, even though I do not think you want to hear this, I think the school board is right. You are the guy for the job."

Football? Really? Grant cared even about that?

But Craig could hardly spit out a reprimand, as he had done with Wes earlier. Not in the face of Grant's enormous kindness toward him.

"I'll keep that in mind." Craig kind of wished he didn't mean it.

Chapter Thirty

SHE DROVE TOWARD HIS HOUSE, THE SILENCE BETWEEN THEM NOT TENSE BUT NOT COMFORTABLE EITHER.

"It's the talk, isn't it?" she finally asked.

He pulled his stare from the window toward her. "What's that?"

"The reason you've been distant. It's this chatter going on about you coaching."

Tension drained from his shoulders, and he sank into the seat. "Some of it, yeah."

"Are you going to apply?"

"No."

"Why?"

He pinned a look on her he was sure she understood to be *don't ask, because you already know why.* They had, after all, had this conversation before.

Lips pursed, she stared ahead. "Did you know Sophie and Lance were dating?"

"I had an inkling."

"You did?"

"Yeah. She got stuck in the mud out that way a few weeks

back. He rescued her. Sounds like the makings of romance, don't you think?"

Her breathy chuckle loosened the remaining tension. "If looks aren't lying, I'd say that cowboy is smitten."

"Can't argue that. And Sophie seems happy. Then again, she's always happy."

Brenna gave him a quick side glance. "Does that bother you?"

"That Sophie is happy? No. It's one of the reasons I like her. Happy people are nice."

This time her glance was more of an eye roll than anything else. "That's not what I meant. You dated her."

"That's a bit of an exaggeration. We went out a few times." Same story that had been repeating for years.

"And?"

"And agreed we were good as friends. The end."

"Hmm."

They rolled up to his house, and she turned into his driveway. She shifted into Park but then sat there, eyes focused on the garage door. Though he probably should have thanked her for the ride and exited the car, he sat there as well, wondering what he was waiting for but willing to simply sit with her in silence.

Finally she turned to him, her blue eyes pleading. "Are we friends, Craig?"

"I want to be." That wasn't completely true. Man, those eyes. That wide-open, vulnerable look. Those freckles splayed perfectly across her nose and cheeks. Those lips...

He forced his attention back to her eyes.

"Craig, I need to say some things."

"Okay."

"Can we go somewhere? To talk?"

"Yeah. Let me go in and check on Mom and the boys, okay?"

The slight part of her lips closed—and why did he keep looking at them?—and she nodded.

A quick check in the house and he found the boys were asleep, and Mom was nearly out too, a rerun of *Matlock* playing on her TV. He told her he'd be gone a bit longer but would be back soon. With sleepy-glazed eyes, Mom nodded.

"There's fresh tea in the fridge," she said.

He filled two metal mugs and took them to Brenna's car. Without a word, she drove toward the stadium. He'd have preferred to go to the river—but maybe there were too many memories there. Maybe Brenna had been wise, picking the deserted football field instead. After they both exited the car, he handed her a mug of tea and followed her into the stands.

As they settled on a bench midway up the stands, the night became a soft quilt around them, the last vestiges of the long-lasting prairie sunset a faint streak of light gray on the western horizon. No longer did crickets provide the background music, as the first hard frost two nights before had left near silence for their meeting. Craig inhaled the chilled air, wondering about the winter to come. Would it be a hard one—full of wind and snow?

And loneliness.

He'd grown tired of loneliness. Tired of always looking for a way to move forward but never finding an opening, always longing for home.

The thing was, when he'd thought about Brenna Blaum, he'd been more than willing to own that he'd loved her. In the past. Back when everything hadn't yet broken, they hadn't yet tasted the bitterness of a relationship gone bad. He'd even been willing to admit that she still stirred a longing in him—but had been more apt to credit memories than current reality for that response.

But sitting there in the blanket of night with her by his side...

The thing was, he still loved her. Hadn't ever stopped.

"We were being honest, right?" Her sudden break into the stillness, and his silent revelation, jarred him.

"Honest?" Was she...did she know? Was she daring him to say what maybe she already knew?

"Yes." Her intake of air rattled as she wrapped one arm around her stomach. "We said we'd be honest. About the past. About what happened between us." Her glance at his face seemed almost frightened. "Did you mean it?"

"Yeah."

Silence. Unease replaced the comfortable part of the night as he tried to imagine what he would say—how could he possibly tell her that after all this time and all the wreckage, that he still loved her and wanted desperately for her to find a way to—

"I was ashamed."

Once again, her voice, her words shattered his thoughts.

***

"I was so ashamed." Her voice cracked as she rolled her fingers into fists. It was a fruitless attempt at control. Tears leaked over her eyelids. "I was ashamed when you broke up with me—even before that—because of the girl I'd become. That's why I've been so angry. It wasn't all at you. I was mad at me because I was ashamed."

Brenna forced herself to meet those penetrating blue eyes. "After those interviews, you were getting so much attention. It was like I suddenly had panoramic vision. When we were apart, all I could focus on were the social media posts, the suggestive—and maybe well-beyond suggestive—comments from other girls about how...how they wanted you. When I was with you, all I could see were the flirty smiles, the glances filled with longing."

Craig sat back, offense clear in his posture. "From me?"

"No. At you."

His chest moved with a long breath, and some of the anger drained from his eyes.

Cool air stirred trees across the field, making their silhouettes dance against the darkening gray sky. Brenna breathed in, hoping courage drifted in the air. "I thought you were losing interest in me. That you saw all those other willing options and—"

He turned, leaving her with his profile, which was twisted with pain and with guilt. After a stretch of quiet, he nodded.

Wrapping her arms around herself, she huddled against that festering pain.

The mug of tea was lifted from her fingers and then those arms, familiar in their strength and tenderness, surrounded her. She buried into the shelter, surprised to discover it was exactly where she'd wanted to be all along.

"I *am* ashamed," she whispered into his chest.

He curled her in closer, and his voice, hushed and soaked with emotion, spoke near her ear. "Me too."

***

She stayed there against him, her tears known to him only because of the wetness seeping through his shirt and the movement of her shoulders. Craig lay his cheek against her hair as he shut his eyes. The past lay behind his eyelids, those moments he wished he'd been better. Done better.

Brenna had been honest, something that she hadn't been willing to be back then. The least he could do was take up that same courage.

"Brenna."

Though she clutched his T-shirt, she pulled away from him, shaking her head. "You don't need to apologize. Craig, I knew what I was doing back then."

Again, he squeezed his eyes shut as the memory of that night—the first time they'd gone too far—blew through his mind, sending fire through his veins and over his skin. He'd known better. Had even tried to stop. Once. But when her fingers had traced a blazing path across the bare skin of his chest and then his stomach, desire had exploded.

She'll be my wife, he'd thought. Which meant he was nothing like the man who had fathered him. And that was good enough for that moment.

Later, when she could barely look at him and he'd tried to apologize, she'd gotten up to leave.

"Brenna, wait. I'm—"

She'd spun into him. Woven her fingers through his hair, then took his lips with hers. The kiss was...sultry?

"Just remember how much I love you, Craig."

In the darkness, she'd moved away. "Brenna, I know you love me—and not because of this."

He'd known something wasn't right. That wasn't Brenna. Brenna was a rule keeper—but more than that, she was sweet. Pure.

That sultry woman? Not her.

Something had been wrong. For months that knowledge had chased itself through his mind. But every time he'd attempted to talk to her about it, she'd closed up. Meanwhile, *just once* turned into *just this one more time*. Again. And again.

Things between had not gotten better. Resentment and mistrust took root. Craig had felt out of control. And he couldn't get his mind or his heart to function on anything correctly. Every part of his life unraveled.

He and Brenna needed a break. No, more accurately put, he needed a break. He could hardly think let alone breathe, and his university coach had to be right. The thing that was spiraling him out of control was the relationship between him and Brenna.

He loved her. But he couldn't deal with her right then, when she was being off and he was being irresponsible.

After I secure a place in the NFL, he'd told himself, *then we'll try again.*

Then he'd find the manhood to talk to her about whatever was going on that had turned her from confident to clingy. From sweet to sultry. They'd work it out and get on with the life they'd hoped for. That Hallmark-movie-perfect romance she'd dreamed about under the twinkle lights during Small Town Revival.

Seven years later, there they were. Both broken and lost. Bad decision after bad decision compounded by a tragedy no one saw coming, and there they were. Finally dealing with it.

"Brenna, I knew." He leaned back, hands on her shoulders. "Maybe I didn't understand all of it, but I knew something was going on with you. And I didn't deal with it. I kept hoping it would go away."

She looked down at her hands twisting in her lap. With a sniff, she nodded.

"I'm so sorry, Brenna." His voice broke.

With a small lift of her chin, she peeked at him. "We were young."

He shook his head. "No. That wasn't why. I was weak, and I didn't want to deal with conflict. Being the popular guy most of my life meant that really, I never had to before. But for the record, Brenna, I loved you. When you told me there was a baby, my panic wasn't because I didn't want to be with you. I did. I wanted forever with you—and truthfully, the idea of a baby was a little exciting. But you had things you wanted to do. Goals and dreams within your grasp. I felt like I'd stolen them. Ruined your future—because I'd been a weak man. A man like the one who had left my mom alone and pregnant. Stealing your dreams for the Olympic trials made the guilt I was already struggling with worse."

Her chuckle was the sad sort. "Didn't matter anyway. I quit

running."

"I know." He brushed the line of freckles on her cheekbone with his thumb. "I don't know why."

"Scottie."

"He wouldn't have wanted you to quit. He loved watching you run almost as much as he loved football—and ice cream."

"I know." Her eyes met his and held. "I lost the love of it, and I couldn't do it anymore." She inhaled and grazed the length of his jaw with her fingertips. "He wouldn't have wanted you to quit either."

"I didn't quit football because of him." He'd quit because the thought of returning to something he'd let become too important—more important than the people he'd loved—made him feel sick.

Her hand fell away, and after a moment, so did her gaze, and she nodded. "I think I knew that too." She blinked, and a tear rolled over her cheek. "How could we have ruined each other the way we did?"

"I don't know," he whispered.

Sniffing, she straightened her posture and smudged the trail of her tear with the heel of her hand. "Is that why you won't talk about coaching?"

Her too then. He sighed.

"We're being honest."

Yeah, but...

He stared at the fifty-yard line below them, trying to figure out how to put words to something he wasn't quite sure of in his own mind. The only thing he knew for certain was that he was not Coach Blaum. Not even half the man Coach Blaum was, and this woman beside him—Coach's own daughter— knew that better than anyone.

"Something occurred to me tonight at the vineyard," Brenna said. "Miss Jane says it's easier to pin the blame on something that won't argue with you than to be honest about your own failures." She wrapped her arms around her shoulders. "You and me—we have both been trying to avoid the thing that we think was our undoing. The reason we fell as people and became someone we'd hoped not to be."

That sounded deep and, well, Grant-esque. Or yes, something Miss Jane would say, bless her wise, experienced heart. He fixed his attention on Brenna.

"I avoided you." She looked at him. "Named all of everything ugly between us your fault, but deep down I think I must have known that the shame I smeared you with was really my own."

"And me?" he whispered, not sure he was ready to hear it.

She nodded toward the field. "This. Football. And maybe even Big Prairie."

Something hard and thick swelled in his throat.

"I think Miss Jane is right. We are more willing to pin our failures on something outside of ourselves than we are to admit that it was us." Her voice broke again. "It was me, Craig, back then. I did things—desperate things—that I thought would make you stay with me. Even though I knew how you felt about sex—how you didn't want to be like the man who'd left your mother. Even though I should have trusted you to be the good man you'd always been. I manipulated you. It wasn't the video of you and Scottie, or the popularity you gained, or football. It was my own insecurity. I'm responsible for the things that I did to you. To us." Her small body quivered beside him, and she pulled in another shuddering breath. "And I'm sorry."

When he lifted his hand, he found he was trembling as well, and with as much gentleness that his billowing emotions would allow, he fingered the plane of her cheeks, cupped the side of her face. "It wasn't just you—not all your fault." He leaned, and when his forehead touched hers, she reached to grip his neck. "I wish I'd been a better man. I wish that I had ignored my coach's advice and married you, that I'd chosen us, not football."

"Craig." Her thumb rubbed the stubble on his cheek, catching the moisture of his tears. "It doesn't have to be a choice. That's what I'm trying to tell you now."

He sat back, searching her face, not understanding.

"You're afraid, I think, that if you go back into that world, you'll get mixed up again. That it will be your downfall all over. But what if you and I own that we made bad choices? Doesn't that leave room for the possibility that those things we've been avoiding—they were *good* things? We just messed them up."

"Okay, that's true, but I don't—"

"Craig, everyone is not wrong when they say you would do well as the head coach."

"They don't know—"

"They do know. They know that not only were you a good player, but you're a good man—not perfect, but good. More than that, they know—they see even now—how good you are with kids. And I think that they know that as much as you could teach them about the game on the field, you can teach them more about success off the field. Don't you know that's what made my dad great? It wasn't his winning record or the many trips to state he made. It was so much bigger than that."

He squeezed his eyes shut. She slid both palms along the sides of his face.

"He taught you to be men. Whether you were in your pads or street clothes. On the field or in the classroom. He showed you character, demanded respect and humility and hard work, and gave you the tools to live well. More than anything else, that's what the people want for their kids—for their program. And *that's* why they want you."

He shook his head as another tear rolled until it met her thumb. "What if I fail again?"

"You will." After a pause, she laughed. "Did you think you

were perfect?"

He chuckled too. "Clearly not."

Hands still trembling, he slid them up her back to her shoulders. "My mom, the boys. I don't think I can do it all alone."

"You won't have to." She leaned in until her nose brushed his.

His pulse ached as the headiness of her touch made the world a beautiful haze.

"I don't think we can be friends, Craig," she whispered.

"I need you to be my friend. My best friend."

She moved again, this time brushing her mouth across the top of his lip, causing his heart to throb with a reckless rhythm and beckoning the slightest groan from his throat.

"I want that too," she whispered.

The warm moisture of her breath grew the longing to know her mouth again, and he slid his fingers into her hair. "You do?"

"Yes. Forevermore, yes. And also..."

Her kiss was more than desire. It was promise. A new beginning. And a return.

"I love you, Craig."

His breath caught, and he had to swallow a lump of emotion before he could whisper a response. "I love you too, Brenna." He brushed at her tear wetting his thumb. "Never stopped. Never will."

Suddenly, and with his whole heart, he was very thankful that the God who mastered making the impossible possible had brought him back to Big Prairie.

Epilogue

CRAIG STOOD ON THE SIDELINES, HAND ON HIS NECK, TAKING IT IN.

On the overhead speakers, Justin Timberlake's "Can't Stop the Feeling" filled the evening air, setting many of the fans still in the stands in motion, as well as all the players and students on the field.

The season had been a success, and now...

State playoffs.

Unbelievable. He couldn't stop the movements of his shoulders, the bounce in his feet as he bopped his way across the field, high-fiving players, band members, cheerleaders, and every other student who wiggled across his path.

Last year he'd come back. Longing for home but not believing that Big Prairie could ever be it. Not ever again.

Now? Well.

On July 20, 1969, Neil Armstrong stepped off the lunar module named *Eagle* and planted a boot where no one had thought possible. The country, much of the world, watched, listened, minds blown. Wonder took over as imaginations were given a whole new level of possibilities.

Man had walked on the moon.

Some sixty years later, Craig still hadn't. Likely never would, which didn't matter because that hadn't ever been on his radar.

As he moved beneath the Friday night lights, that first moonwalk crossed his mind. Because for him, this day—these collective moments in which he walked and breathed and lived—this was his moonwalk.

This was his impossible. Made possible.

He'd never have a full grasp of redemption. That was okay. He never wanted to lose the wonder of it.

Hank Johnson met him about midfield and pumped his arm. "It's good to see you back in the game, Erickson."

Craig nodded. Grinned. "Good to be back."

Honestly, it was. Brenna had been right. He'd blamed football for his choices, when his choices were simply his bad choices.

Craig turned back to the home stands. There she was. Right where she'd always waited after a game, hair tinted with white by the floodlights overhead. Two boys on either side of her, bouncing around, laughing. All of them now sharing his name.

Their gazes collided, and Craig fingered the ring on his left hand.

When he'd been eighteen, this sort of moment had been the hope of everything. Her stare on him, his heart hurting with the kind of pain-pleasure that was a beautiful hallelujah.

I'm going to marry Coach's daughter.

That was what he'd thought back then. Had been the best idea he'd ever had. The best plan he'd ever walked away from. The best hope he thought he'd never get back.

Now, there she was, looking at him. Smiling. No longer the coach's daughter.

Now the new coach's wife.

Craig cut a straight path through the sweaty boys he claimed as his, the young men who looked at him the same way he'd looked at Coach Blaum all those years back.

Don't let me fail them. He prayed as players high-fived, fist-bumped, jumped on to one another in celebration.

The whole time, while moving to the music with the rest of the ecstatic crowd, Brenna smiled at him.

Don't let me fail her. The prayer caused his breath to catch, his heart to clinch. *Not again. Not like before.*

By the time he met her at the fence, his victory grin had dwindled.

"What's this?" Brenna drew a frown over his lips with her index finger. "You won, Coach. Now is the time to smile."

Though the low fence separated them, he drew her head into his chest and held on. Letting go of the boys' hands, she folded her arms around him. "Dad said to tell you 'good game,'" she said. "They'll see you at home later."

No doubt the emotions of everything this day was had worn on Coach Blaum—his father-in-law. His first time back in this stadium, first time ever on the bleachers.

Craig curled around Brenna, words stuck inside. She pressed close. Held him as the silence between them settled against the noise of celebration. Craig wished Scottie was there telling him what he'd caught on video, assuring Craig he'd point out what needed work when they would watch it together. He wished his mom was well enough to have her hand on his arm, pride bright in her eyes as she stood there on that field. She was getting there, but this night game would have been too much. He also wished Brenna's dad was still there, his feet on this turf, his name still listed on the program as head coach.

The truth was, Grant had been right. You couldn't ever go back. But also...

His wife pulled away, cupped his face, and smiled. It was a new day; they had a new life. A redeemed life.

The truth was, you could always go home. Again.

The End

I hope you enjoyed your visit in Big Prairie, hanging out with Craig and Brenna and the boys, and meeting their community. Thank you so much for coming! I'd love it if you'd leave a review on your favorite book retail site or Goodreads, and please watch for more Big Prairie Romances!

As always, it's an honor to share the stories from my heart with you. Don't be a stranger!

 Jen

Other Books by Jen

Rock Creek Romance Collection

Reclaimed

Just as Paul's kindness begins to melt Suzanna's frozen heart, a conflict regarding her land escalates in town. Even in the warmth of Paul's love, resentment keeps a cold grip on her fragile heart.

When romance isn't enough, will Suzanna ever find peace?

The Cupcake Dilemma

"Witty and sweet...an irresistibly fun and flirty read." -Rel, Relzreviewz.com

It all started with an extra assignment delegated to me at school right before Valentine's Day... But before we get too far, let me begin by stating this clearly. I was *voluntold*.

Ordinary Snowflakes

"...I have to pick myself up from the warm gooey puddle I've melted into on the floor. This book is perfection in a novella..." **-Katie Donovan, the Fiction Aficionado**
Someone has noticed me. A secret admirer? A man with a good heart, who sees how much I actually need help, even though I never admit it? Maybe this is the beginning of a beautiful story—a romance full of hope and second chances and love.

The Grace Revealed Series

An alcoholic, a woman of shame, and a pharisee. How far does the hand of grace reach?

"The characters are all impressively multifaceted, engaging with complex emotional strains and difficult issues of allegiance... Rodewald proves to be a formidable new voice."
-Publisher's Weekly (review for Blue Columbine)

"*This is not a simple story... this is raw and real and heartbreaking. In all the best ways that take a book from great to riveting. This is a book that reaches inside your heart, rips it out, and then renews it with the soul-cleansing life-changing miracle of grace.*" **-readingismysuperpower.org** (review for Blue Columbine)

"*When people claim Christian Fiction is superficial and unrealistic, they have not discovered Jennifer Rodewald and her Grace Revealed series... Redemption and forgiveness are hard fought in this story, with raw emotion bleeding from the page. Finding Evergreen is highly deserving of the investment of time and emotion!*" **-RelzReviews** (review for Finding Evergreen)

"*...an incredible story of God's redemption and love that transforms not only the heroine, but everyone around her.*" - **Sydna Masse, President/Founder at Ramah International** (review for Red Rose Bouquet)

"*With Red Rose Bouquet, Jennifer's adept handling of deep subjects has cemented her on my list of must-read authors. I can't wait to see what she tackles next.*" **-Christina Coryell, Author of The Camdyn Series**

Stand Alone

The Carpenter's Daughter

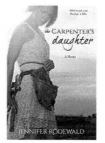

How far is she willing to go to find out who she is?

"*An honest tale of one woman's journey to self discovery that will have reader's searching their own hearts.*" - **Sarah Monzon**

About the Author

 Jennifer Rodewald/J. Rodes lives on the wide plains somewhere near the middle of Nowhere. A coffee addict, pickleball enthusiast, and storyteller, she also wears the hats of mom, teacher, and friend. Mostly, she loves Jesus and wants to see others fall in love with Him too.

She would love to hear from you! Please visit her at authorjenrodewald.com or at www.facebook.com/authorjenrodewald

Made in the USA
Middletown, DE
30 January 2025